FATAL CONCEIT

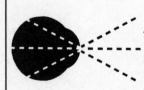

This Large Print Book carries the
Seal of Approval of N.A.V.H.

FATAL CONCEIT

ROBERT K. TANENBAUM

THORNDIKE PRESS

A part of Gale, Cengage Learning

GALE
CENGAGE Learning®

Farmington Hills, Mich • San Francisco • New York • Waterville, Maine
Meriden, Conn • Mason, Ohio • Chicago

Copyright © 2014 by Robert K. Tanenbaum
Thorndike Press, a part of Gale, Cengage Learning.

Thorndike Press® Large Print Thriller.
The text of this Large Print edition is unabridged.
Other aspects of the book may vary from the original edition.
Set in 16 pt. Plantin.

LIBRARY OF CONGRESS CATALOGING-IN-PUBLICATION DATA

Tanenbaum, Robert.
    Fatal conceit / by Robert K. Tanenbaum. — Large print edition.
      pages cm. — (Thorndike Press large print thriller)
    ISBN 978-1-4104-7111-6 (hardcover) — ISBN 1-4104-7111-X (hardcover)
    1. Karp, Butch (Fictitious character)—Fiction. 2. Terrorism—Russia (Federation)—Chechnia—Fiction. 3. Conspiracies—United States—Fiction. 4. Large type books. I. Title.
    PS3570.A52F38 2014b
    813'.54—dc23
                                                          2014018117

Published in 2014 by arrangement with Gallery Books, a division of Simon & Schuster, Inc.

Printed in the United States of America
1 2 3 4 5 6 7 18 17 16 15 14

To those blessings in my life:
Patti, Rachael, Roger, Billy,
and my brother, Bill;
and
To the loving Memory of
Reina Tanenbaum
My sister, truly an angel

ACKNOWLEDGMENTS

To my legendary mentors, District Attorney Frank S. Hogan and Henry Robbins, both of whom were larger in life than in their well-deserved and hard-earned legends, everlasting gratitude and respect; to my special friends and brilliant tutors at the Manhattan DAO, Bob Lehner, Mel Glass, and John Keenan, three of the best who ever served and whose passion for justice was unequaled and uncompromising, my heartfelt appreciation, respect, and gratitude; to Professor Robert Cole and Professor Jesse Choper, who at Boalt Hall challenged, stimulated, and focused the passions of my mind to problem-solve and to do justice; to Steve Jackson, an extraordinarily talented and gifted scrivener whose genius flows throughout the manuscript and whose contribution to it cannot be overstated, a dear friend for whom I have the utmost respect; to Louise Burke, my publisher, whose enthusiastic support, savvy, and encyclopedic smarts qualify her as my first pick in a game of three on three in the Avenue P park in Brooklyn; to Wendy Walker, my talented, highly skilled, and insightful editor, many thanks for all that you do; to Mitchell Ivers and Natasha Simons, the inimitable twosome whose adult supervision, oversight, and rapid responses are invaluable and profoundly appreciated; to my agents, Mike Hamilburg and Bob Diforio, who in exemplary fashion have always represented my best interests; to Coach Paul Ryan, who personified "American Exceptionalism" and mentored me in its finest virtues; to my esteemed special friend and confidant Richard A. Sprague, who has always challenged, debated, and inspired me in the pursuit of fulfilling the reality of "American Exceptionalism"; and to Rene Herrerias, who believed in me early on and in so doing changed my life, truly a divine intervention.

PROLOGUE

Roger Karp arrived outside the Casablanca Hotel off West 43rd a little after eight on a Monday morning. It was no social call. He was the district attorney for New York County and upstairs in the hotel was the body of a man whose death was certain to be the lead story in newspapers and newscasts across the globe. He wanted to be out ahead of the cloud of media locusts that would soon descend upon his city to join their brethren already there.

As he approached the hotel entrance, a glass door opened and the broad coffee-colored face of Detective Clay Fulton appeared. "Morning, Butch," he said, using the nickname that friends, family, and foes alike knew him by. The detective pushed the door open further. "This way."

Karp followed the detective into the elegant lobby of the Casablanca, a boutique hotel a block off Times Square. He was pleased to see that so far there were no media types evident. Several people, presumably hotel employees by their uniforms and name tags, were over by the front desk talking to two plainclothes police detectives. A young woman in uniform cried inconsolably among them.

Fulton pointed to her. "She found the body when he didn't answer the door for room service this morning."

Karp nodded. "Where we going?"

"Sixth floor, room 648."

The two large men, both about six-foot-five though the detective was a bit stockier, crossed the lobby headed for the elevator. A young, freckle-faced uniformed police officer was holding a door open for them. "Good morning, Mr. Karp," the officer said.

Pausing for a moment to get a good look at the young man, Karp then smiled. "Aren't you Jimmy Fallon's son Richie? Wow, seems like it was yesterday your dad was a rookie working in the detective squad for DA Francis Garrahy, and I was a scrub assistant DA. Now you're a cop, too. Like father, like son, eh?"

The young officer beamed. "Kind of you to remember, sir."

"Say hello to your father for me."

"Can't do that, sir, he drank himself to

10

death last year."

"Oh, hey, sorry to hear that; he was a good man."

"Yeah, he was. But you know us Irish cops, if we ain't in church, we're hittin' the booze, though I never touch the stuff myself. Not after seeing what it did to Pops."

"Your mom still with us?"

"Yes, sir. I want her to move in with me and the missus, but we can't get her out of the old house in Queens. She says Pops' ghost keeps her company, and she's afraid he won't be able to find her nowheres else."

"Home is where the heart is, Richie. Say hi to her for me."

"I'll do it. Thank you, sir."

After the door of the elevator closed, Karp shook his head. "Didn't know that about Jimmy."

"Yeah, he got bounced from the force for drinking on the job and hitting a pedestrian with his squad car. Next thing I heard, he went on a binge to end all binges, drank himself into a coma, and never came out. Guess he didn't know what to do if he couldn't be a cop."

"It's a tough job."

"That it is, boss, that it is."

The men fell silent for a moment then

Fulton asked, "Any word on Lucy and Ned?"

Karp shook his head and had to clear his throat to answer. "Nothing new. Not much more than has been in the papers." His voice was husky, and the detective let it be.

The elevator slid open again on the sixth floor and the two longtime friends and colleagues exited. Fulton pointed to the left. "Down here."

They rounded a corner and Karp saw another uniformed officer standing guard outside a room at the end of the hallway. As they walked toward him a door opened halfway down the hall and an older woman in a robe, her face made up with too much eye shadow for that time of the morning, peered out. "Is everything okay?" she asked in a tremulous voice.

"There's been an incident, but it's under control," Fulton assured her. "If you could just remain in your room for a little while longer I'm going to ask an officer to stop by and ask you a few questions, then you'll be free to go."

We'll see about everything being under control, Karp thought as the woman gave a small cry and disappeared. The dead bolt slid home.

Twenty minutes earlier, Karp was just

about to leave his family loft apartment on Grand and Crosby Streets for his office at the Criminal Courts building at 100 Centre Street. He'd been looking forward to the walk. The air was crisp with the promise of fall though it was supposed to warm up nicely into another lovely Indian Summer day on Manhattan Island. *Perfect day for a brisk hike.*

Then Fulton called from the Casablanca. Instead of a pleasant stroll to work, Karp hopped in an unmarked sedan driven by his omnipresent bodyguard, NYPD Officer J. P. Murphy, to take him to the hotel. On the ride uptown, he looked out the windows at the crowds on the sidewalks but hardly saw them in his shock and disbelief over the identity of the victim and the initial report from Fulton regarding the cause of death. "Looks like suicide . . . an overdose. But I don't know, Butch, something isn't right."

Normally Karp wouldn't have responded personally to a suicide in a New York City hotel. But given the prominence of the deceased and certain recent events there was no question that he would oversee this case from the get-go. A small voice in his head even speculated that there could be a connection between the man's death and what had happened a week earlier to his

13

daughter, Lucy. *There's certainly a nexus,* he thought, *however tenuous.*

Nodding to the officer guarding the scene, Karp entered the room ahead of Fulton. Located on the top floor of the hotel, room 648 was a suite with a sitting area that contained a work desk, coffee table, and a couch with two end tables; through wooden double-doors, currently open, was the bedroom. The first thing he noted were the scattered remains of a room service breakfast the traumatized young woman downstairs apparently had dropped on the plush maroon carpeting in the sitting area when she noticed the body on the king-sized bed. He turned his attention to where two crime scene technicians were working at the desk, on which a laptop computer sat open.

"What's up?" Karp asked.

One of the CSI techs, who was using a razor blade to scrape the dried residue of a liquid off the glass-covered desktop and into an envelope, stopped what he was doing and looked up. "Covering our bases, Mr. Karp," he said. "Got a little spill here, looks pretty fresh; probably just some of the scotch he was drinking, but we'll test it anyway."

"I see the bottle. Where's the glass?" Karp asked, looking around.

The technician pointed toward the bedroom. "In there."

Karp looked at the other technician, who was moving his finger on the laptop's touch pad as he watched the screen. "Anything interesting?"

"Mostly making sure I don't lose any information before I shut it down and take it to the lab to look over. . . . There is a note." He moved his finger and then clicked on the pad.

A document file appeared on the screen, blank except for six words.

" 'I'm sorry about everything. Forgive me,' " Karp read.

"Short and sweet," said Fulton, who was looking over their shoulders.

"What was he sorry about?" Karp wondered aloud.

"Wasn't he supposed to testify before a congressional committee tomorrow?" Fulton said.

"Think there's a connection?"

"Who knows? I'm sure the media will tell us soon enough."

"Yeah, but will they get it right?" Karp asked.

"Since when did that matter? So long as they're first and it doesn't buck the status quo."

Karp turned and walked into the bedroom, where several people were working around the corpse. The dead man lay on his back on top of a white down comforter, his head propped on a pillow. He was wearing a silk smoking jacket and long, striped pajama bottoms. His hands were clasped on top of his belly; his eyes were closed and his lips gave no hint of an expression. Except for the pallor of his skin and the absolute stillness with which he lay, he appeared to be sleeping.

Looking down at the familiar face, Karp felt a wave of sorrow pass through him. Here were the mortal remains of a dynamic man, a true American hero that he and many other people around the world respected. Karp couldn't fathom what drove the man to take his own life. *Something he was sorry for.*

"So sad," said a white-haired woman in a long medical coat who was gently examining the body.

"Yes it is. But good to see you, Gail," Karp said.

Assistant Medical Examiner Gail Manning smiled, her kind blue eyes wet in spite of her long service to the New York Medical Examiner's Office where death had been a constant companion. "I always thought of him as a good man . . . sort of above it all," she said.

"I think many of us felt the same," Karp replied.

"I guess he had demons none of us knew about."

"If so, they got the better of him and that's our loss. Can you tell me anything?"

"Well, judging from lividity and his core body temperature, my preliminary finding on time of death, subject to revision, is about ten hours ago."

Karp did the math. "About 10:00 p.m. last night?"

"That's an educated guess. I'll be able to tell more at the autopsy and after running a few tests."

"How'd he do it?"

Manning pointed to a pill bottle next to a glass partly filled with an amber liquid on the nightstand beside the bed. "The old-fashioned way, tranquilizers with a scotch chaser. At least that's what it looks like." Her face screwed up as if she was trying to reconcile her answer with something running through her mind.

"Is there something else?" Karp asked.

"Well, he was drinking a twenty-five-year-old Macallan, a real connoisseur's scotch — can't afford it myself though I would if I could," she began, then her voice trailed off.

"And?"

"I don't know . . . maybe it's nothing, but he apparently emptied the capsules — *diazepam,* better known as Valium, according to the bottle — into the scotch and drank it," Manning said, "as opposed to just swallowing the capsules and washing them down with scotch."

"And that strikes you as odd because?"

"The Valium would have ruined the taste of the Macallan for someone who likes fine scotch, as apparently he did."

Karp looked thoughtful and then nodded. "Great deductive reasoning, Mrs. Sherlock Holmes. I know you're thorough, but let's be extra particular with the toxicology and get me a report as soon as you can."

"Will do . . . uh-oh, what now?" A sudden commotion out in the sitting room made Karp and Manning turn their heads. They could hear but not see the participants engaged in the abrupt loud argument.

"This is a federal investigation, everybody out," a stern male voice demanded.

"Like hell it is," a voice Karp knew was Fulton's growled. "Everybody keep doing what you're doing!"

Karp reached the bedroom door just as a short man in a dark suit and sunglasses attempted to reach for the laptop computer

18

only to be blocked by Fulton. "You're obstructing a federal agent in the performance of his duty," the short man snarled. His identically dressed partner, a taller, younger man who looked like a former college quarterback, stepped forward as if to intercede.

Fulton half-smiled as he met the younger man chest to chest. "Yeah, and you're in New York City, which makes it an NYPD investigation until I say it ain't."

Everybody in the room turned when Karp walked out of the bedroom. "Mind telling me what this is about?" he asked the short man.

"Mr. Karp. I'm Special Agent Jack Robbins and this is Special Agent Ricardo Fuentes, FBI. This is now a federal case. I want that computer and I want everybody out of here, and that includes the big guy."

"On what grounds?" Karp inquired mildly.

"National security. I'm sure you're aware of the identity of the deceased. The president has asked the FBI to investigate and that computer may contain sensitive materials that require classified clearance to view," Robbins replied curtly. "And I'm sure your techno-geek there doesn't have that clearance."

Karp's eyes narrowed. "The president

19

asked you to investigate? I just heard about this thirty minutes ago. How'd the president know and get you guys involved so quickly?"

The agent frowned. "I'm not at liberty to discuss that."

"In other words, you don't know because they don't tell guys at your level those sorts of things," Karp said, walking over until he was towering over the smaller man. "Whatever that computer may or may not contain, regarding national security, it may also hold evidence relevant to the cause and manner of the death of the deceased."

"Evidence? Investigation? This isn't a homicide."

"We're in the preliminary stages of determining precisely what has occurred, and your presence is, quite frankly, highly suspect. Nevertheless, since I'm the chief law enforcement officer in New York County everything remains under my jurisdiction and authority. So until I determine otherwise, NYPD will be the custodians of all the evidence, particularly the computer."

Robbins glared up at Karp. "I'll get a federal court order," he said through clenched teeth.

"You do what you think you have to do, and I'll see you in court," Karp responded. "In the meantime, Detective Fulton, I want that computer locked up at the DAO. I'll make it available for these gentlemen to look at there in your presence *after* you and the fine young computer savant behind you have had an opportunity to examine it. I'm sure the two of you will disregard any alleged sensitive materials bearing on national security."

"You'll regret this, Karp," Robbins hissed.

"I doubt it," Karp replied nonchalantly. "Now you're obstructing the NYPD and DAO from performing their duties. So either remove yourselves, or I'll ask Detective Fulton to escort you out of here in handcuffs and deliver you to the Tombs, where you can call your bosses to come bail you out."

The agent started to reply but then looked at Fulton, who was grinning, and decided against it. "Let's go, Fuentes, let the local yokels have their day," he sneered. "We'll be back, and with a federal SWAT team if we need it. Then we'll see who ends up behind bars."

When the agents stormed out, the others in the room broke into a loud cheer. "Way to go, Mr. DA," Manning shouted.

"Yeah, kicked a little fed behind," the technician at the computer added. "My mom's the only one who gets to call me a techno-geek. Computer savant, I like that."

"All right everybody, back to work," Fulton said. He turned to Karp. "That *was* fun."

"Enjoyed it, but they will be back. Work fast and like I said, get that computer down to the evidence vault and make sure you put in place a security team. No outside agency looks at that computer without my written authorization. I'm going into the office now; I've got some catching up to do."

Fulton followed him into the hall where Karp paused for a moment. "I wonder who called those guys?"

Fulton shrugged. "Some young cop who wants to join the bureau and play G-man so he tipped them off hoping it would be noted on his resume."

"Yeah, perhaps," Karp said, then gave his friend a sideways look. "But, Clay, I share your initial instincts; this whole thing is wrong. I can feel it in my bones."

"Yeah? Me, too. I was hoping it wasn't something I was coming down with."

Karp smiled. "The intuition flu, maybe. Anyway, let's make sure we run this thing to the ground. Talk to the neighbors, check out the employees yourself. Maybe I *am* coming down with a bug but something about this has made me queasy."

1

Eight days earlier . . .

The fat man in the light blue jogging suit lit a cigar as he sat back behind a desk in the office of his palatial home outside of Washington, D.C. After a few puffs to get the Mancuso going, he turned his attention to the enormous television mounted on the wall across the darkened room.

Beyond the heavy drapes pulled across the windows, it was midafternoon on a sunny day in wealthy Loudoun County. But halfway around the world, it was nighttime where a Predator drone circled three thousand feet above the scene displayed in black and white infrared images on the television. Only seconds behind real time, ghostly figures of human beings showed up clearly as they ran across open spaces or ducked behind corners of a dark cluster of buildings and vehicles. Several fires also blazed away in white-hot pixels — one clearly a truck, another on a roof — and bursts of brilliant ellipses he knew were tracer rounds raced back and forth across the screen.

A half hour earlier when he was rudely interrupted during an afternoon quickie with his mistress to watch the events as they unfolded, the firefight between the attackers on the outside and the besieged defenders inside the buildings had been intense. But the defenders were clearly outnumbered and outgunned; without help the outcome had been inevitable. Now almost all of the sporadic shooting was coming from the attackers, including shots apparently fired at figures lying on the ground. *Executing the wounded,* he guessed. *Good, this is FUBAR enough already, we don't need any witnesses.*

"How long ago did you say this started?" the fat man asked. A short, neat man in black-rimmed glasses, wearing a three-piece vested suit, standing off to the side of his desk and also watching the screen, looked at his watch. "Almost three hours ago," he replied. "State Department got an encoded radio transmission about 1300 hours our time, 0300 Sunday there, from the compound stating that they were under attack and requesting help. State called me and scrambled an NSA drone from the airbase in Turkey. I called you after that."

"Good," the fat man said as he studied the cigar. "Then what?"

The neat man pushed his glasses up his nose and looked over at a very large, hard-looking younger man sitting in a chair in a dark corner of the room watching the television intently, seemingly oblivious to their conversation. "More calls for assistance but those stopped right before I got here. The drone was over the target and could have fired on the hostiles, but I did what you said and told them to stand down."

"A necessary evil," the fat man replied with a shrug. "We aren't supposed to be there, right? At least not doing whatever it was in the hell you were doing. We don't know who we would have been shooting at and that's not our airspace. We need to keep this under wraps if at all possible. . . . What about the Russians?"

The neat man shrugged. "Somebody in the compound also sent a general distress call to the Russian army base near Grozny, but . . . um . . . there was no response," he replied. "I finally got through to the Russian embassy and told them that our 'trade mission' in Zandaq had been attacked. One of their undersecretaries got back to me on my way over here and said that apparently the post's communication system had been down for repairs, but they were sending a counterterrorism team to 'investigate.' It's a pretty good hop to the compound, and they won't be there for at least another hour and by that time . . ." He stopped and looked at the television. There were no more signs of resistance from the buildings; some of the attackers were still running about, but others appeared to be just milling around. "It's over," he concluded simply.

The fat man looked at the screen. In some ways he looked like just another overweight limousine liberal; the sort who sat around in coffee shops in Birkenstock sandals over white socks and tie-dyed rock concert T-shirts while talking to their stockbrokers on their smartphones. He wore his hair, which he dyed ash blond, swept back and longish, and his well-scrubbed, hairless face with its round pink cheeks and full lips looked almost boyish. He was sixty years old and with the toadying press liked coming off as an affable political geek holdover from the late sixties. But he was shrewd, ruthless, and committed to his far left of center politics, and right now, his weak blue eyes glinted with anger behind the round wire-rim glasses he wore.

"It may be over in fucking Chechnya," he

26

growled as he stabbed his cigar at the screen, "but it's not fucking over here. In fact, the shitstorm hasn't even started here, but it will if we don't keep a lid on this and know what we're going to do to distract the voters if anything does get out." He took a long drag and blew the smoke at the ceiling. "So tell me again what the fuck we were doing there?"

The neat man, Tucker Lindsey, cleared his throat. He didn't like the fat man, detested him as a matter of fact. *A crude, obese, arrogant asshole from the Midwest,* he'd described him to his former colleagues at the State Department. Certainly not a member of "The Club" that permeated the entourage around the president, as well as his cabinet and appointed posts, particularly at State. *Not an Ivy League man,* he thought with disdain.

In a world that made any sense, there would have been no way that he, a Harvard Law grad and the president's national security adviser, should have to answer to the boorish tub of goo. But Rod Fauhomme was the president's re-election campaign manager, probably the best in his dirty business, and with the election only three weeks away, orders from the top were that the corpulent politico was calling the shots on

27

anything that might affect the president's run at a second term.

"Officially, it's a trade mission," Lindsey said. "A deputy chief of mission from the U.S. consulate in Grozny, the capital of Chechnya, reaching out to the locals. In reality, DCM David Huff and a small security detail drove to Zandaq, a small, out-of-the-way town in southeastern Chechnya, to meet with one of the leaders of the Chechen separatist movement." He nodded at the television screen. "What you're looking at there is a small gated compound about five miles from town that we lease as part of an agricultural and cultural outreach program run by State."

"And why are we meeting with this Chechen separatist?"

"To work out a quid pro quo deal," Lindsey said. "He helps us get arms to the rebels in Syria; in exchange he keeps some to get rid of foreign fighters — mostly Islamic extremists — and the Russians; we also agree to support their bid for independence from Russia at the United Nations."

"Do we care about their independence?"

"To some extent where it meets our foreign policy goals; but it's a dangerous world out there, a constant juggling act. These Chechen separatists are Muslim but they're secular and moderate; they're a better counterbalance to extremist Islamic states than any government we could have created on our own. Plus they hate the Russians with a passion, and anything that distracts the Kremlin can't be all bad."

"Why not just give the guns to the Syrian rebels openly? Everybody knows we want Assad out of there; nobody likes the guy."

Again, Lindsey shrugged. "The usual walking a tightrope when it comes to the Middle East. We don't want to be seen as toppling yet another government in a Muslim country. And if the weapons wind up in the wrong hands after Assad's out — i.e., killing U.S. soldiers in some other place or bringing down an airliner in Munich — we need to be able to deny it was the administration."

"Then why Chechens? Why not just tell the Israelis to do it?"

"The Israelis have the same concern about where the arms will eventually wind up and also don't want them being traced back to them. Imagine how it would go over in Tehran or Cairo if the Arab press got wind of the Israelis' providing arms to rebels to topple Muslim governments. . . . To be honest, we're also yanking the Russians' chain a little bit. They're not helping us out with

Syria, or with the damn Iranians, so we're stirring the pot in their backyard."

Fauhomme shook his head. "Jesus, don't you spooks ever get tired of 'stirring the pot'? It never seems to pan out, or is Iran-Contra such a distant memory that the lesson has been forgotten?"

Stung, Lindsey countered. "No more than you get tired of manipulating voters."

"Yeah," Fauhomme snorted. "But I get results."

"No offense," Lindsey replied tersely, "but you have no idea what has worked and what hasn't. All you hear about is the occasional foul-up that is bound to happen now and again, but believe it or not, we have reasons for doing what we do that might not be apparent to someone who isn't in the loop."

Lindsey made his last comment pointedly, but Fauhomme just brushed it off with a wave of his cigar. "If I want in the loop, I'll get in the loop," he replied. "But we have experts, like yourself, to muck it up just fine on your own."

The fat man rubbed his face with his pudgy fingers. He had been in the political game for most of his adult life. The son of an auto worker and avowed communist, he'd joined Students for a Democratic Society when he arrived on a college campus in Illinois in the late sixties. But when the SDS wasn't radical enough in its plans to topple the Establishment, he'd signed on with the violent Weathermen faction, hoping to plant bombs and kill cops.

However, times changed and he and his fellow "revolutionaries" decided that they would have a better chance of bringing down the corrupt capitalist system if they worked insidiously from the inside. So he turned to the political party most closely aligned with his politics, even though the party leadership was far too close to the middle and away from the left for his tastes. Then he made a name for himself as a "community organizer." That was where he'd met the president, a kindred spirit, and a few years later ran his first political campaign for alderman.

Fauhomme had gone on to run other campaigns for candidates who fit his left-wing profile, but always dropped whatever else he was doing if the then-future president called asking for help as he climbed the ladder from state to federal offices. He was a true believer, and what he believed in was a socialist America, whether its population chose to identify itself that way or not. The men and women he helped elect were those he thought would push the United

States further to the left with every election cycle.

Over the past few years, it had helped that the opposition party seemed bent on self-destruction, trotting out pathetic candidates who seemed to relish snatching defeat from the jaws of victory. It went hand-in-hand with his favorite campaign ploy, which was to attack the candidate on a personal level and avoid talking about the real issues whenever possible. With the economy in shambles, two foreign wars, and massive debt, the opposition should have run away with the upcoming election. But instead, the other party selected a candidate who fit the stereotype Fauhomme himself had worked to convince the low-information masses was their biggest enemy — wealthy, out of touch with working people, and part of the good old white boys' club that was "holding them back" and unfairly hoarding all the wealth. Toss in a few Neanderthal candidates to spew insults at minorities and women — which the opposition party had not countered successfully while Fauhomme, with the help of a willing media, used to paint the entire party with the same broad "mean-spirited" brush — and that runaway victory was instead a double-digit lead in the polls for the president.

Still, not everyone in the country was buying the bullshit he was spreading. Many *were* paying attention to a stagnant economy, trillion-dollar deficits, runaway entitlement programs, the haphazard and dangerous foreign policy, and a steady encroachment on rights and traditional values. Not everyone believed that the government could spend its way out of a deep recession or trusted the manipulated employment numbers. Thus the election was not a shoo-in for Fauhomme's man either.

In fact, three weeks earlier, the normally wooden opposition candidate had delivered a surprisingly passionate performance in the first debate that had centered on the economy and had the president up against the ropes by its end. The drubbing had shown up immediately in the polls with the opposition closing that double-digit lead to mid-single digit. Reeling from the disaster, Fauhomme immediately fired the team appointed to prepare the president for the debate, even though the real problem had been the candidate's arrogance.

As a result, two nights earlier the president had rebounded with a strong showing in the second debate, which had centered on foreign policy and terrorism. For reasons even Fauhomme couldn't fathom, the opposition candidate backed off attacking the weaknesses in the president's policies, saying that "in these dangerous times, we need to come together and present a united front to America's enemies." *Bullshit,* he'd thought when he heard that, *you are the enemy.*

The president's performance had for the moment stopped the opposition's momentum, but the losses in the polls had not been regained. The one thing the campaign did not need now was a debacle like the one playing out on the television screen.

"Okay, so we're playing games with the Russians and trying to clandestinely get weapons into the hands of God-knows-who to get rid of Assad, probably in violation of U.S. and maybe even international law . . . business as usual for you national 'insecurity' types, I get it," Fauhomme said. "But I got an election hanging in the balance, and if we lose, not only is it over for the president, it's over for you."

He let his warning sink in as he stared at Lindsey until the little man looked away. He smiled slightly and stole a glance at the younger man in the corner, a former Marine named "Big Ray" Baum who'd been drummed out of the Corps for brutal acts against civilians in Afghanistan. Baum was smirking, having listened to the exchange.

"Do you think the Russians could be behind the attack?" he asked, turning back to Lindsey.

"I wouldn't put it past them. The attack looked pretty organized, but some of it was haphazard and took a long time considering their superior numbers and firepower, not the discipline you'd expect to see from Russian special forces masquerading as insurgents. But the Russians certainly wouldn't have been happy if they found out what our 'trade mission' was really about and could have got someone else to do their dirty work for them."

"So what will they do now after their 'investigation' turns up dead Americans?" Fauhomme asked.

"They'll blame it on the separatists," Lindsey replied. "The more they can link the separatists with terrorism, the more they can crack down on the movement. Officially we'd have to go along with it; we don't say anything about the brutal things they do to 'terrorists' in Chechnya, and they don't say anything when we take out someone with a drone strike. This little incident is going to give them a free pass to go to town on those poor bastards."

Fauhomme nodded at the television screen. "So I take it you don't think these were the separatists?"

"Doubtful," Lindsey replied. "We were there to make arrangements to give them weapons and back them up at the UN. They had nothing to win by attacking us and everything to lose, especially when the Russians let loose on them with our blessing. The bad guys are more likely foreign fighters — Islamic extremists from other countries who flock anywhere Muslims are fighting a secular government or infidels. They're probably Al Qaeda or linked . . ."

"WRONG!" the fat man shouted as he sat up suddenly in his seat. "They're not fucking Al Qaeda!"

Lindsey furrowed his brow. "What do you mean? There's a good chance that they are. One of the reasons we assigned this to Huff was we've been getting reports about Al Qaeda increasing their activities in the area, coming over the border from Dagestan, and . . ." He was interrupted again when Fauhomme slammed a meaty palm down on his desk and pointed his cigar at Lindsey. "Al Qaeda doesn't exist as an effective terrorist organization anymore," he hissed. "The president said so on national television two days ago. Or don't you remember the last debate? That's when he told John and Susie Q. Public and 300-plus million of their fellow citizens that one of the finest moments of his administration was eradicating Public Enemy Number One, fucking Al Qaeda. Therefore, Al Qaeda doesn't exist."

"We warned the president against making too broad a statement . . ."

"I don't give a rat's ass about your warning . . . we needed to give the masses something after the first debate debacle, so we gave them the death of Al Qaeda and now we can all sleep safe in our beds tonight thanks to *this* administration."

There was a knock at the door of his office, which opened before he could reply. A beautiful young brunette woman in a silk dressing gown poked her head in. "Is everything okay, honey?" she asked the fat man. "I heard a bang and I . . ."

"Get the fuck out!" Fauhomme exclaimed. "Jesus, Connie, how many fucking times do I have to tell you to stay out of my office when I'm in a meeting!"

The young woman's face crumpled and it looked for a moment like she might cry, but she quickly ducked back out. Fauhomme continued to look at the door for a moment as if she might try to come in again, and then shook his head. "Jesus, what a ditz," he exclaimed. "Great in the sack, but that plane's flying without a pilot."

"Uh-oh, what have we got here?" Baum interrupted.

The other two turned to look back at the television. Although the images were small and grainy, they were clear enough; a crowd of armed men were pushing and shoving three prisoners toward the open area between the main building and the compound's outer fence. They could see that one of the captives appeared to be a slightly built woman; the others were definitely larger males. One of the men suddenly turned on his captors and began to fight, but he was quickly clubbed to his knees and then dragged forward to where they were all forced to line up side by side.

A man, apparently the terrorist leader, stepped in front of the prisoners. He then turned and looked up and appeared to be staring right at the Predator. Holding up a finger, he tracked the circling drone that he could hear but not see as though to say he knew he was being watched. He then turned back to the captives.

Walking over to the prisoner on his left, a tall man, he pointed his gun as if he was going to execute him. But then he lowered the gun and stepped over to the female captive, where he seemed to say something to her. He then reached out and appeared to touch her face before moving on to the last male prisoner, who was still on his knees. The leader pointed his gun at the prisoner, who looked steadily up at him; there was a flash and the prisoner pitched sideways and lay still.

"Jesus," Lindsey muttered.

"Better for us if those sons of bitches kill all of them," Fauhomme replied.

Lindsey frowned. "What the hell kind of man are you? Those are Americans."

"What kind of a man am I?" Fauhomme repeated rhetorically. "I'm a man who sees the big picture, and sometimes sacrifices need to be made for the greater good. I'm the man who cleans up everybody else's fuckups, including you James Bond wannabes. And I'm a man trying to win an important election that could determine the course of this country for the next century."

Suddenly there was another knock at the door. "Yeah, what is it?" Fauhomme shouted.

When the door opened a clean-cut young man poked his head in and looked at Lindsey. "Excuse, sir, but you said to let you know if there were any more communications from Chechnya," he said as he walked in and shut the door behind him. "We just learned that a call was placed to the U.S. embassy in Moscow about ten minutes ago. The caller left a message." He held up a small digital recorder. "Want to hear it?"

"Yeah, Augie, go ahead, play it," Lindsey replied.

Augie pressed a button and a young woman's voice, cracking with strain and fear, entered the room. "This is codename Wallflower. We are at the compound in Zandaq. We've been attacked and overrun. They're trying to get in. I don't think it will be much longer. They are not Chechen; they're speaking Arabic, several native Saudi speakers, a Yemeni, not sure of the others, but I repeat, they are not Chechen. . . . I'm with David Huff." The woman's voice paused and a loud pounding could be heard. "They're here," she said, then the phone went dead.

Lindsey motioned for Augie to leave. "Let me know if anything else comes in."

"Who the hell is Wallflower?" Fauhomme demanded.

Lindsey shook his head. "Couldn't tell you. There was no one with our people using that codename. In fact, I didn't think there were any women on the mission."

"Well apparently there is, and it's somebody who knows the difference between a Saudi and a Yemeni speaking Arabic," Fauhomme retorted. "She sounded American."

"I'll have to ask around, see if some other agency was in the area," Lindsey said. "So what now?"

"I want every copy of that fucking tape. And nobody, I mean nobody, says anything about it; it doesn't exist." Fauhomme stopped talking and looked at the television screen, where the remaining two hostages were being herded onto a flatbed truck. "Tell the drone operator to light 'em up," he said.

"Light who up?" Lindsey asked.

"The hostages, who the hell do you think?" Fauhomme said. "We've got a hostage situation, and I won't have this administration's chances of re-election pulling a Jimmy Carter on me. They need to go!"

Lindsey punched a number into his cell phone. "Take out the truck with the friendlies," he said quietly. "Yeah, you heard me right, the friendlies; in fact, take them all out, as many as you can, but make sure you get that truck. Am I clear?" He put his cell phone down and looked back at Fauhomme. "Then what's our story?"

"Our story is that our peaceful trade mis-

sion was attacked by Chechen separatist terrorists, a cowardly betrayal of heroic Deputy
Chief of Mission Huff and his brave security
team, who were trying to offer the hand of
friendship and instead were stabbed in the
back," Fauhomme said. "There were no
survivors. I'll bet the Russians will back us
on this, but they'll be bending us over a barrel for the next decade as payback."

"Something's happening with the drone,"
Baum said.

They all looked at the television screen
just as it wavered and then went to black.
At the same time, Lindsey's phone buzzed.
"Yeah?" he answered, then cursed. "What
the hell do you mean you lost contact? Get
it back!"

A minute later, the screen blinked on
again but all that could be seen were the
buildings and vehicles, as well as a couple
of bodies, now only slightly warmer than
their surroundings, according to the drone's
infrared electro-optical sensor. There was
no sign of life.

"Where in the hell did they go?" Lindsey
asked and got back on his phone. "Goddammit, expand the search area," he yelled.
"Do I have to tell you everything?" He
ended the call with an angry push of a button and looked at Fauhomme. "They're

gone," he said.

"And you, my friend, are a master of the obvious," Fauhomme said and stubbed his cigar out. "Just make sure they stay gone."

2

"On two, go out about five yards, stop, wait for my fake, then take off and hook around the lady with the baby carriage . . . after that go long."

"You've had me go long the last two plays," Giancarlo complained, "and Zak had me covered both times."

"That's why he won't expect it again," his dad, Butch Karp, said with a wink. "Sell the short route; then when he bites, use the baby carriage to brush him off. We'll burn him, baby."

Giancarlo rolled his eyes and shook his head. He and his dad were down 28–0 to his mom, Marlene, and his twin brother, Isaac, better known as "Zak" or, as he was referring to himself during this Saturday afternoon family game of touch football in Central Park, "The Glue-meister."

Zak was the main reason for the lopsided score. Although born only a few minutes before Giancarlo, the "older" sibling was bigger, stronger, faster. In fact, Zak was one of the better athletes in the New York City school system, the starting running back and middle linebacker on their high school football team and starting pitcher and center fielder for the baseball team.

All in all, Giancarlo didn't mind the accolades Zak garnered for his physical prowess. In fact, when they weren't battling over the things teen-aged brothers squabble about, he was proud of his sibling. Early in their boyhoods, Giancarlo had seen the writing on the wall when it came to who was going to be the superior athlete, and he was cool with it. Not that Giancarlo was terrible, by any means — he'd made the varsity baseball team, though most of his game-day participation was spent riding the pine. Still, his brother was college athletic scholarship material and he clearly was not. However, Giancarlo more than compensated with his musical abilities on a half-dozen instruments and superiority in academics. Zak struggled with his grades, mostly because of inattention rooted in a firm belief that he was headed for a pro football or baseball career.

Both boys were movie-star handsome with the soulful brown eyes and black curly hair from their Italian mother's side of the family. Zak was a little more rugged and already waking up with a five o'clock shadow, while Giancarlo's features were more delicate. Neither had their father's height, or his Slavic facial characteristics and gray, gold-flecked eyes. There was even a long-running and mostly good-natured argument between their parents about whose athletic genes Zak inherited.

Back in the day, their father was a highly recruited high school basketball player who'd been compared to former Celtic great Bob Cousy when he starred in his freshman year at the University of California–Berkeley. However, a freak knee injury during practice ended his college, and potential pro, playing careers, relegating him from then on to pickup basketball games and first base for the New York County District Attorney's Office softball team. He worked out on weights and swam when his busy schedule allowed, which wasn't often, and tried to get in quick-paced walks when his bum knee cooperated. But even he admitted that his cardio conditioning wasn't all it should be.

Meanwhile, the boys' mother, Marlene Ciampi, was no slouch as an athlete. A fit, lithe woman even into middle age, she'd grown up wrestling and boxing with her brothers, as well as running track and playing basketball and tennis for the women's teams at Sacred Heart High School in Queens and then in college at Smith. After quitting the District Attorney's Office, she kept herself in shape throughout motherhood and beyond, when her career path led to creating a security firm for VIP clients, as well as working as a sometimes confrontational advocate for abused women. Now as a defense attorney and private investigator, she still put in fifteen to twenty miles of running per week, swam, and played tennis and racquetball. Several times this afternoon she'd easily sidestepped her husband's rush attempts (after he'd counted "one Mississippi, two Mississippi, three Mississippi") and passed the ball to Zak, who did the rest by eluding his brother on his way to four touchdowns.

Giancarlo had resigned himself to there being no hope of winning the game, which meant listening to his brother gloat for the rest of the afternoon and evening. Still, Zak was so competitive that one score would dampen his enthusiasm for rubbing it in, and he might even take it so hard that he'd go into a sulk and not speak for hours. So with that one small hope to cling to, Giancarlo turned back to where the football lay

47

on the grass waiting for him to hike it to his dad.

"Come on over here, Butta-fingas," Zak taunted his brother in his best faux Bronx accent.

"Yeah, let's see whatcha got there, Noodle Arm!" Marlene yelled at Karp.

The boys squared off. Marlene got into a sprinter's pose, ready to run her husband down like a dog as soon as she counted off her third Mississippi. Karp looked around as if he was Joe Namath looking over the Baltimore Colts defense. He noticed the plain-clothes cop, J. P. Murphy, an unwanted but necessary accoutrement of being the district attorney of New York County, standing over on the sideline, watchful but enjoying the warmth of an Indian Summer day. All around the edges of the Central Park meadow, elms, maples, and oaks were hitting their stride with the season's vibrant display of reds, yellows, oranges, purples, and golds. But the grass was still green and slightly in need of mowing, and the temperature beneath the bright blue sky was more reminiscent of early summer than the chill gray of approaching winter.

This was Karp's favorite time of year, especially when playing a game of touch football with his family in the park. The October games had been a tradition since the twins were young boys, and the only thing missing was his daughter, Lucy. But she was a grown woman living in New Mexico with her fiancé, Ned Blanchett, both of them working for a covert antiterrorism agency. They hadn't heard from her in a while but that wasn't unusual when she was on assignment, and all he knew was that her family missed her.

"You're mine, Karp," Marlene snarled.

"Don't bet on it, Ciampi," Karp growled back. "By the way, next score wins."

"What! No way," yelled Zak. "You're down twenty-eight–zip."

"Oh, let the babies have their way, Zak," Marlene said. "We'll shut these pansies out, then run the ball down their throats. The taste of victory will be that much sweeter."

Zak laughed. "Yeah, you're right, Mom. Go ahead, *losers;* we'll spot you the twenty-eight points!"

"Down, set, hut one, hut two . . ." Karp barked out the signals.

Giancarlo snapped the ball and began his route with Zak backpedaling to stay with him. Marlene began her count. "One Mississippi, two Mississippi . . ."

Karp cocked his arm as Giancarlo stopped

and turned to face him. Smiling, Zak began to move to get in front of his brother to intercept the throw. At the same time, Marlene reached her third Mississippi, and with a primal scream, ran for her husband.

Anticipating the fast but undisciplined attack of his opponents, and using it against them, Karp faked the throw to Giancarlo. Marlene stopped charging and jumped in the air with both arms up to block it; meanwhile, with a shout of triumph, Zak cut under Giancarlo's route. But instead Karp held on to the ball and took two steps forward while his wife's momentum carried her past him.

Giancarlo then turned and streaked toward where a young woman was sitting on the grass next to a baby carriage and texting on her cell phone. Yelling in surprise, Zak turned to follow his brother, who waited until the last moment before cutting hard to the right and around the woman and her infant. Zak suddenly found himself facing the choice of either running through or leaping over the baby carriage. When the young woman looked up, surprised to see a nearly two-hundred-pound teen-aged boy bearing down on her precious infant, she screamed, which brought Zak to a complete halt while his brother ran on.

With the proverbial eye in the back of his head, Karp knew that his wife was bearing down on him. He lofted the ball toward what, in his best estimation, was the point Giancarlo would reach on the other end of the trajectory; a moment later, he felt Marlene's hands push him just below the waist. They both stood watching as the ball sailed in a perfect arc to settle into Giancarlo's outstretched hands as he raced on to the end zone; he crossed it with the ball held aloft in celebration.

"TOUCHDOWN!" Karp and Giancarlo shouted at the same time. "WE WIN!"

"PENALTY!" Zak protested. "Not fair! You can't use a lady and her baby to set a pick!"

"Really, Butch, what kind of a human being uses a baby . . . a *baby,* for God's sake . . . just to score in a football game?" scolded Marlene.

"I was sure Zak would stop in time," Karp said with a smile and a shrug. "Besides, all's fair in love and football. Now let's see, what did we bet on the game?"

"Win or lose you were going to treat us all to cherry cheese coffeecake at Il Buon Pane," Marlene answered.

Karp's response was interrupted by the approach of their quarreling sons. "That was pass interference!" Zak complained.

"The lady and her baby weren't on our team, I had to go around them, too," Giancarlo countered. "Face it, you lost, we won."

"No way, we get a chance to tie you!"

Giancarlo shook his head. "I believe the rule was 'Next score wins.' It was sudden death. Game over."

Zak turned to his mother. "Mom!"

Marlene shrugged. "Sorry, Zak, but we agreed. It was pretty low and they'll have to live with the shame, and besides, we know who really won this game."

The answer didn't satisfy Zak. He frowned at his dad. "Aren't you supposed to be a role model or something?"

Karp smiled. "Consider that a good life lesson. Don't let your ego get in the way of making smart decisions. And once you got your opponent on the ropes, keep him there until he goes down; let him off and all it takes is one lucky punch."

"Doesn't sound like much of a role model speech to me," Zak grumbled.

Laughing, Karp was about to goad his son some more when Officer Murphy shouted and waved, "Uh, Mr. Karp! I have a call, says it's urgent!"

"Who is it, J.P.?" Karp asked. Rare were the calls that weren't "urgent," though in reality most could wait for him to enjoy a couple of uninterrupted hours with his family.

"It's Mr. Jaxon," Murphy replied, walking toward them.

Karp and Marlene stared at each other with frowns. S. P. "Espy" Jaxon was an old family friend and had once been an assistant district attorney with the New York office, which was where they'd met. But Jaxon had grown tired of dealing with criminals on that end of the justice system and, saying he wanted to be "more proactive," joined the FBI. He'd eventually risen to the rank of special agent in charge of the New York City office, where he'd been when the World Trade Center was attacked on 9/11. Soon after, he'd been asked by someone apparently so high up in the federal government that Jaxon reported only to him, or her — Karp had never asked or been told who — to head up a small, covert antiterrorism group whose main objective was rooting out sleeper cells that had infiltrated the nation's major law enforcement and intelligence agencies. Unlike those agencies, Jaxon's had not been placed under the umbrella of the United States National Security Agency, created in the aftermath of 9/11, and operated quietly behind the scenes.

Given a free hand to form his team, Jaxon had been careful to choose men and women from the FBI and other agencies that he knew personally and trusted implicitly. He was also looking for "outsiders" who didn't have a federal "jacket" and therefore were below the radar of enemies foreign and domestic. These had included several friends of Karp and Marlene, as well as their daughter, Lucy, a "polyglot" capable of fluently speaking more than sixty languages, and her fiancé, Ned Blanchett, a simple ranch hand when he met Lucy but whose natural abilities as a sharpshooter and cool head in perilous situations had made him a perfect fit for Jaxon's team. It was a dangerous job, and the mention of Jaxon's name in the context of an "urgent" message wasn't something Karp and Marlene wanted to hear.

Karp trotted over to meet Murphy, who handed him his cell phone. "Thanks, J.P.," he said. "Hey, Espy, what's up?"

"Where are you?"

The abruptness of the response warned Karp that this was not a social call. "In Central Park with Marlene and the boys."

"I need to see you, and Marlene, right away."

Karp felt a chill run down his spine. Over

the years, his family had been the target of a wide assortment of violent criminals, from sociopathic serial killers to paid assassins to vicious terrorists of many persuasions. "Does this have to do with Lucy?"

The pause on the other end of the line told him all he needed to know. "Yes," Jaxon replied. "But I don't want you to assume the worst. I do need to tell you some things that are best said in person. When will you be home?"

"Can we meet at the loft in twenty?" Karp asked. He glanced over at Marlene, who was standing thirty feet away studying his face while the boys continued to argue about the game.

"I'll see you then," Jaxon replied. "And, Butch, it might be best if the twins were doing something outside of the apartment. What I have to say is for you and Marlene only, and you might want a chance to process it all after I leave before the boys start asking questions."

"I understand. See you in twenty," Karp replied, and pressed the button to end the call. Marlene's serious expression hadn't changed but the boys were used to their dad getting urgent calls and hardly noticed. He called them over and said, "Duty calls; your mom and I need to meet Espy back at the loft. Apparently, he wants to go over an old case and it can't wait."

"But I thought we were going to get cherry cheese coffeecake and see the Sobelmans at Il Buon Pane," Zak complained.

Golda and Moishe Sobelman, the proprietors of Il Buon Pane bakery on 29th and Third, made the best cherry cheese coffeecake in the Five Boroughs, and quite possibly the world. So good, as was the conversation with the Sobelmans, that it wasn't something Karp passed up lightly. "Sorry, guys," he said with genuine regret while getting into the daypack they'd brought and fishing out his wallet. "Tell you what, how about you guys grab a cab over to Il Buon Pane and gorge yourselves on me. And take in a movie afterward."

Zak pouted. "Nah, I think I'll just go home and raid the fridge. Maybe play some Xbox."

However, Giancarlo, the more perceptive of the two, had been studying the interplay between his parents' faces and nudged his brother. "C'mon, it'll be fun. And we can go to a movie or a museum."

Zak started to grouse again but he looked from his brother's face to his dad's and nodded. "But I'm not going to the stupid Museum of Modern Art again. I don't get how most of that stuff got in a museum in the first place."

"I love you, bro." Giancarlo laughed. "The best stuff's on the top floors of MOMA but it wouldn't hurt you to see something new. If it's not a painting of some guys hacking at each other with swords, it's not art to you."

"We all have our own tastes," Zak sniffed, and snatched the cash his dad was offering. "There's a new *Die Hard* movie playing at the Turtle Bay Theater. So how about some cherry cheese coffeecake and a little Bruce Willis 'yippee-ki-yay'?"

With that the boys were off and running for a taxi. Marlene waited until they were out of earshot and turned back to her husband. "Okay, what gives?"

"Espy wants to talk to us, alone. It's about Lucy, but he said not to worry," Karp said, fudging a little bit on the difference between "don't assume" and "don't worry."

Marlene blinked back the fear he'd seen leap into her eyes and nodded. "Let's go."

At Karp's request, Officer Murphy hit the lights and siren and they made it back to the old brick warehouse building on the corner of Grand and Crosby Street in ten minutes. But they still didn't beat a black sedan already parked across the street and

57

the man who got out of the front passenger seat.

For the most part, Jaxon looked his usual secret agent self, with his crew-cut pewter-gray hair, tan, chiseled face, and icy blue eyes. But the customary perfect smile was missing and the silver stubble on his face and dark circles beneath those eyes suggested that he hadn't had much sleep or time to freshen up when he awoke.

Seeing the grim look on his friend's face, Karp didn't wait for him but turned and stepped up on the landing outside the steel security door on the building's Crosby Street side and punched in the entry code. The bottom floor of the building was allegedly occupied by a Chinese import-export business, though there rarely seemed to be any customers, or workers, for that matter. And they knew that it was actually owned by Tran Vinh Do, a former Viet Cong leader and Vietnamese gangster who had befriended Marlene and due to a few odd twists of fate now worked with Jaxon and his agency.

The Karp-Ciampi family loft was on the top floor of the building, accessible strictly by a keyed elevator that ran from the secure entryway inside the steel outside door only to their floor. There was a fire escape on the outside of the building, but it was only accessible from a small deck off their living room.

Jaxon caught up with Karp and Marlene at the elevator and they rode it to the fourth-floor loft without saying anything beyond a quick greeting. They stepped into a small vestibule outside the front door while Butch fumbled at his keys as he tried to calm himself for whatever he was about to hear from Jaxon.

During the car ride over, he and Marlene had held hands but otherwise didn't talk much and looked out of their respective windows lost in thought. They knew Lucy's job held risks that had nearly cost her her life before, and that someday they might receive a call that no parent with a child in harm's way wanted to hear. But Lucy was a patriot and when asked by Jaxon to join his team as an interpreter, believed that she was doing her part for her country and that in some way was also tied to the larger apocalyptic struggle against evil.

When the key finally slid home, Karp opened the door and led the way into the apartment that opened up into one large area that comprised the living room and a kitchen, exposed brick walls, and hardwood floors, obstructed only by big wooden posts that ran eighteen feet between the floor and the rough wooden beams across the ceiling. On the far side of the room was a hallway leading to three bedrooms — the master, another large room with bunks occupied by the twins since birth, and Lucy's room, painted pink and populated by dolls as if a little girl still lived there.

Karp walked into the living room area and sat down near the window in the overstuffed leather chair the kids referred to as "dad's throne" and pointed to a large matching couch around the corner of a glass coffee table. "Have a seat, Espy, you look like you could use a nap."

Meanwhile, Marlene had walked into the kitchen. "Can I get you something to drink?" she called over.

"Water would be great," Jaxon replied.

Marlene returned with three glasses of water and placed them on the coffee table as she sat down on the couch next to Jaxon. She tried to smile but her hand trembled as she picked up a glass and took a small nervous sip.

"I'll get right to the point," Jaxon said, leaning forward and looking at each of his friends. "Last night, a U.S. State Department compound in Chechnya was overrun by a heavily armed force in what was apparently a fast-moving, well-coordinated attack."

Karp furrowed his brow. "I didn't see anything on the television this morning," he said, pointing to the large flatscreen attached to a wall opposite the couch.

Jaxon rubbed his eyes and face tiredly before nodding. "We just got word a few hours ago; not much detail, and what we're hearing is all over the board. We got a quick briefing, but if State and the CIA know more than I just told you, they're not telling us, which wouldn't be unheard of. The White House is expected to make some sort of announcement in a couple of hours. I'm told it will be short and won't have a lot of details . . ."

"So what's this got to do with Lucy?" Marlene interjected, unable to control her fear.

Jaxon reached over and placed a hand on her shoulder. "We think she and Ned were in the compound when it was overrun."

3

"Are you ready?"

Lucy Karp picked up her head at the sound of the woman's voice in front of her. She could not see who spoke but knew her. Even if she hadn't worn a heavy cloth sack over her head, the woman wasn't . . . she groped for the right word in her foggy mind . . . *"real" isn't the right word, she's real enough, maybe "corporeal" would be better.*

"Have you prepared yourself for what's ahead?"

Taking a series of rapid breaths in and out, Lucy tried to clear her head. She was exhausted — physically, mentally, emotionally. She couldn't remember the last thing she'd eaten or, as she licked her parched lips, her last drink of water. She hadn't slept in . . . *How long has it been? More than one night. Two? . . .* The bare lightbulb that hung above the chair to which she was tied had not been turned off since she was first brought to the room from the compound outside Zandaq.

Trying to recall the events that led to her current predicament, she was reminded of a terrible loss. "Ned," she croaked. "What happened to Ned?"

"He's in the hands of God now," the woman in the room with her replied, "and no longer your concern."

Lucy sobbed. "No . . . please."

"Lucy!" the woman snapped. "Focus! It's important that you listen, remember, and survive what's to come."

"Please forgive me, St. Teresa, but I don't want to survive," Lucy cried quietly. "If he's gone, there's no point." She tried to remember what happened, searching for any reason to hope.

She and Ned, along with a four-man team, all former military and hand-selected by Espy Jaxon, had surreptitiously crossed the border into Chechnya from Dagestan more than a week earlier. The plan was to meet with a Chechen separatist leader named Lom Daudov to enlist his aid in hunting down an Al Qaeda terrorist mastermind named Amir Al-Sistani, otherwise known to his followers as The Sheik.

Daudov had no great love for Americans; it didn't help that they looked the other way when Russia sent tanks and troops into Chechnya to stamp out the republic. However, according to Jaxon's sources, Daudov hated the Islamic extremists who'd come to Chechnya to fight for their own reasons and saw them as trying to usurp the nationalist movement for a theocracy, to say nothing of their brutal acts against civilians, which hurt the separatist cause in the court of world opinion.

In Dagestan, the country to the east of Chechnya, the team had been met by a young woman, Deshi Zakayev, who said she would be their guide in Chechnya. However, the first week after they crossed the border had been spent moving from place to place only to learn that when they arrived at each new destination Daudov had already been there and gone, or had never showed up at all. Zakayev explained that "Lom" was one of the most wanted men in Chechnya and being difficult to track was what kept him safe.

"The Russians have a large price on his head," she said. "But being a ghost is also part of his strategy, by convincing spies that he will be in one place when he is striking in another. Did you know that his name, Lom, translates to 'lion'? He is the lion and the hope of a free Chechnya. Don't worry, he will meet with us, but we must keep moving until he feels it is safe."

Traveling mostly at night, always on little-used rural back roads or even trails through the heavily wooded, mountainous region, sometimes on horseback, as well as on foot and in the occasional borrowed truck, they continued the game of cat and mouse. Then on Thursday evening, a week after they first crossed the border, the team assembled in a clearing where they'd camped to discuss whether to declare the mission a failure and return to the States. Lucy, as the team's interpreter, had gone to Zakayev with their decision to pack it in.

"Not yet, please. I was just about to tell you," Zakayev, who had been to a nearby town to get her next instructions, said. "Tomorrow we will be taken by a lorry to a location where in two days' time, on Saturday evening, Lom Daudov will meet with you."

"Why two days?" Lucy asked.

Zakayev shrugged. "Because that is how long it will be."

Lucy reported back to the others, who decided to make one more attempt to rendezvous with the separatist guerilla leader. "If he doesn't show, we're done," she went back and told the young woman.

Riding in an old Russian transport, the team arrived the next night at a walled and gated compound near the town of Zandaq. Hustled inside, out of sight of any prying eyes, they'd been surprised to learn that another group of Americans was already there, Deputy Chief of Mission David Huff from the U.S. embassy in Grozny and his security detachment. The tall, middle-aged diplomat had not been particularly forthcoming about his purpose other than to say he was there on a "trade mission to better our relations with the locals and help them normalize relations with Moscow and the West."

"I must say, we've been waiting here for more than a day but so far the man we're trying to meet with hasn't showed," Huff complained. "Now we're told it's going to be Saturday evening." He said he was just as surprised to see them but seemed to know enough to not ask questions, and Lucy didn't volunteer any information.

So they waited, risking discovery. The Russians were apparently aware of Huff's presence and purported reason for his visit to the region. But Lucy, Ned, and the rest of their team were in Chechnya without permission, even if their purpose was to apprehend, or kill, a terrorist. Like some old

Mission: Impossible episode, Jaxon had told the team that if they were caught by the Russians, the American government would deny sending them. *And all for one man,* Lucy thought, *Amir Al-Sistani.*

The situation was shaky. After their arrival, the other members of Lucy's team had met with Huff's men and weren't happy about the security situation. For one thing, they were surprised that the men traveling with Huff were so lightly armed — nothing heavier than M4 carbines — in such a dangerous part of the world. The U.S. State Department had long ago warned American citizens against visiting the region. There were a multitude of factions fighting the Russians in Chechnya. Some were no more than organized crime syndicates and warlords intent on plundering the country; others fought to create an Islamic state; and still others were Chechen patriots who wanted a secular government that wasn't under the control of Moscow, though even they came in many guises, from socialists, to moderate Muslims, to republicans. When the factions weren't battling the Russians, they were often warring among themselves. The wisdom of traveling about such a country with only a small, lightly armed security team was questionable.

Relying more on stealth, Lucy's team wasn't much better armed. Ned carried an M24, bolt-action sniper's rifle, just in case they found Al-Sistani and there was no way to capture him, but the other men carried Russian-made AK-47s so that wearing native clothing, they might pass as locals without close inspection. But they had to travel light and sought to avoid confrontations.

Although she was sure that Ned kept some of his reservations to himself so as not to frighten her, he did tell her that the ex-military men on both security teams weren't happy about their position from a tactical standpoint. The compound was enclosed by a thick, eight-foot-high stone wall with only one iron gate leading in or out; however, it was surrounded on three sides by thickly wooded hills from which an enemy could move close and then fire down into the complex. While sufficient, perhaps, to deter ill-equipped and poorly led brigands, the compound had clearly not been built to turn back a determined assault.

"Who are these separatist guys anyway?" Ned complained.

"Well, they'd describe themselves to you as patriots, like George Washington," she said. "After the Soviet Union fell apart, the separatists declared Chechnya an independent republic. But the Russians — who don't want to lose Chechen oil refineries and pipelines — weren't having it. The Russians claim Chechnya is a state in their Russian federation and doesn't have the right to secede and they've fought two wars over it. The Chechens actually won the first one in 1996, though the Russians essentially destroyed the country's infrastructure and economy, and even after the peace treaty was signed they stationed two brigades here. Then in 1999, the Russians attacked again, using the pretext that it was necessary to stop Chechen terrorism and organized crime. There was a series of bombings in Moscow that killed about three hundred civilians; the Russian government blamed separatists, but there's pretty good evidence the bombs were planted by the Russian Secret Police to justify the military campaign. This time they were able to gain control over most of the territory and cities, and set up a pro-Moscow regime. They were brutal on the civilian population and most of the best-known separatist leaders were killed, including a former president of the republic. But the separatists keep waging a guerilla war that the Russians haven't been able to break."

Never one for politics, Ned accepted the explanation and went off to scout the area around the compound with other members of the security team. As she waited, Lucy tried to get to know the two Chechens in the compound. One was her guide and the other was a small, thin man, Bula Umarov, who Zakayev said was one of Daudov's advisers. He'd been sent ahead to begin the discussions with Huff's "trade mission," which Lucy suspected was more than it seemed.

Zakayev introduced Lucy to Umarov when they found him sitting alone in an interior courtyard of the main house, and she'd taken an almost immediate dislike to him. He had a pockmarked face and feral, shifty eyes — "like a Harlem rat," she later told Ned — and wouldn't look directly at her. That in itself wasn't unusual in a Muslim country where men were often uncomfortable around Western women, and he was polite enough. But something about him made her skin crawl, and she'd noted a quirk about his way of speaking that troubled her as well.

Lucy not only spoke flawless Chechen, she also had an ear for local dialects and couldn't quite place his. "What part of Chechnya are you from?" she asked after speaking to him for a few minutes.

Something had flashed briefly in those rodent eyes. Alarm or fear, she wasn't sure, but something that put him on alert before he smiled slightly and nodded. "I am from Mozdok, on the northwest side of the country," he said.

"Ah, I see," Lucy replied. "I'd like to visit there sometime to expand my knowledge of Chechen regional differences; there is an ever so slight variation in how you speak that I've not heard before."

Umarov had just stared at her for a moment, during which time Lucy noticed how Zakayev turned her head ever so slightly to study his face. *She doesn't trust, or like, him either,* Lucy thought.

"Perhaps, I can explain that," the man said. "I was raised in an orphanage with children who mostly spoke Russian. Maybe I picked something up from them, though no one has ever remarked on it before."

"Yes, that could explain it," Lucy said. "It is very slight. I doubt anyone else would notice, but languages are sort of my thing."

Saying that he needed to get back to his talks with Huff, Umarov had quickly excused himself and then avoided Lucy for the rest of the evening and the next day. However, several times she'd caught him looking at her, though he'd quickly averted his eyes.

On the other hand, Lucy had enjoyed having some quiet time to talk to Zakayev, a beautiful young woman whose facial features were a fine mix of the many different ethnicities that at one time or another called Chechnya home. Russians. Mongols. Turks. Cossacks. She had a slight Asian tilt to her sea-green eyes, widely spaced in a round, bronzed Slavic face, and long silky black hair that most of the time she covered with a scarf. When they'd been traveling from place to place there hadn't been much of an opportunity to get to know her, but the two young women hit it off now that there was time to relax.

Zakayev described herself as a Chechen patriot and vehemently contended that the Russians were the terrorists, not the separatists, "Though we have been guilty of allowing extremists into the movement that cost us world opinion with their acts. That is why Lom is so adamant about cleansing our ranks of those who fight for their own ends, not our country." She described seeing Russian tanks roll through, and sometimes right over the top of villages, and watching as Chechen men "and sometimes women" were lined up and shot "as a warning" to others.

"Our women are raped, and our men are executed or rounded up and sent away never to be heard from again. Meanwhile, the Russian government is in league with crime syndicates to rob us of our wealth," she said angrily. "Yet the West does nothing except go along with the Russians, who call us the terrorists when we try to carry the fight to their cities and their populations as they have done to us. But we are not so different from you Americans when you fought for independence against a larger, more powerful army that tried to put down your desire for freedom with brutality. Back then it was the British who broke down your doors without justification, arrested your men, abused your women, burned your crops, razed your towns, and hung your patriots in an attempt to terrorize you into submission."

Zakayev burned with the zeal of a partisan. But she was also a young woman, only a few years older than Lucy, and she had many questions about what life was like for an Amercian woman. "Someday I would like to see America," she told Lucy after dinner Saturday night. "But Chechnya is my home and we will build a democracy here that will show you Americans a thing or two about freedom when you have to fight for it."

They all waited up Saturday night for Daudov, but he didn't appear. Zakayev had apologized profusely. "I was assured he would be here," she said. "I never would have sworn such a thing to Allah if I had not believed it. To be honest, I am worried. I am going to the town to see if I can get word."

Lucy heard the concern and fear in the young woman's voice and wondered if it was a product of hero worship or something more . . . womanly. "We can't wait any longer," she told the young woman. "Perhaps he had other, more pressing matters. If you're not back by morning, we'll have to leave." Zakayev nodded and left the compound, after which Lucy went to bed.

The best part about being in the compound was that she and Ned got to share a room, and a bed. They'd fallen asleep in each other's arms, as was their habit, but only slept a few hours before he suddenly sat up in bed, waking her.

"What's the matter?" she asked sleepily. But he didn't get a chance to answer before what sounded like a fierce gun battle erupted outside.

Ned jumped from the bed, pulled on his pants, and strapped a sidearm to his waist. He then flung open the carrying case for his rifle and quickly assembled the parts, not bothering with the scope. "Stay here," he ordered, and started to run from the room. He stopped and turned to look at her. "I love you, Lucy. No matter what, I'll be back for you." Then he was gone.

Soon she heard the regular, paced booming of Ned's gun — louder and deeper than the other rifles. He seemed to be on the roof of the building but moving from position to position. Meanwhile, bursts of automatic fire and explosions filled in the blanks around his shooting.

The battle raged for nearly two hours. Then there was a knock on the door of her room and Jason, a former Navy SEAL on her team, hurried in. He was wounded in the side of his chest, she could see the blood soaking into his shirt, but he seemed not to take any notice as he yelled to her. "Come on, Lucy, I'm getting you out of here!"

Jason turned and led the way through the building and across the courtyard to the main house at the back of the compound where she knew Huff was staying. Shots fired from the wall behind her indicated that the attackers had not yet breached the perimeter. She could also hear Ned and another defender shooting from the roof of the building she'd just left, and at least two more were on the roof of the building she now entered. Her escort walked her quickly down to a room at the end of the hallway and knocked on the heavy wooden door, which was opened by one of Huff's security men.

"Stay here," Jason said before turning to the security man who let them in. "We need you outside." The two men then left and Lucy bolted the door.

Turning around, she saw Huff standing behind a radio operator who was sitting at a desk with his communications equipment laid out in front of him. The radio operator kept typing messages into a keypad, but after a moment would shake his head as apparently there were no responses. Meanwhile, Huff kept urging him to try again and grew more agitated every time the shooting intensified. "Call the goddamn Russians," he yelled at the man at one point.

The firefight outside waxed and waned. At times the shooting and explosions that rocked the house and caused debris to fall from the ceiling and walls seemed so intense that Lucy wondered how the defenders could hold out. But then she'd be reassured by the low, powerful report of Ned's gun and continued firing from the roof above her. Occasionally, the shooting stopped, and she dared hope that the attackers had been beaten off and the door would soon open and Ned would be there with his lovely, homely face and "shucks, ma'am, weren't nothing" grin. But then the shooting would resume.

Finally, there was no more shooting from the roof above them, only the sound of Ned's gun and whoever was with him on the other building. Then there was a deafening explosion that rattled the walls and was followed by a silence so complete that her heart faltered and tears welled up in her eyes. *Oh, Ned,* she thought, though she had no other words for the fear that gripped her. The radio operator got up and grabbed his rifle. "I'll hold them off as long as I can," he said, and stepped out of the room.

Huff collapsed into a corner and covered his face with his hands and began moaning. Suddenly, shooting erupted in the hallway. The screams of the wounded and angry shouts in Arabic told her that the radio operator had ambushed the leading attackers. But the reprieve didn't last long. There was an explosion outside the door, a torrent of shots, and then the sound of a half-dozen voices outside the door speaking in Arabic.

The attackers began pounding on the door. "Do you have a way of calling the U.S. embassy in Grozny?" she demanded of Huff.

"My cell phone," he cried. "But it's not a secure line."

"Who the hell cares now," Lucy shouted. "Call and give it to me."

As though moving in a dream, Huff pulled out his phone, punched in a number, and handed it to Lucy. "No one will answer at this hour," he said.

Lucy whirled away from the diplomat and stood facing the door as it shivered with repeated blows. "This is codename Wallflower," she said, speaking into the phone. "We are at the compound in Zandaq. We've been attacked and overrun. They're trying to get in. I don't think it will be much longer. They are not Chechen; they're speaking Arabic, several native Saudi speakers, a Yemeni, not sure of the others, but I repeat, they are not Chechen . . ."

The pounding on the door grew louder. A crack appeared in the wood at the hinges. "I'm with David Huff." The door burst inward. "They're here," she said as a hooded man with a rifle leaped into the room. He saw her and struck her in the stomach with

78

the butt of his gun, doubling her over and sending the phone flying to the ground where it came apart in pieces.

Other men raced into the room and soon Huff and Lucy were being herded from the room, stepping over the body of the radio operator, and out of the building where they were joined by Jason, who was now bleeding from several wounds, including a gash on his head. As they got to the front of the compound, Jason turned on their captors, striking one in the throat as he grabbed for the man's gun. But he was quickly clubbed to the ground before he could shoot and dragged along with the others.

As they stood in the half-light of several fires and what remained of the compound's electric lights around the walls, a man stepped in front of the captives. "Welcome to the future Islamic Republic of Chechnya," he announced. He stopped talking and appeared to be listening.

Far above their heads, Lucy heard a loud humming as if a horde of angry bees was circling. While she had never seen or heard one before, she knew it was the sound of a drone. *Good,* she thought, *I hope they send a missile to take all of these assholes to hell.*

However, the hooded man just laughed and looked in the direction of the sound.

He raised his hand and pointed. "Ah, we are being watched," he said as his finger continued to trace the flight of the drone. "I hope they've enjoyed the show so far, though apparently whoever is watching either can't, or won't, help you. But no matter." He walked over in front of Huff and pointed a handgun at his head.

"Please," Huff screamed, "I'm here on a —"

"Yes, yes, a 'peaceful trade mission,' is that not what you told the Russians?" the hooded man said in perfect boarding-school English. "But I know what you are doing here. Tsk tsk . . . always conniving and plotting for others to do your dirty work, you Americans. But I cannot allow you to arm my enemies in Chechnya, those ignorant peasants who claim to be followers of the one true faith but in fact by their actions are apostate. Unfortunately, Daudov was not here to share your fates, but at least this infidel plan has been . . . how do you say . . . nipped in the bud."

"What are you going to do with me?" Huff asked, his voice trembling.

"Do?" the hooded man asked. "Well, I MIGHT KILL YOU NOW!" he shouted and stuck the gun out at the diplomat, who cried out in terror. The man laughed derisively. "Or I think for now, I will keep you and see what you are worth to the American government. If not so much, then I will shoot you with pleasure."

The hooded man stepped over to Lucy. The eyes beneath the mask narrowed. "You look vaguely familiar," he said. "Do I know you?"

Lucy's eyes hardened but she said nothing. It had taken her a moment to recognize his voice, because she had not expected the hunted to become the hunter, but she knew then that the hooded man was Amir Al-Sistani.

He reached out to grab her chin and turn her face toward the light from one of the fires. Then he laughed. "Allah be praised! What sort of miracle is this! I did not recognize you in the dark, but I see now — the narrow face, the large nose, the pretty lips and eyes," he said, then snorted as he looked her over. "The boyish body. You're the little interpreter I met many years ago in New York City before you and your friends ruined my beautiful plan to destroy your country. What a surprise we should meet in Chechnya, eh! I guess there is more to you than languages." He let go of her chin and his voice hissed like a snake's. "But we'll have more time to talk about that later."

Al-Sistani then stepped over to Jason, who was still on his knees and laboring from the beating he'd taken and his wounds. The terrorist pointed his weapon. "Accept Allah as the one true God and me as his representative on Earth and I may spare you," he demanded.

Jason looked up at his captor and the barrel of the gun. Neither his eyes nor his voice wavered. "Fuck you and the camel you rode in on, asshole."

Al-Sistani's gun barked once and Jason pitched over to the side. *"I guess he did not want to convert,"* he said, and laughed again. He then looked back up into the night sky in the direction of the drone. "Quick," he shouted to his men in his native Arabic. "The Americans may not be content to just watch for much longer, put the prisoners in one of the trucks, then split up. We'll meet again later at our camp." He hesitated and pointed at Lucy. "And be careful what you say in front of this one, she speaks the language of the Prophet and others as well."

The prisoners were quickly bound and heavy cloth hoods yanked down over their heads before they were thrown into the bed of a small truck and covered with a tarp.

The vehicle sped away from the compound, the sound of the drone disappearing behind them.

They rode in the bed of the truck for many hours, bouncing over rough roads, stopping only once so that — by the sounds of it — their captors could relieve themselves on the road, then fill up the truck's gas tank from jerry cans before climbing back in to resume the drive. The captives were given no such consideration and eventually Lucy gave in to the call of nature.

Bruised, damp, and in shock, Lucy fell into a stupor as the miles passed. She tried not to think about Ned but couldn't help it. *He's dead or badly wounded,* she thought, *or he would have never stopped fighting or trying to save me.* She hoped that somehow he had survived. But just before the truck left the compound, she heard several shots ring out and the sound of men laughing and talking in Arabic about "putting the infidels out of their misery," and she cried for her man.

When they at last arrived at what was apparently the terrorists' base, Lucy was separated from Huff and dragged, still hooded, into a building and down several flights of stairs to the room where she was tied to a hard wooden chair. Then she was left alone without food or water. The light-bulb had been kept on, and indigenous music played incessantly from the hallway where her guards apparently passed the time, to deprive her of sleep. If she tried to nod off, one of her unseen captors would enter the room and slap her until she cried out and blood ran from her split lips. But no one spoke to her, or asked her any questions.

Her mind seemed lost in a fog so she wasn't quite sure what to make of it when she sensed another presence in the room. She had not heard the door open or the sound of footsteps. But then she felt enveloped as though in a warm blanket and a sense of calm descended on her. Even though her eyes were covered and her brain addled by lack of sleep, dehydration, and grief she knew who it was. "St. Teresa," she whispered.

Ever since she was a child, in times of stress or danger Lucy had experienced what, for lack of a better word, were "visitations" from a woman dressed in a blue hooded robe, St. Teresa of Avila, a sixteenth-century martyr. The apparition had a kind face, and she was pretty and Spanish and full of grace, and would appear to warn

Lucy of impending menaces, or counsel her through perilous events, or simply comfort her in times of great need. As a child, Lucy had simply accepted the presence as her guardian spirit. As a young woman, she wondered if the psychologists she talked to were right and that the manifestation was simply a psychological coping mechanism. But in her heart she knew that St. Teresa was as real as sunlight, if just as difficult to hold.

It had been years since the saint had appeared, even though Lucy had certainly experienced stressful, dangerous times. She wondered if that was because she'd outgrown the need for such help. But now she appeared again and Lucy realized that the last time she'd seen her, Al-Sistani had been in New York to set into motion his evil plan.

"Shhhh, child," whispered the familiar voice in her ear. "Don't let them hear you."

"I'm afraid."

"Though you walk through the valley of the shadow of death, fear no evil: for He is with you."

"I'm heartbroken."

" 'Cast your cares on the Lord and He will sustain you; he will never let the righteous fall.' Now you must put your fear and grief aside. Are you ready? Have you prepared yourself for what's ahead?"

"Ned," Lucy croaked. "What happened to Ned?"

"He's in the hands of God now, and no longer your concern."

"No . . . please."

"Lucy! Focus! It's important that you listen, remember, and survive what's to come."

"Please forgive me, St. Teresa, but I don't want to survive. If he's gone, there's no point."

"Where there's life there's hope, child. There is not much time, HE is coming. Listen, what do you hear?"

"Nothing. I hear nothing, only the sound of my wounded heart."

"You must listen beyond yourself. Someday it will be important. What do you hear?"

Lucy stopped talking and was still. At first she didn't know what she was listening for, but then she heard a voice somewhere far above her. "I hear the muezzin calling the faithful to evening prayers," she said. "I'm in a mosque! The basement of a mosque!"

"Excellent, my child. Do you hear the guards praying outside your door?"

Again Lucy grew still, and what had been an indistinguishable mumbling became words. "They are from Dagestan. And seagulls! I hear seagulls! We're near the Caspian Sea. The music they were playing included a linginka, a Dagestani folk song. We are in Dagestan!"

"Keep listening, child, remember, and then be prepared when the moment comes." Lucy felt a light touch on her cheek as though the apparition had brushed her with her lips. "Be strong. He will neither fail nor abandon you," the saint said just as the door opened.

A hand grabbed the top of the hood and roughly yanked it off. Lucy blinked in the harsh glare of the lightbulb, and it took her eyes a moment to focus on the face of the man who stood in front of her. His features were all Saudi and reminded her of a predatory bird, with his large hooked nose and black intense eyes set close together in a dark face; his black mustache and beard were kept closely cropped, framing his gleaming white teeth that now showed as he smiled at her.

"Ah, my little bird," Amir Al-Sistani said. "At last we come to you. I'm so sorry to have kept you waiting, but I had some errands to run. I trust your accommodations have been to your liking. No? Oh, well, I will have to speak to management about that. It's so hard to get good help these days." He leaned down so that his face was only a few inches from hers. "Tell me, what brings you to Chechnya?"

Lucy said nothing, so Al-Sistani continued. "I know you were not with the deputy chief of mission's party. You were smart not to tell him anything, by the way, he started squealing as soon as he got a look at my friend Raad here," he said, nodding over his shoulder to where a very large, bare-chested man stood holding two large ten-gallon containers, "and his knife, and he hasn't stopped talking yet. Not exactly a paragon of that famous American courage. So I know all about this plan to meddle in the affairs of Syria and at the same time arm my enemy, Lom Daudov. But why are you here?"

"Go to hell," Lucy said.

Al-Sistani smiled, but then as fast as a cobra he slapped her hard across the side of her face. "I guess we will have to do this the hard way," he said apologetically. "Bula, will you come in here, please?"

Lucy turned to look as the door opened again. Umarov stepped into the room. "I sensed that you were evil," she said in Chechen.

Umarov smiled and shrugged. "I suppose that would depend on your point of view."

Al-Sistani laughed. "I see you have met my spy," he said. "But please, let us speak in Arabic or English, my Chechen is rudimentary at best. . . . As I was saying, Umarov helped set up this little ambush, though I must say I am disappointed that one of my intended victims was not present." He turned to glare at Umarov when he spoke.

Umarov stopped smiling and fear crossed his eyes. "Daudov told me himself that he would be there. I had no other word or way of letting you know before the fighting began."

"You are forgiven, Bula," Al-Sistani said. "It still turned out well. And now you will have the privilege of assisting me." He nodded to the large man, who walked around behind Lucy and placed the containers next to the chair as Al-Sistani replaced the hood. Raad then tilted the chair backward until her feet were above her and her head was down near the floor.

"Bula, if you would do the honors," Lucy heard Al-Sistani say. The next thing she knew, water was being poured over the cloth in front of her face and she couldn't breathe. Every time she tried to inhale, it felt as if she was drowning. She kicked her feet and struggled against her bonds until she felt the ropes cutting into her skin.

Then suddenly the chair was set back upright and the hood pulled from her face. She gasped for air.

"Now will you answer my question?" Al-Sistani asked lightly.

When Lucy didn't reply, he put the hood back on and she was tilted back again. This time they drowned her until she was on the verge of passing out, her desperate struggles growing weaker, then suddenly she was sitting up again and gulping in lungfuls of air.

Al-Sistani patted her cheek. "Catch your breath, little bird, it is time to chirp, or would you care for another bath?" he said with his face pressed close to hers.

"Would you mind backing up, you have foul breath," Lucy croaked.

This time Al-Sistani snarled and the water torture was resumed. As Lucy felt herself start to lose consciousness, she suddenly felt the serene presence of St. Teresa again. "Tell him, child," the saint said. "It's okay, the important thing is that you survive. Tell him."

Lucy screamed as best she could through the water that filled her mouth and throat. The chair was placed back on all four feet. But this time the hood was not removed and she still had to fight to get any air.

"What was that, little bird?" Al-Sistani

asked. "Did I hear you try to speak?"

Lucy coughed and nodded her head. The hood was removed and she sat for a moment panting.

"And what was it you wanted to tell me, little bird?"

Lucy looked up and into the evil man's eyes. She smiled. "We came here to kill or capture you, you son of a bitch."

In the split second it takes to blink, doubt filled and left Al-Sistani's eyes. He sneered. "Apparently you're not very good at what you do. Instead, it's your friends who are feeding the crows, and Bula here tells me your boyfriend is among the carrion."

Lucy tried to hide her reaction but knew by his smile that her grief was transparent. For a moment she wished that he'd drowned her. But then deep inside herself a voice urged her to live on so that if she got the chance, she could kill the man herself.

"Shall I slit her throat?" Raad asked his master.

Al-Sistani appeared to think about it for a moment, then shook his head as he turned to leave. "No, not yet. She and the other one may be useful. But I promise, when the moment is right, you may wash your blade in their blood."

4

Karp was lost in thought as he arrived at the Criminal Courts Building. So engrossed was he in looking down at the sidewalk that he nearly bowled over the small man in the dirty stocking cap with the pointy nose and Coke-bottle-bottom-lens glasses who'd stepped in front of him.

"Hey, what . . . piss shit . . . do I look like a . . . whoop oh boy . . . tackling dummy?" Dirty Warren Bennett exclaimed, as only a man with Tourette's syndrome could.

"Oh, sorry, Warren, I wasn't watching where I was going," Karp said to his friend, who owned the newsstand in front of the massive gray edifice, which housed the city lockup known as the Tombs, the grand jury rooms, clerical departments, the courts, the judges' chambers, Legal Aid Offices, and the offices of the district attorney of New York County.

"Well, that's . . . whoop whoop tits . . .

obvious." Dirty Warren laughed as he peered up at his much taller friend. Then he frowned. "Hey, Butch, you . . . whoop oh boy . . . okay?"

Karp looked into the magnified pale blue eyes of his worried companion. *No,* he thought, *I'm not. My baby girl and her fiancé are missing in action in a far-off country and there's nothing I can do about it.* But he said, "Yes, thanks for asking. You got the *Times* and the *Post*?"

"Of course," Dirty Warren said. "When . . . fucking-A . . . don't I? Are you sure you're . . . whoop whoop . . . okay?"

"Yeah, just a little preoccupied."

"Good, good. Whoooooop. Hey, try this one out. In *The Brothers Karamazov* what is the verdict at Dmitri's trial?"

Karp frowned. "Why'd you pick that movie?"

"Huh? I don't know, I rented it . . . scratch my balls bitch . . . the other night from that classic video store on Bowery. It's about . . ."

"I know what it's about," Karp replied.

"Well, my my somebody . . . tits and ass . . . got up on the wrong side of the bed," Dirty Warren said slowly. "You sure you're . . . whoop . . . okay?"

Karp patted his friend on the back. They'd been playing the movie trivia game ever since he'd met the little news vendor more than a decade earlier. He'd never lost a round either. But today he just had no heart for it. "Sorry, Warren, I've got a lot on my mind. Some other time, okay?"

"Yeah, sure. Here's your . . . bullshit whoop . . . papers. Nah, keep your money, least I can . . . asswipe oh boy ohhhh boy . . . do for a friend who's having a rough morning."

"And you're a good friend, Warren," Karp responded. "We'll catch up later. By the way, Dmitri was innocent, but the jury found him guilty." He turned and walked away from the worried news vendor and headed for the main entrance of the courts building. He intended to go through a side entrance on Leonard Street where a private elevator reserved for himself and judges carried him up to his eighth-floor office. But he'd been so preoccupied with Lucy that, after inadvertently almost knocking Warren to the ground, he decided just to go in the front entrance at 100 Centre Street.

The building wasn't open to the public for business until 8:00 a.m., a half hour away, but a security guard let him in. He crossed the lobby and pressed the button for the elevator before glancing at the front page of the *New York Times*. Most of the articles were related to the upcoming elections. The top story was about yet another gaffe the presidential challenger had made at a fundraiser. It was an ill-advised attempt at humor that had come off as insulting to women, and of course the *Times* — and, Karp suspected, the rest of the media would follow suit — had taken it out of context and blown it out of proportion to make it look as though the candidate had intended it in some callous way. The *Times* quoted the president's bombastic campaign manager, Rod Fauhomme, as saying the challenger was "out of touch and out of time" with voters.

As he read, Karp shook his head. He'd met the president's opponent and thought of him as a good family man and astute captain of industry, more interested in righting the ship of state with sound economic policy than in engaging in a war of empty words. He was overmatched when it came to rhetoric and disinclined to get into personal attacks, though he was consistently portrayed as "mean-spirited" and the pawn of corporations and Wall Street. Combine that with a cheerleading media that fawned all over the president without even the pretense of objectivity and it was a wonder that some pollsters still gave him a slugger's chance at a come-from-behind victory.

The president's poor showing at the first debate had been met with open dismay and alarm by a shocked media, which then rallied to make excuses for their man. Many insisted that he was tired from the "unfortunate necessity" of attending fundraisers in Hollywood but coincidentally engaged in the day-to-day necessities of his job, and truly surprised by the "lies and half-truths" of his opponent's debate points. The president had then come back in the second debate on foreign policy — a subject that the challenger admittedly had little experience in — by claiming to have almost singlehandedly destroyed Al Qaeda and the threat of Islamic extremists while negotiating for "a safer America than when I came into office four years ago."

Easy, Butch, Karp cautioned himself, *presidential politics will be what they are; you've got enough to deal with right here at home.* He looked for news about what the media now referred to as the "Chechnya incident." He found it relegated to the bottom of the page and there wasn't much. A brief recap of what was known: that about 3:00 p.m. EST, a U.S. State Department compound in a remote area of Chechnya had been overrun by unknown assailants, who, according to some sources "in the administration who requested anonymity because they aren't cleared to talk about the situation," had been identified by Russian authorities as Chechen terrorists connected to "criminal elements."

Karp's heart skipped a beat when he read "there are no known survivors," but he forced himself to read on. The remainder of the short story reported that the president was going to address the nation that morning from the Rose Garden. Except for a brief statement Sunday that he was "monitoring the situation" and keeping up with "a fluid and evolving situation," the administration had declined to comment to that point, "preferring to wait until the facts come in."

"Good morning, Butch."

Karp was surprised to hear the familiar voice behind him. He turned. "Good morning, Espy," he replied, searching the agent's face for clues to whether he came bearing good tidings or bad. But there was nothing he could read in the blue-steel eyes or set jaw, so he asked, "Any news?"

Jaxon nodded toward the elevator door that had just opened. "Let's go talk in your office, if you don't mind."

The men were alone on the ride up to the

eighth floor, but they kept their conversation light except when Jaxon asked how Marlene was taking the situation. "Hard," Karp replied. "She's taking it hard. I don't think she's slept much since Sunday and paces around a lot. You and I both know how tough she is, but yesterday I found her in Lucy's room sitting on the bed crying. I think the worst part is not being able to do anything about it; that's bad enough for me, but Marlene's first reaction to almost any stress is to take action. Not knowing and not being able to go rescue her baby girl has her on edge."

Jaxon nodded. "Well, I may have some news that will help," he said, but waited until they exited the elevator, walked down the hall, through his office's reception area, and into Karp's inner sanctum.

The office was a throwback to another time when Karp's mentor, the legendary DA Francis Garrahy, sat behind the immense mahogany desk that dominated the shadowed room with its dark wood paneling, leather-upholstered seats, and a wall filled from floor to ceiling by a bookshelf lined with law books and classics. Even the window coverings were heavy green drapes that Karp now pulled back to let in the morning light before he sat down at the desk as Jaxon settled into a chair across from him. Although Karp didn't himself partake, there was a faint odor of cigars and scotch lingering from days gone by.

"So what's this life ring you're tossing us?" Karp asked. He meant the question to sound more matter-of-fact than it came out, but Marlene wasn't the only one whose nerves were frayed.

Part of the difficulty was there was no one to talk to about their fears. They explained their melancholy to the boys as an old friend having passed away. And the only person Karp had told about the situation was Fulton. Marlene had called Karp's cousin, Ivgeny Karchovski, a former Russian army colonel and, more germane to the issue, the head of a criminal syndicate in Brooklyn's Little Odessa. She hoped that his connections in Russia might be able to find out more than they were getting through official channels. She said he'd gotten back to her but other than reports that his former employer, the Russian army, was cracking down hard in Chechnya, there wasn't much. *I would not want to be associated with the separatist movement in Chechnya right now,* Marlene quoted him. He also told her that it was possible that Al Qaeda in Chechnya was involved.

"I still don't have a lot," Jaxon said. "Those NSA pencil-necks and the CIA goons are playing this close to the vest. It's 'need to know' basis and because they weren't told about our mission — and are scratching their heads over reports that there may have been another agency in the area — I don't have a way to ask a lot of questions. However, one thing that jumped out at me from the most recent report they cared to share was that the preliminary — and I emphasize *preliminary* — news from the Russians on scene is that there are no female victims among the dead. It's not much . . ."

". . . but I'll take it," Karp finished the sentence for him. "Anything else?"

"Yeah, there's one more item of note, though I hesitate to make too much out of it. If you add the people with the other team to ours, not counting Lucy, it would appear from the tally that several male bodies have not been recovered by the Russians either. Again, we need to view this with caution; there were apparently fires, explosions, and heavy weapons involved in the attack, and some bodies may not be . . . intact. But I guess what I'm saying is that there remains hope that Lucy survived and that there are male survivors, too."

Karp closed his eyes and nodded. "Thanks for bringing me the news, and Marlene will be grateful, too. So if Lucy's alive, and possibly these men, they may be hostages?"

"It's a possibility," Jaxon said. "In which case we can hope to negotiate their release."

"I thought we didn't negotiate with terrorists?" Karp said. Again his voice sounded harder than he intended.

"Normally it is the policy of the United States not to negotiate hostages for prisoner exchanges or untenable demands," Jaxon agreed. "However, that's not to say our government won't make concessions on 'humanitarian grounds' with some backdoor bribes. And to be honest, there have been quiet prisoner exchanges handled through third parties in the past."

Karp put his hands behind his neck and sat back as he regarded his old friend. "So you want to tell me what my daughter was doing in Chechnya?"

Jaxon held his gaze and then nodded. "I'm sure you understand that this is all highly classified," he said, "but she was with a team trying to apprehend, or kill, Amir Al-Sistani."

At the mention of the terrorist's name, Karp's eyes widened. Several years earlier, Al-Sistani had arrived in New York City ostensibly as the mild-mannered business manager of a Saudi prince who happened to own one of the largest hedge funds in the world. He knew his daughter had even met the man at a mosque in Harlem where she'd played the part of an interpreter for the prince's visit.

Outwardly meek and obsequious, Al-Sistani had worked his way into the prince's favor for the purpose of controlling the hedge fund in order to use it to destroy the U.S. economy. On the day that the prince rang the opening bell at the New York Stock Exchange and began a tour of the facility, Al-Sistani set his plan into motion by first short-selling his employer's holdings, causing the market to tumble. He then attempted to blow up the computer system that protected the New York Stock Exchange from crashes. He also tried to destroy the computer's backup at a secure facility across the East River in Brooklyn.

The plan was a work of pure evil genius. If it had run its course, the market would have been unable to avoid the free fall and would collapse, which like a row of dominoes, would have then caused banks to fail, businesses to close, and rioting. Chaos and panic would have enveloped the United States and then the world as other markets and economies followed America over the precipice.

In the rubble of Western civilization, Al-Sistani apparently dreamed of a massive uprising in the Islamic world as secular governments were overthrown in favor of a one-world government run according to Islamic law. Armed with nuclear weapons from Pakistan and Iran, this unified Muslim world would step into the void to vanquish and subjugate the West. It would be the beginning of a modern Caliphate with Al-Sistani as the caliph. No small dream, and the dominoes all had to fall just right, but he'd come within seconds of succeeding with at least the initial phase of his plan. But the disaster was averted thanks to the courage of some of the mosque's congregation, as well as well-timed intervention by others, including Karp, Marlene, Lucy, and Jaxon and his team, culminating in desperate gun battles in the bowels of the stock exchange and the building across the river.

After Al-Sistani's subsequent apprehension, Karp had planned to charge him with murder. However, he'd been persuaded by Jaxon to wait on the indictment so that the feds could swing a deal with Al-Sistani to learn who in the U.S. government, and particularly its law enforcement and intelligence agencies, might have assisted him in the attack on the stock exchange. It was believed that a powerful, secret cabal of politicians, businessmen, and military leaders had been working with him to further their own plans to seize control of the U.S. government in the pandemonium of an economic meltdown.

However, Karp and Jaxon both were blindsided when the umbrella national security agency made a quick deal to extradite Al-Sistani to Saudi Arabia to stand trial for the murder of the Saudi prince he'd worked for and murdered in the stock exchange. The trial had been a farce. Al-Sistani was a hero in the Muslim world for his attempt to destroy the United States, and the Saudi government had caved in to public pressure and acquitted him of the charge. Instead, the public relations machine of the Kingdom had gone along with the lie that the prince had actually been killed by overzealous American law enforcement.

"As you know, Al-Sistani's release from prison was greeted with wild jubilation by Muslims worldwide," Jaxon said. "However, he knew we'd be coming after him again and he went into hiding. We've been looking for him for years, hoping to hand him back over to you. We followed a trail of rumors from Yemen to Libya and the tribal regions of Pakistan. Then about six months ago, we started getting reports that he'd shown up in Chechnya to take over Al Qaeda operations there. Our intel was that he is planning to create an Islamic state from which to rebuild his megalomaniacal dreams."

"Which is why my daughter . . ."

". . . as the team's interpreter . . ."

". . . and Ned . . ."

". . . and four others, all good men . . ."

". . . were in Chechnya the same time as Huff and his trade mission."

"That was purely coincidental, though we don't know the 'trade mission's' real purpose — I suspect it was more than a cultural exchange. For that matter, we don't know why Lucy and her team were in Zandaq and can only assume it was connected to their mission. For security reasons, we'd had no communications with them since they crossed the border from Dagestan."

"So did they know where Al-Sistani is hiding?"

"All we had was that he'd been seen quite a bit in the southeast region of Chechnya, near the border with Dagestan," Jaxon replied. "But the plan was to try to make contact with a separatist guerilla leader named Lom Daudov and persuade him to help them find Al-Sistani."

"Why him? Aren't these the guys the Russians are saying were behind the attack?"

"The Russians would blame Christ's crucifixion on Chechen separatists if they could, and to be honest, some groups associated with the independence movement have committed some pretty heinous acts," Jaxon said. "But the movement is made up of many different groups, each with their own agendas. In truth, it's a civil war and there's been a lot of brutality on both sides. But the worst of the atrocities — a school massacre in Grozny and a theater takeover in Moscow that ended badly, both of which by the way we know our friend Nadya Malovo was involved with — seem to have been committed by the Islamic hardliners, most of them foreign fighters committed to jihad, and possibly the Russians themselves to justify occupying Chechnya."

"So what's the difference between the extremists and this Daudov?"

"He's a devout Muslim in his spiritual practices," Jaxon said, "but from what little we know of his politics, he and others like him — all of them Chechen — want to establish a secular democracy. Apparently, as Al Qaeda's influence has grown in Chechnya with the influx of foreign fighters, he got alarmed that the bid for independence was being co-opted by extremists trying to create an Islamic state. We don't know much about Daudov, he's sort of an enigma, but we're told that his basic philosophy is 'Chechnya for Chechens; everybody else get the hell out!' In particular there is no love lost between him and Al Qaeda, which is suspected of having tried to assassinate him in the past. Which brings us to why we wanted to meet with him and see what he might ask in exchange for helping us bring Al-Sistani back to the States for trial."

"But the president said at the debate that Al Qaeda doesn't exist as a viable threat anymore."

"That's politics. Centralized leadership in Al Qaeda was always more philosophical than tactical; Al Qaeda operates as semi-autonomous groups dedicated to one goal, creating a world Islamic state. As such they are alive and well, if under pressure from our attacks."

"It all sounds like risky business to me, this mission to enlist Daudov's help," Karp noted.

Jaxon looked down and then up again. "You're right," he said. "It was. Very little isn't anymore, it seems." He paused and his voice grew husky. "I wasn't going to let Lucy go on this one, but I've got a small agency and nobody else who spoke Chechen. The success of the mission would depend on being able to negotiate with this Daudov and she knew it, so she insisted. Of course, now I wish . . ."

As Jaxon's voice faltered, Karp felt sorry for his friend. Jaxon was Lucy's godfather and sure to hold himself responsible for what had happened. "I know this weighs on you. But Lucy is a strong-willed young woman. She told me on more than one occasion how proud she was to be working for you. She said she felt she was really making a difference."

Jaxon looked up, his eyes brimming with tears. "Thanks, Butch. I guess the best thing to do right now is hope and say our prayers."

The moment was interrupted by a knock on the door. "Come in," Karp called.

The door opened and the beehive hairdo and heavily made-up face of his receptionist, the widow Darla Milquetost, appeared. "Oh, sorry, Mr. Karp," she said. "I knew you were here because the light was on, but I didn't know you had a guest so early. Good morning, Mr. Jaxon."

"Good morning, Darla," both men said at

the same time. "What can I do for you?" Karp added.

"I was just going to tell you that the president is about to go on television to talk about this terrible thing in Chechnya."

Karp looked at his watch and then sat up, grabbing the remote control from his desk and pointing it at the television across the room. "You're absolutely right. Thank you for the reminder."

Milquetost disappeared and the television blinked on just as the president approached the lectern in the Rose Garden. "My fellow Americans," he began, "I come to you today with both a heavy heart as well as firm resolve. As we all know by now, on what was a pleasant Saturday afternoon for most of us, a peaceful U.S. trade mission in Chechnya was overrun in the dead of night by what our friends in Russia have identified as a loosely organized group of criminals and extremists bent on preventing the normalization of the natural relationship between these two peoples. This attack was carried out quickly, without warning or provocation, and in brutal fashion, and brave Americans, there to offer the hand of peaceful cooperation, were murdered. Our Russian friends have secured the site and have launched a vigorous investigation into this terrible event. Unfortunately, at this point, we must report that there are no known survivors, including the mission's leader, Deputy Chief of Mission David Huff, who was stationed at the U.S. embassy in Grozny."

The president paused as he looked out over the assembled media to allow the cameras to capture the very presidential moment. "These murderers," he continued at last, "paint themselves as peace-loving Muslims in search of independence. But do not let their rhetoric fool you, they are little more than thugs and vicious criminals who hide their deeds beneath a cloak of Chechen patriotism and use terror to bully and intimidate the majority of citizens in Chechnya who want nothing to do with them. Our friends in Russia have known the truth for many years, and suffered horrible atrocities at the hands of these cowards. Unfortunately Sunday morning in Chechnya, we learned their truth the hard way. But let me be clear, with the help of the Russian authorities, we will leave no stone unturned, no effort short of the maximum, until the perpetrators are caught and brought to justice."

The president then opened the floor to questions from the media. Picked to begin was a talking head for one of the major networks. "Mr. President," the man asked in his best "I'm a serious journalist" voice, "you said the attack was carried out quickly. How fast are we talking about and could our people have been saved?"

"Well, Dave, we're still sorting through the reports," the president replied, "but our best information is that it was over from start to finish in a half hour, maybe less. We scrambled an unmanned aerial vehicle, a fully-armed drone, as soon as we had any indication of trouble, and had two fighters standing by at an airfield in Turkey. But by the time the drone arrived, our people were dead and the killers were gone. The attack occurred in the early morning hours and apparently caught our people off-guard; I'm sure they gave a good account of themselves, but they were overwhelmed in very short order. The Russians also sent a tactical assault squad — I should point out that Chechnya is a Russian state and under their authority — to help, but again, it was already too late."

Another member of the media, the White House reporter for the *New York Times,* waved his hand in the air like a schoolboy who thinks he has the right answer. He knew he was going to be called as it had already been worked out with the president's press secretary, Rosemary Hilb, but he was excited just the same when the president pointed to him.

"Yes, Josh?"

"Is there anything to the possibility that the Iranians may have been involved?"

The president frowned as if he'd been hit by a tough question he hadn't anticipated, much less one that had been planted by Hilb. "Let me say this about that . . . we have no direct evidence that the government of Iran was involved in the attack. We do know, however, that as a matter of policy, they are a rogue nation that believes in meddling in the affairs of other countries and in terrorism as a means of achieving their political ends."

The president had hardly reached the end of his sentence when a tall female reporter with a mane of blond hair, wearing a bright red dress that matched her lipstick, raised her hand and shouted for attention.

"Is that who I think it is?" Jaxon asked.

Karp nodded. "The inimitable Ariadne Stupenagel. But it doesn't look like the president is going to call on her."

In fact, the president turned away from Stupenagel and pointed to a young woman who wrote a column for a lightweight online news agency. "It's Diane, right?" he asked with his famously charming smile.

The reporter blushed at the familiarity and seemed to forget her question for a moment before remembering. "Do we have any specific idea of who these killers might be?" she asked coquettishly.

"Well, Diane, that's a good question," he said with another smile. "Again, the information is frustratingly limited, but one name has emerged as a 'person of interest.' Lom Daudov. He's one of these extremists masquerading as a patriot that I talked about before. Our understanding is that he was seen in the area that day. He is already wanted by the Russians, and the legitimate, duly elected government of Chechnya, for previous violent, criminal acts. As an American, I believe that this man has the right to be considered innocent until proven guilty, but he's certainly a suspect and we're very interested in his quick apprehension."

At the mention of Daudov, Karp had looked at Jaxon, who furrowed his brow but said nothing.

The president held up his hand as if he was going to end the press conference.

"MR. PRESIDENT! Is it possible that the attackers were not separatists but foreign fighters linked to Al Qaeda in Chechnya?"

113

It was Stupenagel again, this time shouting so loud into the television camera microphones that the president couldn't ignore her without its being too obvious.

The president scowled. "We have received no reports of any kind, that I am aware of, suggesting that Al Qaeda played any part in this attack. As I stated clearly during the debate more than a week ago, Al Qaeda as a viable terrorist organization doesn't exist anymore. At my direction, we chopped the head off the snake, and without the head, the body dies. I think sometimes, some people — or political parties — like to trot Al Qaeda out as some sort of bogeyman to frighten the American people. But the days of that terrorist organization being a real threat came to an end after I came into office. I understand there are always rumors — their genesis, well, I think we all know who has something to gain by trying to discredit this administration — but just because Chechnya is predominantly Muslim, and these killers may in fact be Muslim, at least in name, that doesn't make them Al Qaeda. And perhaps, Ms. Stupenagel, we should be sure of our facts before repeating them in a public forum."

The brash reporter ignored the public scolding. "Mr. President, would you care to comment on reports that the Russians, and their puppet government in Chechnya, are using this as a pretext to crack down on a popular uprising?"

"I don't think it's appropriate for me to comment on how the Russians, and the legitimate government of Chechnya, go about the business of apprehending criminals," the president snapped. "We've had no credible reports of any human rights violations, and as I think even you, Ms. Stupenagel, would have to agree, this administration has repeatedly gone to bat for oppressed people all over this world. Now, thank you all for coming. I believe Ms. Rosemary Hilb will take a few more questions."

With that the president turned and left the podium. A short, fierce-looking woman with jet black hair, pale skin, a gray pantsuit, and a "don't fuck with me" look took his place. Hilb answered questions in short, clipped, safe sentences and then announced that the press conference was over like a sergeant dismissing a company of new recruits.

Karp turned off the television. "What do you think?" he said.

Jaxon looked troubled. "Something doesn't smell right," he said. "I still have to wonder why Daudov would attack a 'peaceful trade mission,' not to mention my team, when we were there to talk to him about getting rid of one of his enemies. If anything, he's been cultivating world public opinion in his battle with the Russians."

"I can't say how I know," Karp added, "but Stupenagel's comment about the Russians' using this as an excuse to crack down on separatists fits what I've heard from a very reputable source on the region. So was her remark about Al Qaeda."

"I believe it," Jaxon said, then smiled. "So the long arm of Butch Karp stretches halfway around the globe, eh?"

Karp, thinking about his wife and his cousin, Ivgeny Karchovski, simply replied, "I just happen to know someone who knows someone."

"Well, Ariadne seemed certain of herself," Jaxon noted. "I mean, the girl has never lacked for sources. I wonder how concrete her information is and where she got it."

"Might be worth asking her," Karp said. "But she has this thing about protecting her sources and gets her back up when asked. She is a sucker for a good-looking guy, however, in spite of being betrothed to my office manager, Gilbert Murrow, so you might turn on the old Jaxon charm."

"I tried that a few years ago with her, hoping she'd reveal a source." Jaxon laughed. "But all I got out of it was a big bar bill and a proposition that I'm still not sure is physically possible."

5

Rod Fauhomme hoisted himself up from his chair and lumbered across the room with his hand extended when the fit-looking man with the tan, chiseled face knocked and entered the office in the West Wing of the White House. "General Allen, good of you to join us," he said in his best midwestern "damn glad to meet you" voice.

Lt. Gen. Sam Allen regarded him for a moment with his cool hazel eyes and then nodded. "Thank you. I didn't realize you'd be here when Mr. Lindsey asked me to drop by. I thought this was a security matter, not politics," he said, and turned to face the president's national security adviser, who stood up at his desk but remained next to his chair.

Fauhomme let the snub slide off him like grease on a hot skillet. He was used to the rich and powerful regarding him as a political hack, useful when the going got tough, and paid to do a dirty job so that they could keep their hands clean and have someone else to blame if something went wrong. *Like a plumber called in to unclog a toilet,* he thought as he dropped his hand but continued to smile at the general. They were also afraid of him, and with good reason; he was the kingmaker and whatever it took was what he did. *That's okay, pretty boy, as long as you play ball with my team I couldn't care less what you think of me. But step out of line and I'll crush you like a grape. AND enjoy doing it.*

Over at his desk, Tucker Lindsey suppressed a smile at the slight to Fauhomme. *Way to put the son of a bitch in his place,* he thought. However, he remained standing next to his chair for a reason, which was to establish the pecking order. He was the president's NSA, and one of his most trusted friends and advisers during his first term in office; Allen was "just" the acting director of the CIA and an outsider in the administration. Lindsey wanted to make sure the man knew who he had to answer to; it was at Lindsey's suggestion that the president submitted Allen's name to Congress for confirmation and Lindsey could make sure that nomination was withdrawn, too.

Some in the president's entourage of advisers thought Allen was an odd choice in the first place. By all accounts, the general seemed at best apolitical and certainly had never evinced any of the left-leaning views of the administration. But the agency director before him, a political-payback appointee from the first term, had resigned in disgrace after being caught in a child pornography sting by D.C. police. It was a public relations nightmare with the president's re-election campaign in full swing and already taking hits for the economy and a series of foreign policy gaffes. They needed to come up with a replacement whose reputation on both sides of the aisle, as well as with the American public, was unimpeachable. And who better than an American war hero?

As the press was fond of writing, Lt. Gen. Sam Allen was a soldier's soldier. He eschewed politics and even stayed away from the jockeying for position and publicity common among the military hierarchy, in which generals vied to become celebrities with an eye on lucrative television contracts as "military experts" after retirement. Instead, throughout his long and illustrious military career, Allen had quietly done his job, honoring his oath to protect the Constitution and serve at the behest of whoever was his commander-in-chief.

His resume couldn't have been better, or cleaner. He was a West Point man; graduated head of his class. In 1991, he served in Operation Desert Storm, where he earned his first Silver Star. Twenty years later, he had a chest full of medals, though except on formal occasions the only extraneous emblems that appeared on his uniform, other than his symbols of rank, were the dual parachutes of the 101st Airborne. The public knew him as the general who saved the administration's bacon in Afghanistan when it looked like the Taliban was going to send the U.S. home in a press-orchestrated, Vietnam-like defeat.

When the former agency director got caught literally with his pants down, Lindsey had suggested the president consider the recently retired Allen as a quick way to stop the bleeding on the scandal. He thought that if Allen later proved difficult from a policy standpoint, he could be replaced after the "Child Porn Spy" incident was forgotten. Lindsey knew that Allen was his own man, that he'd done his job for his men and his country, not any political party or politician. So he was somewhat surprised and pleased that Allen was so obviously interested in the job and expressed his gratitude at even being considered for the short list of potential replacements; he'd been even more appreciative when the president settled on him in September as his nominee.

After Lindsey thought about Allen's reaction, it made sense. The general was a man of action who was not looking forward to quiet retirement. Heading up the world's most powerful spy agency beat planting roses and writing his memoir. *We'll see how appreciative,* he thought as the general crossed the room to greet him. *And if he's not, Fauhomme has another trick up his sleeve. Our good general is not as lily white as he would have us believe.* "Thanks for coming, Sam," he said, holding out his hand. "Have a seat. How's the missus?"

"She's well, thank you," Allen replied a little tightly. "To be honest, I haven't seen her much lately. We've both been so busy. I've been trying to get up to speed at the agency and putting out fires. And she's busy with her charity work, and when she's not, she spends most of her time on our little farm in Vermont. But everything's fine."

Allen's voice caught a little at the end, but he didn't notice the quick look between Fauhomme and Lindsey. He blinked hard and then got down to business. "Anyway, you wanted me to come see you about my testimony before the congressional committee on Tuesday," he said.

Lindsey nodded. It was Thursday, five days since he and Fauhomme watched a well-organized terrorist attack overrun a State Department compound and murder Americans as if it was a television show. Ever since then they'd been in scramble mode to control what information was released and how the media portrayed it. It was unlikely that the truth would never come out, but the election was only two weeks away so delay, delay, delay was the strategy. After the election, it wouldn't matter.

On Tuesday, they watched the president's performance with satisfaction from Lindsey's office. The boss had stuck to the agreed-upon talking points: the enemy struck with no warning, the attack was over in a half hour or less, there was no time to render assistance. He'd emphasized that the Americans were there on a peaceful trade mission, and when that female reporter tried to interject Al Qaeda into the conversation, the president put her in her place. And he handled the whole thing with a lot of plausible deniability — "it is my understanding at this moment" and "that I am aware of" — that could be reconstructed at a later time as circumstances dictated.

"I did like the touch about setting up Iran as the straw man here," Fauhomme had said after the press conference was over. "Everybody's afraid of those crazy Iranians and this is just the sort of stunt the American public expects from Tehran. The press will dig up some old stock footage of Ahmadinejad ranting at the United Nations and that will be the story that everybody assumes is true."

Since the Rose Garden press conference, however, there had been a number of small issues that had to be dealt with. The day after the president's comments, the BBC had reported that locals from the nearby village claimed to have heard firing from the direction of the compound more than an hour before the official time given and that it had gone on for nearly two hours. The European news agency Reuters then added that some witnesses reported hearing the buzzing of a drone over the village during the height of the battle.

The task of dealing with the reports had mostly fallen on Rosemary Hilb as the mouthpiece of the administration, with Fauhomme calling the shots behind the scenes. She complained to Lindsey that at times she felt like a woman with a garden hose trying to put out a forest fire by running from one tree to the next.

The administration was, she told the media, not ruling out any possibilities, recognizing that in the "fog of war" it often took time and "careful winnowing of the chaff from the wheat" for the full truth to emerge. "Having said that, these unsubstantiated reports that the attack began sooner, and lasted longer, conflict with the timing of when we were made aware that there was a problem and immediately responded." She'd noted that reports of small-arms fire, including for "nighttime hunting," were not "uncommon in that part of the world." She implied that the simple villagers of Chechnya had condensed the events of the night so that hearing a few unrelated shots, then the actual attack, and finally the arrival of the drone "all seemed to occur at approximately the same time."

As usual, the administration's cause was helped by a compliant and lazy U.S. media that asked few penetrating questions and couldn't be bothered to dig for the truth. Instead, they preferred running with the official storyline and Fauhomme's script that the separatists were a bunch of murderous criminals and terrorists. With the help of the administration, as well as a Russian government only too happy to supply old film footage, the major networks and cable shows all cobbled together "documentaries" about school massacres and bombings in Russia by the evil separatists. In the meantime, the press completely ignored the truth about villages razed by Russian tanks, summary executions, indiscriminate aerial bombings and artillery shelling, as well as the disappearance of "suspected terrorists" who were never heard from again.

It didn't hurt that a large segment of the public, particularly younger supporters of the president, got its news and formed their opinions by watching "talk" shows on the Comedy Channel in which the hosts at times pretended to be serious journalists asking tough questions, but retreated to the "I'm just an entertainer" excuse when they got the facts wrong.

These comedian/journalists were soon joined by the mainstream press in mocking senators and congressmen of the opposition party who, citing the conflicting reports on the "Chechnya incident," called for hearings. Fauhomme had hoped that with enough ridicule the opposition would forget about the hearings, but surprisingly they'd stuck to their guns. The hearings were set to begin Monday with Tucker Lindsey and Helene Vonu, the assistant secretary of state specializing in that part of the world, appearing first and then General Allen testifying on Tuesday.

At Fauhomme's insistence the administration had circled the wagons, and a pointed memo had been sent to the affected parties reminding them to stick to the agreed-upon talking points and nothing more. Of the three administration officials subpoenaed, only Lindsey knew the real truth. Vonu, a strikingly beautiful Greek-American and career diplomat with an eye on the secretary of state cabinet position in the second term, would be making the rounds of the Sunday morning news talk shows and visiting the editorial boards of the major newspapers; she'd even scheduled an appearance on one of the Comedy Central shows in an effort to reach young voters and make sure they were in the fold.

By and large, Fauhomme had told Lindsey, the situation was under control. The hearing might be contentious, with a lot of posturing on both sides — after all, it was an election year — but nothing would come of it "so long as we all pull together as a team," the politico had written in his memo.

Actually, the hearings could work in favor

of the campaign, he noted in a private conversation with the NSA director. After the three administration officials testified, there were more than a dozen other people who'd either been subpoenaed or asked to appear voluntarily, ranging from experts on the region to security "specialists" who could be expected to make the usual, self-serving statements about inadequate preparations or tactical "mistakes" that had led to the slaughter but were meaningless now.

Allegations would be made and countered; impromptu press conferences in the halls of Congress would materialize, with each side complaining that the other was using the death of Americans at the hands of terrorists for political gain. And in the end, nothing would come of it, and nothing new would be divulged, at least nothing the opposition could make stick. In the meantime, the identification of the bodies in Chechnya would be dragged out. Again the Russians were cooperating, and the American team had been warned in no uncertain terms that they were not to release the results of their findings until the president and his advisers had an opportunity to review the report. Between the opposition senators and congressmen, and those in the president's party, the questioning, bombast, and posturing could well eat up the weeks before the election.

The biggest concern was the hostages, if they were still alive. So far there'd been no word or demands, which was making them all nervous. Meanwhile, they were working on a plan to "eliminate the problem," as Fauhomme euphemistically put it.

Then Allen called Lindsey that morning and threw a wrench in the works. He said that he'd received information that there might be more to some of the reports than was being credited. Enough, he said, that he felt obligated to expand on the talking points in his testimony so that they included these new developments.

Feeling panic rise in him like bile, Lindsey told Allen that he needed to talk to the president. But when he hung up, he called Fauhomme, who'd told him to arrange the meeting that afternoon in Lindsey's office.

"So, Sam, I asked you to come over so we could follow up on our conversation this morning about these . . . uh . . . alleged developments from Chechnya," Lindsey said to Allen.

The general frowned and glanced over at Fauhomme. "I'd judge these matters to be classified."

Fauhomme leaned back in his chair with

a patient smile and patted a fat leg with the manila envelope he was carrying. But it was Lindsey who spoke. "Mr. Fauhomme has the full confidence of the president and is often briefed on classified matters so that he can best advise the president when it comes to this important election."

When the general seemed to hesitate further, Fauhomme leaned forward and showed the general his cell phone. "I'll call the boss and get him to tell you it's okay, if it would make you feel any better."

The general thought about it for a moment and then shook his head. "That won't be necessary."

Fauhomme grinned and leaned back again as he looked over at Lindsey. "Thank you for that courtesy; we're all friends here and trying to do what's best for this country. Now let's hear what's going on."

The general pursed his lips before speaking. "I don't know quite how to say this, I'm not used to the ways of the Beltway yet, so I'll just go with my military background and spit it out. It appears that we may not have heard the full story from the State Department, or they may be unaware of some parts of it, at least not at the top. But my guys have learned that a series of encoded messages was sent from the compound in Chechnya through one of our spy satellites more than an hour before our 'official' estimate of when the attack began."

"Maybe these messages had nothing to do with the attack," Lindsey suggested.

"At 0300 hours?" Allen replied. "Besides, the messages continued through the attack and coincided with the reports that villagers heard shooting throughout that time."

"What else?" Lindsey asked.

"There was also a cell phone call placed from someone inside the compound to the U.S. embassy in Grozny almost two hours after that initial series of messages. So someone was still alive in the compound."

"Any idea who placed that call?" asked Lindsey.

"Or who received it, IF it was actually made and not just some blip caused by explosions or some such thing?" Fauhomme added.

Allen shook his head. "There's no record of it in the official file," he said. "All we know is that a call was placed. I'd like to have my guys on the ground in Grozny make some inquiries at the embassy."

"It was early in the morning," Lindsey said. "Maybe no one picked up. IF it was a call rather than, as Rod noted, a blip caused by the fighting. Then again, maybe a message was left and it's been missed in all the confusion; tell you what, I'll place a call to Grozny myself. What else you got?"

Allen leaned forward in his seat. "Now I admit that we don't have the best intel on the ground in Chechnya, an oversight that I'll be working on, but we are hearing from several sources that the Chechen separatist party is claiming that this guy, Daudov, was not responsible for the attack. They're blaming foreign fighters under the direction of Al Qaeda in Chechnya."

Fauhomme frowned. "I haven't seen any stories about that in the press," he said. "Why aren't these separatists holding a press conference or something to profess their innocence?"

"From what I understand, they've all gone underground until things settle down," Allen responded. "We've had a couple of reports that the Russians are hitting them pretty hard already; mass arrests and even paramilitary action against villages known to have separatist leanings."

"Good," Fauhomme said. "Maybe the Russians will find out something useful, which is more than what I'm hearing here so far."

Allen's face hardened at the rebuke but he kept his voice in control. "I'm not saying that any of this is the truth. However, I will be under oath at the hearing, and when asked to divulge everything I know about the attack, I think these items should be added to our talking points. If this comes out later, and it looks like we were trying to hide something, I think the embarrassment to the president and this administration would be worse than conceding that our knowledge of what happened can change as the facts continue to come in."

"Well, that's where you're wrong, General," Fauhomme said. "These . . . rumors . . . will only add to the confusion of the American people, and right before an election that I believe, as do many others, including the president, is pivotal to the future of this country. If we have to backtrack and say that it now appears that — oops, we made a mistake, the attack may have started earlier and lasted longer than we first said, the president's opponent will blow it out of proportion with 20/20 hindsight. He'll raise a hue and cry about why we didn't respond faster to save lives."

"And if it's true, why didn't we?" the general asked.

"No one here is saying it is true," Fauhomme replied. "It's just another rumor. But that won't matter to the other side."

"Well, is it true?"

Lindsey answered. "General Allen, while you're new to the CIA and civilian intelligence gathering, I know you're no neophyte when it comes to the concept that sometimes in war hard decisions need to be made and that the public simply can't be told everything, for reasons of national security."

It took a moment for Lindsey's comment to sink in, but then Allen frowned. "This wasn't any 'peaceful trade mission,' was it?"

"No, General, it wasn't," Lindsey replied. He then explained.

When the NSA director finished, Allen's eyes blazed with anger. "You played with fire and when it got out of control, you left Americans to twist in the wind. . . . And you want me to lie about it under oath."

"That's international politics for you," Fauhomme said. "It's a dirty world out there, and sometime you have to get down in the mud and tough it out."

Allen looked at Fauhomme with disdain. "What would you know about getting down in the mud to tough anything out? You're dirty, but it comes from inside you."

Lindsey tried to strike a conciliatory tone. "Look, Sam, the attack happened and there's nothing we can do about it. We still don't know if it was spur of the moment, or because the bad guys got wind of the mission and didn't like it. We're not even sure who was behind it; there are a lot of factions over there, and it could have been any one of them. But if we go out there and say it could have been Al Qaeda, a week after the president was on national TV saying Al Qaeda doesn't exist, he's going to look like an idiot, and he does not want to look like an idiot. All we're saying is let's stick with the talking points for now and let this ride until after the election. We'll continue to gather the facts, and then after all the votes are counted we can issue a complete, reasoned report on what happened . . ."

"Minus the truth about what we were actually doing there," Allen said.

"If you're going to worry about bending rules," Fauhomme retorted, "you're working for the wrong agency."

"Maybe I am," Allen said. "I'm not naïve. I understand that a lot goes on with national security that has to be kept from the public. But this time Americans were murdered, and the public has a right to know who was behind it."

"People died, what does it matter who killed them?" Fauhomme scoffed. "They're dead."

Allen regarded the fat man coldly for a moment, as if trying to decide whether to beat the crap out of him. "Does it matter who killed Americans?" he asked rhetorically. "It sure as hell does to me. One, I want to know which sons of bitches I'm going to wipe from the face of the planet. Two, I want to know if they belong to an organization that attacked this country and murdered more than three thousand people and has sworn to murder Americans — men, women, and children — whenever they get the chance, and I will continue to root out every last one of them until, as the president said prematurely, that organization ceases to exist. And three, I want to know who, if anybody, put them up to it and hold them accountable as well."

"No one is saying that we don't find out exactly who was responsible and take them down after the election," Lindsey said. "It's a matter of what we tell the American people now. I think what Rod meant by his comment is that if the public feels safer believing that Al Qaeda is kaput, why not let them continue to believe it? Plus, if we are dealing with Al Qaeda here, why let them know that we're on to them?"

"I don't know," Allen responded. "I guess your way of thinking assumes that Americans need to be lied to and sheltered like imbecile children. As for tipping Al Qaeda in Chechnya that we're coming for them, they know we'll find out — they're not exactly shy when it comes to taking credit for their crimes — so why the subterfuge? Except it's all about the president's image and this election."

"Need I remind you that if the president loses this election it's unlikely the next president will keep you on as the director of the CIA," Fauhomme said.

"Maybe some jobs aren't worth the price," Allen retorted. "I'm not lying to the committee."

Fauhomme looked at Lindsey, who looked away. "That's right, lying is only okay if it's convenient to you, isn't that right, Allen?" the political boss sneered.

Allen furrowed his brown. "What the hell do you mean by that?"

Fauhomme's face hardened as he tossed the envelope on Lindsey's desk in front of the general. "The name Jenna Blair ring a bell? I believe you met her at that little party I threw over the Fourth of July on Long Island."

Allen blinked and the anger faded from his eyes and was replaced by a troubled look. "Quit playing games."

"Not a game, General," Fauhomme said. "Look inside."

Picking up the envelope, Allen opened it. He reached in and pulled out a half-dozen eight-by-ten photographs. As he did, Fauhomme smiled.

After glancing at the photographs, Allen placed them back in the envelope and put it on the desk. "These are just photographs of me with the young woman you named," he said quietly.

"If you mean they are not you and Ms. Blair en flagrante in some bed, you're correct," Fauhomme replied. "However, a photograph of you kissing the young woman, who I don't believe is your wife of twenty-odd years, in front of the Casablanca Hotel on West 43rd, as well as holding hands in the hotel lobby while waiting for the elevator that will be taking you to your little love nest, doesn't leave all that much to the imagination either."

"You son of a bitch," Allen said.

"I've been called worse," Fauhomme replied with a chuckle. "But I'm serious as a fucking toothache about this. I'm trying to get the president re-elected because we, I mean he, has some unfinished business and that's far more important than what some cavemen in the Middle East do or that some

138

holier-than-thou general — who's getting a little extramarital loving on the side — doesn't want to lie to Congress. And if that means resorting to blackmail, I'll fucking resort to blackmail. In case you're still not getting it, or you think this would cause a backlash against this administration so I wouldn't dare do this, we won't be the ones tied to exposing your little peccadillo. Some lucky dipshit in the press corps will receive the photographs anonymously and will jump all over this story. Of course, it will be an embarrassment to the president, who'll make a few statements about fully supporting you, but in the end he'll have to ask you to withdraw your nomination 'for the good of the country' and your family. In the meantime, your wife and children will be put through the wringer. Ever had the press camped out on your lawn? It's no fun. And your wife . . . tsk tsk . . . that poor woman's face will be on the cover of every supermarket tabloid from the Atlantic to the Pacific, heck, she might even make the cover of *Time*."

Fauhomme let the imagery sink in and appeared to be enjoying himself as the general hung his head, his hands clenching and unclenching. "And then there's Miss Blair . . . you in love or is she just some snatch? If you give a shit about the girl, you won't put her through this."

"That's enough, Rod," Lindsey interjected. "You've made your point." He leaned over his desk in the direction of the general. "Look, Sam, just stick to the talking points as we've agreed on and this all goes away. The president will be re-elected, your nomination will sail through, you handle your private life privately, and you kill the sons of bitches who caused this problem in the first place with the blessing of the president."

Allen didn't respond. He just sat slumped over, looking at the floor.

"So, General, time's up," Fauhomme said. "What's it going to be? You going to play ball with the team that drafted you, or you want to be traded to the other side, baggage and all?"

Allen stared at Fauhomme, his eyes full of contempt, but he nodded. "You win," he said. "I'll stick to the talking points."

Fauhomme grinned. "Now there's the team spirit." He glanced over at Lindsey, whose face registered his shame. *Fuck him,* the fat man thought. *I thought these spook types would have more balls.* "You're dismissed, General," he said with scorn.

Without a word or another glance at either

man, Allen got up and left the office. "Jesus, I hated to do that," Lindsey said when the door clicked shut. "What if he decides to take the hit and goes to the press?"

Fauhomme laughed, a cruel, barking sound. "The press? Those lazy herd animals that used to be the Fourth Estate?" he scoffed. "They'll report what I tell them to report, and the public will think what I tell them to think. I'm not worried about the press . . . at least not most of them, and the ones I would worry about are few and far between. We just have to make it through the election."

"What about Allen? You really think he's going to play ball?"

Fauhomme narrowed his eyes and glanced at the door the general had just left through. "Yeah, I do," he said. "A good man like that putting his poor cast-aside wife through what will happen if he doesn't? Not to mention the shame and embarrassment that will destroy his legacy?"

He paused to think some more. "Still, you're right, I don't like wild cards." He stopped talking and punched in a number on his cell phone. "Yeah, Ray," he said. "I want you to follow our little bird for a few days until we get through this hearing. I want to know where he goes and who he meets with. We got his phone tapped and an intercept on his cell? Yeah? Good man. Keep me posted. What's that? . . . We'll cross that bridge when we come to it, for now just watch him."

Fauhomme hung up and smiled at Lindsey. "Never fear, Big Ray Baum is on the case," he said, and lit a cigar. "I just love election season, don't you? Really gets the competitive juices flowing."

6

Ariadne Stupenagel paused to let her eyes adjust to the dark interior of the White Horse Tavern. As always, a lot of memories flooded in any time she walked into the bar, even on a sunny Friday afternoon in autumn, which wasn't the usual time of day she'd frequented the place.

A fixture in the Village since it opened in 1880 as a longshoreman's bar, the tavern had gained its reputation as a place where writers and artists gathered beginning in the early 1950s when Dylan Thomas made it his home away from hotel. Legend had it that Thomas, whose likeness graced several paintings now hung behind the bar, drank himself to death there, though he actually went home to the nearby Chelsea Hotel and succumbed several days later. Beat writer Jack Kerouac had been tossed out of the White Horse so many times that the message "Jack Go Home" was still scrawled on a wall of the men's restroom. And other luminaries who had tipped back a few there included Norman Mailer, Bob Dylan, Jim Morrison, Mary Travers, and Hunter S. Thompson, as well as a host of New York's lesser-known artists and journalists, including Stupenagel, who had first joined them longer ago than she would ever admit.

As a drinking destination for the famous and infamous, the White Horse had become a tourist destination, taking some of the "locals' hangout" flavor out of it. But it was still a nostalgic place for her, especially because she was there to meet a former lover whom she used to have drinks with there when they were both in New York. They'd met in the 1980s when she was a "younger" journalist reporting from various war zones in Africa; he'd been a young army major with the 101st Airborne working "black ops" trying to hunt down various African war criminals. They'd become lovers on one hot, sweltering night in Nairobi and then repeated the performance in various places around the world when her job as a journalist and his job as a soldier brought their paths together. She'd gone on to make a name for herself as a Pulitzer Prize–winning reporter and he'd risen through the ranks to lieutenant general and given his last command overseeing the stabilization of the U.S. presence in Afghanistan. A year earlier he'd retired, only to be named acting director of the CIA after his predecessor got caught trying to meet up with someone he thought was a twelve-year-old girl but who turned out to be a Silver Spring, Maryland, police detective.

As her eyes adjusted, Stupenagel caught a glimpse of herself in the big mirror that ran the length of the old-fashioned wooden bar. At least in the half-light, she saw the same tall, beautiful woman with the wild blond hair and the cherry red lipstick that was her trademark. Her date had told her that he would prefer not to attract any attention, so she'd toned down the usual high heels and revealing low-cut blouses she also favored for a light sweater, denim jeans, and flats. She hoped that the lines she knew were around her eyes and mouth wouldn't be too noticeable and then chided herself. *After all, Ariadne, you're happily engaged to a wonderful man, and Sam's been married for twenty years.* She ordered a beer and headed to one of the back rooms, where she took a seat in a high-backed booth where she could watch the door.

She recognized Sam Allen the moment he walked into the room. He was wearing a disguise that might have fooled most people — a loose, dingy old army sweatshirt and faded blue jeans with a beat-up Yankee ball-cap and dark, nondescript sunglasses. He was carrying a beer, trying to look nonchalant, but he couldn't hide the ramrod-straight posture or square shoulders when he turned to face her. He wasn't very tall, just over six foot, which had her beat by only a couple of inches, but he was one of those men whose presence always made even larger men seem to shrink by comparison. She could tell that he still had his athlete's body — he was famous for his morning runs with his officers in Afghanistan, and woe to the younger subordinate who couldn't keep up — but she was thinking about another sort of stamina that had always been impressive when he spotted her and headed back to the booth.

Stupenagel stood and they hugged. Breathing in the old familiar scent of him, she noted that the loose clothing wasn't covering up any extra padding, and the same muscles she remembered so well were still present. She was grateful, however, to see that the lines around his eyes were deeper than hers and his day-old beard had as much salt as pepper in it. Still, he was a gorgeous man, and she wondered what her fiancé, Gilbert Murrow, would think of a mulligan.

"Hello, Ari," he said, using the nickname that only he had ever dared, "you look as beautiful as ever."

Trying not to melt into a puddle of female gooeyness, Stupenagel smiled and rolled her eyes. "I guess vision is the first of the senses to go," she said. "But a little blindness in an old beau never hurt a girl."

Allen smiled and sat down across from her with his back to the door. Anyone walking in would not see him without coming back.

"So how's Martha?" Stupenagel asked, thinking that inquiring about his wife was the best way to throw cold water on her fantasies.

Allen's smile faded. "She's fine," he said. "The kids are gone, and I'm busy with the new job, so she spends a lot of time on her farm in Vermont."

Stupenagel smiled. "Sounds like a happily married older couple. She's on the farm and you're in D.C." Then she saw the look on his face. "What's wrong, Sam?"

For the first time since she'd known him, Allen looked vulnerable. "It's been a while since Martha and I have lived as husband and wife," he stammered.

Suddenly, Stupenagel knew what was troubling him. "You're having an affair." She hadn't meant for her comment to sound so shocked. She'd had plenty of sexual encounters herself, including with more than a few married men, some of them quite famous or important. But Sam Allen had never seemed the type. She'd been surprised when she returned from covering a war in Central America many years earlier to learn that he'd married Martha Philpott, who she learned was a New England blue blood. The one time she met her, Martha didn't seem the sort to have captured the romantic interest of the hot-blooded warrior she'd sweated up the sheets with in Kenya and beyond. But when she'd gotten over her disappointment, not that she'd ever believed that nuptials were in their future, she realized that the other woman was the perfect military wife; a good mother to their two children, an asset on the arm of her husband at the social gatherings so important to an officer with aspirations. And Stupenagel knew that Allen's one weakness was ambition.

Allen hung his head and nodded. "I hate that word," he said. "I met someone and fell in love."

"While you were married . . . that's an af-

148

fair, Sam," Stupenagel said. *Again with the judgmental tone, Ariadne. You're no paragon of virtue.* "And for someone in your position . . . if the press got wind of that . . ." She let her voice trail off.

"I'm being blackmailed, Ari."

Stupenagel sat back with a scowl on her face. "Some shithead threatening to spill the beans on your girlfriend to bollix up your confirmation if you don't give them what they want?"

"That's part of it," Allen said. "But these aren't just any blackmailers."

Stupenagel frowned. "How do you mean?"

Allen looked around behind him, then turned back. "You've heard the official story about Chechnya?"

Stupenagel's eyes narrowed. "Yeah, sure. I was at the Rose Garden when the president gave his little talk."

"Well, not everything is as it is being laid out," Allen said in a low voice. "I think the wrong guy might be getting the blame."

"It wasn't this Daudov?"

"Maybe, maybe not," Allen replied. "That's what the Russians are saying, but they've got it in for him for their own reasons. I've heard some rumors that the attackers were foreign Islamic extremists, not Chechen at all, and tied to Al Qaeda."

"I knew it," Stupenagel hissed. "That means the prez stood up there and lied."

"I don't know that he knows," Allen said. "I'm hoping that if the Al Qaeda information is true, and I believe it is, it's the low-life advisers around him that are keeping him in the dark. I guess I'm still naïve enough to want to believe that the president of the United States wouldn't knowingly lie to his constituents, particularly when there are murdered Americans lying dead in another country."

Stupenagel snorted. "I haven't been that naïve since Nixon," she said. "But it would be a hell of an embarrassment if a week after he says Al Qaeda is kaput, they show up and wipe out an American trade mission."

"That's something else," Allen said. "I don't believe that this 'trade mission' was just some goodwill gesture to the locals."

"What do you mean?" Stupenagel said. She could feel the woman who a moment ago was all gaga over an old lover turning into the journalist.

"Just a hunch, but the powers that be are awfully close-lipped about it, considering I'm the acting head of the main intelligence agency," Allen said.

"So what else you got?"

"I also have reason to believe that it wasn't

some spontaneous strike that caught our people asleep and was over quickly. I think the reports that they may have held out a few hours, plenty of time for us to have scrambled air support from our bases in Turkey, are true. And that report from Reuters about villagers saying they heard a drone during the fight? There may be some truth to that as well."

Stupenagel whistled. She was all journalist now. "This is incredible. If it's true, the administration is lying through its collective teeth." She thought about it for a moment. "I'd sure as hell like to know what that so-called trade mission was really about and what it has to do with what happened."

"So would I," Allen replied, "and I'm going to find out."

"What are you going to do in the meantime?"

The troubled look returned to Allen's eyes. "I don't know," he replied. "My inclination is to say what I know at the hearing on Tuesday. But I've been told in no uncertain terms to let it go until after the election or . . ."

". . . or somebody exposes your affair, which pretty much dump-trucks your confirmation."

"And hurts people I care for very much."

151

Stupenagel reached across the table and held Allen's hands with her own. "I'm sorry, Sam," she said. "You're a good man and whatever happened to you and your wife, that should be between the two of you. I'm not saying an affair was the way to go about changing your life, but I know these things can get complicated."

"Thanks, Ari," said Allen as a tear formed and rolled down his cheek. "I knew I could find an understanding shoulder to cry on, but I made this bed, no pun intended, and I'll deal with the consequences. I just need to figure out the best way, and timing, to do that."

"So who are these people who are black-mailing you? I mean I can guess, but how high up does this go?"

"High, but I'm not sure how high, and I'm not ready to speculate on that with a journalist, even one I've seen naked."

Stupenagel laughed. "You've seen more than that. So can I use this?"

"You mean for a story?"

"That's what I do, Sam. If you want, I'll just say it came from a well-placed source."

Allen shook his head. "They'll know who it was. Let me think about it. If it was just me, I'd say go for it, confirmation be damned. But I don't know yet if the president deserves to take a hit on this. And more important, I have Martha and the kids . . . and Jenna . . . to think about."

"Jenna. That's her name," Stupenagel said, feeling a prick of jealousy again. "She must be something for you to have risked your reputation and career."

"She is."

"Does she feel the same way about you?"

Allen thought about it, then nodded. "I think so. She's quite a bit younger and maybe it's all just pillow talk, but she says she loves me. Maybe I'm a fool but I believe her, and I feel the same."

"So what are you going to do about that?"

"What I should have done years ago, ask Martha for a divorce, and then see if I can talk Jenna into marrying me."

Stupenagel smiled. "I keep feeling these little fits of jealousy, but I'm happy for you. I've actually met a really great guy and we're getting married next spring."

Allen pointed to the diamond ring on her left hand. "I saw the rock, congratulations."

"So putting on my journalist hat, can I get a little head start on the rest of the buzzards if you decide to lay it all out there at the hearings? I work for a weekly now, and we go to press Monday night and we're on the streets Tuesday morning."

"How about I let you know Monday? If I tell the committee everything, I think these people may follow through on their threat, but I'll beat them to the punch by talking to Martha and Jenna Monday night. Then I'll give you a call and fill you in on what little I know. Deal?"

"Deal."

They spent another half hour talking about old times and then Allen said he had to leave. "Jenna and I are going to spend the weekend at the cabin. You remember the cabin?"

Nodding, Stupenagel laughed. He was referring to a rustic cabin in a lake community called Orvin, located in upstate New York, that had been in his family for generations. They'd spent several long weekends there when they were young, swimming in the lake, drinking wine and whiskey, and making the floorboards beneath the bed creak like a million crickets. "You mean you're taking another woman to our special place?"

Allen laughed, too. "It will always be our special place, just in another time. You remember how to get there?"

"I believe I could find my way," Stupenagel said, then wiggled an eyebrow. "Surely you're not suggesting that I join you and

Jenna for a little debauchery? My, haven't you gotten kinky in your old age!"

Allen laughed aloud. "I don't think I could survive that," he said. "I'd stand a better chance against a hundred angry Taliban insurgents, not that it wouldn't be a great way to go. But no, I just wanted to see if you remembered where it is." He paused and this time he grabbed her hands. "If something were to happen to me, I'd want someone to look in on Jenna for me. Make sure she's all right. Would you do that?"

Stupenagel frowned. "Something like what? Do you think you're in danger?"

"No, I don't think so," Allen said. "These are pretty nasty people, but they're counting on their scheme to keep me quiet. They'll try to ruin me if I say something they don't like at the hearing and count on the witch hunt they can drum up among your brethren in the media to slander me and bury what I tell the committee. I'll be done with the CIA and going through hell with Martha and the kids, but I don't think they'll do more than that. But who knows, maybe I'll get run over by a bus on my way to the Capitol. I'd just like to know that someone will look in on Jenna if something does happen."

"I don't like it, Sam, anybody willing to

blackmail the acting director of the CIA would probably stoop to just about anything," Stupenagel said. "But okay, you got an address and a phone number?"

Allen pulled out his wallet and handed her a business card. "Yeah, it's all here on the back." He stood up and she joined him, giving in to an impulse to kiss him quickly.

"Be careful, Sam, I want to see you and your bride-to-be at my wedding," she said, choking back tears.

Wiping the tears from her face, Allen stepped back. "Hey, I've dealt with tougher hombres than these people — the Taliban were no pushovers, you know. I'll see you on the flip-flop, Ari, and give you a call Monday night."

When Allen left through the back door, Stupenagel sat down and finished her glass of wine, thinking about the past and what her old flame had just told her. With a sigh, she got up and sauntered up to the bar to pay her bill. A big, younger man, the sort you'd see in an aftershave commercial, sat at the bar. He hadn't been there when she came in but smiled at her in the mirror. She looked down and noted the tattoo of a bulldog with USMC stenciled below it.

"Jarhead, eh?" she said.

The man glanced down at his arm and

smiled. "Yeah, in another life," he said. "So what's a good-looking woman doing out all alone on a Friday afternoon?"

"Just met up with an old friend," she said. "He left."

"Got time for a new friend?"

Smiling, Stupenagel patted his cheek. "I'm old enough to be your slightly older twin sister," she said. "But I'm going home to my fiancé."

"Lucky guy," the man said. "Maybe some other time."

"I doubt it, handsome, but it's a mixed-up world we live in and stranger things have happened."

"Damn straight about it being a mixed-up world. Good luck with the boyfriend. If you change your mind, I'll be here for a while longer."

Stupenagel sighed. She paid her bill and glanced one last time at the mirror. The young man was watching her with a slight smile on his face. He winked. She laughed and shook her head as she turned and left the White Horse and temptation behind.

7

Jenna Blair heard the musical notes coming from her computer that meant someone was trying to contact her and hurried over to her desk. There were only two people in the world she talked with via webcam, her mother in Colorado and her lover.

As she sat down, she moved the mouse on its pad to bring the screen to life. She smiled when she saw the lean, tanned, handsome face of Lt. Gen. Sam Allen smiling back at her. "Hi, baby," she purred. "I was just thinking about our weekend at the cabin. That was sooooooo nice. I love you so much."

The little lie hung there in the air like a soap balloon. Actually, the weekend at the cabin *had* been nice, as it always was when they were together, but both of them had been preoccupied. He'd spent a lot of time in his office, and she'd gone for walks around the lake to think. She didn't know what was troubling him — it could have been any number of things, from divorcing his wife to the upcoming congressional hearing. He said he needed to talk to her about what was on his mind, but that it had to wait until Monday. In the meantime, she knew what was troubling her — her conscience.

"I love you, too, sweetheart. I'm glad we had that time together, even if I was tied up with work," Allen replied.

"That's okay, my love. I wasn't all there either. I'm not complaining, and you were there when it counted, if you know what I mean."

Laughing as his girlfriend wiggled her eyebrows suggestively, Allen shook his head. "You're incorrigible."

"Are you saying I'm too much?"

"No, not at all. I'm flattered and grateful that you find me attractive, and happily satiated every time we see each other. Forgive me, honey, I didn't mean that."

"That's better. I'm in love, Sam. I can't get enough of you." She pouted. "I can't believe we're in the same city and we're not going to sleep together."

"Is what you do called 'sleep'?" he said with a chuckle, then yawned himself. "Excuse me, don't know where that came from,

I guess I am tired."

"You're not getting old on me, are you?"

"Never. I just ordered room service — lasagna — and my old buddy, Pete, sent a bottle of Macallan twenty-five-year-old scotch to keep me company. Should be just the thing to put me to sleep, as soon as I wrap up my little speech," he said, and took another sip.

"Well, in the meantime, you just be your sexy self for me, and I'm going to record you while you type. Then if you're a good boy, I'll give you a show when I get out of the shower," Jenna said, reaching for the mouse to turn on her webcam's recorder. She was putting together a montage of photos and videos — at least the PG-rated stuff — to show her parents when she went home to Colorado for Thanksgiving, which was when she planned to tell them that their daughter was dating the director of the CIA. She was going to give him a copy, too, as a surprise.

He frowned. "I don't know why you'd want to record this."

She wrinkled her nose. "Because I'm going to blackmail you with it someday."

Allen yawned again. "You want to talk now about what you said at the cabin?"

Jenna shook her head. "No. I'm going to

go hop in the shower. I think you need time to think about this, so I'll wait until Monday for your answer."

With that, Jenna stood and let her robe fall from her naked body. She could almost feel his eyes on her as she walked away with a laugh. But reaching the bathroom, her hands went to her face and she sobbed.

As with many other young women with looks and talent, Blair had come to the Big Apple hoping to make it in musical theater on Broadway. But like most of those other young women, she quickly learned that what passed for superior ability in Denver, Colorado, was not necessarily going to stand out in a town filled with other aspiring singers, dancers, and actresses. There had been a few modeling jobs, but they were always going to be limited — petite, fit, and pretty rather than leggy and gorgeous, she wasn't tall enough or exotic enough for runway shows. Most of her modeling gigs had been for television and billboard campaigns as the wholesome, girl-next-door type with enough curves and playfulness in her blond looks and lively hazel eyes to hold the attention of male consumers. But most women, one modeling agency director told her, would find her "intimidating." "You're just too much like 'one of the guys' — a very sexy one of the guys, I must say, and I'm gay — for our Manolo heels and Gucci purses customers. They *know* they can't keep up with you. But I'll call when we're selling Old Spice aftershave."

She'd kept her hand in the acting business by answering cattle calls for "crowd scenes" and choruses on the big stage and bit parts in off-Broadway productions. But part-time actor's wages and modeling didn't pay the rent on her two-bedroom East Harlem walk-up, even with two roommates.

What had allowed her to squeak by was working as a bicycle messenger delivering important packages and letters between businesses in Midtown Manhattan. She'd been into mountain biking in her home state of Colorado, so she had the legs, stamina, and bicycle survival instincts it took to be a NYC messenger. Something of a daredevil, she actually enjoyed dodging cars and pedestrians as she powered her way from the Upper West Side to Wall Street. But as her dreams of a career on the stage faded, she started thinking about what she was going to do when her legs gave out or she wanted to do more than subsist. And the more she thought about it, the more pursuing a law degree at NYU appealed to her, but it cost a lot more money than she had to spend.

Then Connie Rae Lee, one of the girls she'd met and befriended at a cattle call to be flying monkeys in the hit play *Wicked,* had called one day four years earlier wanting to know if she was available to attend a party "with some very important people who might be able to do you some good."

Lee was a free spirit who, when they met, made her "real" living as a yoga instructor. Tall and willowy with long tresses of dark, layered hair and stunning blue eyes, she got a lot of offers from men but was keeping an eye out for one with money. "As Mama always said, it's just as easy to marry a rich man as a poor one, and you get to go more places," she informed Blair when they went out on the town.

Apparently this theory had worked for Lee, who had found herself a rich boyfriend, a big-time political honcho named Rod Fauhomme. "He's overweight . . . okay, let's call it fat . . . and he has a temper," she told Blair over coffee one morning, "but he's not bad-looking and says he's going to take care of me. We go to a lot of fun events, and we just got back from Hawaii. Besides, he's gone half the time to Washington, D.C., so it's not like I have to put out all the time. . . .

I could do worse."

Lee hadn't sounded very convincing, nor had Fauhomme apparently offered an engagement ring yet. But he had put her up in an expensive town house on the Upper West Side, paid her bills, and gave her a nice allowance. The first time Blair had seen her after she moved into the new digs, her friend was wearing a thousand dollars' worth of new clothes, shoes, and accessories. She was also sporting the fading remnant of a bruise on the side of her face.

"What's that?" Blair asked, pointing to Lee's cheek.

"Oh, this," Lee said, quickly placing a hand to her face to hide the mark. "It's nothing. Rod likes it rough sometimes and he gets carried away. But it's all good. He's going to take me to a dinner at the White House after the president's inauguration. He'd take me to the inaugural ball, but he says it's kind of a stuffy affair and I wouldn't be comfortable. So we'll just go when we can get a little more of what he calls 'face time with the prez.' You know he was the president's campaign manager, right?"

It was shortly after that conversation that Lee called with the offer to attend the party. It sounded like fun, so Blair had said, "Why not?" And didn't think anything of it when

Connie added, "You could make a lot of good connections at these parties, so don't be afraid to show off those pretty titties, girlfriend, if you know what I mean."

The party was in the penthouse suite of the Carlyle Hotel on Manhattan's ritzy, fashionable Upper East Side. She was suitably impressed as Connie pointed out the various movers and shakers in the room, including the mayor, two major Broadway stars, a producer, a Hollywood actor known for his left-wing politics, two congressmen, a slew of very wealthy attorneys, bankers, and CEOs, some with their bored, "cosmetically altered" wives and others with beautiful girlfriends who looked to be about half their ages. And, of course, Rod Fauhomme, whom she'd never met, but he nodded at her and winked when Lee pointed him out across the room talking to the mayor.

Not long into the party, Lee introduced her to an Israeli businessman named Ariel Shimon. He was short, fiftyish, with silver taking over his jet-black hair at the temples, but trim, charming, intelligent, and dressed impeccably in a tailored Armani suit. He was immediately taken with her, especially the parts of her below her chin; his eyes drifted to her cleavage as they spoke and lingered there like tourists at an art gallery.

It wasn't long before he was making suggestive remarks and obviously trying to get her drunk, which the more she got, the more she laughed at his jokes and innuendoes.

After about an hour of this, Jenna saw him talking to Lee over by the bar. They were both watching her before he turned to order drinks. Lee walked over with a knowing smile on her lips. "So how are things going with Ariel?"

"Other than he hasn't looked above my breasts since we first shook hands and seems to like making a lot of bedroom jokes, I'm having fun. He's a hoot," Blair replied with a laugh. She looked around the crowded room. "Boy, you weren't kidding when you said there were going to be a lot of important people here."

"Yes, and Ariel's one of them." She turned and nodded toward the bar, where the man of the moment was staring back at them with a drink in each hand. "You know he's worth a few gazillion, something to do with Israeli defense contracts, and he contributes a lot of money to political action committees whenever Rod asks." She paused and winked. "He's also pretty good looking."

"And old enough to be my dad."

"A very rich, very handsome dad, if you ask me. Besides, Rod's thirty years older

166

than me and as long as he hasn't been drinking too much, he's a better lover than most of the boys I've dated," Lee said. She hesitated, then reached out and touched Jenna's arm. "Ariel's going to be in town for a couple of weeks and would like to date you."

"I think he's married," Blair pointed out.

Lee scoffed. "To some boring professor of archeology in Tel Aviv. That's a long ways from New York."

"So what do you mean he wants to 'date' me? I take it you mean the sort of date that ends up in bed."

Her friend giggled. "It could be fun, and it would be profitable. Some people I know are willing to pay you five thousand dollars a week to keep Ariel happy while he's here."

Blair's jaw dropped. "These 'people' are going to pay me five thousand dollars a week to 'date' a filthy rich Israeli business-man? I believe that's called prostitution."

"Oh, come on, Jenna, tell me those aspiring actor losers you meet aren't expecting sex for buying you a slice of pizza and a beer."

"It's not guaranteed, and not many of them succeed," Blair said. She was smiling, but then she frowned. "This is why you invited me, isn't it?"

"Call it an opportunity, Jenna," Lee replied. "You need money. Ariel needs someone to show him the sights, in and out of bed. And these people I mentioned are willing to pay for it."

"These people, what do they want in return?" Blair asked suspiciously.

"Nothing much. They mostly want Ariel to have a good time. But they'd also like information. They'd be interested in anything he might have to say about Israeli-American relations, the president, the Israeli government, his business. Anything that comes up, no pun intended."

Lee giggled at her own joke, but Blair wasn't smiling anymore. "This just keeps getting better. You want me to sleep with a big campaign donor *and* spy on him?" She shook her head. "I can't do that."

Patting her on the shoulder, Lee said, "Give it some thought. You'd be helping yourself and helping your country."

"Helping my country?"

"Yes," Lee replied, completely serious now. "It's a dangerous world and the more information people like the men in this room, like my boyfriend, Rod, can get, the better they are able to make good decisions to protect the rest of us."

"That's quite the speech," Blair said. "But

why does Ariel want me? There are a lot of beautiful women in this room, and a million more in the city."

Lee shrugged. "He chose you. Guys like him don't always go for the supermodels. If all they wanted was a beautiful whore in bed, they could buy that anytime. You've got a nice butt, great ta-tas, and a pretty face, and guys like him also want somebody they can jog with in Central Park or play a game of tennis with, and then go dancing at Club 21 before hopping in the sack at the end of the day."

Blair laughed. "Wow, you've really given this some thought," she said. She hugged her friend. "Thanks, but I got an early morning. I'm going to catch a cab."

Lee looked disappointed, but then smiled. "Well, think about it, would you? It'd be a fun couple of weeks and pay your rent for a few months."

"Yeah, sure, I'll think about it," Blair had replied, never intending to give it another thought. When she left, she looked over her shoulder and saw Lee talking to the Israeli. He looked angry, but when she gave him a little wave, he smiled slightly and waved back.

The next day she arrived home from work tired and sweaty to discover she'd been sent three dozen long-stemmed red roses. "Who'd you sleep with?" one of her room-mates asked. "I hope you got the lead role."

"I have no idea," she'd replied. Then she read the card: "Thanks for the conversation and your charming company. I'd love to see you again. Ariel."

A half hour later, her cell phone rang. Caller ID didn't say who it was from so she didn't answer it until the third time whoever it was called her back. It was Ariel Shimon. He wanted to take her out to dinner. "Please," he begged. "I don't know anyone in this great big city, and I hate eating alone. Pretty please. I'll take you right home afterward, no hanky panky. I promise."

So she agreed. He picked her up in a stretch limousine an hour later and took her to dinner at Asiate. After a bottle of Armand de Brignac champagne, two bottles of Grgich Hills Cabernet, and a dinner of stuffed lobster tails, asparagus, and the most melt-in-your-mouth crème brûlée she'd ever tasted, Jenna was feeling no pain. And Shimon had been a perfect gentleman, only lightly caressing her bustline with his eyes from time to time, but otherwise keeping her entertained with funny or fascinating stories about Israel. She didn't see the bill for the dinner, much less the limo, but she was sure that it was more than she made in a month. She was half-considering whether to take him to bed for his efforts, but he took her straight home as he'd promised and stopped at a pleasant but not overpowering kiss before asking if she'd see him again the next night.

In fact, Blair didn't sleep with him until the third date. They'd gone dancing at S.O.B.'s and he certainly hadn't moved like any fifty-year-old she knew. And no young men her own age had his charm or flair. She learned that he'd been in the Israeli army and had been decorated for heroism; he had two young boys he loved very much, but he didn't talk much about his wife other than to describe her as "distant and cold." At the end of the evening when he asked if she wanted to see his suite at the Plaza, she said yes.

Ariel turned out to be as good a lover as he was a dancer and a soldier. Heroic, in fact. At the end of the first week of their affair, Blair got a call from Lee. "I hear you and Ariel are hitting it off," she said. "That's great!"

"Where'd you get that from?"

"He talks to my boyfriend all the time," Lee said. "Political stuff mostly, I think, although they go into Rod's office for it, and I don't hear much. But he did tell me that he really likes you."

"That's nice," Blair said, feeling a warm glow. "I like him, too."

"You'll like him even more when you check your bank account," Lee said. "And don't worry, you don't even have to report it to the IRS. It's taken care of."

"What? What are you talking about?" Blair asked. She was sitting at her computer so she got online as they talked and logged in to her bank account. "Oh, my God. There's five thousand dollars in there that wasn't there this morning!"

Lee laughed. "Did you think I was lying?"

"How'd you get my bank account?"

"Oh, ve haf vays, dahling," Lee said, and laughed again. "Really? I mean, look who we're talking about here. Rod's an important guy; he tells me that all the time."

A chill ran down Blair's spine. *They can get into my bank account?* But she was also realizing what the money would mean to paying the rent that month. *And putting a little away for law school,* she thought. Then her conscience spoke up. "No, really. I can't accept this. I'm having a good time with Ariel, and he's already spent a fortune taking me out."

"He can afford to take you to dinner in

Paris if that's what he wants, and the five thousand dollars isn't even his money," Lee assured her. "At least not directly. It's worth it to some people that Ariel is happy with you. He's been really easy to deal with, Rod says. Think of it as being paid as a goodwill ambassador between our countries."

These "people" meaning Rod, Blair thought. "Ambassador . . . new word for 'escort,' but I can use the money."

"That's the spirit," Lee said. "Now, have you given any thought to what I said about letting me know the sorts of things he talks about?"

"You mean like, 'oooh do that again'?" Blair replied sarcastically.

"No, silly. But anything else?"

This is the payback. "Well, he was talking about the Israeli government considering buying fighters from France . . ."

So having sex for money, and reporting what her lover talked about over dinner or after a bout in bed, began. Two weeks and two more paydays later, Ariel presented her with a diamond-studded tennis bracelet worth at least as much as what had been transferred into her bank account.

"I'm going home tomorrow, my love," he said as they had drinks at the Pegu Club.

Blair felt a pang of disappointment. She'd

grown to like Ariel, and she was sad to see it end. "So will I get to see you the next time you're in New York?" she asked.

Shimon smiled and touched her cheek, but then he shook his head. "It's better to keep these things short and sweet," he said. "Otherwise one person or the other forms an attachment that is simply impossible. In Israel I am a respected businessman with a wife and two children and possibly politics in my future. I cannot risk having my enemies discover I have a mistress. So this is good-bye. It's been fun."

It was all Blair could do not to cry, at least not until he'd dropped her off at her apartment. She understood their affair was a temporary thing, but he'd been so cold and made her feel so cheap. She sobbed all night, but then in the morning felt better about the whole thing, especially when she looked in her bank account and discovered an additional five thousand dollars she hadn't expected.

"A bonus for good work," Lee explained later that day. "Rod is very very pleased with you. You'll go far."

Blair learned what Lee meant by going far the next time she was invited to another glamorous party and introduced to another lonely, rich, and important man who was visiting New York City. At first, still stung by Shimon's callousness, she resisted, but then she shrugged. *We're using each other,* she thought. *I use him for the money; he uses me for my body. We both get what we want.*

Over the next several years, there'd been a dozen such men. Each time it had been easier to accept the money, and she no longer cried when they left. She even let herself believe it a little bit when Lee would babble on about how her information was helping the men who advised the president. A year earlier, she'd started law school and moved into a nice two-bedroom apartment in the Chelsea district that she shared with another law student. *I'll do this until I get through school,* she told herself as each man wined, dined, and bedded her before leaving.

Then three months ago, Lee had called to invite her to her apartment. "Rod wants to talk to you," she said.

When Blair arrived at the apartment, she found that her friend was gone but Fauhomme was there. *"I wanted us to have a little private chat,"* he said as he fixed himself a drink at the bar. "Get you anything?"

"An India Pale Ale if you have it," Blair said.

Fauhomme raised an eyebrow. "I wouldn't

have pegged you for an IPA type," he said as he opened the refrigerator and got out a bottle.

Blair held out her hand. "No? What type would you have pegged me for?" She didn't like the man, who'd grown fatter since she'd seen him at the first party. She knew he was a son of a bitch who liked to slap Lee around and verbally abuse her. Her friend had recently confided that the cruelty was getting worse, but she was mostly worried that he was thinking about getting rid of her. "He thinks I'm stupid because I could give a shit about politics, and because I'm nice. But I'm not stupid and I see things and hear things." The other woman's pretty face contorted into an angry mask. "And he better not fuck with me, or I'll nail his fat ass." Then she'd started to cry.

Fauhomme shrugged. "I hear you have expensive tastes."

"Sometimes I prefer a vodka martini, Grey Goose, shaved ice, very dry," Blair said. "But nothing like a good ol' IPA on a hot June day."

"To each their own," he said, raising his glass in a toast. "But as I was saying, I wanted to talk to you privately about a very important matter. First, I want to thank you for all you've done to help us keep our important visitors . . . um . . . happy. Your . . . efforts . . . have not gone unnoticed by people at the very highest levels. It may not seem like it to you but you are performing a great service to your country."

Blair felt her face burning. The fat man seemed to be choosing his words carefully but letting her know that essentially all he was saying was "thanks for being a whore." Even Shimon had not made her feel as cheap.

"Thank you," she said icily. "I've met some very interesting people."

Fauhomme smiled, not a very pleasant expression on his face, and his eyes didn't smile with his mouth. "Yes, you have." He pointed at the couch in Lee's living room. "Let's have a seat."

When they were settled, he looked at her intently and then asked, "Have you heard of a man named Sam Allen?"

Blair looked surprised. "The general? Of course, I read about him in the *Times*. He was in Afghanistan and a hero. I think I saw that the president is putting him in charge of the CIA?"

"I see you're well read, that's good, that's very good," Fauhomme said. "Yes, he's currently on the short list. If the president nominates him, his name will be submitted to Congress for approval. That may not happen until after the election in November."

"I see," Blair said. "So what does this have to do with me?"

"Right to the point, I like that, pretty and smart. I suppose then that you're aware that the former CIA director left under a cloud?"

"He was a child molester, right?"

"Looks that way," Fauhomme said. "Unfortunately, the president appointed him, so that sort of thing comes back as egg on his face."

"I should imagine."

"Yes. Anyway, so when the president was looking for his replacement, he wanted to be extra careful to choose someone who would be above reproach. Someone with no skeletons in his closet, and that brings me to General Allen. Everything we know about him suggests that he is that sort of man. Distinguished. Heroic. Upstanding. . . . But of course we thought that about his predecessor, which goes to show you never know what a man might be hiding."

Blair suddenly realized where the conversation was headed and was shocked. Not by Fauhomme so much, as she knew he lacked any morals, but that the president had such men working for him. She liked the president; she was young and idealistic, and wanted to believe what he said about the country going forward "together." The other major party didn't appeal to her, nor did it seem to want to; its members appeared content to just be portrayed as angry, wealthy white people, rednecks, religious fundamentalists, and bigots. She felt that for whatever reason, racists and misogynists gravitated to the other party, though she recognized that it was unfair to paint the whole party with the same brush.

The media seemed to favor the president, and she assumed that was because they knew what they were talking about. But looking at the fat man, she wondered if it was all a lie. "You want me to spy on the guy who might someday be the director of the CIA by going to bed with him?"

Fauhomme studied her for a moment as he rattled the ice cubes around in his glass. "I'm trying to protect the president. The director of the CIA is a very important position in a dangerous world; a mistake like the last guy makes us look foolish to our friends overseas and weak to our enemies. At home, it reflects on the president's decision-making. We're getting to the backstretch of this election campaign and the president can't afford to look foolish, weak, or inept."

"The article I read said General Allen was happily married," Blair noted. "If he's this fine, upstanding man that you say he is, wouldn't it be a red flag if he's willing to have an affair with a little floozy like me?"

Fauhomme chuckled. "Very astute, but it's not necessarily a deal-killer. I have it on good information that the general's marriage is on the rocks and has been for a long time. I suppose you could attribute that to the long deployments overseas and the stresses of his job. And I don't know if you've seen photographs of Mrs. Allen, but she hasn't exactly worked at staying youthful and attractive. The general's young for his age, and after all the pressure he's been under . . . and what he's going through now in his personal and professional life . . . he could use a diversion, so long as it didn't get into the media. And we're all discreet adults here."

"Wow," Blair said. "You people have a lot of words for it; first I was a goodwill ambassador, now I'm a diversion." She shook her head. "How did I ever get into this? Passed around like a cheap bottle of whiskey so that you know what these men are talking about in bed. I admit, I've had a good time; most of these men would be fun to date even if I wasn't being paid. But I don't know, this is different . . ."

"You'll be paid one hundred thousand dollars . . ."

Blair gasped. "What did you say?"

"Fifty thousand now," he said. "Fifty thousand after the election, win or lose."

"That's a lot of money."

"It's an important task, and it's not like he's 'looking' for a woman, not like the other men you've met; you may find it tougher to . . . seduce him. But I need you to try. I cannot risk another bad choice for such an important position. It would be absolutely deadly at the polls. I'm asking you on behalf of the president."

"He knows?" Blair asked.

"What the president does or doesn't know is none of your business," Fauhomme said. "It's my job to get him elected."

Blair thought about it. A hundred thousand dollars would ensure the law degree and give her a nest egg when she left the business of sleeping with Fauhomme's targets. "So how would I meet him?"

Fauhomme grinned and got up to pour himself another scotch. "I'm having some people over to my place at my beach house on Long Island for the long Fourth of July weekend. Should be about ten couples. The general will be there by himself, and Connie will make the introductions. There should be plenty of opportunities to use your feminine wiles."

"What if he doesn't like me? At least not like that?"

"You still get fifty thousand, but I'm expecting nothing less than your best."

"What do you want me to find out?"

"The usual," Fauhomme said, sitting back down on the couch next to her. "Anything we might not have been able to find out about him through the usual ways. You know, any weird sexual preferences, a gambling problem, uses heroin. But we also need to know that he's a team player."

"What do you mean?"

"What I mean is the general has a reputation for not being interested in politics, which is fine," Fauhomme said. "But we need to know that he'll back the president when push comes to shove and will keep his opinions to himself if he disagrees with the administration."

"So how will I know that?"

"You don't need to know," Fauhomme said. "Just tell us anything that comes up and we'll make the judgment call. Does he talk behind the president's back? Is he in line with our foreign policy goals? That sort of thing. Anything you can imagine damag-

182

ing this administration if it was to come out in the press. Just keep good notes and tell us everything; you never know what offhand comment might mean something combined with other information."

Fauhomme leaned toward her until all she could see was his fat face and intense eyes. "So do we have a deal?" It was framed as a question but it sounded like a demand.

Blair felt a twinge, but she wasn't sure if it was fear or conscience. Whatever it was, it didn't stand a chance against a hundred thousand dollars. "I'll come to the party and meet him and see where it goes from there."

The fat man leaned back with a wide grin. The intensity in his eyes was replaced with a cheerful twinkle. "That a girl," he exulted. "Connie will see that the money is deposited in your account by the evening. And we'll see you, and that cute little tush of yours, in Long Island."

The weekend of the Fourth rolled around and Blair was met outside her apartment building by a limousine that took her to an enormous Cape Cod–style home set on several acres of prime Long Island beach property. There were several other smaller cottages — "for guests," the driver said — on either side of the main house, all on the ocean. She was taken to one, where she found a fruit basket along with a bottle of champagne chilling in a bucket of ice and a note that read, "Cocktails at 6, main house. Dress up! Good luck. Connie and Rod."

At 6:10, having wiggled into a tight black silk dress that showed off her cleavage and her round butt, Blair wandered over to the main house, where she found the other guests chatting over cocktails in a large room off the back deck. A black man in a white tuxedo was playing the grand piano over in a corner and singing Cole Porter when she walked in. She would never forget how her eyes went immediately to the general, who was talking to two couples and Connie near the bar. He wasn't the tallest man in the room, maybe a shade over six foot; nor was he the most expensively tailored, though he was no slouch, and she suspected he would have made a blazer straight off the rack at Macy's look good. But something else she would always remember about him was how other men seemed to shrink, or fade, in his presence.

It took her a moment to realize that Lee was trying to get her attention. Her friend waved her over. "Oh, Jenna, there you are," she gushed. "Everyone, this is my friend Jenna Blair, a future attorney, fabulous actress, and Xtreme sports athlete — guys, do not try to compete with this girl, she's an animal. We're like best friends forever. Jenna, this is Senator and Mrs. Harry Dodd, and this wild man is Barnabas Radcliff and his . . . fiancée, am I right? . . . Lydia, and I'm sorry, Lydia, but I didn't get your last name? Swales? Lydia Swales."

"Barney to you, lovely lady," Radcliff said, taking and kissing her hand.

"Barney is the senior partner in a big law firm on Fifth Avenue," Connie said. "And a very good friend of the president, as well as of me and Rod."

Radcliff smiled at the introduction. He was good-looking, wearing a small ransom in jewelry, including a Louis Vuitton watch, and in his sixties. His fiancée, Lydia Swales, appeared to be Blair's age and smiled humorlessly as he fawned over her. Blair wondered if Swales was also working for Fauhomme as a "goodwill ambassador." Lydia's obvious displeasure didn't dissuade her beau. "When you get out of law school do come see me," he said. "We're always looking for good young talent . . . in the firm, that is."

Everybody laughed at his little innuendo. Everyone but Swales and the man Connie turned to now. "And this hunk is General

Sam Allen, though I'm sure you recognize that handsome face."

Allen hadn't laughed at the lawyer's sleazy intimation. Instead, he held out his hand, a nice hand — not too soft, but not dry and calloused, a man's hand, and that of a man who knew how to grip a woman's hand without crushing hers or being condescendingly light. "Nice to meet you, Miss Blair," he said. "But 'Sam' is quite enough."

"Only if you'll call me Jenna, or Jen," she replied with a smile.

"Agreed."

Of course it had been arranged so that they sat next to each other for dinner. That, too, was a night she'd never forget. She'd been around some attractive, self-assured men over the past four years since Ariel Shimon, but Allen was a cut above any of them. He was as handsome as any movie star, though much more real, and had a voice that sounded like deep musical tones when he spoke. He smiled often with his perfect white teeth and laughed in a way that never sounded strained or faked. And not once — at least not that she caught — had his eyes drifted to her chest.

He at least acted as if he was genuinely interested in her life and her observations. He'd been to the Rockies and liked mountain biking, rock climbing, and skiing — her three greatest outdoor passions — as well as surfing and, as he joked, "jumping out of perfectly good airplanes." He didn't talk down to her, or brag about himself, or make any sexual comments.

In fact, he excused himself early from the after-dinner gathering. Blair found herself disappointed, not because of the additional fifty thousand dollars that depended on seducing him, but because she really enjoyed his company.

"How'd it go?" Lee asked after Allen left the room.

Blair shrugged. "Okay, I guess. But I don't think you need me. If that guy's got skeletons in the closet, they're the good kind. We didn't talk about the CIA much but he did say he's excited about the job and appreciates the president choosing him."

"That's all good, but keep trying. You'd be surprised what some men can hide from everyone," Lee said, as if she knew. "Rod said to tell you that Sam runs on the beach at 6:00 a.m. I take it you brought your running shoes?"

The next morning, Blair was on the beach in her running clothes and was stretching between two dunes when she saw the general come out of his guest house and head for the harder sand at the water line. He didn't see her as he ran past, and she took a moment to note the trim torso and finely muscled legs.

She ran after him, and though she was in good shape and he seemed to be running effortlessly, she had to work hard to catch up. "Good morning," she panted as she drew alongside him.

Allen looked over and smiled. "Good morning, Jenna. You're up early." He wasn't even breathing hard.

"You know what they say about running being good for hangovers?"

He looked puzzled. "No, what do they say?"

"I don't know," she said. "I was hoping you did."

Allen laughed. "I've had my share of hangovers, and done quite a bit of running. But I try never to combine the two. You are much braver than I am."

They settled into a pace, and she was sure he slowed down for her. As they ran, he seemed to be in the mood to talk. He talked about his two sons; Billy, who was in West Point, and Roger, who had just graduated high school and was going to be a freshman in the fall at Cornell. "He wants to be a doctor."

"What do you think about that?"

"It's great," Allen said. "Somebody in this family ought to be into healing people instead of figuring out how to kill them."

Allen went quiet after that last remark for a half-mile or so, then apologized. "I'm sorry. That was a little heavy for this early in the morning. I guess I've been to too many bad places and seen too many bad things. I'm still learning to let go of some of that. But to be honest, while I'm proud of my son at West Point, I'd rather he didn't have to see the things I've seen; I don't want him to someday have to write a letter home to some wife or mother who's never going to see her husband or son again. I'd rather he didn't have to make the types of decisions I had to sometimes. I wouldn't have minded if they both wanted to be doctors. And even without the bad things, the army isn't the best life for anyone who wants to be a good father and husband."

"Where's your wife?" Blair asked impulsively.

They ran on a dozen more steps before he answered. "Not here," he said, and then he took off. "Come on," he yelled over his shoulder, "race you back to the house."

She wouldn't have stood a chance even if he hadn't bolted away from her. When she

189

ran up gasping for air, he'd already recovered and was looking at the waves. A minor meteorological disturbance off the Eastern Seaboard had stirred up four-foot waves. "Do you surf?" he asked.

"Not well, but I like trying," she said. "You suggesting . . . ?"

"Meet you back here in a half hour. They have wet-suit tops and boards at the main house; I'll bring the gear for you, too."

"Oh, my God, five miles running in the sand and now the man wants to surf." She laughed. "You're going to kill me!"

"I don't think there's any danger of that," Allen replied and ran off.

At the designated time, Blair was back on the beach wearing a formfitting two-piece swimsuit. This time his eyes did wander appreciatively over her body.

"Nice muscles," he said with honest admiration.

"Likewise," she said, taking in his broad shoulders, smooth, muscular chest, and six-pack belly. She noticed a deep indentation in his upper chest just below his left shoulder and pointed. "What happened?"

Allen looked down and frowned. "That's a very minor example of what a round from an AK-47 can do to the human body. I was lucky. It went through without hitting any major blood vessels, though it did a number on my shoulder blade where it came out." He turned and showed her the indented, puckered exit scar. "Gross, huh?"

Impulsively, Blair reached out and gently touched the old wound. "No. It's sort of a beauty mark. It's part of what makes you who you are." She looked up into his eyes just as he blinked hard as if he'd been reminded of some old pain.

"I've . . . uh . . . never heard it put quite that way," he stammered.

"I do believe you're blushing, General," Blair replied.

Allen laughed. "Nah, I just fry in the sun. Anyway, enough war stories, surf's up!"

They spent the morning surfing before going to their respective cottages to shower and then met again in the main house for lunch. "Ah, here's our surfers," Fauhomme bellowed as he and Lee approached the pair. "Kowabunga, dudes!"

Allen glanced quickly at Blair in a way that told her he found the fat politico as disingenuous as she did. But he smiled and said, "Jen here is trying to remind me what it's like to be young, which is tiring."

"Well, you both looked great out there, a regular Frankie Avalon and Annette Funicello," Fauhomme said, and slapped Allen on the back.

"Who?" Blair asked.

"Before your time," Allen replied.

"Indeed," Fauhomme echoed, and then looked across the room. "Look who decided to join our gathering. The president's national security adviser, Tucker Lindsey, and his . . . um . . . 'friend,' Ike something. I can never remember his last name. Lovely couple, and Tucker is sharp as a tack. Good man to work for, Sam."

"It's my understanding that the director of the CIA answers directly to the president," Allen replied. He'd said it quietly but pointedly.

Fauhomme's smile froze for a moment but then relaxed again. "Well, let's say you'll be working closely together, but the president does rely on Tucker's opinions. I'm sure he'll rely on yours after you get to know each other, too. In the meantime, we're a team and we all try not to step on each other's toes." He cut off any follow-up remarks by turning to Lee and saying, "Let's go say hello to Tucker and Ike." With that, Fauhomme grabbed Lee's elbow rather forcefully and guided her across the room toward the two men.

Watching them go, Allen asked, "How did you say you met our host?"

Blair bit her lip. "Well, I've known Connie for five or six years. We're pretty good friends. She started going out with Rod about four years ago. And, uh, sometimes I get invited to their parties. I'm really not in these people's league."

Allen tilted his head slightly and looked into her eyes. "No, you're way above it."

Looking back, that might have been the moment she fell in love with Sam Allen, though she would not have believed it at the time. "Do you know Tucker Lindsey?" she asked, attempting to regain her composure. She'd met Lindsey at a few parties and had never liked the man; she thought he was arrogant and looked down his nose at everyone. She wasn't sure if he knew about her arrangements with Fauhomme. She got the impression that he did from the way he could hardly be bothered to say hello when they'd meet, and that might be the only thing he said to her the entire event.

"Yes," Allen said. "Actually, he's the one who recommended me for the CIA job, though I didn't know him at that time. We've had quite a few conversations since."

"You don't seem to be all that impressed."

Allen's eyes narrowed as she looked back at him, and she wondered for a moment if he'd guessed the game she was paid to play.

But then he smiled wryly. "You're very intuitive, Jenna Blair. It's probably not fair; I haven't spent enough time with Mr. Lindsey to really know him, and to be sure, he is very smart and sure of himself. . . . Let's just call it an old soldier's distrust of civilians when it comes to military decisions."

"Why is that?"

"Because men like him are good at starting wars that soldiers like me and my son, and many other sons, have to fight." He put a finger to his lips. "But shhhhhhh . . . let's not talk politics, war, religion, or the CIA this weekend. I've had enough of all of it to last me another lifetime."

After lunch Allen said he was going back to his guest house to "lie in a hammock and read a good book. I haven't had much time for that lately, and you've about worn me out."

Blair would never be sure if it was because he saw the look of disappointment on her face, but then he added, "I know it might not be too exciting for a young woman of your energy levels, but if you have nothing else to do, find something to read and come on over. There are two hammocks and I was going to make up a pitcher of mojitos."

She surprised even herself by how quickly

she said it sounded like the perfect way to spend the afternoon. By the end of the second mojito they'd put their books down — he was reading *Atlas Shrugged* and she was devouring a romance novel — and were chatting amiably across the space between their two hammocks. She told funny stories about being a struggling actress in New York City, and he told funny stories about being a soldier from Africa to Afghanistan. She noticed, however, that he avoided what he referred to as "war stories."

Fourth of July dinner that night was a catered affair on the beach complete with a wet bar and a Benny Goodman–style orchestra. Blair had changed into a simple white cotton dress that accentuated the positives of her figure and rose to way up her thigh. As she walked up to where the party had been set up inside twinkling lights that had been strung up around the perimeter, her eyes again went immediately to where Allen stood talking to several men. He was dressed in long khaki shorts and a loose, white cotton top. He broke from the others when he saw her and met her halfway across the sand between them.

"Were you spying on me?" she said as she reached out and tugged on his shirt. "We look like twins."

"That's what I do," he said with a laugh. "But don't worry; your secrets are safe with me."

"And yours are with me, O man of mystery," Blair replied.

Except they aren't, are they, Jenna. Her conscience had taken that moment to show up on her face.

"Are you okay?" Allen asked, suddenly concerned. "For a moment there you looked like something you ate wasn't agreeing with you."

Smiling weakly, Blair shook her head. "I'm fine," she said. "I just think I need something to eat. Some crazy man has been running my body and mind ragged all day."

After wolfing down a cheeseburger, potato salad, beans, and two more IPAs, Blair announced that she was stuffed. Having inhaled several double shots of scotch with his meal, Allen was ready for hyper-libido-laced romance.

"Wow, I'm impressed," Allen said. "How do you fit it all in that little body?"

"I'm like a hummingbird. I burn the calories off faster than I can put them in."

"The envy of women everywhere. So let's go burn some more."

Before she could protest, Allen had led her out onto the sand in front of the orchestra where several other couples were dancing. She'd never learned to dance "old-fashioned," but Allen was a wonderful teacher and guide. Pretty soon he had her moving as if she'd been doing it all of her life. They danced off and on as the sun set and darkness fell. Then they grabbed two large beach towels from a table and sat next to each other on the moonlit beach near the waterline to watch the fireworks display that Fauhomme had arranged.

That was the first time he kissed her; leaning in close after one explosion for a sweet, quick brushing of lips. She was ready for more, but he turned and watched the next explosion overhead as if it had never happened. A few minutes of that and she grew impatient; she stood and picked up her towel, holding her hand toward him. "Come on," she said. "I need to walk this cheeseburger off." Allen didn't say anything but stood up and grabbed his towel, and they strolled off down the beach.

Somewhere out of sight of the others, their hands met and fingers intertwined. She led him to a spot between two large dunes tufted with sea grass. There she turned and this time kissed him, long and deep. He responded with hunger, but she pushed him away with a laugh. In the next moment, she

197

lifted her dress off in a single movement, turned and dashed for the water, unclasping her bra and dropping her panties as she ran.

"What are you doing?" he yelled after her, looking back up the beach to see if anybody was walking toward them.

"Skinny-dipping! What does it look like, you old fuddy-duddy!"

Watching the naked young woman dive into the waves, Allen started to run toward her, stripping his clothes off. "Fuddy-duddy?" he yelled in mock outrage. "I'm not a fuddy-duddy!"

Soon they were competing at trying to catch waves. He would later admit that he was "painfully aware" of her body as they floated on the swells. But he didn't try to touch her. That didn't happen until a wave cast them both onto the shore at the same time, the power of the water rolling their bodies together.

The next thing Blair knew, she was in his arms, kissing him as the receding wave hissed around them. "This is like that old movie . . ." she whispered, her voice husky.

"From Here to Eternity."

"What?"

"That's the name of the movie you're thinking about, *From Here to Eternity,* it's the scene where Burt Lancaster and Deborah Kerr are lying in the surf . . ."

"Shut up and kiss me again, Sam."

The large beach towels they had brought came in handy when they moved to the secluded spot between the dunes and consummated what had begun the evening before when he'd first looked into her eyes. Later, they lay together, her head on his chest and a leg stretched over his body, lost in thought and spent. "You know I'm married and things are complicated right now . . ." he said as he stroked her hair.

"What? Not even a tennis bracelet?" Blair sat up and hugged her knees. Suddenly she was tired of what she'd become.

"Tennis bracelet? I don't understand? I was just trying to say that my marriage has been over for many years, though it took meeting you, and tonight, to realize that I need to do something about it. What I meant by 'it's complicated' is that I need to think about how to navigate these waters I suddenly find myself in, both in regard to getting a divorce — I want to make it as easy on my wife as I can — and this CIA job. I hope this doesn't sound like I have too big an ego, but I think U.S. intelligence agencies need someone who can bring a soldier's eye to the decisions that are made.

Anyway, my country means everything to me, and I'm not done serving her."

"Never mind, I get it; I'm a big girl," Blair said bitterly as she stood up and started putting her clothes on. "I had a great time today and the sex was pretty good, too. We should be getting back to the party."

Standing when she did, Allen took her by the shoulders and turned her so that the moonlight lit both of their faces. "I had a great time today, too, the best I've had in a long, long time. And the sex was more than pretty good; I know it and you know it. I'm not trying to get rid of you. I want to see you after this. I shouldn't — the possibility of hurting people I care about and losing this appointment worries me — but I do. I've been waiting for someone like you for more years than I care to remember, and I don't want to lose whatever potential we have. If you want to wait to see me again until after I'm divorced and we don't have to sneak around, I'll understand. But now or in the future, I want to see you."

Maybe that was when she fell in love. Certainly it's when she'd decided to give Fauhomme back his fifty thousand. Even if things didn't work out with Allen, she knew she was done with the lifestyle.

Blair wiped at the hot tears that were running down her cheeks, and sniffled. "I want to see you, too. I think we can be careful . . . until you're divorced."

Allen pulled her against him and kissed her tenderly. "I don't need your answer tonight," he said. "I want you to think about this. If something gets out in the press it could be messy, not just for me and my family, and the president, but for you. The media are a bunch of jackals when they get hold of something like this. Either way I will be asking my wife for a divorce this fall when my youngest son leaves for college. After that I don't . . ."

"Sam."

"Yes, Jenna."

"Shut up and kiss me again."

The next morning, Allen got up at five so that he could sneak out of her cottage and back to his own. He had to get back to Washington, D.C., and left soon afterward. He texted her from the airport: "I miss you already." She texted back: "I missed you as soon as you left my arms this morning."

Two hours later, she was in her cottage packing to leave when there was a knock on the door and Fauhomme entered. "I hope you enjoyed yourself this weekend," he said.

"It was very nice, thank you." Still basking in the glow of new love, Blair meant what she said and even smiled at Fau-homme; after all, he'd brought them to-gether.

"So am I to understand that you and the general were playing a little beach blanket bingo?"

The warm glow faded. "I'm giving your money back," she answered quietly. "Like I said, you don't need me. The guy's a straight-arrow, and he's definitely got the president's back."

"A straight-arrow, except for doing the naughty bit with you," Fauhomme replied. "Or was that a onetime thing? *Wham bam, thank you ma'am.*"

Blair stopped packing for a moment and hung her head. "I'm not spying on him for you," she said, and looked up.

Fauhomme's face flushed slightly, his eyes hard. Remembering the bruises on Lee's face, Blair thought he might hit her. *I'll kick his fat ass if he tries,* she thought. But then to her surprise, he smiled.

"Okay," he said with a shrug. "I can see you really like the guy, and I could tell he really liked you. If you don't mind me ask-ing, are you going to see each other still?"

Blair was reluctant to answer but felt that if Fauhomme was going to be nice about it, she should be, too. "I think so," she said.

"He's got to be careful until he gets divorced and this confirmation goes through. He really wants the job."

"And he'll be good at it," Fauhomme said. "I believe that Tucker Lindsey is going to suggest that the president appoint him acting director and see how that works out for a bit. Then, if there are no issues and everybody's happy — including the general — we can proceed with making it permanent."

Blair smiled. *Maybe Porky Pig isn't so bad,* she thought.

"In the meantime," he said, "be discreet, please. I'd hate to see what would happen if it got out that he was having an affair."

The way Fauhomme said it, Blair wondered for a moment if it was a veiled threat. But then he added, "Maybe the four of us can have dinner sometime when we're all in New York. I know Connie would like that."

She relaxed. "I'd like that, too."

"Good, then we'll make it happen. In the meantime, your secret is safe with me, my friend."

8

"Well, in the meantime, you just be your sexy self for me, and I'm going to record you while you type. Then if you're a good boy, I'll give you a show when I get out of the shower."

Sam Allen frowned. He was photo shy and the webcam taping made him uncomfortable; if it had been anybody but Jenna . . . "I don't know why you'd want to record this."

She wrinkled her nose. "Because I'm going to blackmail you with it someday."

Allen yawned again. "You want to talk now about what you said at the cabin?"

Jenna shook her head. "No. I'm going to go hop in the shower. I think you need time to think about this, so I'll wait until Monday for your answer."

Allen nodded. If he could have, he would have reached through the internet to pull her to him and hung on for all he was worth. He was from a different generation and a different era, and yet no woman — not his old flame Ariadne Stupenagel, nor his wife when they first married — had ever matched him so well.

Allen wondered at first if everything he'd felt that Fourth of July weekend had been a combination of loneliness, sun, waves, booze, and a beautiful, willing young woman. But starting that next week with a flurry of texts, emails, and late-night telephone conversations, the relationship had grown like a wild rosebush, sending out new tendrils and blossoms every day, even when he had to spend most of his time in Washington, D.C.

Considering their age difference, they were amazingly compatible. Physically he was a match for most men half his age; he ate right and was diligent about keeping himself in shape. So he had no problem keeping up with her boundless energy. He was well-read and delighted to discover that she liked reading as much as he did, though she preferred her books to be a mix of entertainment and education, while he pretty much stuck to biographies, history, and the classics. They both liked old movies and being outdoors, whether it was hiking, skiing, rock climbing, or mountain biking.

She was a wonderful combination of youthful innocence in the way she looked at the world, yet amazingly insightful and mature for her age.

As much as their schedules allowed, especially after the president appointed him acting director and her law classes began again in September, they got together on weekends and the occasional weeknight. Sometimes she traveled to Virginia — he felt it was too risky to meet in the capital because of the omnipresent media — and they stayed at a bed and breakfast in the Shenandoah Valley. Or he'd catch a flight to New York City and she'd meet him at the Casablanca, where the manager was a former army buddy.

The first time he brought Jenna to the hotel, his friend didn't bat an eyebrow. Then when Jenna was otherwise occupied, they'd had a chance to talk and Allen explained that she was more than just a fling. His friend had leaned close and said, "Hey, I can see that. It's been a while since I seen you with that dopey 'I'm in love' face, but I remember it from back in the day. So I'm happy for you no matter how long it lasts. You are henceforth Mr. and Mrs. Sean Stibbards at the Casablanca. Some of the staff will know, of course, but they're a good bunch and keep their mouths closed."

Twice before the past weekend they'd gone to a rustic cabin in upstate New York that had been in his family for generations. She said it was her favorite place to be with him, and he had to agree. They could relax and not be looking over their shoulders, fearing discovery.

As their intimacy grew, Jenna told him that he had to stay her lover forever. "You've ruined me for 'boys' my own age." He admitted that he'd had some great lovers in the past but never the combination of lust and love that he felt with her.

Of course, when they weren't together he was plagued by guilt and worry. He'd been raised to believe in the concepts of duty, responsibility, and faithfulness — both to his country and to his wife. When he talked to Jenna, he didn't try to blame the failure of the marriage on Martha.

"We both checked out on each other," he said. "I was into my career and gone a lot of the time, and she put herself into the kids. I don't know exactly when it happened, but one day we woke up and there was nothing left of 'us.' We were still friends, and we could talk about most things, especially the boys. But the feeling you want to have for the most important person in your life, it was simply gone. I'm sure this is going to hurt her, no one likes to be 'left,' but I don't think it will be unexpected and maybe even a relief so we can both move on with our lives."

"You sure you just didn't need to get laid, and maybe you're still in love with her?" Jenna asked. She'd said it lightly but he knew by the fear in her eyes that she was serious. He shook his head. "I love her . . . as a friend and as the mother of my children," he replied. "But I am *in love* with you. And if you'll have an old coot like me, I want to spend my life with you."

He showered her with flowers, small gifts, and letters filled with flowery professions of love. Jenna called him her poet-warrior and said she was surprised and then enchanted to meet a man with his achievements and proven courage who could yet open up and be vulnerable.

"I have to admit that's not easy for me," he replied. "I've learned to bottle a lot of that up; in fact, before I met you, I was pretty sure I was done with love. But I'm trying because I want you to know everything about me."

When September arrived and his younger son went off to college, he told Jenna that he was going to file for divorce. But she

208

urged him to wait until after his confirmation hearings, which had been delayed until the election was over. "You know if word gets out that you've filed, the press will start snooping around," she said. "If they find out about me, it will ruin your chances, and the press will put your wife through hell, too."

So they settled into a holding pattern: committed to each other while holding out for the election, followed by his confirmation hearing, followed by divorce, followed by . . . forever.

Then the American trade mission was attacked in Chechnya. Except for quick telephone calls to check in with her, they didn't get much of a chance to talk and he'd been reluctant to say much over the phone. He told her he was preparing for the hearing before the congressional committee.

Then he went to the meeting with Tucker Lindsey and Rod Fauhomme expecting a substantive conversation about what he'd been hearing regarding the attack and the need to alter the administration's "talking points." He'd never expected to be told to keep his mouth shut or risk having his affair with Jenna exposed, his family devastated and hounded by the media, and his job with the agency dead and buried.

As a general he was used to making life-and-death decisions quickly and with certainty. But as a man trying to juggle the dissolution of his marriage and an exciting new lover on one hand, and believing that the agency needed his direction on the other, he was torn and unsure. Part of him said to go along with the plan, lie by omission at the congressional hearings, get confirmed, and *then* take out the bad guys with the trash. *It will probably take that long to identify them anyway,* said one of the voices in his head. *What does it matter if they pay for it now or later?*

The other voice said that no good could come of lying when foreign policy depended on it. Not in Vietnam, or Iraq, or Afghanistan. Lying had cost too many lives and too much of the nation's wealth. *You took an oath to defend the Constitution, and that doesn't include perjuring yourself to Congress or failing to tell the truth to the American people.*

There was a third voice, too. Not an unkind or accusatory voice, but the voice of his conscience when it came to his marriage. Strangely, he had no regrets about his relationship with Jenna. Conscience told him that he should have divorced his wife first, but his heart pointed out that he hadn't planned on meeting someone like her. He believed in fate and that it was their destiny to meet and fall in love. However, he did feel guilt over the pain his wife and family would experience when he filed for divorce. Especially if it was preceded by learning the truth from some sneering reporter and then having it spread across the media world like a flu virus. It would take a long time to heal those wounds and could also damage his relationship with Jenna, as the remorse for the pain he caused ate away at him.

He still wasn't sure which voice he was going to listen to when he flew to New York on Friday morning and called Ariadne to make plans to meet at the White Horse. He wanted to see her for two reasons. One was that he wanted to talk to someone about Jenna and knew she'd understand without being judgmental, even if all he was really after was acceptance. More important, Stupenagel was the best investigative journalist he'd ever known. If something did happen to him, whether by accident or commission, he wanted her to know where to dig to find the truth. He'd given her enough hints to get her started if he wasn't around; she'd have to figure out the rest on her own, but if anyone could do it — and have the courage to go public with it — it was Ari.

On the drive north with Jenna, he hardly noticed the fall colors except to respond absently to her appreciative comments. He'd been too consumed with studying his options as he would have been before a battle, though he mostly knew what he was going to do by the time they pulled up to the cabin.

"I'm having lunch Monday with Pete Oatman," he said as he brought their bags in from the car. "He's the superintendent at West Point and an old friend; I want to run some things past him, but need to have my ducks in order. Then I hope to see my son after lunch. I'm going to tell him about the divorce."

"Is that what's bothering you? The divorce? Honey, I still think you should wait until the right time . . ."

Allen reached over and took her hand. "There is no 'right' time for something like that," he said. "There is only now. I'm tired of the subterfuge. I'm not good at lying. I want to be with you. But what's going on with me has more to do with the hearing, even if that does concern you, too, than my divorce. I just need to think it through."

"It's okay," she said. "I've got a lot to think about, too."

He looked at her curiously, but they both put it out of their minds that first night over a bottle of pinot grigio as they sat on the front porch of the cabin watching the moon rise beyond the little lake. Nor did it come up again when she woke in his arms the next morning with the light pouring in the master bedroom's window.

As promised, he'd spent most of Saturday morning and the early afternoon in his office with the door closed. At about one o'clock, she made lunch and came to let him know it was ready. She knocked but didn't wait for him to answer before walking in. He was standing in front of an open wall safe that had been built behind the bookshelf. Her sudden appearance startled him; he didn't want her to see what was in his hand, so he quickly put it in the vault and closed the safe.

"Oh, sorry," she said. "I made tuna sandwiches and I . . . well, I didn't mean to intrude."

"No, that's okay, Jen," he said, and nodded at the safe. "Come on over, let me show you how this works." He swung a set of faux book covers over the safe to hide it.

"Just like in the movies!" she'd said.

They both laughed. It was an inside joke from the night on the beach that they used often. "Yeah, just like in the movies," he repeated. He showed her how pulling out the faux copy of *The Last of the Mohicans* produced a clicking sound and then the phony books swung out again. "Great-grandpa Ben Allen built this; he was a fan of James Fenimore Cooper; it's where I keep all my important papers."

"I love that book and the movie with Daniel Day-Lewis. But that's your business. I didn't mean to barge in."

"I don't mind. In fact, I was planning on showing you."

She looked at him quizzically. "I'm glad you want me to know all the family secrets," she said, then she bit her lip. "I have a secret that I need to share with you, too."

Allen studied her face for a minute and then put a finger beneath her chin and tilted her mouth up toward his. "Can it wait until Monday night?" he asked, and then kissed her. "We do need to talk, but after I see Pete Oatman. We can spend the night at the Casablanca and pour our guts out before making wild passionate love; then I'll catch an early flight down to D.C. How's that sound?"

Her eyes clouded by tears, Jenna nodded. "Yes. It can wait until Monday."

That night he'd been particularly melancholy as he sat in the big chair in front of the fireplace with Jenna cuddled up on his lap like a cat, closing her eyes and even purring as he stroked her hair. They'd been quiet for several minutes when he cleared his throat and shifted a little so he could see her face.

"You know, I'd give it all up for you, Jen," he said. "Maybe I should forget about the job. We could get married and live here. I could open a fly-fishing shop and you could hang your shingle in town and practice law. Or just knock around here with me and the kids."

"Kids?" she said, raising an eyebrow.

"Only if you want them, of course," he said, hugging her closer.

They were quiet for a moment, then she said, "It sounds nice, but you wouldn't be happy."

"I'd be happy if I was with you. What if I decided to write a book instead of going to Washington?" he said. "Would you be willing to give up the exciting and glamorous life as the spy chief's wife in D.C.?"

"In a heartbeat."

"Think of all the intrigue and fancy black-and-white parties you'd miss."

She snuggled in closer to his chest. "I do look great in black. But I have all the

215

intrigue I need right here." More silence, then, "You're not ready to open a fly-shop or sit in an old cabin writing a book with a bunch of toddlers running around. Maybe at first you'd be okay, and maybe we'd be okay because we love each other so much. But you'd always wonder if you could have made a difference at the agency. You'll always be a soldier, Sam." She sighed. "Besides, the next president will probably kick you out and then we can retire to our little piece of heaven on the lake."

He laughed and hugged her closer. "You're right," he said. "I don't think I'm cut out for the politics surrounding the job. I probably won't even make it through this president's next term, *if* there is a next term."

They drove back to New York City early Sunday afternoon. He dropped her off at her Chelsea apartment and said he was going to stay at the Casablanca. "I'm probably going to be up all night working on my testimony, then I need to get a copy printed for my visit with Pete. And you are far too distracting to have in a hotel room."

She pouted for a moment, then kissed him. "I'm tired anyway," she said. "I don't have class tomorrow, but I have some things to think about before our talk." She started to get out of the car and then turned back to him. "No matter what happens tomorrow, no matter what you need to tell me, or what I have to say to you, I will always love you, Sam."

"I love you, too, Jen. Nothing's going to happen tomorrow that we can't deal with. I'll get on the computer later this evening to say good night."

He worked all day on his testimony and then went to the hotel's business office to print a copy. As he was walking past the front desk, the clerk smiled. "A friend of yours dropped something off for you. He said his name was Peter." She set a bottle of twenty-five-year-old Macallan scotch on the counter.

Allen laughed and picked up the bottle. "Just what the doctor ordered. I think I'll go to my room and give this baby a trial run."

Back in the room, he ordered room service and then poured himself a healthy tumbler of the scotch. He took a sip and furrowed his brow; there was just the slightest medicinal aftertaste that he wasn't used to, but he shrugged. *Probably something I ate earlier throwing my palate off a bit.* He was working on putting the finishing touches on a letter to his sons when there was a knock on the door.

"Room service," said a male voice.

"Let yourself in," Allen called out as he typed in a revision. He hardly glanced at the room service waiter who came in and placed the tray on the coffee table.

"Anything else, sir?"

"No . . . I see by the tat that you were in the Corps."

"Semper Fi, sir."

"Booya. Airborne here."

"Brothers in arms no matter what branch."

"Damn straight, soldier. Care for a drink?"

"I'd love to, sir, but I'm on duty and they frown on that sort of thing. Some other time."

"You bet. Do me a favor, put 20 percent on your tip and let yourself out."

"Yes, sir. Have a good night, sir."

"You, too," Allen said, and turned back to his computer. *Ten o'clock, time to check in with Jenna,* he thought as he took another sip of scotch. He wrinkled his nose; it still seemed a little bitter, but he decided the lasagna he'd ordered would round it out. He turned on his computer's video cam and dialed her up.

"Are you saying I'm too much?" she asked.

"No, not at all. I'm flattered and grateful that you find me attractive, and happily satiated every time we see each other. Forgive me, honey, I didn't mean that."

"That's better. I'm in love, Sam. I can't get enough of you." She pouted. "I can't believe we're in the same city and we're not going to sleep together."

"Is what you do called 'sleep'?" he said with a chuckle, then yawned himself. "Excuse me, don't know where that came from, I guess I am tired."

"You're not getting old on me, are you?"

"Never. I just ordered room service — lasagna — and my old buddy, Pete, sent a bottle of Macallan to keep me company. Should be just the thing to put me to sleep," he said and took another sip.

He frowned. "I don't know why you'd want to record this."

She wrinkled her nose. "Because I'm going to blackmail you with it someday."

Allen yawned again. "You want to talk now about what you said at the cabin?"

Jenna shook her head. "No. I'm going to go hop in the shower. I think you need time to think about this, so I'll wait until Monday for your answer."

Allen watched as she stood and then dropped her robe, displaying the body he enjoyed so much. He shook his head and poured himself another tumbler's worth of scotch and took another sip. He sloshed a little as he attempted to put the glass back on the desk. He shook his head. *Man, time to hit the sack.*

He tried to stand but suddenly his legs felt weak and he sat back down. *No way two drinks puts me away like that,* he thought. He looked at the bottle and recalled the bitter aftertaste. Suddenly, he knew what was happening.

"I'd love to, sir, but I'm on duty and they frown on that sort of thing. Some other time."

Barely able to keep his eyes open, his mind growing fuzzy, Allen willed his hands back to the keyboard and typed a short email. He sent it and then reached forward so that only a blank page showed. His hands fell to his sides and he slumped back into the chair just as he heard the door open.

"Room service . . ."

9

By the time Karp got back to his office after leaving the Casablanca and the body of Lt. Gen. Sam Allen, he knew he had his hands full with a high-profile homicide case. In spite of the killer's efforts to make it look like a suicide, it didn't take Fulton's "intuition flu," or Assistant Medical Examiner Gail Manning's remark about how a scotch aficionado would have avoided the bitter taste by not emptying the pills into the drink, to recognize the deception.

Suicide simply didn't make sense. For one thing, it just didn't mesh with what he knew of Allen's character — a decorated soldier who'd retired at the pinnacle of his career and was embarking on another that at least publicly he seemed to covet. While anything was possible, nothing about the man indicated he was the sort to kill himself even if he was "sorry for everything" — whatever that meant. *A man like him would "face the* music," Karp thought. And even if for some inexplicable reason Allen had decided to take his life, he wouldn't have chosen to do it in such a public manner, in a hotel room in New York City, putting his family and friends through the media storm that would follow.

The question then became who killed the general and why. Over the course of his military career and in his position as the acting director of the CIA, Allen would have made enemies, as well as been a prime target for assassination. However, it was reasonable to rule out a terrorist action, as they would have wanted the publicity of killing such an important individual.

Poison, if that was indeed the cause of Allen's death, had been a tool of the spy trade for eons. Somehow Karp doubted that the general had been induced to swallow enough Valium to kill him — after all, there'd been no sign of a struggle — and thought it likely to have been used to cover up the real cause of death. *Gail will find it in the toxicology,* he thought, *especially now that I've asked her to look beyond the obvious.*

So who then? Why? He was supposed to testify before the congressional committee tomorrow. Could it be related to that? And who would have the arrogance to think that they could murder the acting director of the CIA and get away with it? The questions raced through his mind as Officer J. P. Murphy drove him south toward the Criminal Courts Building. He tried to call Marlene to tell her about Allen; she'd been out for a run when Fulton gave him the news that morning. But she didn't answer her cell phone.

The news outlets had reported that there were no female bodies identified and several males were unaccounted for in Chechnya after the attack. The absence of "bad news" had lifted Marlene's spirits at least for the moment. She was convinced that Lucy and Ned were alive. "They were probably together doing something outside the compound," she explained. "Maybe they've been captured or are on the run, but I can feel they're alive . . . I don't know how I know, maybe it's the mom in me, but I know."

Karp didn't want to dash her faith; he hoped she was right. But he knew that in what the administration kept referring to as the "fog of war," the information that Jaxon was getting was agonizingly incomplete. And since the initial report, the fact that there'd been nothing new was demoralizing.

Believing that their daughter needed her, but unable to do anything, Marlene reverted to a darkened mood. He didn't know what she'd make of the news about Allen and what, if anything, it had to do with the compound being overrun in Chechnya — and Lucy's disappearance. He didn't know what to make of it himself.

When he got to his office and was settled in behind his desk, he reached for a yellow legal pad. Whether it was for a trial or just to help him think through a problem, he always found that jotting down notes on a pad helped his thought process. He listed the chronology of events since the attack in Chechnya, such as he knew them from either the media — meaning the administration — or Jaxon, leading up to Allen's death the day before he was scheduled to testify. Up to this point, as far as he knew, the general had refrained from making any comments other than to say that the CIA was continuing to assess what happened as information became available. He refused to be baited by the growing criticism, particularly from the president's opponents, that "once again" American intelligence gathering had failed to identify and deal with a threat.

Most of the administration's statements

had come through Rosemary Hilb, the irascible press secretary, and Helene Vonu, the assistant secretary of state specializing in the Northern Caucasus and Russia. Vonu, in particular, had been the public face of the administration on television and in newspaper reports. But she mostly stuck with the administration's talking points: the attack occurred without warning, was over swiftly, and was carried out by Chechen separatists in a "brutal act of terror." She and others like Fauhomme had lauded the president's "close cooperation" with Russian authorities as proof of his fitness to lead "in the international arena."

On the Sunday-morning political talk shows, Vonu expanded a little, saying, "These terrorists — masquerading as patriots — are trying to disrupt U.S. attempts to mediate a political solution" between "disgruntled" Chechen factions and Russia. When the sole member on one of the panels who occasionally was critical of the administration renewed the question of whether Al Qaeda was involved, Vonu openly scoffed. "Al Qaeda Al Qaeda Al Qaeda," she said, smiling and shaking her head as though scolding a not very bright student. "Let's trot out the big bad bogeyman of Al Qaeda to sell newspapers and television ads, shall

225

we? Our Russian friends will back me up on this one; Al Qaeda was not behind this attack. It just seems to me that some people have a hard time accepting that other forms of terrorism exist that aren't Islamic extremism–motivated or somehow connected to Al Qaeda. The terrorists behind this attack are little more than warlords and organized crime syndicates who don't want to see a legitimate, democratically elected government in power in Chechnya."

Rod Fauhomme made the rounds, too. He complained that the congressional hearings were "clearly a partisan attempt to discredit the administration in the run-up to the election. The president's opponent took a big hit in the last debate, which happened to be on foreign policy. The opponent knows he has no foreign policy experience, and unlike the president would be lost in the current situation. So all he — through his proxies on the congressional committee — can do is invent straw men and attack while cooler heads are handling the situation in co-operation with the Russian government. It's the difference between statesmanship and gamesmanship."

Karp picked up the television remote and clicked on the twenty-four-hour news channel just as a photograph of Allen appeared

226

above the text: BREAKING NEWS! CIA DI-
RECTOR ALLEN DEAD IN NEW YORK HOTEL.
So it's out, he thought, but in the next
instant his attention was diverted by what
sounded like a brawl in the reception area
outside his office, followed by a sort of wild
scrabbling at the door before it cracked
open.

Standing up, Karp could see Darla
Milquetost valiantly fighting to keep the
intruder out. "I don't care who you think
you are; you can't just barge in on Mr.
Karp!"

The tall blond woman on the other side
of his receptionist ignored the shorter
woman and yelled over the top of her head.
"Karp, we need to talk!"

"You need to make an appointment like
anyone else!" Milquetost complained. "You
are such a rude person!"

"Beat it, Darla, this is important," Ariadne
Stupenagel said, using her greater size to
leverage her way past and into his office.

Darla clutched Stupenagel's elbow as she
looked at Karp. "Shall I call security?" she
asked hopefully.

Karp shook his head. "No, thank you,
Darla. Sorry, Ariadne, but I'm not in the
mood to deal with the media just now . . ."

Stupenagel pointed past him to the television screen. "It's about Sam."

"Sam?" Karp replied with a frown.

"Sam Allen. We were old friends," Stupenagel explained. "I talked to him Friday, and I think you might want to hear what I've got to say before it appears in my newspaper tomorrow."

Still frowning, Karp nodded at his receptionist. "It's okay, Darla, let her in."

Milquetost glared up at Stupenagel. "Okay, but I'll be right outside if you change your mind." She let go of the journalist and left the room.

Karp shook his head. "You really do need to quit antagonizing Mrs. Milquetost. She's just doing her job." His voice faded as Stupenagel crossed the room and sat down in the leather chair across from Karp's big mahogany desk and crossed her long legs. "First, I want your assurances that this goes no further, particularly in regard to the slimeballs in the press," she said. "This is *my* story."

"So this is about getting a scoop," Karp replied with a frown. Just then Ariadne's normally tough-as-nails reporter's eyes welled up with tears; she covered her face with her hands and sobbed.

"Hey, Ariadne, I'm sorry. You said he was a friend, I wasn't thinking." He grabbed a box of tissues as he walked around his desk and handed her one.

"Thank you," she said softly. "Sorry. I got a call a half hour ago from a friend who works at the hotel. I just . . ." She stopped for a moment to catch her breath. "I couldn't believe it. I just saw him Friday."

"Yes, you were saying that I should hear," Karp said as the intercom suddenly buzzed, followed by Milquetost's annoyed voice.

"Mr. Karp, your wife is here to see you."

Karp looked at Stupenagel, who said, "I called her. I know about Lucy."

The door opened and Marlene walked in. Stupenagel stood and the two women embraced. They'd been friends since they were college roommates at Smith. Stupenagel had been the wild child while Marlene was more conservative due to her strict Italian Catholic upbringing in Queens, but still the unlikely pair had formed a lasting bond.

Marlene was aware of the love-hate relationship between "Stupe" and her media-averse husband, but she knew even he had a grudging respect for her talents as an investigative journalist. And several times in the past, she had "done the right thing" and held stories or passed on information — sometimes against her aggressive journalistic principles.

"Hi, sweetheart," Karp said when Marlene broke away from her friend. "I take it you're here due to whatever Ariadne has to say about General Allen's alleged suicide."

"It wasn't a suicide," Stupenagel spat. Suddenly, the tears were gone, replaced by a fierce glare. "I've known Sam a long time. He wasn't the type . . ."

"People change. I'd guess he was under a lot of —"

"Sam was the sort of man who thrived on pressure," Stupenagel retorted. "But even if not, I talked to him two days ago. He wasn't suicidal, though he certainly had a lot going on in his personal life, and he was damn mad about the Chechnya situation and prepared to do something about it at the congressional hearings."

Karp and Marlene listened quietly for the next twenty minutes while Stupenagel told them about her conversation with Allen. The more she spoke, the grimmer their faces became.

When she was done, Marlene let out a low whistle. "Well, if what he said about Al Qaeda being involved is true, and someone high up is lying about this 'trade mission' and the failure to respond to protect American lives, I can understand why the administration wouldn't want this to come out in the hearings right before the election. You think he was killed to prevent any deviation from the administration's version?"

"It's the only thing that makes sense to me," Stupenagel replied.

"I don't know, Stupe," Karp said. "You say he was being blackmailed — supposedly by someone in the administration — to keep his mouth shut or his wife would find out about his affair. Maybe the choice between lying at the hearing or putting his family through hell was too much for him so he took pills as a way out?"

"And killing himself wouldn't be putting his family through hell?" Stupenagel shook her head. "You would have had to know the man, but he was going to tell the truth and was prepared to take his lumps."

Marlene abruptly got up from her chair and walked over to the window behind Karp and looked out at the streets. "I knew there was something fishy about the whole explanation regarding what happened in Chechnya. And this proves it, at least to me. I think you're right, Ariadne; I don't think he killed himself. But those sons of bitches put my daughter in harm's way, and if I can prove it . . ."

Both women turned expectantly toward Karp. "I have to admit that something wasn't right when I went to the hotel this morning. Clay and I both felt it," he said. "I'm waiting on the toxicology results and Fulton's investigation, but I think you're right; this wasn't a suicide. But intuition and even Allen's telling you he was being blackmailed is a long way from proving who would have been behind it. I'd rather the killer, or killers, not know that we're on to them. So, you going to run with the story?"

Stupenagel considered the question, then shrugged. "I'm going to write up what I got," she said. "But it's pretty dicey. Sam can't back me up and my editor may be a little hinky about saying that he was killed because of what he was going to say at the hearing. I need corroboration, a second source; so I guess that buys you a little time." She looked up at the television and did a double-take that caused Karp and Marlene to look, too.

The photograph of a young woman now appeared with the headlines about Allen's death. "That's Jenna," Stupenagel said.

"Who?" Karp asked.

"Sam's girlfriend, Jenna. Sam showed me a photograph . . ." Her voice trailed off as she listened to the newscaster.

"FBI officials are asking the public for help in locating this woman, Jenna Blair," the newsman said. "According to an FBI spokesperson, she may have been the last person to see General Allen alive and is being sought for questioning. Anyone having information is asked to . . ."

"Think she knows something?" Marlene asked.

"I don't know," Stupenagel replied. "But even if she doesn't, I'd say we better find her before whoever was blackmailing Sam does." She turned to look at Marlene. "Care to do a little investigative work with your old buddy?"

Marlene's eyes narrowed. "You bet." Both women again looked at Karp. "Any thoughts, Butch?" his wife asked.

Karp thought about it and nodded. "Yeah, starting with a telephone call to Jaxon."

"That's a start," Stupenagel said. "I think we're going to need all the help we can get."

10

Blair woke up, stretched, and rolled over to look at her smartphone on the nightstand. She stuck out her lower lip and pouted when she didn't see the usual "good morning, sweetheart" text she got from Allen whenever they were apart.

Eight o'clock. Oh, well, he had to get going by five to meet his buddy at West Point and he's preoccupied with the congressional hearing. I'm sure he spaced it. Still, a girl's got to put her foot down. No good-morning text and last night he couldn't stay awake long enough for me to get out of the shower.

In fact, he'd already gone to bed, lights out, when she emerged from the bathroom after her shower wearing an emerald green satin shift he particularly liked on her. The screen on her computer had gone dark in sleep mode but she noted that it was still recording the signal sent from Sam's webcam. Thinking he might be awake, she moved the mouse and her screen blinked on. His chair was empty and the room was mostly dark; there was only enough light coming in the windows to cast shadows.

"Sam?" she'd said quietly, not wanting to wake him if he was asleep.

There was no answer. She turned off her computer. "Good night, my love, sweet dreams," she whispered. She didn't have classes or work in the morning and could sleep in, but she was tired and went to bed. Then she started thinking about the conversation they were going to have and was soon wide awake, tossing and turning in the dark.

Blair was not at all as sure as he was that nothing was going to happen on Monday that they couldn't deal with. She wasn't worried about what he was going to say; probably nothing worse than that he'd decided he couldn't see her until after his confirmation hearings. But *she* was going to have to tell *him* that she'd slept with and spied on important men for money and had been about to do the same with him. She would have been willing to bet her soul that she knew who had the greater sins to confess and the guiltier conscience.

At first she had tried to believe that she could get away with not telling him about her recent past. She never heard from any of her former "dates," and didn't expect to, as she was one of the skeletons in their closets. But as the weeks passed and summer had turned to autumn and their love had grown, the weight of her secret dragged on her conscience. He kept talking about a future together, even hinting at marriage. "Or just knock around here with me and the kids . . ." She wanted all of that, but she knew that the strain of keeping her secret, always living in fear that he would find out, would ultimately destroy their relationship whether or not he ever learned the truth.

And if it ever came out in the media, it would destroy him and his career. She could visualize the *New York Post* headline: CIA DIRECTOR MARRIES "PRETTY WOMAN." *Only it wouldn't be funny and it wouldn't end like a fairy tale.* She knew she had to tell him and let him make the decision. Still, she hesitated, in part to hold on to him for just a little bit longer, and in part not wanting to hurt him while he was under such pressure with the "situation" in Chechnya.

It had consumed him since he got the news while they were staying at the Shenandoah Valley bed and breakfast. They were sitting on the inn's front porch admiring prize Morgan horses grazing and racing in the pastures while enjoying the sunset when the call came from CIA headquarters in Langley, Virginia. "Yeah, what's up?" he asked, then frowned and sat up. "What time did this happen?" he asked, looking at his watch. Then he cursed. "Why am I just now hearing about this?" Apparently he didn't like that response any better. "Goddammit, I don't care if it's a 'State Department and National Security Agency matter,' we're the goddamned Central Intelligence Agency and we need to get on top of this now! Check the satellites, and if we have any sources on the ground, I want to know what they know and I want to know it yesterday. Is that clear?" He looked at his watch again. "I'll see you in two hours, that's 19:45, and I want to know why it took them two hours to let us know."

Sam hung up the phone and patted her knee. "Sorry, babe, but I've got to go," he said. "There's been a problem. I need to go into the office and it may take some time. You can stay here if you want and I'll send a car back for you in the morning. Or, I'll have the driver drop you off at Dulles and you can catch a flight home tonight."

She chose to go home and then except for a few brief webcam conversations and his "good morning" and "good night" texts, she'd hardly heard from him during the week.

If he was tired and a bit frayed around the edges when he spoke to her on Wednesday morning, his mood darkened considerably after he met with Tucker Lindsey. "And that son of a bitch, excuse my language, Rod Fauhomme was there." She could feel his smoldering anger, but he still wouldn't talk about it. Instead, he asked if she would go to the lake cabin with him for the weekend. "I have a lot of thinking and work to do," he said. "But I'd love it if you'd go and keep me company. Just knowing you're near me and that I'll wake up with you in the morning makes me happy."

That was the sort of thing he was always saying that melted her every time. "I'd love to go," she said. "I'm not complete when I'm not with you." And she meant what she said about the weekend, it was special, it was always special with Sam. No one else had ever made her feel as safe and loved. But she'd also needed the alone time walking around the lake to think, and if this was to be the last time, to commit it to memory.

Sitting on the porch waiting for him to be done in his office, she watched a pair of loons on the lake playfully chasing each other over and under the water, rubbing necks and grooming each other; she wished life was anywhere near that simple for her and her man. She fantasized that Sam would listen to what she had to say and forgive her and choose to be with her. But then that voice, the one that tried to warn her back to when she was letting Ariel Shimon wine and dine her, sighed. *Who are you kidding, Jenna? Surely you don't think even this kind of love can overcome that. This isn't the movies.*

As they drove back from the cabin to New York on Sunday afternoon, her mind had been on the tangled web of her life. Not only did she have to confess her own sins, but according to Sam their relationship was also tied up with what happened in Chechnya — and between Sam and Fauhomme. Just the thought of the leering, piggish face of the president's campaign manager filled her with foreboding. "Your secret is safe with me, my friend."

After Sam dropped her off, Blair felt the need to talk to someone. But the only person she could confide in about Sam was Connie Rae Lee. They only talked on the telephone since the Fourth of July party, and Connie was always turning the conversation toward Blair's relationship with Sam. She figured that Connie was digging for any little bits of information she could use for Fauhomme, but since she kept the conversation to "girl talk," she didn't feel she was betraying his confidence. And the things Connie said about Fauhomme — his drinking and abusive behavior — made her feel as though she ought to be able to talk to her friend candidly.

"I think I have to tell him, Connie."

"I don't know, Jenna," Lee said doubtfully. "I mean, what would you do if he told you that he'd slept with some other women for money and that's what he was going to do with you when you met?"

"I know, I know," she replied and started to cry.

"Look, honey, I don't see why you need to tell him right now, if ever. I mean, how's he going to find out? I'm not going to tell him, and Rod's not," Lee said, then changed the subject. "What do you think he wants to talk to you about? The divorce?"

"I don't know, maybe," Blair sniffed. "Or it could be something to do with this hearing."

There was a brief pause on the other end of the line. "How do you mean?"

"I'm not sure. The whole time up at the cabin he was preoccupied about it and said he needed to work on what he was going to say. He wants to run it by his friend, Pete Oatman, the superintendent at West Point, tomorrow. It wasn't anything specific he said, but he made it sound like somehow I was involved. Apparently, he and Rod and that guy Tucker Lindsey had it out the other day."

The other end of the line was quiet before Lee spoke again. "I'm sure that was all just a heated strategy meeting . . . happens all the time in politics. They're all so macho. But it's going to be okay, honey. I've got to go. Let's talk tomorrow."

Sometime after two in the morning she had finally fallen asleep and dreamed of Sam. In her dream, she walked out of the cabin and saw him standing naked on the small dock that went out into the lake with his back toward her. The loons were swimming nearby making their haunting calls when he turned. She saw that his face was lined with worry and his eyes were sad, but when he saw her, he smiled and all the cares melted from his face. "I love you, too, Jen. Nothing's going to happen tomorrow that we can't deal with." Then he walked to the end of the dock and dove into the still, dark waters. That's when she woke up.

Blair got out of bed and dressed, then grabbed her laptop and left the apartment.

On mornings she didn't have to be anywhere, it was her habit to head to the STIR coffee shop on the corner where she'd read the online news reports and catch up on emails. She noted that the flower shops along her street were slow putting their fragile wares on the sidewalk until the day grew warmer, another sign that winter was on its way.

Instead of sitting outside, she chose the warmth of a small table near the window, where she settled down with an Americano and blueberry scone. After scanning the headlines, mostly about the election now only a week away and the start of congressional hearings on "the Chechnya incident," she checked her emails. Near the top, beneath the usual spam advertisements was one from Sam; she looked at the time it was sent. *While I was in the shower.* She opened it happily, expecting some poetic love note, but all it said was: "No matter how long it takes, no matter how far, I will find you. 121078. Call Ariadne Stupenagel. 212-804-5438."

A line from The Last of the Mohicans? *121078? My birthday? Ariadne? His old girlfriend? Obviously means something to him, but it's a mystery to me.* Smiling, she returned to the rest of her emails. There was one from her mother with the usual small talk about what was going on at home and pointed questions about when was she going to visit "with your new beau." She felt a stab of guilt; she hadn't told her parents much about Sam, not his name, just that he was "a little older" and "works for the government." And "he treats me better than any man I've ever known." Her parents had never been the sort to pry, but she could tell her mom's curiosity was driving her crazy. They'd been very excited when she told them she had been accepted to law school, but never asked her where she was getting the money for it. That was her business.

There was another email from her agent letting her know about a cattle call for a new Broadway production "that might even include a few lines." In the past, such a call would have reinvigorated the dream until the next disappointment, but that dream didn't matter to her anymore. What she wanted was to pursue her law degree and allow her relationship with Sam to go wherever it was meant to go. *If we can just get through tonight,* she thought, but that brought tears to her eyes. *It's impossible.*

After about an hour at the coffee shop, she was ready to go home when she noticed several people had gathered below the small television mounted near the ceiling in a corner of the shop and were watching raptly. Then she saw Sam's face appear on the screen. At first she assumed that it had to be a story about his impending testimony, but when she saw a middle-aged woman cover her mouth and shake her head she was filled with dread. As if pulled by a magnet, she rose from her seat and walked slowly toward the television.

Before she even heard the broadcaster's voice she read the text below Sam's photograph. *General Allen dead in New York hotel.* She absorbed the news like a fighter taking a blow to the solar plexus. She couldn't breathe and felt woozy; her eyes filled with tears. She had to be reading it wrong. Then she heard the broadcaster: ". . . source close to the investigation indicated — and this is only speculation at this point — that General Allen took his own life."

Suicide? The word burned into her brain like an ember. *He* chose *to leave me?* She felt sick, as if she might throw up, and turned back toward her laptop, stumbling against a chair before reaching her table and gripping the edge so as not to fall down. Taking a deep breath and letting it out, she closed her laptop and put it in its case and then walked out of the door in a fog.

He's not dead. This has to have something to do with Fauhomme. A small desperate cry escaped her mouth as she picked up the pace back to her apartment.

Punching in the security code to get into her building, she suddenly thought of the strange, cryptic email he'd sent. *I will find you.* That's it. It was some sort of code to let me know he was okay and will explain later. *He wasn't suicidal, he couldn't . . .* She remembered the webcam recording. Maybe he'd said something when she was in the shower that would shed more light on what was going on.

Blair rushed into her apartment and started up her desktop computer, calling up the recording. She fast-forwarded it until she reached the point where she left to take her shower.

"I don't know why you'd want to record this."

"Because I'm going to blackmail you with it someday."

"You want to talk now about what you said at the cabin?"

"No. I'm going to go hop in the shower. I think you need time to think about this, so I'll wait until Monday for your answer."

Sam looked sleepy. Then he spilled his

drink. *Something's wrong.* He tried to stand up but couldn't. *He looks drugged.* Shaking his head as though to clear his mind, he leaned forward and typed something before collapsing back into the chair. The sound of a door opening and a voice, "Room service . . ."

"Help him," she whispered, but then watched in horror. The man was not there to help Sam. He was there to kill him.

She remained focused but trembling while her body convulsed in agony. When her stomach stopped heaving, she wiped her dripping nose and sat staring at the now blank screen. She shook her head and reached for her phone, punching in the only number she could think of to call at that moment.

"Connie, oh, my God, Connie . . ." she gasped when her friend answered.

"Jenna! Where have you been? I've been trying to get ahold of you! You've heard . . . ?"

"He . . . he . . . oh, God help me . . ."

"It's so terrible. Did you have any indication that he would do . . ."

"He was murdered!" Blair cried out.

There was silence from the other end, then, "What do you mean? We're watching the television and they said . . ."

"I don't give a fuck what they said on the television," Blair shouted. "I saw it happen!"

"What? Honey, I know this is a shock but . . ."

"Listen to me, please just listen to me. We were talking on the webcam and I was recording our conversation. I left to take a shower but I didn't turn off the recorder. I didn't watch it until just now and . . . oh, God, please don't let this be true . . ."

Connie was quiet so long that Blair wondered if the connection had been lost. But then she came back on the line. "Have you told anybody else about this?"

"What? No, I called you . . ."

"Good," Connie said. "Listen, Rod's here and I told him what you said. He's worried that if what you say is true, it might be connected to this thing in Chechnya and you could be in danger. Don't go anywhere; he's going to send someone over to your apartment right away who will get you to safety. He said don't call anybody, not even the police can be trusted."

"Please hurry," Blair begged, then burst into tears. "I don't want to live without him."

As she waited to be rescued, Blair threw some clothes into a daypack and alternated between sobbing and gasping for air. *Dead.*

Sam was dead. Murdered. And still her mind searched for any reason to hope.

Packed, she stationed herself at her window where she could see the street in front of the apartment building. A tall, muscular man wearing a black T-shirt and dark glasses got out of the front passenger seat and walked swiftly up to the door. She started for her front door when he buzzed her apartment but then detoured to her desktop computer. One of the assets of living in that building was a video feed from the security camera at the front door. But he was looking down and she could not see his face. "Hello?"

"Miss Blair, I was sent by Mr. Fauhomme," the man replied, still without looking up.

"Thank you," she whimpered, and was about to hit the button to buzz him in when she looked at his right arm. *I've seen that tattoo before,* she thought, and knew in that instant where she'd seen it. Fear rose like bile in her throat and threatened to overwhelm her.

Think, Jenna, her inner voice demanded. *He's coming here to kill you.* "I just got out of the shower and need to dry my hair," she said. "Come on up. I'll leave the door open."

Blair ran into the bathroom and turned

on her hair dryer before leaving the room and closing the door. She then grabbed her pack and jammed her laptop inside before opening the alley-side window and climbing out onto the fire escape.

The hair dryer ruse must have worked for a bit, because she had just reached the final ladder to the alley when she heard a curse above her. "Stop right there," a man's voice above her shouted. Then he was on the fire escape and rushing down after her. "She's on the fire escape . . . the alley . . . don't let her get away!" he yelled into a cell phone.

Blair burst out of the alley just as she saw the sedan's driver — another young man in a black T-shirt and dark glasses — emerge and start for her. In terror, she raced across the street, dodging traffic and running past the coffee shop.

Then up ahead she saw a bike messenger, a former boyfriend, who was just getting off his bicycle to deliver a package. "Joey!" she screamed.

Joey turned at the sound of his name and smiled as he saw Blair running toward him. Then, seeing her face, he frowned. "What's up, Jenna . . ."

"I need your bike!"

"What?"

"That guy behind me wants to hurt me. I

have to get away. Please, Joey . . ."

"Sure," Joey replied, handing her his bike. "Just lock it up — 7, 19, 23 — call and let me know where . . ."

"I will," she said, already up on the pedals and starting to pump for all she was worth. She could hear her pursuer's footsteps pounding on the street. She looked back in time to see Joey step in front of the first young man, with the second man, the one with the tattoo, closing as he shouted, "Goddammit, I'm a federal agent, stop!"

"What's your problem," Joey demanded.

Thwarted and with his prey riding swiftly away, the first young man struck Joey in the stomach, doubling him over, and then kneed him in the face, sending him back against the building.

Sorry, Joey, Blair thought as she pedaled furiously around the corner.

The man with the tattoo on his forearm ran a few feet past the fallen bike messenger. "FUCK!" he screamed and then got back on his cell phone. "She's on a bike headed south on Seventh Avenue . . . wearing a blue top and khaki shorts. I don't care what it fucking takes, she has to be stopped. I need that computer."

11

The small, olive-skinned man with the large hooked nose and wearing a traditional Arabic *keffiyah* headscarf smiled out from the television screen. "*Allahu akbar,* I am Sheik Amir Al-Sistani," he said with a small, condescending bow of his head. "I am sure you are familiar with the name." His dark eyes hardened. "Your plan to stop me has failed, as has your attempt to arm the heretic separatists who resist Allah's will that I establish the Islamic Republic of Chechnya."

He shrugged. "It doesn't matter to me that you intended to bring down the apostate government of Syria, except that it is further proof to my Muslim brothers that you Americans will do anything in your hatred of Islam. But hasn't that always been the way in your arrogance and conceit?"

Al-Sistani waved his hand, apparently at the cameraman, who panned back to reveal that the terrorist was standing behind two blindfolded individuals seated with their wrists bound in front of them. One was a tall man and the other a young woman.

"That's David Huff," Lindsey told Fauhomme.

"Who's the girl? And what does he mean, our 'plan to stop him'? I don't even know who the fuck he is," Fauhomme said, pausing the recording.

"Hell if I know who the girl is; we assume she's the one who tried to call the embassy during the attack. But who she is and what she was doing there, we don't have a clue. Al-Sistani is the guy who tried to take down the New York Stock Exchange a couple of years ago. We extradited him to Saudi Arabia and they turned him loose . . ."

"Another national security fuckup. Let's listen," Fauhomme said.

The Arab continued. "However, I realize that this would be something of an . . . embarrassment . . . to your president should he be forced to acknowledge that Al Qaeda not only continues to exist," he said mockingly, "but indeed, we are quite capable of striking at our enemies wherever we find them — in Zandaq or in the heart of his sinful cities. Or should I say that if you cut the head off the great serpent of Allah, another will grow to replace it."

Again he made a small bow as he walked out in front of the two captives. "So, where does that leave us? It is quite clear to me that this embarrassing situation would greatly harm the president's chances of re-election. But I do not care who is in power — and in fact I may prefer such a weak and ineffectual administration to another — so perhaps we may strike a deal that benefits us both? You will deliver to me, at a place of my choosing, the great Sheik Omar Abdel-Rahman, currently held in your federal prison in Colorado, or the next recording will be distributed worldwide and will include . . . Raad, take your place . . ." A huge, bare-chested man stepped in behind the young woman and placed a large, curved knife at her throat. ". . . the slaughter of these sheep!"

As the young woman felt the blade, she screamed. "Please help us!" she cried out, raising her bound hands in front of her chest as she pled. "O lion of God, save me!"

Seemingly surprised, Al-Sistani at first scowled as he looked back at the young woman, but then laughed cruelly as he turned back to the camera. "So you see, the American harlot wants to live," he said. "Imagine the effect on voters should I not only reveal that the U.S. administration has been lying to them, but its lies led to the horrifying death of this poor child and your embassy lackey. You have one week to deliver Sheik Abdel-Rahman to a place I will name later."

Al-Sistani made a cutting motion across his neck at the cameraman. When nothing happened, he snarled, "Turn it off, you idiot!"

The screen went blank. Cursing, Fauhomme hurled the channel changer at the television. "I can't fucking believe this shit!" he bellowed. He glared at Ray Baum, who stood in a corner of the room, recalling when the assassin told him that the girl had gotten away.

"I thought you knew what the hell you were doing!" he yelled.

"I do," Baum replied. "I did what you told me to do, make it look like a suicide. I got on his computer and wrote the note. I swear there was nothing on his screen like he was webcamming with her but she must have been recording. I didn't see it . . ."

"And we're lucky she called Connie. But you managed to botch that, too."

"She was pretty clever and bought herself time with that hairdryer excuse," Baum countered. "I don't know how she made me.

I kept my face down in front of her security camera."

"Well, it must have been something, because she ran like a rabbit, and now I have to sweat bullets."

"So why does this Al-Sistani fuck want this sheik, Abdel whatshisname?"

Lindsey grimaced. "Omar Abdel-Rahman, better known in the U.S. as 'The Blind Sheik,' is probably the world's most venerated cleric in the eyes of Islamic extremists," he said. "He was behind the first attempt to bomb the World Trade Center back in 1993 and is in federal custody. If Al-Sistani can force the U.S. to hand him over, it would be a huge public relations coup for him and probably give him a leg up in the Al Qaeda hierarchy, maybe even make him the new number one. Jihadists the world over would flock to his banner."

Rubbing his temples, Fauhomme felt a migraine coming on. The recording he'd just watched had been delivered to the U.S. embassy in Grozny that morning and transmitted from there to Lindsey's office in the White House. He felt a sudden chill that his old Romanian grandmother would have attributed to someone "stepping on your grave." He thought of himself as above superstition, but he had to admit that this whole mess was spinning out of control.

He had placed a call Monday morning to his man at FBI headquarters and told him that Allen was dead and that the bureau needed to take over the investigation, which of course would lead nowhere. But then the New York district attorney, Karp, had sent them packing. He wasn't too worried about the general's laptop. As incompetent as Baum had proved to be in getting to Jenna Blair, the muscle-head was sure that he'd inserted a computer virus in Allen's machine that would destroy the hard drive as soon as anyone tried to open the files.

At first Fauhomme worried about Karp, a man he knew only by reputation. He knew that he was no friend of the president or his politics. But there was only a week to the election, and after some initial concerns about what Karp would do and how fast, he knew there wasn't much the district attorney could do before the election. Then, when the president was back in power, and with the help of the media, they'd deal with Karp; the man was up for re-election in two years and it was high time he was voted out of office.

The big concern, the one that could throw a wrench into the machine before the election, was Blair, or more accurately, whatever it was she had on her computer. It had been forty-eight hours since Baum lost her, and despite a federal "Be On The Lookout" bulletin distributed nationally to law enforcement agencies as well as airports, bus stations, and the media, there'd been no reported sightings. The agencies had been told that the computer contained highly classified material and was not to be examined, under stiff penalties. And "the person of interest in this case is not to be questioned but detained and held for federal authorities."

"What's the latest with the Russians and finding this joker, Al-Sistani, and the others?" Fauhomme asked.

"After this came in I called my contact at their embassy," Lindsey replied. "I'm meeting with him tomorrow. He indicated they have a man on the inside but are waiting to hear from him."

"What the hell is taking so long? Can't you people get off your asses?"

Lindsey's eyes narrowed. "I'm not the one who murdered an American general, or . . ." he said, looking over at Baum, ". . . got myself recorded doing it."

Baum's expression of barely concealed contempt didn't change, but Fauhomme pointed a fat finger at Lindsey. "No, you are the one who created this fuckup in the first place. But it's water under the bridge. We have a mess and we need cleanup on aisle four before the voters go to the polls. Let this Russian know what we expect and that we need it in a hurry."

"And if the Russians can't help, what are we going to do about Al-Sistani's demands?"

Fauhomme looked as if he'd been asked an incredibly stupid question. "Why, we'll give him the old fart. Say it's on humanitarian grounds or some such bullshit. I mean, they bought it about that guy who blew up the jet over Lockerbie, Scotland, didn't they?"

"And if it comes out that we were blackmailed into it by a leader of Al Qaeda, which as you pointed out doesn't exist anymore?"

"I don't give a shit," Fauhomme said, "so long as it's after next Tuesday. My job is to win this election. Besides, we'll spin it that the president knew all along that Al Qaeda was still a player, but he was trying to lull them into a sense of security until we were betrayed by these separatists."

"Think the press will buy it?" Lindsey said skeptically.

"Hell yes," Fauhomme snorted. "They're

already complicit in the cover-up for not asking questions in the first place. They'd have to swallow their overblown egos and admit that they didn't do their jobs. You think that pack of hyenas are suddenly going to become good journalists? In what hole have you been hiding? They'll lap up anything we feed them that will get them off the hook. If it's going along with more lies, they'll go along. Now what about the girl?"

"We have surveillance on all of her known acquaintances, including her folks in Colorado."

"Have you talked to them?"

"Yes, we told them that she and Allen were 'friends,' and that we were concerned about her well-being."

"They believe it?"

"Who knows." Lindsey shrugged. "According to my guy, they hadn't heard from her since last Friday. They were obviously worried, but he couldn't get a reading on whether they were hiding anything."

"I assume we've got all these phones tapped?"

"Of course, and if she sends an email we'll track it back to the IP — internet provider — address and we'll know where she sent it from," Lindsey said. "We've frozen her bank account. So she's going to be out of money pretty quick. We'll find her."

"You'll let me know when you do," Fauhomme said, and glanced at Baum. "I'd prefer if Ray took her into custody, as well as her computer."

"I understand that 'took into custody' is a euphemism, and this girl won't be making any court appearances," Lindsey said. "But what are you going to do if some other law enforcement agency gets to her first? It's going to look pretty funny if she dies after they turn her over to your goon here."

"Watch your mouth," Baum snarled.

"Watch yours," Lindsey shot back. "Who the fuck do you think you're talking to? I have a hundred goons like you I can call right now. If my boss hadn't put your boss in charge until the election, I might do it just for kicks. And remember, the election is over next Tuesday."

Baum considered an angry comeback but thought better of it and shut his mouth. But Fauhomme laughed. "All right, boys, the testosterone is getting a little thick in here. As for your question, I think you were the one who pointed out to me that it's a dangerous world out there, and accidents do happen, even suicide."

"What if she goes to the press before we

can get to her?"

Fauhomme's lips twisted. "I've thought about that and I have a plan. I'm going to call one of my pals in the press and tell him — completely off the record, of course — that Allen and Blair were 'special friends.' Not much more than that. I'll feed him what more I want him to have as circumstances dictate. That will get the hyenas' attention off of Chechnya; nothing they like better than a good sex scandal, it's easier than covering real news."

Lindsey shook his head and blew out his breath. "So we're still going to destroy his reputation and do that to his family."

"What? You suddenly developing a conscience?" Fauhomme scoffed.

"He was a good man, and a great soldier. It's a shame it had to come to this."

Fauhomme glared at him. "And it's a real fucking shame that the guy you chose for the job was not a team player. If you'd done a better job of vetting him we wouldn't be having this conversation or be knee deep in manure." He stood up from his desk and indicated the door. "Now if you'll excuse us, I need to talk to Big Ray here . . . alone."

After Lindsey left, Fauhomme turned to Baum. "Once we have the girl and her computer — and we're sure there're no loose ends that could come back to haunt us — she's going to have an accident, am I clear?"

"Crystal, sir."

12

Stupenagel arrived with Marlene outside the apartment building in the Chelsea district, using the address for Jenna Blair that Allen had given her. She stepped forward and pressed the buzzer. A woman answered timidly.

"Who's there?"

"Ariadne Stupenagel. I'm looking for Jenna Blair or her roommate."

"Stupenagel? Aren't you a reporter? I've read your stories."

Stupenagel raised an eyebrow as she glanced at Marlene. "Yes, but —"

"I don't want to talk to the press," the woman interrupted. "Jenna's gone, and I don't know anything. Leave me alone."

"I was about to say that I'm not here as a reporter," Stupenagel spoke quickly. "I was a friend of Sam Allen's, and he asked me to look in on Jenna if something happened to him."

There was a slight hesitation. "How do I know you're telling the truth?"

"Well . . . let's see . . . I can tell you they met on July Fourth at a party on Long Island, and they've been seeing each other ever since. I know she's a law student and is from Colorado . . ."

"You could have got that from someone else . . ."

"But Sam told me on Friday. Then he was going away to his cabin and was taking Jenna with him." When the other woman didn't respond she continued. "I've known Sam for more than twenty years, and I know he loved her very much."

The other woman sighed. "She loved him, too. Now they're acting like she had something to do with . . . with it."

"Who's 'they'?"

"The FBI agents and that other guy. They told me not to talk to anybody."

Stupenagel looked up at the security camera. "I don't want to frighten you any more than you already are, but I'm worried that Jenna could be in danger. I loved Sam . . ." She choked up and had to start over. "I loved Sam, too. They can't order you not to talk to someone else. And in this case it might be the safest thing to do for everybody, especially Jenna."

"Who's that with you?"

"My best friend, Marlene Ciampi. She's an attorney and a private investigator. She's trying to help, too."

The other woman sighed. Then the security door buzzed. "I don't know what I can do, but come on in."

The two friends made their way up to the apartment, where a pretty, young brunette stood waiting for them outside the door. "I'm Sharon," she said, holding out her hand. "Sharon McKinney."

When they were seated around a coffee table in the small living room, McKinney was the first to speak. "I spent Sunday night at my boyfriend's place," she explained. "I didn't know about Sam until I got back to my apartment about nine in the morning, maybe a little after. Jenna was gone and that guy was here."

"Do you know who he was?"

McKinney shrugged. "He showed me an identification card that said he was a federal agent of some kind. I think his name was Ray or Dave . . . something like that. He didn't let me see it for long."

"Did he say what he was doing?"

"Looking for Jenna. He said she was wanted for questioning about Sam's death. That's the first I'd heard of what happened." McKinney stopped talking and reached for a box of tissues on the coffee table. "It's just so terrible. But I know Jenna didn't have anything to do with it. And she was here all night."

"You're sure of that?" Marlene asked.

"Well, I talked to her after she got back from the cabin. Then later on we were texting when she said that Sam was trying to talk to her on the webcam and she had to go."

"You still have that text?"

McKinney nodded. "Yeah, I'm bad about not erasing texts. I probably have a few hundred old ones on my phone."

"Do me a favor and make sure that you don't erase that one," Marlene said. "In fact, if you wouldn't mind, forward me a copy so that we have a record. It could be important to Jenna later."

"This guy who was here, can you describe him?" Stupenagel asked.

"Yeah, tall, good-looking, built like an athlete — the sort of guy who'd catch your eye if you were looking for a boyfriend, which I wasn't, and in fact he kind of gave me the creeps."

"How do you mean?"

"I don't know how to describe it," McKinney replied. "I mean on the outside he was nice enough; he didn't yell or threaten me. But I got the feeling there was something just beneath the skin, like he was really angry and had to fight not to show it."

"Anything else you can think of about him?"

McKinney started to shake her head no but then stopped. "He had a tat on his right forearm. It was the Marine Corps emblem; my boyfriend has the exact same one. Hey, what's the matter? Did I say something?"

The young woman was looking at Stupenagel's face, which had gone pale. "The guy at the White Horse bar," she half-whispered. "He was following Sam." She recovered and urged McKinney to go on.

"Something just didn't seem right about him," the young woman said. "I was getting suspicious but then these two FBI agents got here; they seemed to know who he was. I could tell they didn't like him either and he left pretty quick."

Stupenagel leaned forward and grabbed McKinney's hand. "Do you have any idea of where Jenna went? You need to be honest, Sharon, her life could depend on it."

Looking more frightened, McKinney denied knowing. "The FBI agents asked me, too. I just don't know. Maybe home to Colorado . . . one of her other friends . . .

maybe Connie Rae Lee."

"Who's she? Does she live in New York?"

"Yes. She's some big-shot political guy's girlfriend. I guess he's like the president's campaign manager or something like that."

Stupenagel and Marlene exchanged glances. "Mind if we look around a little?" Marlene asked. "Maybe we'll see something that gives us a clue."

"Go ahead, but between that Ray guy and the FBI agents they went through everything."

While Stupenagel started out in the living room and kitchen, Marlene followed McKinney to Jenna's bedroom, where she walked over to the desk. "You said Jenna was going to get on the webcam with Sam. I don't see a computer. Did the agents take it?"

"We both just have laptops; mine's in my bedroom," McKinney said. "She must have hers with her. I know the men didn't take it, and that first guy asked me where it was. He was interested in whether she had any recording equipment. I didn't tell him, because I thought it might get Jenna in trouble, but she did have an app in her computer that would let her record webcam conversations. She liked to tape Sam and then played them back over and over when he was gone. That girl was really in love."

"I take it this is Jenna and Sam," Marlene said, pointing to a framed photograph above the desk just as Stupenagel walked up behind her.

"Yes, I think it was taken at the lake."

Suddenly, Stupenagel clutched Marlene's elbow. "I think I know where she is! No wonder Sam asked if I remembered the way."

Marlene immediately understood and turned to McKinney. "We've got to run. With your permission, I'm going to call Detective Clay Fulton. He works for the New York district attorney, who happens to be my husband, and is the most trustworthy cop you'll ever meet in your life. I'd like you to tell him everything you told us, including showing him that text."

McKinney looked scared but she nodded. "If I can help . . ."

Marlene reached out and patted her shoulder. "You've already been a big help. Clay will make sure that you're okay. He's not afraid of anybody."

With that the two women were racing out the door and down the stairs headed for Marlene's pickup truck, which she'd parked a block away.

"I should have known he didn't start talking about the cabin just for old times' sake," Stupenagel said as they pulled away from the curb. "He was letting me know I should go there if something happened to him."

"So you think she'd go there, too," Marlene said. "Why? Wouldn't that be an obvious place for someone to look for her?"

"I don't know," Stupenagel replied. "It's just a hunch. But we won't know until we get there. None of us — not me, not Butch, not Clay, not you — believe Sam killed himself. So he was murdered. And if this guy was following him three days before, I'll bet he had something to do with it."

"Then he came looking for Jenna," Marlene added. "And the FBI agents knew him."

Stupenagel whistled under her breath. "How high up does this go? If it's the same guy, and I'd bet my entire shoe collection it is, he follows Sam to the White Horse, where Sam tells me that someone in government who doesn't want him to tell the truth about what happened in Chechnya is blackmailing him over his affair with Jenna. Jesus, Marlene, I think we need to find her before he does."

"The Finger Lakes area is a good four-hour drive," Marlene said. "Think we ought to call the cops up there and ask them to see if she's at the cabin."

"No way," Stupenagel said. "If I'm right about Sam's death being a hit ordered from somebody in the administration, who you going to call that you can trust? They're being told that Jenna is wanted for questioning. If they find her, they'll turn her over to the first guy with a federal badge. Then what do you bet something happens to her?"

"You're right, but I'm going to call Clay and tell him about Sharon and what we're up to," Marlene said. "And I'm going to let Butch know, too."

Driving Interstate 81 north, the two women spent the first couple of hours talking: Stupenagel about Sam Allen; Marlene about Lucy and the possible connection to his murder that seemed increasingly likely. Then they lapsed into silence and passed the remaining miles looking at the foliage that was already starting to wane, lost in their own thoughts.

The chance to take action of any sort was a welcome relief to Marlene after the hell she'd been going through worrying about Lucy, but with nothing she could do about it. Much of her emotional energy was spent convincing herself that her daughter, and Ned, were alive. She pestered Ivgeny Karchovski to keep asking his contacts, but all they'd done was confirm that there were no females among the dead and that there were at least two missing males.

Just the evening before the president had made a big deal of meeting with the family of Deputy Chief of Mission David Huff. The family had little to say about the meeting except that the president told them that he would do everything in his power "to find out who did this and bring them to justice."

But, Marlene thought, *if he already knew who was really behind the attack — and it wasn't who his flunkies were saying it was — that means he's lying about what he knew and when he knew it regarding the murder of American citizens. And to do that to a victim's family? Unconscionable.*

Marlene called Fulton first and filled him in so that he could get right to Sharon McKinney. She then called her husband and did the same.

"Be careful," he said. "If what you're saying is true, you've got an elephant by the tail. I've got Jaxon coming by this afternoon. He called from D.C. to say he was flying in and wanted to talk."

"About what?" Marlene asked hopefully.

"Didn't say. He was obviously avoiding

272

talking about whatever it is over the telephone."

"Let me know. Whatever it is, I want to know."

"I will, sweetheart, just keep believing."

As they drove, Stupenagel tried calling the number she had for Jenna Blair. When there was no answer, she texted that she was a friend of Sam's and wanted to meet. But again there was no reply.

"Actually, it might be a good thing if she has her phone turned off," Marlene said. "Otherwise someone looking for her — someone with the power to force the phone company to cooperate — could triangulate her position from cell towers."

"Think she's that savvy?"

"So far she's managed to elude the FBI, and your friend with the tattoo," Marlene pointed out.

"At least we hope she has," Stupenagel replied. "For all we know, he's already found her."

The women arrived in the tiny town of Orvin just before five o'clock. Stupenagel tried to find the road on the far side of town that would lead to the cabin, but after a couple of false starts admitted that the town had changed a lot "and I'm a little lost. But I know where to go. We passed the post office and if you want to find someone in a small town, that's where you ask."

When they got to the post office there was only one vehicle, a police car, parked in the lot. The building was deserted, too, except for the woman behind the counter, who was talking to a uniformed officer whose shoulder badge identified him as a town constable. "What can I do for you?" asked the short, plump, middle-aged woman. Her hair, which was nearly white, framed her open, pleasant face. "We're getting ready to close."

"I won't take much of your time," Stupenagel said. "It's been a long time since I've been here and I needed directions to a friend's cabin."

"Who are you looking for?" asked the constable, who was on the chubby side himself.

Stupenagel bit her lip. "Well, actually, I'm looking for just the cabin . . . my friend passed away recently . . . you may have heard about General Sam Allen?"

The couple exchanged glances, and the smile disappeared from the constable's face. "If you don't mind me asking, what's your interest in Sam's place? He was well-liked in this town; people respected his privacy and will continue to do so now that he's gone."

Stupenagel tried to explain. "Like I said, I'm an old friend of Sam's. We used to come up to his family's cabin, and I just wanted to —"

"Hey, I remember you!" the postmistress exclaimed. "You were Sam's girlfriend, the big tall blonde with the red lipstick!"

Stupenagel smiled. "That's me."

"I was a waitress at the Egg's Nest restaurant, and you two would come in for breakfast sometimes. Geez, what's it been? Twenty years?" the woman said.

"Longer. But I remember the Egg's Nest," Stupenagel said with a laugh. "Is it still in business?"

"Yep. Still the same place with the crazy art on the wall and the same crazy owner. I'm Nancy Spooner — I run the post office — and this rotund Sherlock Holmes is my husband, Tom, the town constable, though there's not a whole lot of crime to keep him busy, so he's usually in here pestering me."

"Why, that's not true! Just the other night I had to capture that raccoon that was getting into Mrs. Thatcher's garbage, and he was big and mean," Tom Spooner said with a grin, and held out his fleshy, plump hand. "Tom Spooner."

"Ariadne Stupenagel. And this is my friend, Marlene Ciampi."

"Are you a friend of Sam's, too?" Nancy Spooner asked Marlene.

"No, I'm just along for the ride."

"Terrible what happened," Tom Spooner said. He shook his head. "Didn't seem the kind of man who would take that road out of here."

"I agree," Stupenagel replied.

"And now they're looking for that young woman," Nancy Spooner said. "We saw her once with Sam at the Egg's Nest. Seemed nice and he doted on her — one of those spring/winter things, I guess. Tom here got a bulletin saying to be on the watch."

"Have you seen her?"

Tom Spooner shook his head. "Nope, and not much of anybody else either. After we heard about Sam, we've been expecting the press to come snooping around like they always do, but I guess Sam kept the old family place a pretty good secret. You're the first outsiders I know about who've come looking."

"Well, I was just thinking about Sam, and this is a good time of the year for a drive to see the fall colors, so I thought I'd come and say good-bye to some great memories," Stupenagel said.

Marlene looked at her friend. She knew that Stupenagel was trying to get information without engaging the locals' curiosity. But she also knew that Ariadne was telling the truth; Sam's death had really hurt her.

"Well, it can be tough to find," Tom Spooner admitted. "Nice piece of property with that little private lake, but isolated. Come on out to the car and I'll show you on a map. I'd take you out there myself, but I have a date with the missus and I'm hoping to get lucky!"

"In your dreams, old man," Nancy Spooner said, laughing.

"I'm sure we'll do fine if you can point me in the right direction," Stupenagel said. "It's still pretty light out, and I think I'll remember once I get on the right road."

"Well, I can do that for you. But that road can get a little rough in the dark and there's essentially no cell service once you leave town, so you might want to get back before it's too late."

Twenty minutes after looking at the constable's map and getting directions, Stupenagel and Marlene were bouncing along a dirt road through a dense forest. The area was sparsely populated with the occasional cabin and they saw few people.

"Was always more of a summer crowd out here, so a lot of these are vacation homes and get boarded up in the winter," Stupenagel said.

"Good place to hide out," Marlene said. "But for how long? If she's on the run, she'd have to figure that sooner or later somebody will look for her here."

"I just hope we're the first," Stupenagel said.

When five minutes later they pulled into the drive of an old cabin fronting a small, pretty lake, it appeared that no one was there. It was getting toward dusk and there were no lights on, and there were no vehicles parked outside.

The women got out of the car and walked around the cabin looking in the windows. Then they went up on the front porch, where Stupenagel knocked on the door. There was no answer nor sounds coming from within.

Marlene tried the door and to their surprise, it opened. "I guess it won't hurt to look around inside," she said.

Inside the cabin was dark. But then Marlene pointed to something; a laptop computer case lying on the dining room table. The computer was missing.

Walking as quietly as they could, they

made their way to what appeared to be an office. This time it was Stupenagel who noticed the open wall safe set into the bookshelf. Then Marlene pointed to a laptop open on the desk next to a small pile of papers and two DVD cases. There was also a small jewelry box off to one side. But then a voice behind them warned, "Stop . . . don't make me shoot you!"

13

Karp was waiting on the subway platform at the Whitehall Street station near Battery Park when he was suddenly aware of a horrible odor. He looked behind him and immediately recognized its source — a hulking man who waved at him with one hand while a finger on the other hand probed his nose. "Oh, hello, Booger," he said. "I didn't know you were going to be meeting me tonight."

As tall as Karp and outweighing him by at least a hundred pounds — it was difficult to say as he wore many layers of cast-off undergarments and coats — the Walking Booger, as this particular street denizen was known, resembled a dirty bear. Every visible inch of him, and there wasn't much that was, from his hands to his filthy face and massive head was covered with thick wiry hair; two small brown eyes glinted out of the tangled fur, completing the bruin analogy.

" 'Ello, 'utch," the giant replied pleasantly, though the nasal excavating hindered his speech. " 'Irty 'arren ask me 'oo 'elp."

Karp smiled. Despite his appearance and lack of personal hygiene, the Walking Booger was another of the homeless people frequently seen around the Criminal Courts Building who seemed to watch out for him and his family like some sort of ragtag guardian angels. The citizens of New York City had no idea about the many times when Dirty Warren and the Walking Booger, as well as their other sidewalk compatriots, had helped thwart the aims of criminals and terrorists. Most "normal" citizens pretended not to see the street people, or gave them a wide berth, but over the years he'd met many who except for their circumstances were as upstanding as any of their fellow New Yorkers.

Although it was early evening, there weren't many other people on the platform, and those who were kept their distance from Karp and his odiferous companion. So they were alone when the train slid up to the platform and they entered the last car, as Karp had been instructed an hour earlier.

This latest adventure began shortly after Karp spoke to Marlene about her quest up north, when Espy Jaxon had arrived at the office. He came bearing the proverbial good and bad news in the form of a DVD he held up to Karp and then walked over to the entertainment center and inserted the disc.

"I received this via government courier a couple of hours ago," the agent said. "I have no idea who sent it but apparently someone in either the State Department or the CIA doesn't like what's going on. I'll warn you, some of it's pretty tough to watch, but it also gives us reason to hope."

Jaxon picked up the remote control from Karp's desk, turned on the television, and hit the play button. A face Karp recognized with revulsion appeared on the screen.

"*Allahu akbar,* I am Sheik Amir Al-Sistani. I am sure you are familiar with the name. Your plan to stop me has failed, as has your attempt to arm the heretic separatists who resist Allah's will that I establish the Islamic Republic of Chechnya. It doesn't matter to me that you intended to bring down the apostate government of Syria, except that it is further proof to my Muslim brothers that you Americans will do anything in your hatred of Islam. But hasn't that always been the way in your arrogance and conceit?"

Jaxon paused the recording. "So apparently we now have an idea of what the other

282

group was doing at the compound. Some sort of arms deal with the separatists and connected to a plan to topple the government of Syria." He pushed the play button again.

Karp could not contain the gasp that escaped his lips when the camera panned back, revealing his daughter sitting next to a man Jaxon explained was David Huff from the U.S. embassy in Grozny. He hardly heard Al-Sistani's taunts and felt hot tears come into his eyes as the bare-chested man put a knife to Lucy's throat.

"It's okay," Jaxon assured him. "Nothing happens. He's using them — as well as his threat to embarrass the administration — as hostages to barter for Abdel-Rahman's release."

"That doesn't mean he won't eventually kill them," Karp said, trying to keep the emotion out of his voice. "Particularly if the administration won't 'deal with terrorists,' as we discussed before."

"I won't sugarcoat it, you're right," Jaxon said. "And to be honest, I don't think the administration wants them back. Al-Sistani is right about the embarrassment it would cause, especially with less than a week to go before the election."

"So what do we do? Give this to the press?"

"I thought about it," Jaxon replied. "The American people certainly deserve to know the truth. But even if the media would follow up — and that's a big question, the way they pander to this administration — it could backfire and we'd lose Lucy and Huff. The congressional hearings on Chechnya were postponed because of Allen's death and there's no way they'd reconvene before the election, so there's no one on the other side of the aisle to get at the facts. The administration and its lackeys would deny deny deny until after next Tuesday, and then stonewall and say it was a national security issue. And as we've discussed, they could fall back on the public policy that the U.S. does not make deals with terrorists, while expressing great remorse — at least when the cameras are rolling — about the 'brave Americans' sacrificed for the cause of freedom. In the meantime, Al-Sistani might carry out his threats to kill the hostages to prove he was serious and give him standing in Al Qaeda."

Karp bowed his head. "So there's nothing we can do?"

"I didn't say that. I want you to watch part of the recording again from when Lucy screams."

Reluctantly, Karp kept his eyes on the screen as "Raad" placed his knife at Lucy's throat.

"Watch her hands," Jaxon said as Lucy cried out.

"Please help us! O lion of God, save me!"

A moment later, Karp knew what Jaxon was alluding to. There had been something about her desperate scream that had struck him as so not like Lucy; she'd faced danger before, and because of her deep faith had always accepted the possibility of death with an amazing degree of calm. Now as he watched her, he knew why this was different. "She screamed to distract Al-Sistani from what she was really doing," he said.

Jaxon smiled. "That's our girl. Nerves of steel, and it's not just any sign language that could be picked up by whoever watched that tape. It's Native American sign language. I didn't even know that she was conversant in it. But when I saw this, I was sure she was trying to say something; I know some American Sign Language, but it wasn't until I showed it to John Jojola that we found out what she was doing. He, of course, recognized it right away. Smart girl; apparently, she didn't want the usual intelligence agencies who saw this to know what she was saying — she doesn't trust them any more than we do — and was hoping that somehow I, or I should say, Jojola, would see this."

Shaking his head over his daughter's courage and quick thinking, Karp realized that she'd placed her faith in a slim chance that it would pay off. A former Special Forces guerilla fighter during the Vietnam War, Jojola had been the chief of police at his home on the Taos Indian Reservation in New Mexico when he met Marlene and Lucy several years earlier. Marlene and Lucy had gone to New Mexico on a sabbatical, where they became involved with Jojola, who was trying to catch a serial child killer. A deeply spiritual man in the ways of his people, Jojola had shared his beliefs with the women and educated them in the customs and rituals of his people. As their friendship grew, he met Jaxon and joined the team with Lucy and Ned Blanchett.

"So what did she say?" Karp asked.

"Well, as you might imagine, Native American sign language does not translate as literally as American Sign Language, but the gist is that she's being held in a 'holy building,' or site, near 'big water' to 'the east of the battle.' Putting it together as best we can, we think that means she's being held in a mosque near the Caspian Sea, probably in Dagestan, which is a hotbed of Islamic extremism and an easy place for Al-Sistani to hide out."

"Sounds like a big place to start looking," Karp noted. "I take it there are a lot of mosques in Dagestan."

"There are, but it's a relatively small population, most of which is clustered in urban areas. We think she mentioned 'big water' because she is aware of her proximity to the Caspian. There's one more thing. Did you find her comment, 'O lion of God, save me,' to be odd, even for our young spiritualist?"

"I did."

"We didn't," Jaxon said. "The Chechen word for lion is *lom,* as in Lom Daudov, the separatist leader whom the Russians blamed for the attack. He's the guy my team was trying to contact to help find Al-Sistani before Al-Sistani beat us to the punch. Daudov is known to his followers as 'the lion of God,' and 'Lion' was our codeword for him."

"So Lucy was asking him to save her?"

"Yes, I think so, but not directly," Jaxon replied. "She wouldn't have thought that Lom would see this disc or know Native American sign language. I think she's telling us to reach out to Daudov; maybe he knows how to find Al-Sistani."

"What chance do you have of that . . . before it's too late?"

"I can't give you any odds, but it's the only option I see right now. I have a team standing by but we don't know where to find him, much less ask for his help, with our own government blaming him for the attack. The Russians are after him with everything they've got, and no doubt our people are cooperating with them. So he's gone into hiding. Nor can we safely ask the CIA to assist with their local contacts because we don't know the good guys from the bad guys."

"Then I don't get it," Karp said. "How are we going to find Daudov?"

"Well, it's a long shot, but we think we know one person whom Daudov would be interested in using for his own political purposes, which might make him willing to help us rescue Lucy and Deputy Chief of Mission Huff."

"Who?"

Jaxon paused to look long and hard at Karp. "Nadya Malovo, known to Daudov as Ajmaani."

The name settled over the room like a noxious dark cloud. Nadya Malovo was a beautiful Russian assassin who had crossed swords frequently with Karp, his family, and his associates. She worked for the highest bidder, and at one point in the past that had been the Russian government and the Russian mob, for whom she had assumed the identity of Ajmaani, a Chechen Islamic terrorist.

"Why would Daudov want Nadya?" Karp asked.

"If he could get her to tell the truth, and he probably has his ways," Jaxon said, "she's proof that at least some of the atrocities committed in Chechnya and Russia that were blamed on separatists were actually manufactured by the Russians as a pretext for invading and controlling Chechnya. She would demonstrate that the idea of a nexus between Islamic extremists and secular nationalists like Daudov is false."

"So how would we get word to him, even if we had Nadya?" Karp asked.

"We think we can still contact a young woman, Deshi Zakayev, who was our team's liaison with Daudov," Jaxon said. "Because there were no female fatalities, we're hoping she either wasn't in the compound or escaped. If we can get Nadya, our team will be inserted and make contact with her."

"That's a big *if*," Karp said. "I don't even know if she's still alive or how we would pry her out of the hands of David Grale."

One of Malovo's major employers after she left Russia for the United States had been Andrew Kane, an extremely wealthy former NYC mayoral candidate and, more pertinently, an evil mastermind who considered Karp his archnemesis. One of his plots with Malovo had been to blow up a natural gas container ship as it passed beneath the Brooklyn Bridge, only once again to be thwarted by Karp and Company. Kane had managed to elude Jaxon, only to be captured by David Grale, the half-mad leader of a large community of homeless souls known as the Mole People, who lived in the subway tunnels, sewers, and natural caves beneath the city.

Malovo had eventually been caught and sent to a maximum-security federal prison. But she'd plotted her way out of there as well. Almost two years earlier, having claimed to turn over a new leaf, she began assisting U.S. antiterrorism agencies, including Jaxon's, and helped stop several terrorist plots by infiltrating several groups as Ajmaani. However, the entire time she was actually planning her escape while gaining a financial windfall of enormous proportions.

She hatched a plan for suicide bombers to blow themselves up in the crowd at the annual Halloween Parade in Manhattan's West Village. One of the bombers had specifically tried to target Karp, who was the parade grand marshal, and his family. But the attack on the parade and the Karp family was only secondary to her real intention, which was to free Kane from Grale. Of course, her efforts were not motivated by any loyalty or feelings for Kane — Karp doubted that she had such emotions — but by the fact that only Kane knew the account numbers and passwords for offshore banks where he'd stashed hundreds of millions of dollars. However, Grale, who always seemed to be one step ahead of his enemies, had discovered her plan and was waiting for her when she dared enter the inner sanctum of his dark kingdom. Word on the street from the likes of Dirty Warren was that, like Kane, Malovo was now a captive, too.

Years of entreaties by Karp through intermediaries to convince Grale to release his two prisoners to his office for prosecution had been rejected. Dirty Warren said that foul-ups by law enforcement agencies, such as releasing Amir Al-Sistani, even though that was not Karp's fault and he would have stopped it if he could, had soured Grale on cooperating, though he liked Karp personally.

But there was one thing Karp hadn't tried. He looked at his watch and stood up. "I think the only chance we have of getting Malovo is for me to go ask Grale personally," he said.

Standing as well, Jaxon frowned. "That could be dangerous. What I understand from talking to Lucy is that he's subject to wild mood swings, maybe schizophrenia, and sometimes even his followers are afraid of him."

"It's about my daughter," Karp said. "And maybe the country's future. But I need to get to Dirty Warren before he closes up for the day, and it's almost that time. You coming?"

As the two men rode the elevator to the ground floor, Karp wondered how Marlene was coming with her expedition; he hadn't heard from her since she was about to arrive in Orvin in the upstate New York Finger Lakes region. He wished she would have taken at least Clay for backup, but she wasn't willing to wait for him, nor was she sure of finding who she was looking for. "And I don't want to waste his time," she said, "if it's a wild goose chase." But he wasn't too worried; his wife could be as lethal as a venomous snake if challenged, and Stupenagel was no pushover. *She said she wasn't getting good reception,* he assured himself.

They reached the sidewalk just as Dirty Warren was lowering the heavy wooden panel that secured his newsstand for the night. "Why don't you hang back a little," Karp told Jaxon. "He might be more comfortable talking about Grale if it's just me."

As Jaxon waited, he continued forward and called out, "Hey, Warren, got a minute?"

Hearing his friend's voice, Dirty Warren turned toward Karp with a smile on his face but frowned when he saw the situation was serious. "Sure, Butch . . . whoop balls . . . what's up?"

"I need to talk to David," Karp replied. "As soon as possible. It's important."

"What? Whoop!"

"David Grale. I have to talk to him. Tonight. Now."

"Uh, that's what I thought you said . . . oh boy fuck me whoop . . . not possible."

"Why not?"

"Well, for starters, even when . . . oh boy ohhhhh boy . . . David's in a — how should I put this delicately — good mood you don't just drop by for a . . . bullshit asshole . . . visit," Dirty Warren said, the nervous tics that were part of his Tourette's syndrome threatening to take over his face while his torrent of profanity increased. "And he's definitely not in a good mood these days; in fact, he's in very . . . whoop whoop . . . bad mood. Very bad. I don't even go there when he's like this. You never know what he's going to do . . . motherfucking scumbag whoop . . . or who he might decide is 'evil.' And you know what that would mean."

Dirty Warren shuddered at the thought, and Karp understood that his quirky friend was truly afraid. But as he'd just said to Jaxon, his daughter's life was on the line. "Please, Warren," he pleaded. "It's about Lucy. She's in danger."

The little news vendor's pale blue eyes widened beneath the thick lenses of his glasses and then he nodded. "Okay," he said. "But only you. Espy can't go. David doesn't know him."

"I may need him," Karp said. He quickly explained what he hoped to accomplish.

The nervous tics increased, as did his hopping from foot to foot. "Oh, Christ . . . whoop whoooooop . . . that's what you want? Oh, geez . . . ass balls tits whoop whoop oh boy ohhhhhh boy. Well, they still can't go; they'd never even get to David. *If* David doesn't cut my throat for bringing you, and *if* he doesn't cut us both into quivering pieces afterward, and *if* he agrees to let you have Malovo — and I don't think he's going to — he'll provide the escort until she's handed over to your guys on the outside. Personally, I think we're dead men. Give me an hour and I'll call on your cell phone to let you know."

As promised, Dirty Warren called in about an hour. "At first he just laughed at me . . . whoop . . . it wasn't a nice laugh. But then I told him that Lucy was . . . cocks scumbag oh boy . . . in trouble, and he said he'd listen to you but not to get your hopes up."

Dirty Warren said that Jaxon and any others would have to wait in Battery Park, but for Karp to go down into the subway and wait on the platform. "Get in the last car," he said. "You're going to . . . oh boy whoop . . . take a ride. No guarantees you'll be coming back. I hate to say this . . . asswipe bastard . . . because I love the man, but David's crazy."

When they got on the train, Karp saw Dirty Warren sitting in the back of the otherwise empty car. Just before the doors closed, a young black man came running down the stairs intending to get into their car, but Booger grabbed him by the chest and propelled him back out of the car.

The train pulled away from the platform

and headed uptown. Each time it stopped and anyone tried to get on, Booger charged down the aisle shouting at the top of his lungs. " 'Et off! 'Et off!" No one argued with him.

Meanwhile, Karp and Dirty Warren rode silently. The train traveled north and then, shortly after leaving the 42nd Street station, it slowed and then stopped in the tunnel. The train operator's voice came on over the intercom. "We have stopped for a routine maintenance crew to depart. Please keep your seats and stand back from the doors."

Dirty Warren stood up just as the car's doors slid open. "This is where we get off. Watch your . . . whoop whoop . . . step."

Wondering how in the hell Grale was able to command the city subway, Karp followed Dirty Warren and Booger out of the car and down onto the tracks. Then the doors shut and the train moved on. He found himself standing outside a door marked "Authorized Personnel Only" beneath a dim light. It seemed like no surprise when Dirty Warren produced a key that opened the door. Then for the next half hour or so he did his best to keep up with the other two as they made their way through a series of service tunnels — up and down ladders, sloshing through sewers with several inches of foul-smelling liquid in the dark as rats scurried across their path — and natural caves.

Dirty Warren had a small flashlight, which was often the only source of illumination for their path, and sometimes in the dark Karp felt as if he was being watched by unseen eyes. When, during a stop to catch his breath, he commented on it, Dirty Warren told him to ignore it. "It's best not to think about what else and who else . . . oh boy whoop . . . lives down here. Nobody messes with Booger but I wouldn't . . . balls boobs . . . want to come alone, and you should never try."

They were in what seemed to be a large tunnel, though it was so dark that Karp couldn't see his hand in front of his face and could only follow the beam of the flashlight, when a voice spoke up in front of them.

Suddenly a lantern was lit and two men — one short and fat, the other tall and thin — stepped out of an alcove carved into the rock. "Well, if it ain't his lordship, Butch Karp," the tall, skinny one said with a grand bow. "He put me away for robbery once, he did, a loooooooong time ago."

"You deserved it, Clyde," the short, fat one said. "You were guilty as sin."

"Right you are, Bert, right you are. But

turned over a new leaf, I have, thanks to Father Grale, and look at all it's done for me," Clyde replied with a sweep of his hand to encompass their dark surroundings.

"Saved your immortal soul, that's what it did for you, you fool," Bert said. "Now let these good folks pass us by. You are expected, Mr. Karp."

"Thank you," Karp said, nodding.

They walked for another five minutes, at last coming to a cavern the size of a large indoor sports arena. It was lit by hundreds of electric bulbs, and Karp recalled stories he'd been told that Grale's followers included electricians who'd tapped into the subway power lines. Several dozen people were on the main floor of the cavern talking, while children kicked balls and chased each other around; others seemed to be working at tasks, such as sorting food and other items brought down from the world above. He could see many more inhabitants going about their personal lives in what appeared to be small rooms carved into the wall.

They all stopped what they were doing and looked when Dirty Warren led him out into the open space. "Hey, it's Butch Karp!" someone yelled. Others started talking to each other until the cavern buzzed with a hundred voices; those people on the floor drew closer and those in the rooms emerged to see what the fuss was about.

"ENOUGH!" a voice roared from one end of the cavern. "Go about your business!"

The inhabitants didn't need to be told twice. Some cast a fearful glance in the direction the voice had come from. Karp, too, looked that way and saw the man he'd come to ask for a favor. At the far end of the cavern, on what appeared to be a long-abandoned subway platform from another century, David Grale sat slumped in a large, overstuffed chair.

"This way . . . whoop whoop . . . Butch," Dirty Warren, clearly nervous, said. "Mustn't keep him waiting . . . oh boy ass balls."

Karp followed the little news vendor up to the dais, where he stood before the King of the Mole People like a supplicant approaching a feudal monarch. Many years earlier, Grale had been a Catholic layperson whom Lucy had befriended when they worked together in a soup kitchen for the homeless. Ten years his junior, she'd developed a schoolgirl crush on the handsome, gentle man, not realizing that at night he transformed into a religious vigilante who hunted down and killed violent criminals he claimed were actually demons inhabiting the bodies of humans. His dual nature had gone undetected for quite some time before he was found out and had to flee — a wanted man by the police — to a life beneath the streets, where he took refuge among the homeless and unwanted and came to be regarded as their spiritual and temporal leader.

Over the years, Grale had slowly drifted in and out of madness as he vacillated between his better nature and the darkness that made him moody and dangerous. Karp knew that Grale was a serial killer, no matter if his victims "deserved" their fates. However, his views on the man were tempered by the fact that the "Mad Monk of Manhattan," as the journalist Ariadne Stupenagel had labeled him in a recent feature article, had often acted as a guardian angel watching over his family. He was particularly fond of Lucy, and despite his murderous ways, she didn't judge him.

Deeply spiritual, Lucy had long believed that her family's seemingly endless run-ins with sociopaths and terrorists were not just happenstance or solely tied to her parents' professions, but part of a larger war between good and evil. And she saw Grale as an avenging angel of God. "Like it or not, his fate and ours are tied together," she'd once told her father.

Looking up at the man, Karp was shocked by his appearance. He was clad in a plain brown monk's robe, his thin face was pale as moonlight, his dark eyes glittering with fever or madness from their deep-set sockets, and sweat beaded up on his forehead. His hair was long and stringy, and his beard and mustache more unkempt than the last time Karp had seen him. He clutched a handkerchief in one hand on which Karp could see spots of bright red blood. *I heard he was tubercular,* he thought. *Jesus, he looks like death warmed over.*

"Hello, Butch," Grale said in his low, gravelly voice. "Welcome to my home. Forgive my oversight at not having invited you earlier, but we're both such busy people." He laughed but was stopped short by a fit of coughing into the cloth.

"Thank you for seeing me now," Karp replied. But before he could go on, there was a rattling of a chain and a dog . . . no, a man on all fours . . . came crawling out from behind Grale's "throne."

It took Karp a moment to recognize the sorry creature, who seemed to be all skin and bones. The expensively coiffed wavy blond hair had been reduced to a few gray wisps, and the blue eyes that had charmed so many had been reduced to one wildly staring eyeball, while the other was just a white, sightless globe. The man's countenance was hideously disfigured by a botched face transplant he'd undergone many years earlier in order to disguise himself; discolored skin hung like shredded tissue paper on parts of his face while appearing normal elsewhere.

"Kane?" Karp said. The man was evil, but to see him reduced to such an abysmal condition shocked him.

At the mention of his name, what was left of Andrew Kane crawled forward to focus on the tall man standing in front of his master. Then he snarled, pulling his thin lips back from a nearly toothless mouth, and rage caught fire in his one good eye. "Kaaaaarrrrpppp," he hissed, and it appeared he might try to leap on his old enemy. But Grale yanked hard on the chain around Kane's neck, pulling him roughly onto his back.

"Down, dog," Grale growled at Kane, who rolled over onto his side and remained there cowering. Grale then turned back to Karp and smiled, revealing that he, too, had few teeth left in his mouth. "So, Butch, you didn't come all of this way to say hi to me or my dog. My friend Warren tells me you have a request?" His voice grew hard and his face set as if in stone as he finished his sentence.

Karp nodded. "I need to ask you to hand over Nadya Malovo . . . if she is still alive."

"Alive?" Grale asked. "Oh, that devil is alive all right." He leaned back in his chair and shouted. "Bring Malovo!"

After a minute, two large, muscular men emerged from the dark tunnel at one end of the platform. Each was holding a chain, the other end of which was attached to a thick leather collar fastened around the neck of a woman; her hands were bound behind her and her legs were hobbled by knotted ropes. However, if Karp was surprised to see how captivity had reduced Andrew Kane to barely human, he was just as surprised to see how well Nadya Malovo appeared to have handled two years of underground captivity. Her face was pale from the lack of sun and her short, formerly blond hair was now as white as snow, but she stood erect with her head up, and the seductress's body still retained its curves. She regarded him without expression with her sea green eyes.

Grale seemed to guess at Karp's surprise, because he suddenly heaved himself up from the chair and stalked across the platform until he stood in front of the prisoner. He grabbed her beneath her chin and turned her face until she had to look him in the eyes. That's when Karp noticed one other difference in Nadya Malovo. He'd never known her to exhibit fear, but her eyes betrayed that she was definitely afraid of her captor. She quailed and shut her eyes.

"Still alive and still beautiful, no?" Grale said as he released his grip. "Thus Satan's most effective minions are pleasant to look at on the outside while festering with evil beneath the lovely skin."

"She is evil, no doubt," Karp said. "But I'm asking you to release her into my custody."

Malovo's eyes flew open and she looked at Karp with both curiosity and what he took to be hope. But Grale turned and walked over toward Karp until he was towering above him, his eyes glittering with anger.

"Why? So that our so-called justice system can let her go to kill innocent people?" he raged. "Law enforcement had her in its custody before, as they did Andrew Kane and Amir Al-Sistani, and yet she got away!"

"Those were other agencies, not the New York District Attorney's Office," Karp replied evenly. "I've successfully prosecuted many of their associates, as well as a great many other people you believe are inhabited by demons."

Grale frowned. "I'm not blaming you, Butch. I know the sort of man you are — a man of integrity. However, even you do not control everything that goes on in the world at large. I could hand her over to you confident that if possible you would bring her to justice; but there are others out there who might be able to force you to give her up to them. Those men I do not trust."

"I'm not saying they wouldn't try," Karp agreed. "And possibly even succeed — the federal government is no friend of mine. But they won't get the chance, because I intend to hand her over to someone else myself."

Grale's eyes widened and he looked as if he was going to shout him down, but Karp softly added, "David, Lucy's in trouble, a captive of Al-Sistani. The only hope I have to save her is by using Malovo as bait to get her back."

At the mention of Lucy's name, Grale's features softened. His hand passed over his eyes, and when he looked at Karp again, he more closely resembled the gentle social worker who'd dedicated himself to the poor. "I'm sorry," he said. "I forgot that Warren said this was somehow tied to Lucy. My mind seems to wander these days. What can you tell me?"

"I'd rather not say in front of anyone but you," Karp replied. "No disrespect intended, Warren."

"None . . . whoop whoop . . . taken, Butch," Dirty Warren said. "I'm one of those 'need to know' sort of . . . oh boy breasts asses . . . guys. And I don't need to know."

"Please, join me up here then," Grale said, pointing to a stepladder. "The rest of you please excuse us. Take Malovo and Kane back to their cells."

After the prisoners were led away, Karp settled into the chair next to Grale's throne. He then gave a condensed version of all that had transpired since the attack on the mission in Zandaq.

When he reached the part regarding the DVD disc and Al-Sistani's threats, Grale's face grew grim. "I should have slit his throat when I had him in my custody." This wasn't the first time Grale had been asked to rescue Lucy from Al-Sistani. As with Kane and Malovo, he'd once captured the Islamic terrorist, but had then exchanged him for Lucy, who had been kidnapped by Kane.

Finished with his account, Karp remained

silent while Grale sat with his head down and his eyes closed. The mad monk was so quiet that for a moment Karp wondered if he'd fallen asleep, but then the brown eyes flew open and his hands gripped the arms of his chair. "If there's any chance that we can save Lucy, then we have to take it," he said.

With that Grale led the way back to "cells" — holes cut in the walls that had been fitted with steel bars and small steel doors, outside of which stood a guard of four men, including the two muscular men who'd brought Malovo out. He walked up to the cell where Malovo sat on a cot.

"I'm turning you over to the district attorney of New York City," he said. "However, if you and I ever meet again, I will kill you, and it won't be quick; I promise that your torment will last for one hundred days. You are evil, Nadya Malovo, and I don't know that there is any part of your soul that can still be redeemed. But if it's possible, you may find the opportunity to do so in the days ahead. And I hope that you will take it."

Malovo said nothing but looked at Karp. Grale turned to Booger and Dirty Warren. "My men here will escort you and the prisoner," he said. "If she attempts to escape, Booger, please do us all a favor and strangle her."

"I 'romise," Booger replied, holding up his right hand as if taking an oath. "If she 'ries 'oo 'scape, I 'ill 'rangle 'er with my 'are 'ands."

As they turned to go back to the cavern, Andrew Kane suddenly scampered to the front of his cell and put a hand out toward Karp. "Please," he begged, "take me with you. I will tell you everything."

Karp looked at Grale, but the King of the Mole People shook his head. "Not today," he said. "Perhaps someday you will visit me again and we can discuss it. But for now this dog remains in his kennel."

An hour later, a very odd-looking group emerged from the Whitehall station and walked hurriedly toward Battery Park. Even though the immediate vicinity appeared to be deserted — Grale had sent a swift vanguard ahead to ensure it — they moved in a tight cluster so that no one would notice the hobbling, bound woman in their midst.

Once in the park, they approached two black Hummers, from which a half-dozen men emerged. One was Jaxon, another Jojola, with four more, younger men whom Karp didn't recognize, and then, to his surprise, his cousin Ivgeny Karchovski.

"Mr. Jaxon informed me what was going on with my cousin, Lucy," the Russian mobster explained in heavily accented English. "He and I thought, perhaps, that my knowledge of the area and my experience with some of these people might help."

Karp was touched. Their polar-opposite careers kept him and his cousin from open social contact but his fate, too, appeared to be tied to that of Karp and his family. "Thank you," he said.

Smiling, Karchovski said, "This is what family is for, no?"

"Okay, Butch, she's all . . . whoop whooooop oh boy . . . yours," Dirty Warren said, nodding to Malovo's handlers, who detached the chains from the collar.

"I can't thank you enough, Warren," Karp said. "Once again you've proven to be a true friend."

"Well . . . son of a bitch whoop . . . you could let me win at movie trivia one of these times," the little man said with a grin.

Karp smiled. "You wouldn't want me to give you one, would you?"

Dirty Warren appeared to think about it for a moment, but then shook his head. "Nah, fair and square. I want . . . butt boobies . . . to win fair and square."

"I knew you would," Karp replied as Dirty

Warren and the others walked away into the night.

When they were gone, he looked at Jaxon. "The prisoner is now yours," he said.

As one of Jaxon's men stepped forward to place a belly chain around her waist and handcuff her to it, Malovo smiled at Karp. "How do you know I won't betray these men the first chance I get?"

Karp locked eyes with her and then shrugged. "I don't. I don't know what role you're going to play in all of this before the end, but then neither do you. But I hope you'll remember Grale's admonition about your soul."

Malovo sneered. "The concepts of souls, heaven, and hell are for the weak," she scoffed. "What I care about is me."

"Then I hope that you will find a reason to do the right thing if needed . . . for your own sake," Karp replied.

As Malovo was led away to one of the Hummers with the four younger men, Karp reached out and placed his hand on Jaxon's shoulder. "Bring my daughter home, Espy," he said, his voice cracking.

"God willing, Butch," Jaxon replied. "God willing."

14

"Stop . . . don't make me shoot you!"

Marlene and Stupenagel raised their hands and turned slowly around. They found themselves facing a terrified young woman who was pointing a pistol at them. Her hand trembled and their first concern was being shot accidentally.

"Jenna Blair," Stupenagel said calmly. "Take it easy, honey, we're here to help."

"Yeah? Like the last guy? The guy who killed Sam? That kind of help?" As she rattled off her comments, Blair cried and waved the gun dangerously.

"The man with the Marine Corps tattoo, right?" Marlene asked.

Blair scowled and sniffed. "Yeah. Friend of yours?" She aimed the gun at Marlene's head.

"No, but we're pretty sure he has something to do with Sam's death," Stupenagel answered.

A look of doubt passed over Blair's face, then she began to cry again, though she didn't lower the gun. "He had everything to do with it," she sobbed. "I saw him kill Sam."

"You saw him? You were there?"

Blair shook her head. "No. I was at my apartment." She pointed to the laptop on the desk. "But I recorded it with the webcam, though I didn't know it until Monday." The young woman's mood shifted again as she yelled, "You know that, though! You were sent to kill me! Just like he was!"

"No, we weren't," Stupenagel said. "We came here to help you. We didn't know what the people involved in this wanted with you — though it's pretty obvious now — but we knew you were in trouble. Jenna, please point the gun at the floor."

"No!" Blair screamed, and extended her gun hand.

"Jenna, please! I've known Sam for more than twenty years. I saw him last Friday at the White Horse Tavern. He told me about you and some other things. He said you were going to come here last weekend. That's why I thought to look here for you."

The doubt returned to Blair's face and she lowered the gun. "Who are you?"

"I'm Ariadne Stupenagel and this . . ."

Stupenagel's attempt to introduce Marlene was cut short by a sob from Blair, who dropped the gun and covered her face with her hands. "Oh, God, I've been so scared."

"You know who I am?"

Blair nodded. "Before he . . . he . . . he . . . died, Sam talked about you," she said between gasps. "He sent me an email last night with your name and phone number. But I was too scared to call at first. And then when I got here there was no reception."

"Did he say anything, or send you an email last night?" Marlene asked.

"Just a line from *The Last of the Mohicans* and my birthday."

Both older women furrowed their brows. "I don't understand," Marlene said.

"I didn't at first either," Blair said. Then she pointed at the open wall safe. "The bookshelf opens when you pull on *The Last of the Mohicans,* and he changed the combination to my birthday."

"How'd you figure that out?" Stupenagel asked.

"After that guy came to my apartment and I got away, I was at Grand Central trying to decide what to do when I remembered how he seemed to think it was important that I know how to locate the safe. He didn't tell me he changed the combination to my birthday, and it took me a while after I got here and had a chance to think about it, but eventually I tried it and it worked."

"He sort of did the same thing with me," Stupenagel said. "Out of the blue he asked if I remembered how to get to the cabin. We used to . . ." She stopped suddenly, realizing what she had been about to say to Blair.

Blair looked at her curiously, then she knew why the other woman had stopped in midsentence. "You were lovers," she stated.

Stupenagel nodded. "It was a long long time ago, before he was married," she said. "We've been friends ever since, though we'd been out of contact for a while. Still, I knew him pretty well, and I was amazed at how deeply he loved you."

Tears rolled down Blair's face, but she smiled. "Thank you."

"What was in the safe, if you don't mind me asking?"

Blair bit her lip. "Some of it was personal . . . for me." She choked and had a hard time getting the next sentence out, but finally she half-whispered, "I think the rest of it was why Sam was killed."

"You mean what happened in Chechnya?" Stupenagel asked.

"He told you?" Blair exclaimed.

"Some of it," Stupenagel replied. "And that someone was using your . . . your relationship with him to blackmail him."

Blair hung her head. "Yes. It's my fault they could hold that over his head. But you know Sam, I think he knew he had to tell the truth and that's why they killed him."

"Do you know who 'they' are?" Marlene asked.

"Yes. But maybe you should hear it from Sam, and then I'll fill in the blanks," Blair said, and walked over to the desk, where she picked up one of the DVDs and then walked over to the entertainment center and inserted the disc in the player.

Sam Allen appeared on the television screen. "My name is Samuel H. Allen, lieutenant general U.S. Army retired. What follows is a recording of the testimony I intend to swear to under oath in front of the congressional committee hearing on what occurred at the U.S. compound outside of Zandaq, Chechnya . . ."

Twenty minutes later, Allen concluded his statement, "At this time, I apologize to my family, my sons, and my wife for whatever pain I have caused them — that was never my intent and I accept fully that I was wrong to break the vows of my marriage in this manner. However, I cannot, will not, deny my love for the woman whose companionship and love has renewed this old soldier's heart. These people are innocent, and while I will answer any questions about my own conduct as candidly as possible, I hope that the media will respect their privacy."

Allen looked out from the screen and blinked hard. "As a result of both the methods used to try to ensure my silence, as well as my own actions, I feel I have no choice but to step down from my position as acting director of the CIA and withdraw my name from further consideration. Thank you."

When the screen went blank, Marlene and Stupenagel looked at each other and then at Blair. "I guess we don't have to tell you how damaging this would be to the administration and why Fauhomme and Lindsey would stoop to blackmail and murder," Marlene said.

Blair covered her face with her hands and sobbed. "It's my fault he's dead."

Stupenagel moved forward quickly and took the young woman into her arms. "It's not your fault," she said. "Sometimes we just follow our hearts over our heads. These people are ruthless."

"You don't understand," Blair said, stepping away from Stupenagel. "They used me to get to him." She then told them about her past and how she was introduced to Sam Allen and for what purpose. "But I fell in love. . . . I never spied on him and wouldn't take their money."

"I believe you, honey," Stupenagel said. "And believe me, I'm about the last person in this room who should cast any stones. I've done some pretty questionable things for the sake of a story myself. Sometimes we know what we're doing is wrong, but everybody makes mistakes. It's what we do to fix them that matters in the end. But like he said on that recording, he was in love, too."

Blair smiled slightly. "I know," she said, walking back over to the desk and picking up the second disc. Five minutes later all three women were crying and continued after Blair showed them the diamond ring in the small jewelry box.

"That was beautiful," Stupenagel sniffed.

Finally, Marlene pointed out, "We haven't seen what your webcam recorded. Would you mind?"

They gathered in front of the desk as Blair showed them what had occurred in her lover's room while she was in the shower. "Oh, Sam . . ." Stupenagel sighed. But Marlene's face was set and angry.

"What do you think we should do now?" Stupenagel asked her friend.

Marlene looked at her watch. "It's almost ten o'clock," she said. "I'm worried about how we're going to get Jenna and all of this evidence secure and safe; sooner or later, they'll come looking here. I need to call Butch; he'll know what to do and has the power to get it done. Besides, Jaxon was on his way over to see Butch — maybe something to do with Lucy — and I'm dying to know what it was about. I think for now we're as safe here as anywhere; at least I can talk to my husband. But to do that I need to head toward town until I can get reception."

Marlene turned and looked at Blair. "Did you tell anybody you were here or make any telephone calls on your cell phone?"

Blair shook her head. "No, I read somewhere that they can track you with your cell phone so I turned mine off. The only person I've contacted was my mom — I sent her an email about noon from the town library. I wanted to let her know I was okay and not to believe anything until we'd had a chance to talk." She caught the other two women giving each other a quick look. "What? Was that bad, too?"

"Probably not," Marlene said. "But I'm sure they're watching your mom and these people are capable of intercepting her email."

Blair looked frightened. "I didn't say where I was."

"You wouldn't have to," Marlene said. "Every internet provider source, like the library, has a specific IP address that identifies where an email was sent from. They might have tracked it to the library."

Stupenagel raised her eyebrows. "Change of plans?"

Marlene thought about it for a moment. "No, not yet anyway. This place was hard enough to find in the daylight, much less in the dark. I think you two should lie low here, and I'll go to town and summon the cavalry. I have GPS in my truck that will help me retrace our steps so I shouldn't get lost."

Twenty minutes later, Marlene had almost reached the main road into town when a dark SUV headed in the opposite direction went past her. The windows of the vehicle were tinted so she couldn't see inside and she wondered if she should turn around and follow. *Nah, you're being paranoid,* she told herself. *If you try to follow every car that goes by tonight you won't get anywhere.*

Just outside town, Marlene's cell indicated she had service, so she pulled over to the side of the road and called Butch. He didn't pick up. She tried the home number and reached Giancarlo, who said "Dad" had called to say he was working late and wasn't sure what time he'd be home. She was trying to decide whether to call Jaxon when an SUV pulled up behind her.

Looking in her side mirror, she saw Constable Spooner, who got out of his car and walked toward her. She rolled down her window. "Evening, Tom."

"Evening," he replied. "You find the cabin?"

"Yes," Marlene said. "My friend, Ariadne, wanted to spend some time alone sitting on the front porch with her memories. I needed to make a call so I came back to town."

"Well, she might not get much of that alone time," Spooner said. "I just talked to our town librarian at the Lucky Duck bar and grill and she said two federal agents came to her house. They showed her a photograph of Sam Allen's young lady friend and she told them she'd seen her earlier that day at the library. She said she told them the girl might be staying at the cabin . . ."

"What!" Marlene exclaimed, suddenly

picturing the dark SUV. "Did she describe the federal agents?"

"As a matter of fact she did," Spooner said. "Gertie's our town spinster, and if you're male, single, and still alive, she's interested. She was all aflutter about this guy who was apparently a dead ringer for James Bond. I don't know that she got a look at the other one, but she said there were two. Why?"

Marlene turned the ignition. "I'm sorry. I have to go. My friend may be in danger! Those men are killers."

Spooner frowned. "Then maybe I should go with you. Let's get in my car; we'll make better time, because I know the roads and a shortcut. And maybe you can tell me what's really going on. I suspect this isn't all about old memories."

Something about Tom Spooner told Marlene she could trust him. So as he drove, she told him a condensed version of the story.

When she was done, the constable looked stunned. "Holy cow, you girls sure know how to ruin a fellow's romantic plans!" He looked at his radio. "Maybe I ought to call in reinforcements?"

"Please don't," Marlene said, reaching into her purse and pulling out a .45 Colt

321

Mustang Ladies Edition. "I don't know if they have a police scanner in their car. They're professional killers and I think our best chance is the element of surprise."

Spooner glanced at her gun. "Well, I don't know why I'm trusting a complete stranger," he said, "but I do. And you seem like a gal who knows what she's doing, so I'll just follow your lead."

The constable demonstrated exceptional driving skills on the dark, rough roads, and they made good time back to the cabin. Just before they arrived, they came upon a black SUV parked on the side of the road. It was empty.

Spooner turned off the lights of his vehicle before they came into view of the cabin and then turned off the car as it rolled into the driveway. Before he could stop, Marlene had jumped from the SUV and was running up to the cabin. No lights were on, but the door was wide open.

Marlene went in with her gun at the ready. No one was inside, but she saw that Blair's laptop and the evidence from the safe were all piled on the kitchen counter next to the door. She went back out just as Spooner reached the front porch carrying a shotgun.

"Nobody home?" he asked quietly.

"No, and I don't know where they went,"

Marlene replied, desperation in her voice. She jumped at the sound of a shot that came from the woods near the lake and took off running.

Big Ray Baum hadn't heard the other car pull into the driveway leading to the cabin. He was too busy watching the two women digging the hole that would be their grave and idly wondering if he should rape one or both of them. *I haven't raped a woman since Afghanistan and that might be just what the doctor ordered,* he thought. But he decided to wait and see what his partner, Craig, wanted to do when he got done getting the stuff at the cabin together and joined him.

He'd been fantasizing about having a go at the Blair woman ever since following her and the general down the beach during the Fourth of July party, watching her undress and then sitting on the other side of the dune listening to their lovemaking. His boss had been pleased later that night when he reported that the little whore had seduced the target. Fauhomme wasn't as happy the next day when she told him she wouldn't spy on Allen, but when Connie told him later that Blair and Allen were seeing each other, he'd changed his mind.

"Let's get some photographs of them

together and anything else you can get," the politico told Baum. "A little blackmail material can go a long ways toward keeping our 'friend' in line if necessary."

So Baum had followed the couple to the Casablanca and the bed and breakfast in the Shenandoah Valley, snapping photographs and making notations of dates and times. But Fauhomme had him doing a lot of other things, so he'd apparently missed their assignations at the cabin.

Fauhomme had proved to be prescient in regard to Allen's being unwilling to always toe the party line. When it became clear that the general wasn't going to stick to the "talking points," he'd played the blackmail card. But Fauhomme hadn't counted on a man like Allen's sense of honor, probably because he had so little himself.

At first the general had pretended to give in. But Fauhomme's decision to have Baum keep an eye on him until the hearings had paid off. He'd followed him from D.C. to New York thinking that the general was just going to see his mistress. When he saw Allen meet the tall blonde at the White Horse he'd wondered if the general had another girl on the side, though it didn't seem to be his style. So after she left, he asked the bartender if he knew who she was.

"Yeah, that's Ariadne Stupenagel," the bartender said. "Haven't seen her in here for a while. Fine-looking piece of ass even at her age."

"What's she do?"

"Never heard of her, huh? You must not read the newspapers and maybe you didn't see that press conference with the president the other day when she went after him on the Chechnya thing? She's an investigative reporter and a damn good one."

The woman's identity had been alarming. The bartender got suspicious when asked if he knew where she lived, so he left.

Then the situation got worse after Allen picked up his girlfriend and then managed to elude him when he left town for the weekend. Fauhomme had been pissed as hell and tore him a new one. Baum noted the fear in his voice and wasn't surprised when the fat man decided not to take a chance on what the general might tell Congress. "Check with that hotel he likes . . . the Casablanca . . . and find out if he's got a reservation before the hearings on Tuesday. If so, do it there. One way or the other, you're going to have to stop him before he goes before the committee."

Arriving at the Casablanca, Baum had walked into the hotel on Saturday and up to the front desk. He'd said he'd served under the general in Iraq and Afghanistan. "Best man I ever met," he said, laying it on thick. "He said to meet him here and we'd have a drink for old times' sake."

The desk clerk had smiled and looked in the reservations book. "Well, I'm really not supposed to say when General Allen is staying with us — we call him Mr. Stibbards — but since he obviously told you where to find him, I think it's okay. Let's see . . . oh, sorry, he's not due back until tomorrow night. Are you sure he said to meet him here today?"

Baum looked perplexed. "You know, I just flew in from overseas and it's entirely possible that I got the dates mixed up," he said. "I'll be back tomorrow."

The next day he'd returned with the bottle of Macallan scotch he'd spiked with Valium, carefully replacing the seal. "Looks like I might get called out of town," he told the same clerk. "Would you give this to him with my compliments?"

"And who shall I say left it?"

"Peter," Baum said, knowing that a bottle of scotch from Peter Oatman, the commandant at West Point and Allen's friend, would not be suspect.

On Sunday, Baum had waited at a coffee

shop across the street for the general to enter the hotel. After giving Allen enough time to check in, he'd gone back for a third time.

"You're back!" the desk clerk said with a smile.

"Turned out I didn't have to go," he replied. "Sam just gave me a call and said he was here."

"He checked in a little while ago. I gave him the scotch and he said he was going to try some straightaway."

"That's great, thank you," Baum said with his most winning smile. "I'll join him in a bit. Do you have another room? Don't tell him I'm back; I want to surprise him, but I'd like to clean up a little first."

"Sure, I can put you on the floor right below him," the clerk said. "It'll be nice for you two to catch up."

"Yeah, it will be great."

It was Baum who had come up with the idea of lacing the general's scotch, one of his few known vices, to make it appear that Allen committed suicide.

Fauhomme liked it. "We let it slip to somebody we like in the press that he was having an affair with Blair and that she was blackmailing him," he said. "He was about to be disgraced, lose his family, his legacy in

327

the toilet . . . and no way he would get confirmed as director of the CIA . . . so he offs himself." But then the fat man frowned. "What if he doesn't drink enough? Maybe he only gets drowsy or calls 911 in time to get him to the hospital? We'd be fucked."

"I'll get into the room when I think he's out," Baum said, "and give him a hotshot under the tongue to finish him off. This stuff I got is practically undetectable unless you look hard for it, and with the 'obvious' cause of death in plain view, no one will look."

"What about that reporter?" Fauhomme said. "I remember the bitch from the press conference. She's not one of ours."

Baum had grinned. "New York is a dangerous city to live in. A lot of violent crime. I'll take care of her, too."

Everything had gone as planned. Wanting to make sure that Allen was drinking the scotch to incapacitate him, he intercepted the general's room service waiter, gave him a hundred-dollar bill, and said, "I'm an old army buddy and staying on the floor below. They'll tell you at the front desk. I want to surprise him." He'd let himself in with a high-tech skeleton key and even carried on a conversation with his intended victim.

"Care for a drink?"

"Would love to, sir, but I'm on duty, and

they frown on it."

The general was slumped in his chair and all but out when he tilted his chin back and injected the poison beneath his tongue. He then dragged Allen into the other room and lifted him onto the bed, neatly arranging his robe and placing his hands together on his belly as though he'd taken his lethal dose and gone to sleep . . . permanently. He quickly arranged the scene and switched the bottles of Macallan. "Couldn't have the Valium in the bottle," he later explained to Fauhomme, "just his glass." Then he typed the "I'm sorry" note and called Fauhomme saying, "It's done," before leaving the room.

The only thing he wasn't happy about occurred when he was standing outside Allen's door listening for sounds coming from within when a nosy old lady down the hall peeked out. He looked her way but she immediately closed her door without saying anything. *She'll think I was room service,* he thought at the time, but still, she was a loose end.

At least he thought the old lady was all he had to be concerned about. Then Fauhomme called him the following morning. "You moron!" the boss screamed. "Jenna Blair was somehow recording what happened from her apartment. Get your dumb ass over there and take care of it."

Ray Baum wasn't afraid of much, but the idea that he'd been recorded committing murder sent a chill down his spine that nearly caused him to panic. He'd still been in his room at the Casablanca, laughing about all the police activity, when he got the call and rushed out, picking up Craig on the way. He had to admit the girl had been pretty clever, making him think she was in the bathroom drying her hair, buying herself enough time to get away. He'd been living in fear ever since that morning that she'd get her computer to someone in the press, like Stupenagel, or worse yet, New York District Attorney Roger Karp.

Then she made a fatal mistake by emailing her mother. Tucker Lindsey's people managed to trace the IP address, so he drove north to Orvin a short time later. Once there he turned on the charm with a homely librarian whom he followed to her door.

"Sorry to bother you, miss . . ." he said when she came to the door.

"Gertie . . . Gertie Malcom," she replied, trying to pat her hair into place and smile at the handsome stranger at the same time.

"I'm agent Mike Ralston and that's my partner, Bob Kravitz, in the car. We're trying to find this girl." He showed her a photograph of Blair.

"Why, that's General Allen's girlfriend," Malcom replied. "It's such a shame what he . . . well, how he . . . well, you know."

"Yes, it was," Baum replied. "Have you seen her lately?"

"Yes, indeed, just today at the library," Malcom said. "She was using the computer to get online. Did she do something wrong?"

"No, not at all," Baum said. "We just want to make sure she's okay. Do you know where she might be staying?"

"Well, I'd guess out at Sam's old family cabin on Loon Lake. It's pretty hard to find. Why don't you come inside and I'll show you on a map."

"You're too kind," Baum replied.

Five minutes later, he was out the door and heading for his black SUV with Gertie Malcom trotting along behind.

"So you going to be in town long?" Gertie called after him.

"Afraid not, Gertie," Baum replied. "But maybe next time I'm through we can have a coffee or a glass of wine."

Gertie's eyes about bugged out of her head. "I'd like that."

"Okay, well, remember what I told you inside about my presence here needing to be a secret."

"Oh, mum's the word, my lips are zipped. You can count on me."

Baum smiled. "I knew I could. Until the next time."

"Au revoir," Gertie called out and waved as he got in the car. She could hardly wait to head down to the Lucky Duck bar and grill and tell the other locals about her meeting with a secret agent. *No details,* she promised herself. *But it won't hurt to say I got a visit.*

Baum and his partner made a couple of wrong turns on the way, but eventually spotted the place through the trees and matched the number on the Rural Route mailbox. At first the cabin looked dark and abandoned. He cursed, but then Craig pointed out how a small slip of light was escaping from behind one of the heavy drapes over a window in what turned out to be the office.

Creeping up to the cabin, he and Craig kicked in the front and back doors simultaneously and caught the two women by surprise. The big one, Stupenagel, had come at him with a letter opener and gashed him pretty good in the forearm before he disarmed her and knocked her woozy with a blow to the side of her head. He then stuck his gun in her mouth and demanded that

Blair tell him if there was anything incriminating other than what he could see.

The frightened young woman said everything was on the desk, and he could tell from the fear in her voice that she was right now incapable of lying. He left Craig to gather the material and do a search of the house while he marched his captives toward the lake, grabbing a shovel that had been leaning against the front porch.

The moon was full and the walking was easy. They had reached a point halfway down the lake trail when he ordered them to take a detour into the woods. After scrambling through the underbrush, they entered a small clearing only about ten yards off the trail, but far enough, he thought. "Dig," he demanded, throwing the shovel at Stupenagel.

"Why should I?" the reporter retorted. "You're just going to kill us anyway."

"You got that right, bitch," Baum said. "But unless you want me to gut-shoot you first, then dig the hole myself and bury you alive, you'll dig your own grave and make it quick."

So the two women took turns digging one hole. "You can be together for eternity," he said with a smirk.

Baum doubted anyone would come looking for the women at the cabin and they were far enough off the trail to make it unlikely someone would stumble on the grave by accident. He'd toss some debris over the top and the fast-growing forest underbrush would do the rest in short order.

They got down about three feet. Stupenagel was digging while Blair sat on the ground in despair. Suddenly the reporter doubled over in pain. "Shit," she gasped. "It's my ulcer . . . oh, fuck, that hurts!"

Stepping forward, Baum pointed his gun at Blair and growled, "Take over; another foot ought to do it." He realized his mistake in taking his eyes off Stupenagel only a moment before the flat of the shovel blade struck him on the side of the head. The blow dropped him to his knees.

"Run!" Stupenagel screamed as she started out of the hole, intending to finish him off.

Blair took off like a frightened rabbit. But it took too long to climb out of a three-foot-deep grave, and just as Stupenagel emerged, shovel raised for the coup de grâce, Baum recovered enough to point and shoot. He wasn't sure where he hit her, but it was enough to send her sprawling backward and down into the hole.

Baum staggered to his feet just as Craig

came running up with his gun drawn. "The girl's running," he shouted. He pointed back down the trail. "Go around the other side in case she doubles back. I'll run her down this way."

A moan escaped from the grave. "I'll be back for you, bitch," he snarled. Adrenaline and rage fueling his legs, Baum took off in pursuit of Blair.

Marlene almost ran past the spot where Baum had forced the women off the trail, but happened to stop in order to listen for any more sounds following the gunshot. She heard a woman groan. "Ariadne?" she called out softly, her gun ready.

"Marlene," Stupenagel answered weakly from a small distance. "They're after her. Save the girl, I'm okay."

Torn between going to her friend, who was obviously not okay, and saving Blair, Marlene hesitated for a moment. Just long enough for Constable Spooner to come huffing and puffing up the trail. "My friend's over there," she said, pointing. "I think she's hurt. Would you check on her, please?"

Spooner crashed into the bushes and Marlene took off again down the trail. Helped by the moonlight, Marlene flew over the ground, running as fast as she could and grateful for the roadwork she'd been putting in.

Near the end of the lake, she broke into a clearing and saw a man with his back to her aiming down at Blair, who'd fallen or been knocked to the ground. "Hold it or I'll blow your fucking head off," she said.

The man raised his hands, but he didn't drop his gun. "You don't know what you're dealing with," he said.

"I have a pretty good idea, and it starts with you, asshole," she replied. "Now drop the gun."

Then another man spoke up off to her side. "No, you drop *your* gun," he said.

Baum's partner had arrived. "Shoot the bitch," he said. "Then I'm going to get me a piece of this one before I drag her ass back. Looks like we'll need a bigger hole."

Marlene started to turn and fire, knowing that the other man had the drop on her and she'd probably lose. But before she or the second man could shoot, a shotgun roared. And from the corner of her eye she saw Baum's accomplice blown off his feet by a load of double-oh buckshot that caught him in the side of his chest.

At the same moment Baum turned to shoot, and might have won the battle, but

Blair kicked at his legs just as he pulled the trigger, and the shot whizzed by Marlene's head. Her .45's first slug caught him in the stomach, doubling him over; the next shot hit him in the head as he tried to straighten up to shoot, and he was dead before he hit the ground.

Marlene ran up to where Blair lay on the ground crying. "You okay?"

"Yes, thank you, thank you," she said before she broke down into uncontrolled sobs.

Marlene turned as Spooner hurried up and checked the assassin's pulse. Unnecessarily, as it turned out. "Just in the nick of time, constable. I owe you big time."

"You're welcome," Spooner said with a grin. "Your friend back there caught a bullet in her shoulder, but I think she'll live. And boy howdy, she can curse up a storm, told me to get my fat ass on down here."

"That's Ariadne," Marlene said with a laugh as Blair stood and they headed back up the trail. "Thanks again."

"Think nothing of it. Sure beats the hell out of wrestling raccoons. Now what?"

15

Tucker Lindsey pulled up in front of the 13th Street Repertory Theater and got out of the sedan. The street was relatively quiet. He noted the homeless bum pushing a shopping cart loaded with assorted junk on the other side of the street, the hooker leaning against the corner of the building on 13th and Sixth Avenue, and the hot dog vendor on the east side of Sixth Avenue. None of them paid any attention to him.

"Everybody ready?" he said quietly so that only the microphone disguised as a tie clasp would pick up his voice.

"We're in place, boss," a voice said in his ear. "All the exits are covered."

"All right, await my signal," Lindsey said as he approached the front door of the dark theater. "If she runs, take her down. And try not to hit any civilians." He pulled on the handle, half-expecting it to be locked.

Maybe I just hoped it would be, he thought.

This isn't what I signed up for. Never mind that, just stick with the program, Tuck, the girl got in over her head and now she has to be eliminated. Then everybody keeps their jobs; you . . . the president . . . it's for the good of the country. He entered the lobby; it was dark but then the red light over a door leading into the theater suddenly glowed. *And when this election's over, I can tell that fat fuck Fauhomme what I really think of him.*

Two nights earlier, Fauhomme had been in New York at his girlfriend's condominium sweating bullets as he waited for Ray Baum to report that the problem with Jenna Blair had been resolved and that her laptop computer was in his possession. The last they'd heard from Baum was that he'd located where the girl was hiding and was on his way to get her. Then there'd been nothing until Thursday morning's stunning development; Baum and his partner, Craig Rose, had been killed in a car accident.

The constable in Orvin, some hick named Tom Spooner, had called the FBI in Albany and the special agent in charge there had called Lindsey, who'd flown to New York, on his cell phone. They were in Fauhomme's office talking about what to do next when the call from the FBI came in and when Lindsey reached out to Spooner, who'd explained what happened.

"I'm afraid some of our dirt back roads are pretty tricky, especially at night, lots of twists and turns," Spooner said. "Your boys were driving too fast, missed a turn and went head-on into an oak. One of the neighbors heard the crash and called, but they were both dead at the scene. Wasn't pretty . . . like I said, they were driving fast. The driver, I guess his name was Ray Baum, though he was pretty unrecognizable from his driver's license photograph, wasn't wearing his seat belt and went through the windshield. I found his NSA ID card in his wallet but didn't know how to reach you so I called the bureau in Albany. They also gave me a positive ID off their fingerprints."

"I appreciate your efforts. Where are the bodies?" Lindsey asked.

"With the medical examiner," Spooner said, "awaiting a toxicology report. The agent in Albany said he'd be up, because they worked for the federal government. All I can say is that they must have been drunk to be driving that fast on a dirt road at midnight."

Fauhomme handed Lindsey a note with a question scribbled on it, which he'd asked Spooner. "Can you tell me if there was a laptop computer located in the car?"

"No computer," Spooner replied. "I was there at the scene and went through the car at our lot yesterday morning. We recovered two 9mm semiautomatics, wallets, a few personal items, but that was about it. . . . You mind telling me what they were doing in my neck of the woods?"

Lindsey looked at Fauhomme, who wrote down another note. "They were looking for a cabin owned by General Sam Allen. . . ."

"Oh . . . yeah, well, they were close . . . good man, Allen. We were shocked as hell to hear the news."

"We all were," Lindsey said. "Do me a favor and secure the area around the cabin — no one in or out. We'll have another team up there as soon as possible. We are also looking for a fugitive. White female, blond, hazel eyes, about thirty years of age. Her name is Jenna Blair but she may be using an alias."

"Not ringing a bell at the moment," Spooner replied. "We're a pretty quiet little burg, but I'll ask around. Want me to hold on to her if I see her?"

"Just keep her under surveillance if you would; we don't want to spook her before my team arrives. If she tries to leave the area, go ahead and pick her up, but no one — and I mean no one — is to question her.

This is a national security case and we don't want it compromised. Same thing with that computer. If it's located, no one is to touch it; it contains highly classified material."

"Gotcha," Spooner replied. "Don't spook her. Don't question her. Don't look at the computer."

"Perfect," Lindsey said. "Again, I appreciate your contacting me and your cooperation. I'll see that the president is aware of your assistance. Oh . . . and I'm sure I don't need to tell you that for the time being we need to keep our agents' identities quiet and the whole thing out of the press if possible; this is still an active investigation and we wouldn't want to tip off our fugitive if she's in the area."

"Mum's the word," Spooner replied.

As soon as he got off the phone, Fauhomme slammed his fists down on Lindsey's desk. "Son of a bitch! God damn Baum!" he shouted. "Send him to do a simple job, and he runs off the road into a tree and gets himself killed."

Lindsey didn't say anything. He'd never liked Baum — he wasn't part of the NSA "team" and had been issued an identification card only at Fauhomme's insistence and then reported only to the fat man. Still, he would have thought the president's campaign manager would have shown a little more loyalty to his handpicked guy, even if that guy should have still been locked up for what he had done to civilians in Afghanistan.

"And Blair . . . who knows where that fucking whore is now?" Fauhomme continued raving.

"She could still be there," Lindsey pointed out. "Baum didn't get the computer so she might not even know he was around. My guys will find out soon enough."

"We need that computer. We have no idea what's on it or what it depicts Baum actually did," Fauhomme said. "And that girl doesn't make it back to New York, or anywhere else . . . am I clear? It's Thursday, five fucking days until the election. Five days, dammit! I want this problem taken care of before then. Find her!"

He didn't have to; two hours later, Jenna Blair called Fauhomme's girlfriend, Connie Rae Lee, who recorded the conversation once she knew who was on the phone. Lindsey was in his hotel room when Fauhomme showed up and played the recording back with a look of grim satisfaction.

The recording had picked up with Lee exclaiming, "Jenna! We've been so worried! Where have you been? Rod sent one of his security guys to your apartment last week and you were gone. It looked like somebody had torn the place apart!"

"That man . . . the man I told you about who killed Sam . . . he showed up first," Blair responded. "He must have been listening to my telephone calls. I recognized his tattoo on the security camera, but I went down the fire escape and got away. I was so scared; I didn't know who to turn to . . ."

"Oh, honey, you should have called me again," Lee had said. "Rod . . . and the president's national security adviser, Tucker Lindsey, I overheard them talking. They didn't want to worry me, but they think that man works for the terrorists!"

At the word "terrorists," Blair sobbed into the cell phone. "He found me!"

"What?" Lee exclaimed in mock surprise. "Where? Are you okay?"

"Remember that cabin I told you about in Orvin, Sam's place?" Blair said. "I was hiding there, and he still found me!" The young woman had started crying again.

"How did you get away?"

"He saw me leaving the cabin and chased me. I think I lost them, but I can't go back to the cabin! I don't know where to go. I just want this nightmare to be over!"

"Jenna, listen to me. Do you still have

your computer? Rod thinks that's what they're after!"

"Yes. I take it with me everywhere."

"You need to let me know where to find you . . . so we can protect you!"

"I'm scared," Blair wailed. "That man will find me!"

"Jenna! We . . . I . . . need you to get a grip. You remember Tucker Lindsey, right? He's the president's top security guy, you trust him, right?"

"I suppose so."

"Of course you can. And he wants to help. You name the place where you'd feel comfortable and Mr. Lindsey will meet you there. Then he can protect you. Okay?"

Blair sniffled a couple of times. "Yeah, okay. Remember where we first met?"

"The little theater on 13th Street?"

"I have the keys. There's nothing playing there now. I'll meet Mr. Lindsey there. But if I see anybody else — especially that guy with the tattoos — I'll be gone. And I'll send that recording of what happened to Sam to the television stations!"

"I don't understand why you think Mr. Lindsey would want to hurt you?"

"That's not the point. Somebody is following me, and maybe if the media sees what he did, he'll have to leave me alone.

So just do what I said or forget it. I'll move to Canada or something. You'll never find me!"

"Okay, okay . . . I'm your friend, Jenna. When do you want to meet?"

"Tomorrow. Friday. Eight o'clock. Have him come in the front door. I'll meet him inside."

"I'm sure he'll be there. And Jenna . . ."

"Yes?"

"Don't forget the computer. You'll be safe when you don't have it anymore, and Mr. Lindsey can arrange for you to go someplace where you'll be taken care of."

Fauhomme turned off the recording and turned to Lindsey. "I guess you'll be going to the Big Apple."

"You should have asked me first," Lindsey said, and scowled. "I could have handled this with a team in New York. How'd you get that, by the way?"

"She doesn't know it, but I have an app on her phone that records everything," Fauhomme said with a shrug. "Besides, I was standing right there, writing little notes so that she'd ask the right questions. And what was I supposed to do? Have Connie put her on hold while I called you? I had to think of someone she would trust. Besides, I think you're forgetting who got us into this mess in the first place."

"I wasn't the one who sent an amateur to murder an American general in a New York City hotel as a way to get us out of it."

"Touché, Tucker," Fauhomme sneered. "So we all fucked up. Now we all need to unfuck the situation. Right?"

After Fauhomme left his room, Lindsey seethed. A campaign manager ordering the president's national security adviser to run and fetch like a Labrador. But he held his tongue. Blair was expecting to see him; she might cut and run if she saw anyone else. And he had other business with a certain attaché to the Russian delegation at the United Nations; the other part of "unfucking" the situation.

That afternoon he'd met Petyr Avdonin, if that was his real name, on a bench at the Alice in Wonderland statue in Central Park. Just a couple of men enjoying a surprisingly mild early November day while eating a late lunch purchased from the kebab vendor on Fifth Avenue.

Lindsey told him about the tape from Al-Sistani. The man had listened politely and commiserated about the predicament the administration found itself in, but he'd made no real attempt to disguise the smirk that played at the corner of his mouth.

"Have you been able to locate the terrorists?" Lindsey asked between mouthfuls of gyro.

"It has been difficult to locate Daudov," Avdonin admitted. "We have killed a number of his associates, as well as several other terrorist leaders. But he is . . . how do you say, um, popular among the people in Chechnya. They hide him and refuse to betray him. Our man has had difficulty reestablishing contact since the attack. As for this . . . Al-Sistani . . . we believe he is in Dagestan. We have a man with him who plays both sides — the Islamic extremists and the separatists — when really he is Russian secret police."

"So why hasn't he reported in?"

"He is in deep cover and must be very careful about how and when he makes contact. Sometimes is weeks before we hear from him. But it has been long time since attack. We should hear from him soon."

"When you do, we'd like to know the precise location," Lindsey said, without volunteering anything more, but the Russian guessed what he was getting at.

"Yes, of course," Avdonin said. "And if something should happen then to the hostages . . . well, it is a dangerous world, fraught with peril. These terrorists have been known to blow themselves and their hostages to pieces, no?"

"Our people will have died bravely for their country," Lindsey said, ignoring the queasy feeling in the pit of his stomach.

"Ah yes, true patriots," Avdonin said with a sardonic smile. "The few who must sacrifice all for the many." He laughed and shook his head. "You Americans . . . you like to portray yourselves as John Wayne, the cowboy in white hat. Maybe that was true a long time ago, but now . . ." he shrugged and laughed again ". . . you are no different from us, except perhaps we are more honest."

The man's smile disappeared and he looked angry. "We're aware of what your chief of mission was up to," he said quietly but firmly. "And I'm not talking about arming the Syrian rebels. Although the Assad government is good customer for our military weapons, I'm sure we will sell to whoever takes his place. But we are not happy that you intended to arm these criminals who call themselves separatists. This is blatant interference in the internal affairs of the Russian federation."

"What do you want?" Lindsey answered, without bothering to deny the allegations.

"You will cease dealing with these people;

find another way to interfere with the Syrian government if you must," Avdonin demanded, "but stay out of Chechnya, or perhaps the American people would like to know the lies they are being told from the White House on down."

Lindsey didn't respond. There was no need. The Russians would have a free hand in Chechnya and the United States would look the other way no matter what human rights violations might occur.

Except for lights along the aisles and a few high on the walls, the theater was dark when Lindsey entered. "I'm in," he said quietly, "but no sign of . . ."

Before he could finish his sentence, a spotlight up in the balcony illuminated a desk that had been set on the stage. Sitting on the desk was an open laptop computer.

Lindsey whirled and put a hand in front of his face to shade his eyes, but he couldn't see who had turned on the light. "Jenna Blair?" he called out.

"Go look at my computer," a female voice replied from the dark. "It's ready; just hit Enter and you'll see."

Lindsey did as he was told. When he played the recording, he looked back toward the spotlight. "Do you know who the man

350

is?" he asked.

"You tell me. I saw him at Fauhomme's party on the Fourth of July where I first met Sam," the woman replied. "Then he showed up at my apartment after I called Connie Rae and again up at Sam's cabin in Orvin. He chased me when I was driving away from the cabin. I lost him."

"Do you know his name?"

"No. Do you?"

Lindsey didn't answer her question. Instead, he said, "Is this the only copy?"

"Are you kidding me? Of course it is. I just want my life back. I want to be left alone. I want that man with the tattoo to leave me alone."

"You need to come with me, Jenna," Lindsey said. "I can protect you."

"How? Sam was a general and he ran the CIA and they still killed him. How are you going to protect me?"

"We'll put you in the witness protection program. You can't keep running."

"Witness protection? Witness against who? That guy? You know and I know he wasn't acting on his own. Sam told me that people were upset with him because he wasn't going to go along with the 'official' story on Chechnya."

"What people?"

"He didn't say. I think he was trying to protect me. But he said he was being black-mailed . . . because of his relationship with me."

"I wouldn't know about that. What I do know is that you're playing a very danger-ous game, and if you don't come with me now, I can't be responsible for what hap-pens to you."

"What's going to happen to me?"

"Nothing if you come with me."

"What are you going to do with that re-cording?"

"We'll find this man . . . and if others are involved, we'll go after them, too. The FBI will."

"Is that who you're going to give the recording to? The FBI?"

"Yes. It's a bureau investigation now. So are you going to come with me?"

"How do I know there's not a bunch of guys in black suits and black cars outside ready to make sure I disappear?"

"I'm alone, Jenna. Let me help you."

"Give me a minute to think about it," the woman said. "I don't know who to trust."

"Jenna, I speak for the president, and you trust him, don't you?"

Jenna Blair didn't answer. Lindsey gave her a minute to consider. "Jenna? You need to make up your mind." But still there was silence, and then the alarm went off in his head. "Seal the doors," he shouted to his colleagues as he ran for the balcony entrance. "And get in here. I want that bitch now!"

Lindsey looked frantically around the balcony area before running down the stairs to join the men in black suits who moments before had screeched to a stop in front of the theater in their black Hummers and now rushed in. "She's running!" he yelled into his microphone.

"We have people on all the exits," one of his men replied.

However, a half-hour of searching the theater didn't turn up Jenna Blair. They did find a trapdoor in an anteroom off the lobby that led to another trapdoor beneath the stage that performers — or a fugitive — could use to move from one area to the next without the audience seeing them. Another small door beneath the stage opened into an old coal-supply tunnel with exits into the basements of other buildings in the neighborhood.

Informed that Blair had likely made her escape through the tunnel, Lindsey again felt a knot in his stomach. "Find her," he told his team over the radio. "And when you do, silence her."

16

Espy Jaxon studied the young woman who sat across from him at the internet café in Grozny. Deshi Zakayev was young, beautiful . . . and angrily skeptical after he'd asked her to arrange a meeting with Lom Daudov.

"And why should he meet with you?" she scoffed. "Why should any of us trust the United States government? You betrayed your own people on the night of the attack and left them to die and fall into the hands of Al-Sistani. If Lom had not been delayed that night, he would have been killed or captured, too. As it was, we could only watch from a nearby hill as your drone circled overhead for more than two hours and did nothing!"

Jaxon hung his head. "I am angry about that, too," he said, looking back up and into her eyes. "Some of those who died were my friends, as well as my colleagues. The young woman who was captured is the daughter of a friend, and I am her godfather." He nodded at Ivgeny Karchovski, who sat next to him interpreting. "This man here is her cousin."

Zakayev studied Karchovski for a moment with evident distaste. "I do not trust any Russian," she said, then shrugged, "but I liked Lucy. She is kind and it is hard to think of her in the hands of that beast." The young woman's face softened for a moment, but then hardened again. "But that does not mean you can be trusted. Now we are being hunted by the Russians, who stop at nothing, while your government turns its back and pretends not to see. Our cause cannot afford to lose Lom and be turned over to men like Amir Al-Sistani."

Jaxon sighed. After crossing the border from Dagestan, they had been staying on the outskirts of Grozny in the dacha of a "Russian businessman," a former comrade of Karchovski's while they served in the Russian army and one of his partners in his "import-export" business. Now it was Monday evening in Chechnya, and in twenty-four hours and halfway around the world, Americans would wake up and head to the polls to vote. Jaxon wished that his fellow citizens knew more of what really happened in Chechnya so they could take it into account when they cast their ballots. But the administration, or at least its front people, had lied, obfuscated, and diverted attention away from the Chechen debacle.

However, none of that mattered to Deshi Zakayev or the man she was representing. All they saw was the American government's betrayal of its own people and willing complicity in the brutal suppression of Chechen separatists by the Russians. Jaxon needed something more and was glad that he'd brought it with him and his team.

"What if I were to tell you that I have something . . . someone . . . Daudov wants? Someone who could help your cause."

Zakayev frowned. "Who?"

"Ajmaani."

A flicker of recognition flitted across Zakayev's face at the name but she shrugged. "I do not know this person."

Jaxon leaned forward across the table and spoke quietly but earnestly. "I believe you do. I believe that you are aware that Ajmaani, who supposedly was fighting for your cause, is actually a Russian agent, Nadya Malovo. I believe that you are aware that she perpetrated atrocities in the name of your cause to discredit those who yearn for a free Chechnya."

Zakayev pursed her lips. "Even if I was to know this person, what good is she to Lom Daudov?"

"She is proof that the Russian government, in league with criminal elements who want to use Chechnya for their own profit, staged 'terrorist attacks' so that they could legitimize the second war against your country. They used these attacks to influence world opinion; instead of Chechen separatists trying to win their independence, you were labeled Islamic terrorists. They lumped you in with Al Qaeda and other extremists."

The hard expression on Zakayev's face did not change, but Jaxon could see her mind working behind her eyes. "How do I know you are not lying to me?" she said. "Dangling this bait so that you can lure Lom Daudov to expose himself to more treachery. No one we are aware of has seen Ajmaani in several years. We believed she was dead."

"She is not dead," Jaxon said. "She is nearby and I am willing to produce her at the time and place Daudov chooses. I will even take the chance that he will not betray me or my people. We do not have permission to be in this country and risk imprisonment, or worse, if we are found out. But

Daudov must make up his mind immediately; Al-Sistani has threatened to kill Lucy and the other man unless my government hands over the terrorist Sheik Abdel-Rahman, which it will not do."

"Because they will not trade with terrorists?" Zakayev asked scornfully.

Jaxon shook his head. "That is the excuse they will use. But the reality is that these people in my government — the ones who stood by and let the mission be overrun and are going along with what the Russians are doing to you — they do not really want Lucy or Mr. Huff to return and tell the truth about what happened. They would prefer that they die."

Zakayev frowned and seemed to be thinking it over before replying, "Even if Lom agrees to help you, Al-Sistani is a difficult man to locate. He stays mostly in Dagestan among his fellow extremists there, and out of reach of both the Russians and us. It could take time, perhaps more time than Lucy has, to find him."

Jaxon smiled grimly. "I may be able to help there. We have reason to believe that Lucy and Mr. Huff are being held in a mosque near the sea. Satellite surveillance has picked up on some unusual activity at a mosque on the outskirts of Kasplysk. Its mullahs are known for their extremist views and ties to various terrorist groups, including Al Qaeda."

"Have these satellites spotted Al-Sistani?" Zakayev asked.

"No, not him specifically," Jaxon admitted. "However, a broadcast attributed to Al-Sistani is known to have emanated from the general area. And the satellites have picked up the presence of armed men going in and out of the mosque, as well as patrolling the grounds, which seems a little much for just a place of worship."

Jaxon decided to play his last card. "If you will help us, I will personally make sure the truth is told about this story," he said. "But if you do not, and Lucy dies, then I will not care what happens to you, Daudov, or your country. I will remain silent."

The young woman's eyes narrowed but she nodded. "I will take your messages to Daudov. I do not guarantee what his response will be. But whatever he decides," she added, "it won't be because he fears your threats."

With that the young woman stood up from the table. "You will hear from me by this evening." Over by the door, the two rough-looking men in leather coats who had accompanied her got up and escorted her out.

"What do you think?" Jaxon asked Karchovski.

The Russian's eyes flicked from the door to Jaxon. The gangster looked a lot like Butch Karp — same height and build, same Slavic features and gray, gold-flecked eyes, though the right side of Karchovski's face had been scarred during an escape from a burning tank in the Khyber Valley many years before. "Daudov has not stayed alive this long without an abundance of caution and attention to self-preservation," he said. "But my contacts say also that he is a man of honor and dedicated to his cause; Nadya would be a great propaganda prize. I guess we'll see."

Returning to the house of his friend, Karchovski went to check on Malovo, who was being kept in a windowless room in the basement of the house with two armed men guarding the door. He walked down the stairs and found her sitting on the bed set up for her, reading a book by a small electric light. Her ankles were shackled to the bar at the bottom of the bed.

When she saw him, Malovo smiled, her jade green eyes sparkling in the low light. She moved her feet and made the cuffs rattle on the metal bar. "Remember when this was something you and I did for fun?" she said with a laugh. "Or is that why you're here now? Something fast before you turn me over to my killers?"

Karchovski hesitated for a moment. Even in a thick, knitted sweater and long pants, and despite her captivity with Grale, Malovo was still an amazingly sensuous and beautiful woman. "That was a long time ago, Nadya, we were both younger and I, at least, was more susceptible to your charms," he replied. "As for your killers . . . you chose the road that led to this place. I am just checking to see that you are comfortable."

Malovo scoffed. "As comfortable as I can be without being able about to stand or walk or even change positions in bed. But it is certainly better than my hole in the wall in that madman's cave, so I guess I shouldn't complain." Suddenly her face softened and her eyes and expression were that of a frightened woman, as she whispered, "Ivgeny, please, for the love of God, help me. We were lovers once, doesn't that mean anything?"

"It did once upon a time in Afghanistan," Karchovski said. "When you were young and the evil in you had not yet matured. It was there; I knew it was there; you enjoyed your dirty work with the KGB far too much. But I always blamed it on your rough childhood and your KGB trainers. However, we all make choices in our life — free will — and you chose to follow your dark side when you had options."

"I had no choice," she retorted angrily. "I had nothing, and when the Soviet Union collapsed, it was everyone for themselves. You have no reason to talk that way to me; you became a gangster in America. You have killed men."

"I am well aware of my sins," Karchovski replied quietly. "But I never killed with the enjoyment you did, nor is that how I make my living. I will kill to defend those who are under my protection and to defend what is mine. And even then I accept that I will have to answer to my Creator for that. But you, Nadya, you kill for money and for the pleasure you get from watching others suffer and die. You will have your own day in that higher court, and what will you say?"

Malovo laughed harshly. "Don't give me that religious nonsense, Ivgeny. When did you become such a man of God? I remember the former loyal Communist Russian army colonel who believed in the here and now and not some foolish myth about the afterlife."

"Perhaps it was when I was being pulled from a burning tank," Karchovski said with a shrug. "Or maybe getting older, I grew wiser, realized that it was okay to believe in something bigger than myself, something bigger than the state. One thing I do know is that we are capable of change no matter how long it takes, even you."

"First Grale and Karp and now you," she sneered. "This insane idea that I will somehow, and for whatever reason, undergo this miraculous metamorphosis from black widow to butterfly when the time comes."

"You let the old woman's husband live."

Malovo scowled. "Goldie's old man, Sobelman, in the bakery? I saw no point in making the woman suffer; they've only got a few more years."

"But how unlike you to even care," Karchovski pointed out. "And what's more, because you didn't pull the trigger and gave yourself up, you set yourself on the road to federal prison and then Grale's cave after that."

A troubled look passed over Malovo's face, but then she snarled, "An error in judgment, I agree. And it only bolsters my argument that kindness is a weakness that can kill you."

"Or change you for the better. Remember

when we first met in Kabul, you the young woman who could laugh at silly jokes, loved fiercely, who was loyal to her comrades, treated a war-hardened soldier like me with tenderness, and even risked her life to protect the helpless. Or don't you remember saving the children in that Khyber Pass village?"

Malovo shook her head again. "You're a fool, Ivgeny," she said. Then a sly look came across her face and she lowered her voice. "But you're also a businessman, and I have a proposition for you." She glanced toward the stairs. "We can come up with a plan to capture Al-Sistani and then get away from the others."

"Even if I wanted to do that, what would it accomplish?"

"While he was pretending to be the business manager for the Saudi prince, Al-Sistani squirreled away millions of dollars in Swiss banks, so that if his larger plan didn't work, he'd have something to fall back on," she replied. "I'm sure it's what's funding his little religious war now. Give me a few minutes with him, and access to that money will be ours."

"I have all the money I need," Karchovski said. "And having you as a business partner would be like inviting a cobra into my bed."

Malovo reached out and grabbed his arm. "Then we could go back to New York and get Kane away from Grale. I know the way into and out of his lair, though we should kill Grale to eliminate the danger. Kane has the account numbers and passwords to bank accounts all over the world worth billions! We could be rich beyond our wildest dreams!"

The beautiful assassin took Karchovski's silence as his mulling her offer over. She lay back and moved her body seductively on the bed. "And I know you remember what lies beneath these clothes," she purred. "I still know how to give pleasure better than any woman you've ever known. And if you'd like others to join us in our play, I am not the jealous type."

This time it was Karchovski's turn to laugh. "Ah, Nadya, my beautiful evil vixen," he said, wiping the tears of mirth from his eyes. "You never stop trying, do you? But I put you out of my heart and away from my desires many years ago. Your enchantments no longer have any power over me."

Malovo spat at him as she sat upright in bed. "Fuck you, Ivgeny. You were always afraid to take what could have been yours. Fine, my death will be on your head."

"No," he replied, shaking his head. "You

chose to be here, whether you knew it or not; and now what happens to you is up to God."

At that moment there was a knock on the door above and Jaxon walked down the stairs. "Daudov's man returned," he said. "Lom is willing to meet and hear what we have to say. We're to bring her."

"When?" Karchovski asked.

"Now. There's a truck waiting outside. Have you finished talking?"

Karchovski looked back at Malovo, who glared malevolently at him. "Yes. There is nothing more here that needs to be said."

17

Rod Fauhomme had to hide the smirk he felt when he saw Tucker Lindsey nod at him and raise his glass of wine from across the ballroom. *The little shit's happy with me for now,* he thought. *We won — correct that, I won — and because I won, he gets to keep his job. The warm and fuzzies won't last, but not to worry, I've got a nice little insurance policy.*

As he glanced around the president's election-night victory party, he received many similar looks from others whose jobs had been on the line. Along with the president, he was the man of the hour. Some knew more than others about what he'd done to ensure victory. However, all were aware that he was the mastermind who had buried the opponent under a barrage of personal attacks that had little to do with who was more qualified to run the country. At the same time he had skillfully deflected the Chechnya incident, using Allen's "suicide" as a pretext for getting the hearings postponed until after the inauguration. Any efforts by the opposition to raise the issue and attempt to get the hearings going before the election had been met with accusations by the president's press secretary, Rosemary Hilb, of being "inappropriate and insensitive to a fallen American hero and his family."

It had worked like a charm. Then Fauhomme turned around and saw to it that the story about Allen's possible affair with Jenna Blair had been leaked to reporters who could be trusted to report exactly what he told them. As expected, they'd gone along with the program; after all, what they really cared about after the election was access to the president, and if that meant submerging their journalistic ethics, then that was the price of admission to the White House. The result was that the public's attention was diverted from a U.S. mission's being overrun, and Americans killed, to a tawdry sex scandal.

The election results had not given the president a landslide, or a mandate, though with a little massaging and a lot of cooperation from the media, it could be made to appear as one. It didn't really matter; for the next four years, the president and his cohorts in Congress and appointees to the Supreme Court could continue the process of moving the country to the left. Already demoralized before the election, the opposition party could be expected to devolve into assigning blame — to "low-information" voters, to their candidate, to Fauhomme, anything to avoid looking at their own lack of a message that appealed to a worried country and at the pundits who kept them trapped in believing there was no reason to adapt or change. He'd just come from watching one of the postelection news shows, and the opposition party leaders were already cannibalizing their candidate.

Fauhomme raised his glass of scotch to acknowledge Lindsey's toast. The national security adviser had failed to catch Jenna Blair, but at least he'd secured the computer. Thinking about what was on the computer sent a shiver up his spine, though he quickly dismissed it. His own computer forensics expert had examined it and determined that the recording of Allen's death had not been downloaded or emailed. So he had reason to believe there was only one copy, which was now in a bank safe deposit box in Arlington, Virginia. It had Lindsey's fingerprints all over it — his insurance policy should Lindsey ever turn against him.

The other major threat to the campaign had also passed without incident. Through unofficial channels, the administration had made overtures to Amir Al-Sistani to make him believe that an exchange of his prisoners was imminent. Fauhomme could not have cared less about the threat from Al-Sistani to kill David Huff and the unidentified female hostage if Al-Sistani's demands weren't met. *In fact, that would take care of a problem,* he thought. But the danger of Al-Sistani's going public about the attack and negotiations was very real; the American public would not have been happy to learn that they'd been lied to about the Zandaq mission's being overrun, or David Huff's purpose there. Nor would they be thrilled with the administration's covert deal-making with a terrorist regarding the blind sheik.

In the meantime, Lindsey was working with the Russians to make sure that neither Al-Sistani nor the hostages survived to trouble the president's next four years in office. But that was for another day, tonight was for celebrating.

Turning his eyes from Lindsey, Fauhomme noticed an attractive blond woman staring at him. She didn't look away when he made eye contact but smiled invitingly. *Another "politics tramp" who wouldn't have given me a sneer if I wasn't connected.* It never ceased to amaze him that power was such an aphrodisiac, and he had taken full advantage of it over the years. The thought brought him around to remembering Connie waiting for him back at the apartment. She'd wanted to come to the party but had been irritating him lately, so he was punishing her by making her miss the victory party. He blamed her for Jenna Blair's turning out to be such a problem. Now in the flush of victory, he was feeling that he might go home and slap her around before letting her "make it up" to him with whatever sexual act appealed to him at that moment.

I'm getting tired of the demanding bitch, he thought. *Maybe it's time to turn her out on the streets.* But at the same time that the idea of moving on to the next woman interested him, he knew Connie presented a problem. She knew too much. He'd have to talk to Baum's replacement about taking care of the problem.

Fauhomme watched as the blonde handed a note to one of the pages who was working at the party. The young man hurried over to him and handed him the folded piece of paper. He looked at it — a phone number

— then glanced back at the blonde and nodded as he tucked it into his suit coat pocket. He might or might not call, but tonight Connie was the easy target.

Two hours later he was naked and snoring on the couch at his Georgetown apartment when he was awakened by Connie's voice. The last thing he remembered was the sound of her crying in the bathroom, where she'd gone to wipe the blood off her mouth and nurse the new bruises he'd given her. He'd come home from the party and found her pouting and ignoring his demands. She tried to go to bed in a guest room but he followed her in there and violently forced himself upon her. Her protests and screams had just excited him more and he hit her a little harder than he intended and drew blood. Then he left her alone crying.

Still half-drunk, he waved her off angrily. "Fuck off," he muttered.

"Rod . . . Rod, wake up . . . the police are here and want to talk to you."

He opened his eyes and glared at her. "Police?" he asked, then narrowed his eyes in suspicion. "Did you call the cops?"

Connie's bruised face blanched in terror. "No . . . no, of course not," she whimpered. "I was sleeping and heard the doorbell."

Fauhomme felt a sudden surge of fear.

"Did they say what they want?"

"Just that they need to talk to you."

Suddenly a horrible thought occurred to him. *It has to be the president. Something has happened to the president. Assassination?* "Let them in. I'll get ready right away." He hurried into the bedroom, where he pulled on a pair of pajama bottoms and a robe.

When he emerged and entered the living room he saw two men standing near Connie, who was sitting on the couch. One of them, an average-sized white man, was leaning over talking to her as she shook her head. The other, a large black man, had been listening to the conversation but turned as Fauhomme approached and frowned.

"What can I do for you gentlemen?" Fauhomme asked.

The white man stood up and also scowled at him. "I'm Detective Kit Deger, D.C. police," he said. "You mind telling me how those marks got on your girlfriend's face?"

Fauhomme looked blankly at Connie, but internally he was seething. *So the bitch did sic the cops on me,* he thought. *She'll pay for this.* He shrugged and said, "I wasn't around, but she told me that she fell down the steps. Now I have important matters with the president in the morning so if this can wait . . ."

Deger shook his head. "I'm afraid it can't." He turned to the big black man. "Clay, you want to do the honors?"

Fulton smiled grimly and nodded. "You bet," he said. "Mr. Fauhomme, my name is Clay Fulton. I'm a detective with the New York City Police Department currently assigned to the New York County District Attorney's Office. I have two warrants here. One is to search your apartment . . ."

"What! That's outrageous . . ." Fauhomme sputtered.

"The second is for your arrest for the murder of Samuel Allen."

Fauhomme's eyes bugged, then he snarled, "Do you know who you're fucking with!"

"Are you Rod Fauhomme?" the black detective asked.

"Yes, you son of a —"

"Then I know who I'm fucking with and you're under arrest."

It had been a long time since Fauhomme felt real fear, but he felt it now as he looked in the hard brown eyes and impassive face of the detective. "You can't . . ."

"Oh, but I can," Fulton replied. "And I just did. Now I'm going to read you your rights. You have the right to remain silent . . ."

Fauhomme turned to Connie Rae Lee. "Call my attorney," he ordered, his voice rising in fear.

The woman raised her face to look at him, one of her eyes swollen shut and her lip split and puffy. "Call him yourself, you son of a bitch," she said. "I hope you rot in prison for the rest of your life."

18

As she sat tied to a chair in the nearly complete darkness, Lucy was aware of the presence of the saint before she heard the voice of her captor, and apparently high executioner, coming for her. But she knew what the appearance by St. Teresa meant — danger and quite possibly death.

At least that's what Al-Sistani had been promising her all week. Frustrated by the U.S. administration's delays in meeting his demands, he'd threatened to cut her throat "to show I mean what I say. Perhaps when they have a video of you choking on your own blood, they will give me what I want to spare Mr. Huff."

"Go ahead," Lucy said. "But if I die, I know I'm going to be fine. But I will also go to my death with the satisfaction of knowing that my friends will someday track you down and kill you, and where you'll be going is cold, dark, and alone, and it's forever."

Al-Sistani's eyes blazed at her comment. But then he laughed. "You don't have any friends," he said.

Then election day came and went. The incumbent president remained in power. And now she quailed when she heard Al-Sistani enter the basement and speak to the guards.

"Be brave, child," St. Teresa encouraged her.

"I'll try," Lucy replied, though unconvincingly.

After making the video, Al-Sistani had largely left her alone with her hands tied behind her to the wooden chair and her ankles bound to the legs with rough cord. She was fed irregularly, usually some sort of weak gruel that tasted vaguely of chicken broth, and went through long spells with no water. And sometimes she was left to sit in her urine and waste before being brought a dampened rag to wash herself up for a few minutes before being tied again. And there'd been plenty of time to consider her impending death. In fact, through the lonely hours of her captivity she'd heard the guards frequently talking outside her cell, taking perverse delight in knowing she could hear them discuss in broken Russian what it was like to have one's throat slit.

"The lungs continue trying to suck air in through your gaping windpipe," said one. "But then the blood from your severed arteries pours in and you can't breathe. You are drowning in your own blood and dying from the loss of blood at the same time."

"I saw a beheading once," said the other guard. "They used a dull knife and it took a long time to saw through the woman's neck. She kept screaming and then all you could hear was gurgling and choking sounds. It seemed quite painful and a horrible way to die. It can actually take quite a while to lose consciousness, and then your body goes into convulsions, thrashing about on the ground. Just like a butchered animal, no dignity to it at all."

Now, apparently, she was going to find out; St. Teresa didn't make appearances for just any reason. "I don't want to die," she said quietly. "Not like this."

"No one knows the hour and place of their death, my child," the saint responded. "It is not in your hands. Just know that the man who will be appointed your executioner is a friend and you must listen carefully to what he says and obey without hesitation."

There wasn't any more time to ask questions before the key was inserted into the lock and the door swung open. Someone turned on the uncovered bulb swinging above her head, causing her to blink repeatedly as the light shot tiny darts of pain into her brain. Her vision was blurry, so at first she was only aware that dark figures had entered the room, one of whom stood in front of her and another who moved behind and began roughly untying her hands and then cut the bonds that held her feet.

"Get up," said Al-Sistani, the man in front of her.

"I don't think I can," Lucy replied. "I can't feel my legs."

"Raad, help this infidel whore to her feet."

Lucy screamed as the giant man behind her grabbed a handful of hair on top of her head and yanked her up off the floor. The moment he let go, her legs went out from under her and she collapsed to the floor.

"Get up!" Al-Sistani shouted, and kicked her in the ribs.

Groaning in pain, Lucy got to her hands and knees and tried to stand up. She got partway up, took one step forward, and then pitched to the stone floor again.

Al-Sistani leaned over until his bearded face was only a few inches from Lucy's. "You only delay, not prevent, the moment of your death," he hissed, then stood and glared at Raad. "Carry her!"

The giant grabbed Lucy under her armpits and violently lifted her to her feet and then half-frog-hopped her up the stairs and out of the basement, through a long hall, and into the gated courtyard of the mosque. She was brought over to a wall on which a green banner with white Arabic lettering spelled out "Death to the United States" above "Allahu akbar."

"God is great," Lucy mumbled.

Raad spun her around so that she was facing a video camera with the wall and its banner behind her. He let her drop painfully to her knees and took up a position behind her with his arms crossed over his bare chest.

Squinting against the glare of the setting sun, Lucy found herself looking across the courtyard toward the wide gate in the mud wall that ran around the mosque. Loitering inside the walls were armed men, most with full beards and wearing the small round black caps and quilted coats popular among Dagestani men. Beyond the guarded gate she saw some of the locals going about their business, apparently unaware of, or unmoved by, what was going on inside the walls. An old man led a donkey piled high with firewood past the open gate. Beyond him two young bearded men dressed as farmers trudged down the steep road that ran up a hill overlooking the mosque.

Another door opened in a different part of the mosque and Lucy saw David Huff being escorted out into the courtyard by a man on either side of him. When he saw Lucy, the banner, and the camera, he suddenly stopped dead in his tracks and tried to back away from his escorts, who grabbed his arms. "Nooooooooo," he screamed. "No, please, I don't want to die!"

Huff's captors ignored his pleading and dragged him forward while forcing him down upon his knees next to Lucy. He looked at her, his eyes wide in terror, tears running down his cheeks and snot dripping from his nose as he whimpered. "I'll do anything," he screeched, turning his head to face Al-Sistani, who was standing next to the video camera. "Please, I'll tell you anything you want to know."

"Shut up, Huff!" Lucy snarled. His cowardice had somehow rekindled her courage, which had been failing until the moment she heard his first wail. "Be a man."

"I don't want to die!"

"They're not going to kill you, David," she said, fixing his darting eyes with her own steady pair. "You're still worth something to them. But they are going to kill me to make a point. So if you don't mind, I'd like a little dignity for my final moments."

Huff's eyes bugged out for a moment and then they cleared of fear. His terror was replaced with a look of shame. "Kill me instead," he said to Al-Sistani. "It will have a bigger impact. Get the headlines, then they'll deal to get the girl back."

Al-Sistani's response was to grin sardonically. "Suddenly brave, Mr. Huff?" he mocked. "That vaunted Western chivalry toward women? You're deluded; they're nothing but whores to be used and thrown away like garbage."

"Then that's why you need to kill me," Huff replied. "Otherwise you're wasting your time. No one will care if she dies."

Al-Sistani shrugged. "It would seem that no one cares if either of you dies," he said. "Your government has pulled out of our negotiations that might have spared your lives. Perhaps they think I won't go through with my threat. So I need to make an example. But the whore is right; you, Mr. Huff, may still have some value alive once the American public has been shown our little film. Then your people will be forced to make a deal with me and hand over Sheik

Abdel-Rahman."

"What's in that for you?"

"Me?" Al-Sistani repeated, obviously enjoying this bit of theater. "Why, I will be an instant hero in all of Islam. The jihadists will rally to my banner, and I will be the number-one man in Al Qaeda. I will be the first caliph of all Islam in more than two hundred years, and all Muslim governments soon will swear fealty to me. I will be Islam's champion in the ultimate battle against the West, and when it is over, Sharia will be the law of all the lands and I will be their ruler! That's what is in it for me!"

"You're insane," Lucy said mockingly. "No one is going to give in to your stupid demands!" She laughed with as much sarcasm as she could muster. "You hit the nail on the head, genius. They don't want us back; we're an embarrassment. They'll just move you up the list and someday, you're going to wake up in the dark and one of the good guys will be standing over you itching to put a bullet in your fat head."

Lucy said that to rattle Al-Sistani. But when the words came out of her mouth, she knew that part of what Al-Sistani had said was true. *No one came to help,* she thought. *I know some of those messages had to get through. They had a drone. Fighter jets could have been there in minutes. They fucked up, then left us to die to cover up Huff's little illegal arms deal and play out their political deception. And now the administration just wants it, and us, to all go away.*

Al-Sistani stared at her for a moment. "Hear how the whore and the coward stall to prolong their miserable lives. The West is weak! Allahu akbar! Death to the infidels! But first, bring out our special guest."

Still on their knees, Lucy and Huff looked when more men walked out of the front door of the mosque. Four large men surrounded a fifth as they crossed the courtyard. Although the man in the middle walked freely and confidently, and his escorts carried their AK-47 rifles loosely over their shoulders, it was clear that he was a prisoner — or at least being watched very carefully. Behind the five men walked a sixth man whom Lucy recognized, Bula Umarov. *The traitor.*

"Ah, my old enemy and new comrade in arms, Lom Daudov, the Lion of Chechnya," Al-Sistani said sarcastically as he gestured to the man in the middle.

Lucy took a moment to study the man she'd come to Chechnya to find. He was not particularly big, though he carried himself like a larger man; he moved with the smooth strength of a natural athlete and held his head high. His hair and beard were the color of copper and when he walked up to stand next to Al-Sistani she could see that his eyes were an almost unnaturally bright shade of sea-green.

Al-Sistani grinned. "Surprised?" he asked Lucy. "Isn't this the man you wanted to meet? The man you were going to give weapons to if he would help hunt me down? . . . What, no answer? But that's what my man Bula told me before we attacked the compound, and I can always trust Bula. Come here, my faithful lapdog."

The short, skinny man with the pock-marked face did as he was ordered, smiling when he glanced at Daudov, who glared at him with hatred. Al-Sistani saw the looks and tsked. "Yes, it apparently came as a surprise to the Chechen lion that his most trusted adviser was working for me."

"I don't care about that worm. I came to you in good faith today," Daudov growled. "I have offered to lay down our old enmity to fight the Russians together for the good of Chechnya!"

"Ah, yes, the good of Chechnya," Al-Sistani said. "But are you willing to swear allegiance to me and see Chechnya as an Islamic state under Sharia law and my rule?"

"Inshallah," Daudov said. "As God wills. Anything would be better than the blood-stained Russians."

Al-Sistani turned to Lucy and Huff like a college professor about to make a point. "You see, Lom and his partisans were blamed for the attack on the mission, and the Russians have made their lives very uncomfortable, and, indeed, hazardous, ever since. So now he's offering to join his Hands of God brigade with my Al Qaeda jihadis, all under my command. The question is can I trust him?"

"I bring more to the table than just myself and my men," Daudov said. "Or have you never heard of Ajmaani?"

Al-Sistani looked confused. "Of course, I know Ajmaani," he said. "She worked for me when I nearly destroyed the New York Stock Exchange. She's dead."

"She's alive," Daudov corrected him. "She crossed into Chechnya a week ago, and my men intercepted her. She is my prisoner."

"You lie!" Al-Sistani snarled.

"I can prove it. She is here."

"Where?"

"With two of my men in a truck at the top of the hill."

Al-Sistani whirled to look up the hill and then back at Daudov. "Have them bring her," he said. "If you are telling the truth, you will be my right-hand man and rule Chechnya when I am caliph of the world. But if you lie, you will suffer the same fate as these two infidels!"

Daudov turned to one of his escorts. "Shoot your rifle in the air," he demanded.

The man looked at Al-Sistani, who nodded. Raising his gun, the man let off a burst. Almost immediately, a small truck at the top of the hill began to make its way down.

"Bula, do you know Ajmaani by sight?"

"Yes, I was involved in the attack on the school that she planned."

"Then go to the gate and stop the vehicle," Al-Sistani said. "Make sure it is her."

"Yes, my sheik."

"And Bula, the men in the truck are to leave their guns at the gate with my men."

"Yes, my sheik."

Bula trotted over to the gate, where the two guards stepped in front of the truck. He walked up to the driver's-side window, which was rolled down, and looked at the passenger in the back.

"It's her! It's Ajmaani!" he yelled back.

"Bring her," Al-Sistani shouted back. "Allahu akbar! This is a glorious day!"

Bula spoke briefly to the driver and two rifles were passed out of the windows to the

guards. He then jumped up on the side-
board of the truck and rode triumphantly
back across the courtyard.

The truck stopped next to the camera
crew. Two men stepped out, their faces
partly obscured by scarves. The tall man on
the passenger side flipped a switch and
shoved his seat forward; he then reached
into the back of the truck and hauled Ajmaani, aka Nadya Malovo, out.

Al-Sistani strolled up to the woman. "Ajmaani," he said slowly. "It's been a long
time. We heard you were dead."

"I am hard to kill," Malovo replied, regarding Al-Sistani coolly.

Al-Sistani chortled. "Still the same
woman, as hard and cold as steel." He
looked at her bound wrists and frowned.
"This won't be necessary," he said, and
pulled a knife from a scabbard in his belt.
Cutting her bonds, he said, "We have much
to discuss."

"More than you know," Malovo replied.

Smiling broadly, Al-Sistani turned back to
Daudov. "Perhaps I have misjudged you,
my friend," he said. Then a sly expression
crossed his face. "You have reunited me
with someone I consider very valuable. But
there is one last task I would ask of you to
prove your loyalty once and for all."

"What is that?" Daudov replied cautiously.

Al-Sistani looked at the man standing behind Lucy. "Raad, give my new comrade your knife," he said. "Then he will cut the throat of the infidel woman."

"No! The Koran forbids making war on women and children," Daudov argued.

"This is not war," Al-Sistani replied, his face and eyes growing hard. "This is a test of loyalty. Once you are on film murdering this agent of the United States, you will be committed to our cause. There will be no turning back."

Al-Sistani nodded to Daudov's escorts, who raised their rifles menacingly. "It's that or you and your men will die here, and I will still have Ajmaani and the hostages."

"Please don't do this," Huff pleaded.

"Bula, take him inside," Al-Sistani ordered. "I wouldn't want her blood on his shirt; he already has enough of it on his hands." His men grabbed Huff and, led by Bula Umarov, dragged him back inside the mosque. Then the terrorist leader turned back to Daudov. "So, what will it be? Prove your loyalty, or die in Dagestan."

Daudov looked hard at Al-Sistani for a moment, but then nodded. He walked over to Lucy and held out his hand for Raad's large curved knife, before assuming the large man's place behind her. Meanwhile, Raad pulled a handgun from the waistband of his pants and stepped back as he pointed it at the back of Daudov's head.

Clapping like an excited Hollywood director, Al-Sistani nodded to his videographer and then stepped out in front of the camera. "Today is a glorious day for the Islamic revolution in Chechnya," he announced grandly. "I, Sheik Amir Al-Sistani, have accepted the sworn allegiance of Lom Daudov, the Lion of Chechnya, who will join me in the holy fight to overthrow the Russian occupiers and their puppet government and create the Islamic Republic of Chechnya. Today, we renew our dedication to the cause of an Islamic world by taking the life of an infidel American foolishly sent to kill me, only to watch her companions die by my hand. Let this be a warning to the West; we will spare no one who opposes us in our holy fight. We demand the release of Sheik Abdel-Rahman or Deputy Chief of Mission David Huff will share the same fate! Allahu akbar!"

Al-Sistani stepped out of the picture and nodded at Daudov. "Inshallah! God's will be done," he shouted offscreen.

Lucy braced herself as she felt Daudov grab her hair and pull her head back, exposing her neck. "I'm sorry," he said as he placed the knife at her throat.

As she looked up, Lucy heard another voice in her head. "Your executioner is a friend . . . listen carefully . . . obey without hesitation." "I forgive you," she said aloud.

"Then fall to the ground, now," Daudov told her, his voice even but urgent.

Lucy threw herself forward and felt Daudov land on top of her. It wasn't so much what he'd said that kept her from hesitating, but the language he'd used. The Lion of Chechnya was speaking Navajo.

19

Karp stared wearily for a moment at the telephone on his desk when it rang. It was 2:00 a.m. on Wednesday, the day after the election. He knew who the call was from, Clay Fulton, and what the caller would say, that Rod Fauhomme and Tucker Lindsey were in custody. What he didn't know as he reached for the receiver was what would happen now or how it would all end.

After the shoot-out several days earlier, Marlene had called, but she was circumspect in what she was willing to say over the telephone other than that he needed to get to Orvin as soon as possible. So he'd contacted Fulton, who arranged for an NYPD helicopter to whisk them north.

In Orvin, they'd been met by Constable Tom Spooner, who took them to Allen's cabin where Marlene, Stupenagel, and Jenna Blair were waiting. Following a quick rundown from the others, Karp had interviewed Blair with Fulton present. He then viewed Allen's taped testimony he intended to give at the congressional hearings, the private message he'd left for Blair, and the webcam recording of the murder on Blair's laptop.

Afterward he took a half hour to sit by himself on the front deck jotting notes down on a legal pad in the light of a lantern with a blanket around his shoulders. When at last he laid down his pencil, Karp took a moment to reflect on the quiet tranquillity as the eastern sky grew light and the loons called on the lake and contrasted it against the violence that had occurred there just a few hours earlier. *And for what? Power? Ego? Ambition?*

Karp rose and walked into the cabin, where he called the others together around the kitchen table. "I have a plan," he said. "It won't be easy to pull off. We're up against some very powerful people who apparently will stop at nothing — not even murder — to accomplish their goals." He looked at Spooner. "And I'll understand if you decide this isn't your fight." His eyes next fell on Blair. "And it's going to be particularly rough on you."

Blair's eyes narrowed and her jaw set. "You know where I stand."

Karp nodded, then turned back to Spooner, who said, "I'm in. I saw how these guys operate. That's not what I fought for in '68. What do you need from me?"

"Time," Karp responded. "I'm going to need a couple of days before our suspects learn the truth about what happened to Baum and his partner. I have a trap in mind and want them to think the evidence — Jenna's computer — is still out there and so is she. Obviously we have to tell them something, maybe a car wreck, just not that we know they were trying to murder Jenna and Stupenagel and then died in a gunfight with you and my wife. The problem is they'll want to verify the story, and as soon as their people see bullet holes, the whole car wreck scenario will be out the window, and they'll know something's up."

Spooner smiled. "Well, it just so happens that my best friend from high school, who then joined the army with me back in the day, is currently the special agent in charge of the Albany office. I'll give him a call."

And that's how Karp's plan was put into action, beginning with Spooner's conversation with his FBI friend. "I didn't go into detail and he didn't ask," Spooner reported. "But I could feel his eyebrows shooting up even over the telephone line. Still, we didn't do a bunch of crawling around in the jungle together without being able to ask for a favor without a lot of questions. He's going to call Lindsey and tell them I got in touch with him about the car wreck and finding the NSA cards. He'll head them off by saying he's coming up to check on the bodies and get my report, which he'll of course forward back to them. And he'll give them my number. I expect I'll be hearing from this Lindsey fella pretty quick."

As predicted, Tucker Lindsey called Spooner and was recorded. "Same thing with the computer; if it's located, no one is to touch it, it contains highly classified material." Then, with Karp orchestrating the timing, Blair waited for two hours before she contacted Connie Rae Lee, pretending to be panicked by the appearance of Baum and wanting to be rid of the computer. "With just enough 'do what I say or I'll give it to the media' to sell it," Karp advised.

In this, as well as other subsequent parts of his plan, Karp was playing hunches based on what he'd gleaned so far from talking to Blair, Spooner, and Stupenagel, as well as Allen's recordings. For instance, he knew that Connie Rae Lee could be the key to getting to the man behind the curtain — Fauhomme. Clearly she passed on anything

Blair told her directly to Fauhomme. In fact, judging by how quickly Baum had been sent to grab Blair and her computer at her apartment, he suspected that Fauhomme was standing next to her when Blair called.

Karp was counting on a similar situation — either with Fauhomme present or Lee passing on the information quickly and Fauhomme then responding — when he told Blair to place the call to Lee. It had quickly become clear that Fauhomme was present and calling the shots. In doing so the president's campaign manager had further implicated himself, as well as confirming what Karp suspected about Lindsey's being up to his eyeballs in the plots and not some unwitting bystander.

So he knew Blair's story was true. The problem was how to meet his own criteria for prosecution by the New York County District Attorney's Office. Karp insisted before going forward with a case that first there must be factual guilt, not a best guess or "most likely" theory, but a thousand percent certainty. Second, if there was factual guilt then there must be legally admissible evidence to convict a defendant beyond a reasonable doubt. So even if certain of a defendant's factual guilt, if there was insufficient legally admissible evidence then the case would not go forward.

It was all about due process. The difference between factual guilt and having legally admissible evidence was the difference between knowing the truth and being able to legally prove it. For example, the prosecution might have compelling evidence that was the result of a search of a defendant's place of business, but the court might determine that a search warrant was required and without it the defendant's Fourth Amendment rights were violated. Similarly, the court might very well strike down a trustworthy and incriminating statement voluntarily given by the accused if the court found that the statement was the product of a "custodial interrogation" that required Miranda warnings that were not given, thereby violating the defendant's Fifth Amendment rights. In both examples, the defendant was factually guilty, but the evidence was inadmissible and could not be used.

Karp was not willing to deprive any man of his freedom without due process. Not even one he detested like Rod Fauhomme.

It was no open-and-shut case. He was going to have to convince the jury that an American general and acting director of the

CIA had been murdered by a rogue former Marine acting in concert with the president's campaign manager and his national security adviser to cover up a foreign policy debacle that threatened the president's election bid.

He would have Blair's story and the tapes, plus Stupenagel's testimony. But obviously the defense would attack Blair's credibility. She slept with men for money. That was how she'd met Allen. They'd already "let slip" to the media that Allen had been having an affair with her. Obviously, they'd exploit that and use it to obfuscate the prosecution's case.

Baum could be tied to Lindsey through the NSA identification cards. But the defense could claim he was a rogue agent acting for others or in his own interests. Maybe even claim the cards were forgeries. But Lindsey had admitted that the dead men were his agents. The call Karp had Blair place to Connie Lee in which Lee suggested that her friend meet the president's national security adviser to hand over the computer had driven a nail in the defendants' coffin.

However, Karp always operated under the premise that there was no such thing as too much incriminating evidence, so he played a couple more hunches. One was that despite Lindsey's assurances that he would come alone, Karp was sure he would have a team standing by ready to swoop into the theater and take Blair into custody. "But before the guys in the dark suits, aviator glasses, and black Hummers appear, he'll make sure she's in the theater," he noted to the others, looking specifically at Fulton, "which means he'll be in radio contact with his team. I want to know what he says from the moment he arrives."

In addition to wiring the theater so that they could record the exchange between Lindsey and Blair, the NYPD "techno-geek" who'd worked for Fulton was positioned in the building across from the theater when Lindsey arrived. He then quickly located the frequency of Lindsey's radio and recorded everything that was said. "If she runs, take her down."

Of course, any number of things could have gone wrong, such as Lindsey's team going into the theater with him and preventing Blair's escape. That could have been dangerous for the young woman; as Marlene pointed out, it wouldn't be enough to have the computer, the witness would have to be silenced. So a bum pushing a shopping cart, a prostitute on the street corner, and a hot dog vendor — all NYPD cops and part of Fulton's DAO team — were ready to move and prevent any "shot while escaping" scenarios, just in case. But the plan had worked to perfection; Jenna escaped without having to alert the bad guys that the DAO was on to them.

Still, Karp needed to tie Fauhomme to the computer. His assessment of the man's character and paranoia determined it was a good bet that Lindsey had been instructed to take the computer to Fauhomme so that he could see what was on it. So Karp asked the computer expert if there was a way to track the computer's whereabouts, as well as plant a listening device on the machine.

"The problem is that if I just install, say, a GPS device that is constantly broadcasting its position," the computer expert explained, "if someone does even a cursory sweep looking for the device, and I assume they will, they'll find it. Same thing with any physical bug I add to the machine's hardware."

"So it can't be done without being discovered?" Karp asked.

"I didn't say that. What I can do is install a couple of apps in the software and bury them so deep that the bad guys would have to have someone like me go through all that computer language and know what they were looking for to find it. Both of the apps would be 'sleepers' — they won't turn on until someone tries to view the webcam recording. When someone does, the apps will 'wake up'; one will send a signal as to its location and the other will turn on the computer's microphone. I'm betting that only the main guys will be allowed to open that recording file, too. They're not going to want to let just any techno-geek like me see that."

"I believe you're right there," Karp said. "And they think they're getting the computer from a frightened young woman, not a 'computer savant.' That sort of subterfuge probably won't cross their minds. So have we made a copy of the webcam recording?"

The technician shook his head. "No, I waited on that," he said. "If we download it or attempt to send it via email, these guys would be able to know that. So I made a copy the old-fashioned way; I set up a video camera and recorded it. It's not a great copy, but not bad either if they go ahead and destroy the original, which is what I would do."

That plan, too, had worked like a charm. Then he moved swiftly to indict Fauhomme and Lindsey for murder but still waited until after the election to have them arrested.

Although he had questions about how high up the cover-up of the events in Chechnya and Allen's murder went, it wasn't his job to tell the American public whom to choose as their next president. And more important, the fallout from the arrests was going to be immediate and intense; he didn't want to give any credence to accusations that he'd timed the indictments solely to influence the election.

Karp sighed as he picked up the receiver. Tomorrow the firestorm would begin. But tonight he was a father with a missing daughter whose life hung in the balance.

"Yeah?" he said into the phone.

"We have them, Butch," Fulton replied. "And more than we bargained for."

The big man had noticed Fauhomme's girlfriend had a bruised face and noted her venomous statement telling her boyfriend to call his own attorney. So as soon as he'd deposited Fauhomme in the police car along with Lindsey — and told the uniformed D.C. officer to stay in the car and "take notes" on anything they said — he'd gone back up to talk to Connie Rae Lee.

Fulton could be physically intimidating, particularly if he was angry and scowling. But when the occasion called for it, he could be a big teddy bear who put witnesses and sometimes even suspects at ease so that they'd talk freely.

When he first went back into the condominium, Lee had been reluctant to say anything, he told Karp. But he sat her down on the couch, got her a drink of water and a cold washcloth to press on her bruise, and then said that she didn't deserve to be mistreated. He later told Karp that she'd looked like she was about to burst into tears and that's when he added that good people had to stand up to evil in the world or it would continue to be perpetuated.

"She sniffled a couple more times and then the dam broke," he said. "When she started talking, she couldn't stop. You're going to love what she has to say. I'm making arrangements to get her back to Manhattan and over to your office tomorrow."

"Thanks, Clay, get some sleep and I'll see you later today." He hung up the telephone and stood up. He could use some sleep himself. It was probably going to be in short supply in the days ahead.

20

The old man with the donkey laden with firewood hesitated at the gate of the mosque near the two guards, who were smoking cigarettes. He glanced at two young farmers who were quickly approaching.

"Move along, old man," said one of the guards, who nodded at the donkey, "and take your wife with you."

"I don't understand a word you're saying, but I take it that it wasn't very nice," the old man replied as he walked back to adjust the donkey's burden by tugging on a rope.

"Huh?" replied the second guard, glancing at where he and his comrade had leaned their rifles against the wall. "What kind of language are you speaking? Where are you from?"

"I take it neither one of you ugly sons of bitches speaks Navajo," the old man replied. "That's okay, I was just going to suggest that you begin singing your death songs."

He grinned and gave the rope a final pull just as the two young farmers reached the donkey.

The odd thought, *Daudov was speaking Navajo,* passed through Lucy's mind just a second before what sounded like a large angry insect thrummed over her at supersonic speeds, followed by the muted thud of that insect impacting a soft but solid object. The next sounds arrived together — a pained grunt and the noise of a loud rifle from the top of the hill outside the mosque.

Unlike in the movies, Raad was not blown off of his feet by the 7.62mm NATO Ball Special M118LR7 cartridge from the M24 bolt-action rifle fired by the sniper. However, the heavy bullet obliterated his heart before traveling down and out the small of his back. He grunted again, looked down at the deceptively small hole punctured just off-center in his bare chest, dropped his gun, took a step forward, and collapsed. For a split second, nobody did anything except watch Raad die before he hit the ground. Then everybody began to move at once.

But not in time to save one of the guards, who had his gun trained on the driver and passenger of the truck that had brought Nadya Malovo into camp. The top of his head disappeared in a spray of red blood from the sniper's second shot.

Meanwhile the tall passenger, Ivgeny Karchovski, and the driver, Espy Jaxon, dropped to the ground and reached beneath the chassis for the semiautomatic handguns stashed there. They came up firing as the other guards tried to scatter, unsure whether to shoot back or worry about the sniper on the hill first. Two fell to Karchovski and Jaxon but the others got to cover and began returning fire, forcing the pair to retreat behind the truck.

Al-Sistani ran for a low wall, followed by two of his men. Jumping behind the wall, he cowered on the ground while shouting at his men to "attack the infidels!" One man stood and tried to rush the two men behind the truck but was cut down by a bullet that struck him in the stomach, causing him to double over, and a second to the head that finished him off.

Another of Al-Sistani's men, who'd gone inside the mosque with Huff, emerged on the balcony of the minaret above the grounds and began firing down into the courtyard. He was unaware of the sniper lying in the tall grass on the hill and paid for his ignorance with a round that caught him in the torso, spinning him violently around so that he lost his balance and fell screaming to the ground below.

In the meantime, outside the mosque, about the same time the sniper's first bullet was punching a hole in Raad, John Jojola, posing as an old man with a donkey, gave the rope a final tug while the two guards watched in confusion with cigarettes dangling from their open mouths. The firewood fell from the beast, revealing three AK-47 rifles that had been tied beneath the wood; the two young farmers, Daudov's fighters, grabbed them, tossing one to John Jojola.

Further confused by the sound of a rifle and the ensuing pandemonium that suddenly broke out inside the courtyard, the guards were slow in reacting. Then, realizing the danger, they tried to get to their rifles but were just fast enough to die with the weapons in their hands. Jojola and the other two then went through the gate, firing as they ran.

Raad had hardly hit the ground when Daudov jumped up and then reached for Lucy. "Can you run?" he asked.

"I don't think so, my legs . . . they're not working," Lucy replied. Kneeling had not done her any favors and she knew it would waste time to try. "I'll crawl. But leave me, get Al-Sistani!"

Daudov looked at her hard and then nodded. He dove for the gun that had fallen from Raad's hand and picked it up. Glancing back at her, he said, "Inshallah! Go with God!"

"Inshallah," she replied. "You, too. Thank you."

Lucy watched as the Chechen patriot began to race toward where Al-Sistani was cowering, behind a wall, while his men rallied around him. But bullets were digging into the dirt and skipping off walls around her, too, and she knew she had to move to reach safety. Painfully, she began to crawl toward the open door of the mosque, where a certain blue-robed saint stood in the shadows beckoning her.

Ned Blanchett slammed another cartridge home in the M24 and looked through the scope to watch as his fiancée crawled slowly toward the door of the mosque. He could see the puffs of dirt and plaster where bullets struck around her, and he was sure she would die. And yet, while it sometimes appeared as if she was moving through a swarm of bullets, none seemed to touch her. There was nothing more he could do for her but find another target and eliminate as much of the danger as he could.

Although he was terrified for her, it beat thinking he might never see her alive again. During the attack on the Zandaq compound in Chechnya, a mortar round had landed on the roof where he and a partner had set up their defensive position. The blast had thrown him off the roof, but as fate would have it, he landed in the branches of a tree and immediately lost consciousness.

Apparently Al-Sistani's men had not looked up when they were combing the compound grounds executing the wounded and rounding up prisoners. All Blanchett knew was that at some point later, just as the sky was lightening up to the east, he woke up to see the face of Lom Daudov hovering above him.

All in all, he'd been lucky. He'd broken a couple of ribs and had a concussion but all of his comrades were dead, "except for Lucy and Huff," Deshi Zakayev had explained. "But they are in the hands of the man who perpetrated the attack, Amir Al-Sistani."

In the days that followed, Blanchett had been on the run with Daudov, constantly moving from one place to another — a farmhouse here, a city apartment there, and once an abandoned mine shaft that had been converted into a hidden bunker. As pressure from the Russians heated up, apparently with the complicity of the U.S. government, there'd been grumbling among Daudov's men that Blanchett should be used as a pawn in negotiations, perhaps to exchange for separatist prisoners. But Daudov, in consultation with Zakayev, had refused.

He had also refused Blanchett's pleading to be allowed to try to rescue his fiancée. "You wouldn't make it ten miles," Daudov said. "Even if we suspect that Al-Sistani is in Dagestan with the hostages, we do not know where; and going to his camp would be like stepping on a beehive."

"I have to try," Blanchett begged, and looked knowingly at Zakayev. "Please, you would do the same."

Daudov followed his glance to the young woman. "You're not helping anyone if your plan has no possible ending but failure. But I will think on it," he said.

However, before Daudov reached a decision, Jaxon showed up with Karchovski, Jojola, two former U.S.-Special-Forces-turned-agents, and satellite imagery of a mosque and its surrounding compound near the city of Kasplysk in Dagestan. The reunion was short but emphatic.

They'd also brought a "surprise guest," Nadya Malovo. Daudov's eyes glittered with anger when he was introduced to the woman. "You've caused my people a lot of pain and suffering," he said. "Women, children, old men . . . you had no remorse for who would die in your evil plots."

Malovo said nothing. And if she was seen swallowing hard and a tinge of moisture showed in her eyes, it was thought to be fear and nothing else.

Jaxon had been right about the value Daudov would place on Malovo. "She will confess her crimes, and then the world will know the truth about Russian treachery and lies," he said. "The world will have to listen and act. We will have Chechnya for Chechens!"

Daudov was also a man of honor. He could have seized Malovo and left the American team to fend for themselves. But instead he agreed to help rescue Lucy and Huff.

"We couldn't bring a large team and overwhelm them with numbers," Jaxon explained when Blanchett asked where the "rest of the troops" were. "Dagestan is a member of the Russian Federation, and they're not going to like us 'invading' one of their states. So we have to get in and out before the Russians get involved, then let the diplomats and politicians blow hot air after they're home safe."

"Why not tell the Russians where they are and have them rescue the hostages?" Blanchett asked. "They have pros at this sort of thing."

Jaxon and Jojola had looked at each other before the team leader replied, "Let's just say we want the hostages to survive being rescued. We're not at all confident that would happen if the Russians go in." He'd explained briefly what was going on back in the States.

"Goddamned politicians," Blanchett exclaimed. "They're the real terrorists, or are at least aiding and abetting the enemy. I'd like to get them in my sights."

"I understand," Jaxon said. "But let's figure out how to save Lucy and Mr. Huff and get Al-Sistani in your sights first."

The problem was Al-Sistani's beehive. "According to the satellite imagery and our best guess, he's got anywhere from a dozen to two dozen men on the grounds at any one time," Jaxon said. "So charging the front gate is not a viable option."

"We need someone inside," Daudov agreed. "And then must rely on surprise and speed." The Chechen guerilla leader thought about it for a moment and then said he had a plan. "I will send one of my advisers, Bula

Umarov, to tell him that I want to negotiate a truce . . . that I will be willing to put myself and my Hands of God brigade at his command. He'll think that the Russians have finally forced me to join him."

"What if he decides to kill you," Jaxon replied. "You're his main rival."

Daudov shrugged. "He might," he said. "In fact, given time, I am sure of it. But it would at least get me in the compound."

"But you're one man," Blanchett said.

"Haven't you heard, I am the Lion of Chechnya," Daudov said with a laugh.

"I think you can sweeten the pot and, perhaps, even the odds a little more," Karchovski said.

"How is that?" Daudov asked as they all looked at the tall Russian.

"There is someone whom Al-Sistani would consider an even greater prize than you. Ajmaani. But for a different reason than yours," Karchovski explained. "You want to use her to prove the duplicity of my fellow countrymen and win freedom for your country. But Al-Sistani will want her to help him reach a man named Andrew Kane; a man who can access billions of dollars if he falls into his hands, which would go a long way toward funding jihad against the West."

"So I sweeten the pot by taking Ajmaani with me?" Daudov said with a smile.

"And, of course, two men necessary to escort such a dangerous prisoner," Karchovski said, pointing to himself and Jaxon. He then outlined how Jojola and Daudov's men would approach the mosque.

"I'm going into the compound, too," Blanchett demanded.

"You're more valuable performing your speciality," Karchovski replied. "Besides, this will be a complex operation; we need somebody who can see when everyone is in place and choose the moment to set the ball in motion." He pointed to a hill outside of the mosque on the satellite photograph. "This is where you'll set up. Then we will wait for your signal."

"What will that be?" Blanchett asked.

"The death of the first man you shoot," Karchovski replied.

"How will I know who to shoot first and when?"

"That, my young cowboy," Karchovski said, clapping him on the shoulder, "will be up to you and God."

After they'd agreed on the basics of the plan, Daudov had cautioned them, "I am not going to tell Bula Umarov our plan. Only that I wish to meet with Al-Sistani and offer my loyalty. I am not going to tell him about Ajmaani, or our rescue plan."

"Why not?" Jaxon asked.

Daudov glanced at Zakayev. "We have reason to believe that he is a traitor working for Al-Sistani, and perhaps the Russians, too."

"Then why trust him with even that part of the plan?" Jojola asked.

"Because Al-Sistani trusts him and would expect him to ferret out any secrets," Daudov said. "That's how Al-Sistani learned about David Huff's mission, as well as the mission of your people. It's also how he knew that I was supposed to be at the compound that night. Only a delay saved me from being there."

"What about Ajmaani . . . Malovo? What are we going to tell her?" Blanchett asked.

Karchovski thought about it for a moment. "It is difficult to pull wool over eyes of someone like her who is suspicious of all motives," he said. "But Jaxon can tell her that Daudov has agreed to trade her with Al-Sistani for the hostages in exchange for arms from the U.S. She may or may not see through it. I will also tell her that our young sniper friend here will keep her in his sights every step of the way and if she tries to escape, or even attempts to move in the direction of cover, he will shoot her before she can take a step."

Blanchett intended to keep Nadya Malovo in the crosshairs of his scope but decided that Al-Sistani would be his first target when everyone was in place. However, first Al-Sistani had moved so that the shot was blocked by the truck, then Daudov had stepped behind Lucy with a knife at her throat while Raad stood directly behind them.

Blanchett chose a new target. Praying that Daudov would get himself and Lucy out of the line of fire, his finger started to gently press the trigger. Lucy threw herself to the ground and Daudov landed on top of her. At that moment he shot and knew that his target, Al-Sistani's executioner, was as good as dead. He'd quickly worked the bolt, jammed another cartridge home, and sighted on what he'd already determined was the second target: the guard with his rifle pointed at Karchovski and Jaxon.

Blanchett then looked for Malovo, but she was nowhere to be seen in the chaos that erupted. He switched to Al-Sistani, but the terrorist dove over the wall as the 7.62 bullet took out a chunk of plaster where he'd been a moment before. A man had appeared on the minaret and died from the bullet intended for the other two. He then looked for Lucy and saw her crawling through the hail of gunfire as Daudov ran toward where Al-Sistani was cowering.

Lucy was on her own. All he could do was keep shooting.

Jaxon and Jojola saw Daudov racing toward Al-Sistani at about the same time. They began pouring bullets toward the position even as their comrades and Blanchett on the hill continued to engage the others. One of Jojola's accomplices was down and the other wounded, and a glance from Jaxon to Karchovski revealed that the Russian had been hit, though he continued to shoot and it was difficult to tell how badly he was hurt.

Heedless of the bullets that whizzed past him or struck the ground in front of and behind him, Daudov ran toward his archenemy, shooting with the handgun and brandishing Raad's knife in his other hand. One of Al-Sistani's bodyguards stood up and the two men fired simultaneously. A bullet grazed Daudov's cheek, another bullet caught the bodyguard in the throat. The wound threw Daudov off for a moment, and the second bodyguard might have killed him, but the big gun on the hill boomed and the man never got his shot off.

Then Daudov was over the wall where Al-Sistani crouched. The terrorist whimpered when he saw who was standing above him with a knife.

"I give up," Al-Sistani screamed. "I invoke Allah's mercy. You cannot kill an unarmed prisoner!"

With a snarl, Daudov reached down and yanked Al-Sistani to his feet. "I should not, you're right," he said, at which his prisoner relaxed. "But I will have to ask Allah's forgiveness." With that, the Chechen patriot plunged the blade deep into Al-Sistani, driving beneath his rib cage for the heart.

Al-Sistani squealed and wiggled like a stuck pig as his hands clutched at his executioner. His eyes widened in terror and blood gouted from his mouth, then he went limp and Daudov let him fall to the ground.

Only then did Daudov seem to realize that all the shooting had stopped. He looked around. None of Al-Sistani's men were left; they'd all fought to the death. Only the men from America and one of his own were still standing; Karchovski appeared to have been shot in the midsection and was being tended to by Jojola.

Jaxon ran up to him. "Where's Lucy?"

Daudov turned toward the mosque door.

"Inside, I think."

Lucy had reached the shadows just inside the door of the mosque when the apparition of St. Teresa vaporized and was replaced by the very real personage of Nadya Malovo. The assassin was pointing a gun at her. "Get up."

Slowly, painfully, Lucy stood and leaned against a wall. "What are you going to do if I can't?" she said.

"I need a hostage," Malovo said. "In fact, I need two." She tossed a staff used for a Muslim banner at Lucy. "Use this, or I will kill you instead."

Hardly waiting for Lucy, though she looked back from time to time and kept the gun on her, Malovo moved toward the back of the mosque. Suddenly, she stopped next to a door. Outside, the shooting seemed to be growing less; inside, they could hear voices.

"Go out and help Al-Sistani," a voice Lucy recognized as Bula Umarov's said.

"I refuse," a man answered. "I am going to escape out the back while there is still time."

"Oh, no, you don't," Umarov said. Then there was the sound of a shot, a man cried out, and something heavy hit the floor.

Malovo stepped through the door, which led to a small courtyard in the back of the mosque. The man everyone else knew as Bula Umarov stood with his back to her, his gun still trained on a jihadi lying on the ground. A frightened Deputy Chief of Mission David Huff stood to one side.

"Drop your weapon, Sergei," Malovo commanded.

The small pockmarked man straightened as if he'd been shocked and dropped his gun. He turned slowly, then smiled. "My old comrade from my KGB days, Nadya Malovo. I'm glad you made it this far."

"Sergei Nikitin," Malovo replied. "Time has not improved your looks or your memory. We both worked in the KGB, but you were no comrade of mine."

Nikitin shrugged. "Be that as it may, now I work for the Russian Federation secret police and I suggest we leave."

"Why?" Malovo asked.

He started to reach for his pocket, then hesitated when she pointed the gun. "May I show you something?"

"Go ahead."

The spy slowly reached in and pulled out a cell phone. "All I have to do is make a call and my bosses — your former bosses — will have a helicopter pick us up at a prearranged meeting place on the beach," he said. "I'm sure they would love to see you again. But we need to hurry."

"What's the rush?"

Umarov-Nikitin laughed. "You mean other than that, whichever side wins the battle outside, things might not go well for either of us?" he said. "Well, there's always the small transmitter I placed on the truck you rode into the compound."

"Transmitter? What kind of transmitter?" Malovo demanded.

Nikitin pointed to the sky and smiled. "A radar tracking device, courtesy of our new Russo-American alliance," he said. "I received it yesterday and was supposed to arm it when you and Daudov and the hostages were together with Al-Sistani. An American drone will be here any minute, and I suggest we be somewhere else. But first we need to shoot the hostages."

Malovo frowned. "Why?"

"Orders from the Kremlin," Nikitin said with a shrug. "Apparently the Americans don't want them back."

Malovo thought about what he said for a moment, then pointed the gun at Lucy. "Call the helicopter," she said.

Nikitin smiled and pressed a button on the telephone. "I'll be there in twenty minutes," he said. "And I'm bringing an extra passenger."

The spy hung up and pointed to the door leading out of the courtyard. "Shoot them and let's go."

"Sorry, there's been a change of plans," Malovo said, turning to point the gun at Nikitin.

"What? No!" Nikitin shouted, but his next words died in his mouth as the bullet smashed into his brain.

"Go," Malovo said to Lucy. "Take him with you."

"I don't understand," Lucy replied.

"What's not to understand? An American drone has been summoned. It will home in on the radar transmitter and reduce this place to rubble. Now run. Tell the others and save yourselves!"

"Come with us," Lucy said. "I'll tell everyone what you did. You can make a new life."

Malovo smiled. "For such a smart girl, you're really not very bright, are you," she said. A wistful look crossed her face. "There will be no new life for me. And if ever we meet again, or I run across that bastard of a father of yours, do not expect me to be merciful. NOW RUN!"

Huff walked up to Lucy and put his arm

around her shoulder. "Thank you," he said to Malovo.

The beautiful assassin sneered. "Today I did not feel like killing you, but don't press your luck," she said, then considered something. "But I'll be watching you. Do the right thing when you get back to the U.S. or someday you may wake up and find me standing in the shadows of your bedroom."

With that Malovo turned and bolted for the back gate. At the same time, Lucy and Huff hobbled to the front of the mosque, where they were met at the door by Daudov and Jaxon. "We have to leave," Lucy shouted. "A drone is coming to kill everyone here."

"What about Malovo?" Jaxon yelled.

"No time to explain. RUN!"

The three men and Lucy ran from the mosque, yelling for the others to pile into a black SUV — apparently Al-Sistani's ride. With Jaxon behind the wheel, the vehicle spun its tires and raced for the front gate.

As he lay dying next to the wall where he'd taken refuge, Al-Sistani was the first to be aware of the Predator. He heard the buzzing of its small motors high up in the overcast sky. He lifted a finger and traced its circular path above.

Those in the SUV had only made it

halfway up the hill when they heard the whoosh of the first Hellfire rocket. Then a second, third, and fourth. They stopped and looked back as the four explosions rocked the ground, and the mosque disappeared in a cloud of smoke, dust, and flame.

As the others were watching the destruction below, Lucy, who was sitting in the front passenger seat, turned her head to look up the hill. She recognized the sound of the sniper's gun and now the only thing she wanted in the world was to see the man who carried it.

As if by magic, Ned Blanchett rose from the tall, golden grasses that had concealed him and began to walk toward the car. Lucy was out in an instant, willing her legs to move toward him. He began to run and reached her just as she collapsed, picking her up in his arms and looking lovingly down into her eyes.

Lucy reached up and touched his face. "Why, hello there, Ned," she said. "What took you so long?"

21

Waiting in the dark, his wife clutching his hand on the seat next to him as she stared out the window of the Bell helicopter, Karp was reminded of the afternoon in Central Park when he got the call from Jaxon — "I need to see you, and Marlene, right away." How long had it been? Only a month? It seemed much longer and made worse by the lies, the cover-up, the murder of Sam Allen. The Al-Sistani video and the words ". . . the slaughter of these sheep . . ." had haunted his dreams.

With great effort he turned his mind from the image of his daughter with Raad's knife to her throat. Instead, he thought about the day Lucy was born and the mental images he had of her childhood. The precocious little girl who liked pink, dolls, and speaking Chinese and about fourteen other languages by the time she was in high school. He smiled. She had always marched to her own drummer, whether as a prepubescent polyglot or the deeply spiritual teenager who believed that she and her family were in the vanguard of some apocalyptic battle with evil, or the traumatized young woman who'd found love and security with a New Mexico ranch hand only to begin working with him for an antiterrorism agency. *All of it leading to this moment.*

Two hours earlier he'd received a similar telephone call from Jaxon. "I need to see you and Marlene, right away," his old friend had said again, only this time he added, "I think you've been looking forward to this moment for a while."

They hardly had enough time to put on their coats and extract a promise from Zak and Giancarlo to "just this once, please don't do anything requiring an ambulance, fire truck, or the police" before Marlene looked up at the security monitor above the door and announced the arrival of a dark sedan. They hurried into the elevator and down to where a clean-cut, square-jawed young man greeted them politely but quickly ushered them into the car.

The sedan took them to the heliport on the east end of 34th Street at the East River's edge, where they were escorted to a black helicopter waiting in the shadows with its blades already turning. As soon as they were buckled in, the helicopter took off with a lurch and flew into the night to what the pilot informed them was Vermont. They landed next to a small, private runway, where the pilot shut the engine down and said they'd be waiting for about a half hour.

After some initial small talk with the pilot and each other, Marlene grew quiet, looking out her window lost in thought. Karp did the same, staring off at the surrounding black silhouettes of leafless trees against a sky filled with stars. It had been a week since they got the call that Lucy had been rescued and would be home soon, slightly more than that since the grand jury had returned a murder indictment against Rod Fauhomme and Tucker Lindsey.

At the thought of the two defendants, Karp felt anger boil up inside him in a bitter stew. He recalled how he had imagined going with Fulton to arrest Fauhomme and Lindsey in Washington and fantasized about their resisting arrest and the satisfaction he'd get helping "subdue" them.

Revenge was an unusually dark thought for a man who for decades had witnessed the aftermath of the horrific deeds humans do to other humans, the carnage created by depraved men and women. Yet he had never given in to the natural desire for retribution and had insisted on the fair and just application of the law. Even when evil was visited upon his family in the past, he had compartmentalized the emotions of husband and father, putting them to the side so that he could do his job as the chief law enforcement officer of New York County. But vicious sociopaths and murderous terrorists had not evoked the loathing he felt for men in public office, and those who worked for them, who pretended to have the best interests of their countrymen at heart and yet were perfectly willing to sacrifice others like pawns on a chessboard if it suited their selfish purposes.

As anticipated, when news of the arrests got out he found himself caught in a Category Five media storm. The administration, flush with the election victory and aided by its flunkies in the press, had immediately gone into full attack mode. In the next day's news cycle he'd been roundly pilloried as a pawn of the opposition party, which, unable to "win the election fairly," was resorting to "dirty tricks" to thwart the president's agenda "and the will of the American people."

Released, despite Karp's protests, on personal recognizance by a judge known to be friendly toward the president's political party, Fauhomme stood on the steps of the Criminal Courts Building looking aggrieved and self-righteous while his attorney issued a statement. He'd labeled the charges "a partisan fantasy leveled by a politically ambitious district attorney. When the truth comes out regarding the death of General Allen, whom my client held in high esteem, Mr. Karp's incompetence and willful disregard for the truth will be self-evident."

Lindsey sneaked out of the jail the back way and didn't make any public appearances. But he was later defended by the president's spokesperson, Rosemary Hilb. She expressed the president's "full faith and confidence that Mr. Fauhomme and Mr. Lindsey will be cleared of these unfounded allegations and the district attorney's ill-advised and misinformed attempts to link the death of an American hero, General Sam Allen, to events in Chechnya will be shown to be false and politically motivated."

The media happily went along with the official line, asking few pointed questions of the administration or the defendants' attorneys while making no pretense of objectivity in their news stories. As was his habit, Karp remained silent in the face of the increasingly vitriolic attacks, including editorials in New York newspapers that suggested it was time for "new blood and a fresh perspective" in the District Attorney's Office. Not that he wasn't angry. But it wasn't the press that made him mad; not even the reasons behind Allen's murder, though he was disgusted and saddened. His feelings were more personal than that.

"Easy there, big fella," Marlene said softly, "you're going to crush my hand in that paw of yours."

"Oh, sorry, sweetheart," Karp replied with a smile, and released his grip.

Just then the runway lights snapped on and a few moments later, a small black jet landed and taxied over toward them. The aircraft had barely come to a stop in front of the helicopter before Marlene jumped down with a cry and ran across the tarmac. A door opened in the fuselage of the jet and a gangway was lowered; Lucy appeared at the top, saw her mother, and dashed down and into her arms.

Karp followed slowly to allow mother and daughter their moment. But then Lucy saw him and broke from Marlene to fold herself against his chest and the protection of his arms.

"Oh, Daddy, I am so happy to see you," she murmured.

"The feeling is mutual, baby," he replied, blinking back tears and then giving up and letting them roll down his cheeks.

Joined by Jaxon, Jojola, and Blanchett, the happy reunion continued on the helicopter's return flight, and, finally, in the loft where they talked into the wee hours. But they didn't discuss Chechnya or Dagestan. Instead, Karp waited for Lucy to come to him, which she did the next day at his office.

"So any idea where Nadya Malovo went?" he asked her after she finished her story.

Lucy shrugged. "I assume she caught that helicopter that Bula told her about; made up some story about him getting killed and a narrow escape. Whoever was pulling his strings in Russia was probably more than willing to make the trade for Nadya. But just in case she decided to do something else, Ivgeny stayed behind to work with Lom Daudov to try to find her."

Quiet for a moment, Lucy then shook her head. "I don't know why she didn't kill me and Huff. I didn't think she had a drop of mercy or kindness in her blood."

It was Karp's turn to shake his head. "I don't know either. She's a stone-cold killer and everything I know about her suggests that there's only one person she cares about and that's Nadya Malovo. But she didn't kill Moishe or Goldie when she had the chance and intended to in order to get at me; and now she let my daughter live. I hate to say it but I'm grateful. But David Grale said something to her before he let her go — not a threat so much, but that she might still be able to redeem her soul someday. Who knows, maybe his words got to her, but somehow I think we haven't seen the last of Nadya Malovo, and who knows how that will turn out when we do."

Although Lucy tried to maintain her composure through most of the "debriefing," several times she broke down and cried. "I'm so sorry, sweetheart," he said, his heart aching as only a father's can when his little girl is hurting. It had happened far too often to this particular little girl, but he'd never gotten used to life's occasional harsh treatment of her. "It must have been horrible."

"I had my moments," Lucy replied. She wiped at her eyes, and then placed her hand on his arm. "It could have been worse, but I wasn't alone." She then told him about St. Teresa's visitations.

As usual, he listened attentively but didn't know what to make of her experiences with the supernatural. When she first began talking about the saint as a child, they'd brought it up with psychologists, who for the most part had written the events off as just a version of an "invisible friend. Completely normal, nothing to worry about." As an adult, she'd claimed to have been warned or advised by the saint in times of extreme stress, and the therapists had attributed the "hallucinations" to her brain coping with the fear by providing a "protector."

Since childhood Lucy had insisted that the apparition was real, and he had to admit that there were some pretty difficult events to explain away. Such as St. Teresa "telling" her that the "executioner," Lom Daudov, was actually a friend and that she needed to do what he said. And who knew that Jojola would teach Daudov just enough Navajo, which he'd explained had two purposes: "So that only you and Lom would know what was being said and that whatever your physical or mental state — we didn't know what kind of shape you'd be in — you'd know that Daudov was a friend and that you needed to listen and obey immediately."

Karp was not one to participate in religious rituals, but was deeply spiritual and knew there was a lot more between heaven and earth that he didn't know than that he did. If there was a St. Teresa, and she was watching out for his daughter, he was simply going to be grateful and leave it at that.

After several days in New York, Lucy and Ned left for New Mexico. Marlene had gone with them, as had a special guest, Jenna Blair. Putting nothing past those in power who might try to silence the young woman, he and Fulton had been pondering where to stash her until the trial. That's when Lucy suggested the ranch outside Taos. "It's quiet and everybody minds their own business," she said.

When asked what she thought of the idea, Blair gratefully agreed. "I need some place to grieve where I'm not constantly in fear," she said. "A ranch in the Rocky Mountains sounds perfect."

A fan of cowboy movies and especially those starring John Wayne since his own childhood, Karp wished he could have spent a few months on a ranch as well. Instead, he had to deal with the fallout of the indictment against Fauhomme and Lindsey while continuing to build his case against them, as well as run an office of 350 ADAs, a team of NYPD detectives assigned to his office, and a support staff of a couple of hundred.

Almost all of the media accounts were slanted toward the defendants and the D.C. administration. Then two weeks after Lucy returned, Ariadne Stupenagel published a story based on an "exclusive" interview with the "unidentified female hostage" who'd been rescued along with Deputy Chief of Mission David Huff, who was "unavailable" to comment on the story. Her report threw fuel on the already raging rhetorical firestorm, but now some of the flames began to creep in the other direction.

Up to that point, the administration's official response to the rescue had been to take credit for the actions "of a top-secret anti-terrorism team whose bravery succeeded in rescuing the hostages while the president personally ordered a drone attack to assist the rescuers. International criminal Amir Al-Sistani was killed in the strike." Press Secretary Hilb had claimed that the administration had "all along been playing a game of cat-and-mouse with Al-Sistani to buy time for the rescuers to locate our people and carry out their mission."

However, she wouldn't comment on the identity of the female hostage, because only a very few people, such as Karp, knew who she was. Huff had been escorted to the U.S. embassy in Grozny, but Jaxon had spirited Lucy and his team out of Chechnya and even the former chief of mission only knew her first name and that she worked for some top-secret agency. But the administration wasn't about to admit that it didn't know who she was and was happy to let the media speculate that she might have been a Russian or even just a fake setup by Al-Sistani for propaganda purposes.

Very little jibed between Lucy's story and the official version. Not the timeline of events. Not the identity of the attackers. Not the presence of a drone during the attack. Not the ignored requests for help. Not the story of the hostages' rescue.

Stupenagel wrote in detail about Lucy's account of the attack on the compound. "We could hear the drone — Al-Sistani laughed about it after the attack. . . . Even if the messages didn't get through, and I know at least one did, mine, whoever was monitoring that drone knew what was happening and didn't try to help."

Yet, Stupenagel noted, when the drone strike on the mosque in Dagestan was ordered, "the administration could not possibly have known that the captives were safe, and in fact they barely escaped the explosions. It calls into question who the real targets were: Amir Al-Sistani and his Al Qaeda jihadists, and/or the American hostages. Was someone in the administration worried that the hostages might tell a different story about the attack on the mission?"

Those allegations alone would have set the administration back on its heels. But Stupenagel wasn't done. She reported the purpose of Huff's mission to clandestinely supply arms to insurgents in Syria through the Chechen separatist Lom Daudov, sending a seismic ripple through the international community.

Like a wounded beast, the administration lashed out savagely at Stupenagel's story as "a cornucopia of fabrications, specious accusations, and events taken out of context." Hilb told the press that she questioned whether Stupenagel had even talked to the unidentified female hostage and implied that she was taking advantage of the hostage's anonymity to "make up a story out of whole cloth."

Assistant Secretary of State Helene Vonu went on the Sunday morning talk shows and explained that "our understanding of the chronology of events was based on our best available information at the time. We have only just, upon the return and debriefing of Deputy Chief of Mission David Huff, learned that some minor details may need to be revised. However, the basic facts and timeline of events have not changed."

Vonu suggested that the account given by

the unidentified hostage was "misinformed, misguided, or misconstrued." She further intimated that it was possible the former hostage was suffering from "post–traumatic stress syndrome associated with her ordeal" and thus "confused." She privately confided to certain members of the press that "it's possible she wasn't American . . . though I can't say more than that at this time."

Going from one show to the next, Vonu danced around the facts like Ginger Rogers dancing around Fred Astaire. The assertion that a drone was present early on during the attack was "inaccurate," she said, "but it's the policy of this administration not to comment on our unmanned aerial vehicle program for national security reasons." For the same reason, she said, she could not address certain allegations regarding the strike that killed Al-Sistani "without revealing highly classified surveillance capabilities.

"However, rest assured the president was very aware of events in Dagestan as they transpired in real time. And, I might add, it is highly offensive to suggest that the president would needlessly risk American lives."

On another show, Vonu said the administration was "not aware" of any requests for assistance at the compound. Furthermore, attempts to identify the attackers as Al

Qaeda insurgents were "in error.

"The attackers were Chechen separatists working with Amir Al-Sistani, a freelance criminal, as evidenced by his attack on the New York Stock Exchange, whose only cause was his own quest for wealth and power. In order to lure Islamic extremists to his cause and increase his credibility, Al-Sistani may have claimed to be linked to Al Qaeda, but we do not believe he was actually part of the organization," she went on, while the journalist host of the program nodded sagely in agreement. "What the president said prior to election day was true then, and is true now. Al Qaeda is no longer a viable threat, thanks in large part to the president's unwavering war on terrorism in cooperation with our friends in the international community, especially Russia."

Most of the mainstream media spent their efforts attempting to discount Stupenagel's story rather than check it out. They did so by attacking the reporter personally, labeling her a "muckraker" and "yellow journalist" while challenging her use of an anonymous source, even though most of them did the same thing on a frequent basis.

One of the Sunday-morning talk show hosts even demanded that the hostage, "if she indeed said these things, step forward and confirm these unsubstantiated rumors being presented as a news story." The host of a Comedy Central show openly derided the story, complete with a laugh track, while childishly pronouncing the reporter's name as "Stupid-nagel." And the editorial page of the *Washington Post* noted that Stupenagel was "a longtime friend of District Attorney Karp and thus, valid or not, her motives are suspect."

However, the tide was changing. Slowly at first, beginning with a few of the media outlets traditionally opposed to the administration, and then the more independent-minded journalists, other news outlets began to pick up on Stupenagel's report and write stories of their own.

With the deft timing of a bullfighter, Stupenagel followed up on her first report the next week with the account of her conversation with Sam Allen at the White Horse Tavern. And she backed it up with an anonymous source "in the intelligence community with firsthand knowledge of the facts" who confirmed Allen's concerns, including that an armed drone had been on the scene in Chechnya within the first hour "of a three-hour firefight."

The source told Stupenagel that Fauhomme and Lindsey had watched the attack "in real time" and the order to stand down and not assist the defenders had come from them. "In fact, after the hostages' capture, an order was given to fire upon the trucks with the hostages," the source was quoted as saying. "Fortunately, contact with the drone was lost for a few minutes and by the time the Predator was back online, the targets had dispersed. The lost contact may not have been entirely accidental. There were a number of people unhappy with the situation and with the orders to fire on our own people."

As corroboration, the source let Stupenagel listen to a recording of what he said was the female hostage's call for help during the firefight. The source of the tape, a man she simply called "Augie," would not give her a copy. However, she reported, she was able to verify a transcript of the recording with the female hostage, which she then printed.

"This is codename Wallflower. We are at the compound near the town of Zandaq. We've been attacked and overrun. They're trying to get in the room. I don't think it will be much longer. They are not Chechen; they're speaking Arabic, several native Saudi speakers, a Yemeni, not sure of the others, but I repeat, they are not Chechen. I'm with David Huff. . . . They are here."

With the publication of the second story, even the administration's apologists had a hard time dismissing the allegations. The most ardent defenders still tried, including the majority whip in the Senate, who slammed the stories and the opposition's "obsession" with the events in Chechnya and Dagestan and accused the president's detractors of using the situation to avoid "progress on those issues that are of actual concern to the American public." But most of the president's former allies lay low.

In the meantime, the White House press office found itself deluged with a type of hard questioning that they weren't used to dealing with; and the talk show hosts were no longer as accommodating or friendly. Hilb began backpedaling while at the same time denying the allegations and accusing Stupenagel and her sources of lying.

However, Vonu, who seemed to be genuinely surprised that the talking points she'd been given were suspect, now said that while it was official policy not to discuss the drone program, she wanted to clarify something "in the interest of making sure the American public gets the whole truth." She then conceded that an aircraft had been on the scene earlier than originally thought. But she insisted that the drone "was not armed and was only a surveillance aircraft; by the time the drone operators were aware of what was happening, and asked for assistance from fighter jets based in Turkey, it was too late."

Asked by a reporter with the BBC News why the aircraft was on the scene at all, the embattled and flustered diplomat said the CIA drone was responding to "garbled messages" received from the compound by the embassy in Grozny.

When the reporter then pointed out that she'd earlier denied the existence of messages, Vonu said the administration had not been aware of any at the time. "We have since learned that these garbled messages were received."

The reporter pointed out that Wallflower's message "did not seem garbled." Vonu responded that "the message in question — the source and authenticity of which is still being verified — was not sent through 'official' channels . . . and arrived too late to affect the outcome at the compound. In trying to get to the bottom of these bits and pieces of information, we have determined that there may have been a breakdown in relaying that information from the agency to the administration, an oversight that is being addressed as we speak." She blamed the "inconsistencies" of the earlier reports coming out of the White House and State Department on "the fog of war and the exigencies of national security measures that protect all of us."

As criticism mounted, the administration went into full defensive posture. Hilb complained to her favorite *Los Angeles Times* reporter that Augie — "if he even exists" — was mistaken about Fauhomme and Lindsey watching the attack in real time. "It's my understanding that sometime after the attack, Mr. Lindsey received a recorded version from the CIA that was shown to Mr. Fauhomme so that he would be able to counsel the president in regard to his public response to the incident."

She also denied that any orders were given to fire upon the trucks bearing the hostages. "The drone operators were told to track the vehicles so that rescue operations could be initiated but lost them in the mountainous region. It's ludicrous to believe that the president's national security adviser or his campaign manager would order the deaths of American citizens. Just as it's ludicrous to believe that the president would give the order to fire in Dagestan if he didn't believe that the hostages were safe."

The fissures that had appeared in the

administration's cozy relationship with the media after Stupenagel's first story had widened considerably and did not recover. According to public opinion polls, the country was split on who they thought was telling the truth, and in New York the polls indicated a change in what people believed about the charges against Fauhomme and Lindsey: about a third believed that politics were at the root of the charge; a third did not; and another third weren't sure.

Still, it could have been worse for the administration and the defendants. Stupenagel did not write about Allen's affair with Jenna Blair, nor her own run-ins with Ray Baum at the White Horse Tavern and Loon Lake. She left the rumors about the affair to her colleagues to report and told Karp that she supposed that someday she would have to write about the subject, but for now she didn't want to make life more difficult for Allen's wife and sons.

"Besides, it's still just rumors to the rest of the media," she said. "I'm the only one who knows for sure."

However, omitting what she knew about the affair and Baum wasn't entirely due to her conscience. It was also part of a deal she had struck in exchange for her interview with Lucy, along with a little arm-twisting by Karp.

When he first talked to her up at Loon Lake after the shootings, he'd asked if she'd consider waiting to write about what happened. He'd been concerned about major evidentiary points appearing in her stories prior to the trial and tainting the jury pool. "I may also be calling you to the stand as a witness," he explained.

Like any journalist, Stupenagel had balked. "I want to write about the trial, not be in it," she complained. And she also didn't like holding back what she knew. "This is my story. If I don't stay on top of it, someone else will take it. I saw Baum in the White Horse Tavern. He tried to kill me, Marlene, and Jenna at Loon Lake, and Jenna says he's the guy she saw kill Sam. That's *my* story!"

However, after a heated discussion with Karp about "civic duty," and talking it over with Marlene and Lucy, she agreed to testify and limit her stories to the events in Chechnya and Dagestan . . . on one condition: Lucy had to give her an exclusive interview about everything, which his daughter had agreed to on the added condition that she not be identified.

Of course, the lawyers for Fauhomme and Lindsey were infuriated by Stupenagel's follow-up story and their inability to control the feeding frenzy of the media. They vociferously denounced the accounts as "bald-faced lies" and insisted that Karp had to be behind their publication in an attempt to taint the potential jury pool. They filed motions to change venue and to dismiss the indictment, alleging prosecutorial misconduct by denying the defendant a fair trial.

At the hearing, when asked by Karp to establish the factual basis for the motion to dismiss, the defense was bereft of anything tangible and simply resorted to their claim that Karp was politically motivated and was manipulating the system to unjustly accuse their clients. Judge Hart, who'd been appointed to the case, admonished the defense attorneys that without a factual basis to support their motion, it would be denied, and they would be precluded from mentioning it during the trial unless they made an offer of proof that would pass legal muster.

Hart also slapped a gag order on both parties and their agents. The defense attorneys had violated the order many times since, whenever it was to their advantage, for example by offering broad hints to a television talk-show host that "the prosecution's star witness, Jenna Blair, is no innocent young woman and will prove to be an embarrassment to Mr. Karp's plans." Asked to elaborate on that comment, they demurred, saying, "I don't want to try this case in the media, but let's just say that Mr. Karp has placed all of his eggs in the wrong basket. Our clients look forward to clearing their names when the truth comes out."

Two months after her first stories appeared, Stupenagel and her fiancé, Karp's office manager, Gilbert Murrow, met for a private dinner in the family loft on Crosby Street. Stupenagel was just back from her own clandestine trip to Chechnya, where she'd interviewed Lom Daudov for a story that was due out in a few days.

After Marlene's famous lasagna and a couple of bottles of Chianti, Karp asked Stupenagel who Augie was, but the reporter just laughed. "You've gotten enough cooperation out of me, Mr. District Attorney. I don't reveal my sources. But all kidding aside, in truth, I don't know who Augie is; I've only talked to him on the phone. I hope he'll come forward, but I could tell he was pretty worried just talking to me anonymously."

"Why do you think he sought you out?"

"He doesn't like what went on," she said. "I know he wrestled for a bit on whether sacrifices sometimes need to be made in the national interest, and whether this fell into that realm. But General Allen's death did it for him; he liked and respected the man."

"Does he know anything about the murder?" Karp asked.

Stupenagel shook her head. "He says no, but that he wouldn't put it past Fauhomme. He has a harder time believing that Lindsey was involved, though he certainly didn't like the man."

During Karp's trial preparation "Augie" did not reveal himself. Karp questioned whether he'd be able to introduce the events in Chechnya to a jury without a witness who could testify about them. Lucy was out; if convicted, the defendants would be able to assert personal bias on appeal and have a shot at getting another trial. He was resigned to going forward without the important link to a motive. Then, two months before the trial, he got an unexpected telephone call, but it wasn't from Augie.

22

"I've got bad news, it's about . . ." The aloof voice of his attorney, Celeste Faust, bored its way into his brain. Rod Fauhomme closed his eyes and rubbed his temples in agony. He sank back into the overstuffed leather chair that was one of two pieces of furniture in his living room and groaned. His head was pounding from a hangover and Faust's voice was only making it worse. He glanced at the note lying on the coffee table. *I hope they fry you, asshole . . .*

He groaned again. Bad news. Over the past eight months, it had seemed that bad was the only news he got. Now with two months to go before his trial, fate was still piling on.

It began with his arrest on the night he'd been celebrating as the high point of his career to date. The world was his oyster and the POTUS his pearl. Then a large black detective put him in handcuffs and stuck him in a police car next to Tucker Lindsey, who sat there blinking like an owl that had flown into a window thinking it could get to the other side. The NYPD detective, Clay Fulton, had gone back inside the condominium, and when he emerged and got into the car, he turned around and said, "Ever hear the phrase, 'Hell hath no fury like a woman scorned'? Well, that's nothing compared to a woman who's been kicked around by a fat asshole."

One night in the Tombs had been bad enough. At his arraignment the next morning, a friendly judge ignored the district attorney's request that he be denied bail and released him with the caveat that he reside in New York City. He breathed a sigh of relief at the judge's decision. He didn't think he could have handled another night in the jail. The rancid smell of urine, unwashed bodies, and disinfectant, as well as listening to yelling and screaming and insane laughter in the dark, had made for a sleepless night. Then there was the large Puerto Rican with the black facial tattoos in the cell next to his who kept looking at him, licking his lips and telling him, "You look like a pink *puerco*. You understand *puerco*? Is a pig . . . is a nice fat pig. And I'm going to have you for dinner, piggy."

With the inmate's oinking noises still echoing in his mind, Fauhomme walked out of the Tombs in the company of his lawyer, whom he let speak for him while he posed with what he thought of as noble resignation for the cameras. But the nightmare of the jail quickly faded in the sunshine, and he started smiling and joking with the media. "Mr. Karp is apparently hard up to find any real criminals in New York City," he said sarcastically. "Instead of doing his job here and protecting the good citizens of this beautiful city, which I might add voted overwhelmingly for the president, he's trying to point the finger in the direction of Washington, D.C., so you won't notice what a lousy job he's done in the Big Apple. Politics over ethics is standard operating procedure with Mr. Karp."

One of the president's closest political allies, a senator from a state in the Northeast, was waiting for him in a limousine at the curb. "Let me drive you home," the old man said, then looked pointedly at his attorney. "Alone."

At first he thought it was a nice gesture from the senator and, by proxy, the president — like giving a metaphorical finger to Karp and anybody else who thought he didn't have friends in *very* high places. But they hadn't driven five blocks before he got the first bitter taste of what was to come.

With a meaningful look, the senator told him that the president would continue to give him and Lindsey his "full faith and support. But for the sake of public perception, and I'm sure you understand this better than anyone, it would be better if there is no direct contact between you and the Oval Office. Okay?"

The senator didn't wait for an answer. "Now we've arranged for a great legal team headed up by a hotshot out of the Justice Department; her name is Celeste Faust, Berkeley law grad and all that, took a leave of absence just to help you out. She'll make short work of this clown Karp, and you'll have the resources of the federal government helping — on the QT, of course, but count on it. Otherwise, you need anything, anything at all, you call me; the president's got your back."

The comment about not contacting the White House stung, but he didn't let it show. Of course he understood the political necessity for the president to publicly distance himself, he told the senator with a false smile. The midterm campaigns would be heating up in a few months, and it was an important election cycle for the cause.

He didn't want to be a distraction.

That's what he said to the old man's face. But what was really going through his mind was that the president didn't need to send his lackey senator to warn him off, as if they didn't have a lot of history together and a common vision for the country. *If he'd called, I would have given him the advice myself until we get this cleared up in New York. But don't worry about it, Rod old boy, he won't forget that you're the one who got him elected.*

Nevertheless, when he got out of the limo that day at the condominium he leased for Connie Rae Lee, Fauhomme had a queasy feeling in his stomach. He wondered what "full faith and support" and "the president's got your back" would mean in a pinch. He felt suddenly vulnerable, and it didn't help his disposition when he walked in the door to an empty apartment.

He'd expected to see Connie, groveling and begging him to forgive her, but she was gone, and so were all the clothes, jewelry, furniture, and other gifts he'd bought her. It was a kick in the stomach, but he quickly pulled himself together. *So what if the rats are jumping ship,* he thought as he fixed himself a stiff scotch on ice, *nothing to worry about.*

Whether the senator liked it or not, the administration was tied to him, and Lindsey, *like fucking Siamese twins.* If he went down it would be confirming everything the president's opponents were saying about Chechnya and the White House's culpability. The president would surely face calls for his impeachment; some of his fiercest detractors might even try to implicate him in Allen's murder. The administration had no choice but to support Fauhomme and do everything possible to get him off the hook.

I was tired of that bitch, Connie, anyway. He fished the phone number of the blonde from the victory party out of his wallet. *They're all replaceable and only good for one thing. She'll be sorry she left.*

In the meantime, he had more important things to concentrate on. That night he started organizing his defense as if he were getting ready for another presidential campaign. During his first meeting with Faust the next day, he instructed her to go on the offensive with personal attacks on Karp and the witnesses.

"Hire a marketing team to get the word out; here are some numbers for people I've used in the past when I wanted press but didn't want it to come back to me and the president," he said. "And here's the cell number for a guy who can dig up anything you don't want to get your hands dirty with. I got plenty of dirt on Blair already. Now we're going to bury this fucker Karp."

Soon his guerilla marketing team, with the help of his friends in the press, on Capitol Hill, and even a couple of A-list Hollywood actors, were beating the "politics of hate" drum so hard that he wondered if they actually believed it. Using his words, they painted Karp as a political hack, desperate to make a big splash before the midterm elections and beholden to his party's national committee for keeping him in office "despite his dismal record."

The mainstream media obliged. One prominent newspaper columnist essentially ran word-for-word an essay Fauhomme wrote, but under his own byline, skewing the data Fauhomme's "new Ray Baum" — a clever former Army Intelligence goon named Bobby Raitz — had gathered on the New York DAO's track record so as to make it appear that Karp was "tough on minorities" but "willing to make sweetheart deals with wealthy white criminals."

Fauhomme's strategy was to ensure one of two outcomes. The first, preferred result was to cause such a public outcry that, along with a lot of pressure behind the scenes from the White House, it would lay the groundwork for a politically sympathetic judge to dismiss the indictment based upon insufficient and/or tainted evidence adduced before the grand jury. The second was to taint the jury pool; the same thing, of course, that his attorneys accused Karp of attempting.

Both strategies seemed to work well at first. A quick public opinion poll conducted by his marketing team three days after his arrest indicated that a significant percentage of New York County citizens believed that the charges against Fauhomme and Lindsey were "political in nature." The poll was immediately faxed and emailed to all the news outlets by the newly formed "New York Citizens for an Ethical District Attorney." Released in time for the Sunday talk shows, the poll also implied that those people questioned overwhelmingly believed that the charges were part of an orchestrated campaign by Karp's national party to link Allen's death to the events in Chechnya in such a way as to implicate the president in a scandal.

"It is dirty politics at its lowest level," the senator who picked Fauhomme up outside the Tombs said on one of the shows.

Fauhomme was pleased with the initial

results. And Karp made it easy by refusing to defend himself or his office. But then things started to go wrong, beginning with the publication of *the bitch* Ariadne Stupenagel's first story.

The administration had been rocked by the allegations and privately placed the blame on him. "You helped create this problem," the senator complained. "Make it go away."

"Wrong, Senator," Fauhomme corrected the old man. "I was cleaning up a mess that Lindsey and his gang of spooks created, apparently with White House approval. If people had taken care of their own business, we wouldn't be in this predicament."

"So how do we get out of it?"

"Deny, deny, deny, and at the same time hedge your bets — nothing set in stone, a lot of quotes about continuing to look into what occurred and adjusting as the facts are ascertained," Fauhomme replied. "But stress that the president was in control of the situation in Dagestan the whole time and that this female hostage couldn't possibly have known what was going on in the situation room at the White House. Obviously, this woman doesn't want to be identified; we can use that to imply that this story was made up or that she's suffering some sort of mental breakdown due to her ordeal. I don't know why the president of the United States hasn't yet found out who she is. Doesn't matter, throw it all against the wall and see what sticks. In the meantime, find out who the fuck she is, which agency she's working for, and come down hard on her. And, Senator, when in doubt, attack, always attack."

If it wasn't for the murder charge he faced, Fauhomme would have enjoyed directing the tactics from behind the scenes. Karp was the epitome of everything he despised — an honorable, highly capable, street-savvy, self-made man. One guided by ethics and principle, not self-interest, which Fauhomme saw as a weakness. A throwback who believed in American exceptionalism, the fair and just application of the rule of law, and the sanctity of the U.S. Constitution; all concepts to be ignored except when useful to achieve his ultimate goals of swinging the country as far left as it would go.

He'd been particularly proud of "a cornucopia of fabrications, specious accusations, and events taken out of context." And of the talking points he created for Vonu, making sure the talk show hosts got an early copy so they'd know how to steer the conversation.

460

However, there was an initial setback when Judge Charles Hart, Jr., was appointed to the case rather than a judge they'd been cultivating with the promise of an appointment to the federal bench. The chief administrative judge responsible for case assignments recognized the extreme media focus on the case and desperately wanted to avoid a courtroom circus. Judge Hart was the perfect choice.

Celeste Faust shrugged, but the wily, ringwise co-counsel, Bill Caulkin, winced at the news. "Hart's tough and fair," he said. "He demands courtroom decorum. He can't be bought. Not for money, not for a federal appointment. We're going to have to win this the hard way at trial, or not at all."

Then Stupenagel published her second story, this one with the anonymous source who pointed the finger directly at Fauhomme and Lindsey. Suddenly the events on the other side of the world had been linked to them, and if he had any doubts about how that affected his legal case, Faust let him know.

"It goes to motive," she said. "Karp doesn't have to prove motive; it's not a key element in a murder charge. But he knows that jurors expect to hear it, and he'd ignore that at his own peril. Prior to this, the indictment alleged that you and Lindsey acted in concert with Ray Baum to kill General Allen to prevent him from telling Congress about his objections to the White House version of the Chechnya situation. The motive there was to stop Allen from having a negative impact on the outcome of the presidential election. However, this story links you and Lindsey directly to what occurred in Chechnya, and with the cover-up, so now there's another motive — that you were also looking out for your own hides, as well as the president's re-election. So far he doesn't have anybody on his witness list who can testify about what happened, and we'd object anyway to the relevance of allowing any testimony about Chechnya. But a witness like that could be dangerous if Judge Hart allowed it."

Even with the tide turning, Fauhomme didn't panic. This one was going to be won in the trenches, and he was willing to get down and dirty. At a secret meeting with Hilb arranged by the senator, he directed her to start a campaign of pushing controversial social agenda issues to distract the press and the public. It had worked the previous November; he was sure it would work now.

So as the media scrutiny on Chechnya and

its relation to Allen's death grew more intense, at Fauhomme's direction the White House reacted by pressing as many hot-button topics as possible. Gun control. Same-sex marriage. Global warming. It didn't matter if any of the rhetoric actually resulted in any meaningful legislation or dialogue; the purpose was to divert attention.

The senator was pleased when the next polls showed that the public was losing interest in Chechnya. He called Fauhomme to congratulate him. Smiling when he hung up the phone, Fauhomme chuckled and went back to bed with the boozy blonde from the victory party. *Why so surprised?* he thought as he gazed at the plump, snoring figure of his new companion. Wasn't he the master of manipulating the masses? The king of sound-bite public persuasion? *I'm the goddamned man of the hour and they better never forget it!*

Stymied on the legal front, Fauhomme's strategy to make the issue of Chechnya and Dagestan go away to take the heat off the administration didn't work either. A lot of that had to do with Stupenagel and a few other journalists who were willing to do the hard work and weren't fooled by his smoke and mirrors, nor were they worried about their invitation to the next White House press dinner. They simply wouldn't let the story die.

Two months after her first stories, Stupenagel returned from her own clandestine trip to Chechnya to write a feature article on Lom Daudov. The story allowed the separatist leader to make his case for an independent "secular" Chechnya, as well as castigating the Russians for their transgressions. But what really hurt was his account of what happened in Chechnya from his vantage point watching the attack. "I kept waiting for the drone to fire its rockets," he was quoted as saying. "The men on the roofs were pinpointing the attackers' machine guns and mortars with laser targeting. But all the drone did was circle and watch for more than two hours. No rockets. No fighter jets. No help."

Backing up Lucy's story, his account of what transpired in Dagestan was also damning to the White House's claims to have been solely responsible for killing Al-Sistani and rescuing the hostages. And Stupenagel backed him up with more quotes from the anonymous female hostage, as well as an unidentified "member of the rescue party."

Daudov also asserted that he'd been contacted by the U.S. Department of State and the National Security Administration about meeting with Huff, not the other way around. "They were the ones who proposed the arms deal with Syrian rebels, using me as a conduit, in exchange for weapons to carry on our battle for independence. I have no particular interest in Syria, so it would make no sense for me to get involved in the internal affairs of another country's civil war; we have enough to deal with at home. I was prepared to listen and that is all."

The White House wasn't the only government surprised and angered by the story. Ever since the attack on the compound, the Russians had gone along with the administration's account. However, the Daudov story made them change their tune. They vehemently denied the separatist's allegations that the Russian secret police were behind faux terrorist attacks and had a spy working for them with Al Qaeda in Chechnya, But they also had to react to the "news" that the United States government was negotiating with one of the "enemy" leaders of an insurrection in order to arm those fighting against Russian ally President Assad in Syria. It occasioned a strongly worded statement at the United Nations from the Russian delegation regarding "blatant, criminal interference in the internal affairs of other nations" and a threat to discontinue talks on "issues of mutual concern."

Meanwhile in the White House press office, Rosemary Hilb scrambled to do damage control, with Fauhomme yanking her strings. At a hastily called press conference, she denied that the president had tried to take credit for killing Al-Sistani and freeing the hostages. "Although I will say that as commander-in-chief he is ultimately responsible for the actions of the heroic Americans who were on the ground. Of course, we can't talk about the details regarding the part that the unmanned aerial vehicle played, but any accusations that American lives were purposely targeted are patently false." She also said that Daudov was lying and that he'd initiated contact with "U.S. operatives" about the arms deal. "It would not have gone any further than listening to what he had to say," said Hilb, who described Daudov as "more pirate than patriot."

However, Stupenagel's report from Chechnya was not so easy to dismiss with clever wordplay. The Sunday *New York Times* published an in-depth piece looking at the chronology of events from the attack on the compound to the hostage rescue mission. That had led to a harsh opinion piece on the editorial page taking the president to task. "At one point, he even lied to the parents of David Huff and the Americans killed in the compound when he told them that they would get to the bottom of who committed this act of terrorism while tears streamed down his face and he hugged them. He already knew who was behind the murders and that Al Qaeda was involved. The act put on by the commander-in-chief was as morally repugnant as it was false."

The administration hadn't just taken hits from the press either. The congressional hearings had resumed with a whole new attitude. Not only was the opposition party no longer demoralized, they were energized and on the attack. Even some of the president's former allies on the subcommittee had distanced themselves by trying to appear as if they, too, were disturbed by the administration's official take on the events. They'd all been particularly hard on Helene Vonu when she appeared before the committee, hammering away at discrepancies in the White House version while she defended herself by saying she'd been given a set of talking points to read and that she wasn't responsible for the content. Concerned that she might be wavering, Fauhomme sent word through the senator that if she wanted the plum position as the U.S. representative at the United Nations, she needed to continue to stand her ground.

Yet for all of Fauhomme's machinations, within a few months of having won the election, the president's ratings in the polls had plummeted to an all-time low. There was even grumbling in some congressional offices about impeachment. Fauhomme knew that such an event was unlikely while the outcome of the trial was still in doubt; the president still had his powerful supporters in Congress, assets in the media, and the wealthy elite in the entertainment industry. However, even the suggestion that the president was in trouble staggered the administration's cachet.

Many foreign governments — former friend and foe alike — no longer took the president seriously and were obviously looking ahead at whoever would take his place. Various Al Qaeda factions in the Middle East and North Africa struck targets, particularly American, as if openly mocking the president's declaration of their demise. Eventually, Hilb had to concede that "despite the president's effort to eliminate the top echelon of Al Qaeda, small splinter groups operating autonomously but still calling themselves Al Qaeda are, perhaps, more prevalent than previously thought."

At the same time the weak economic recovery the president had touted during the election as "a sign that our policies are working" completely stalled as consumer confidence plunged with his poll ratings. In fact, his entire second-term domestic agenda went nowhere; no one was going to champion bills or speak out on behalf of causes connected to a lame-duck president.

Fauhomme felt the repercussions of the pressure on the president. The conversations with the senator were no longer cordial and were barely civil. Rosemary Hilb quit taking his advice and stopped taking his calls. Even his supposed friends in the media and on Capitol Hill weren't returning messages. There were moments of self-doubt that made his chest tighten before he could fix a drink and remind himself that he was smarter than all the rest. *This is just a temporary setback,* he'd tell himself as he took deep breaths between gulps of scotch.

Then more bad news was shoveled onto the mountain of crap he was already climbing when his attorney, Faust, called him one afternoon to let him know that Connie Rae Lee had stabbed him in the back. "Ms. Lee is now a prosecution witness," the attorney said in a clipped monotone. "We're waiting on the district attorney to provide us with a transcript of her interview, but I assume this is not going to be good news."

Fauhomme cursed and threw his cell phone across the room. He hadn't expected this. In fact, ever since his arrest he'd thought she'd come crawling back begging him for another chance. He'd even put off buying new furniture, believing that she would return with all of her belongings. When she didn't throw herself on his mercy, he'd tried calling her. She answered but said she didn't want to talk to him. "This is your last chance, bitch. Come back now or else. . . . And you better keep your mouth shut if you know what's good for you." The line went dead, and the next time he called, the number was disconnected. He asked a friend in the FBI to see if he could locate her, but the "friend" had been noncommittal, and later said he couldn't get involved.

The telephone call from Faust regarding Lee's betrayal filled him with fear and rage. *After all I did for her,* he thought that night as he drank himself into a stupor. *She was a nobody before I met her. Little whore.* He imagined strangling her or, perhaps, throwing her off the balcony. But while entertaining those fantasies, he also brooded over

470

the person he blamed for the nightmare his life had become. He hated Butch Karp and imagined how he'd get even someday when he was back in the driver's seat with the president.

Especially after Faust reported to him what Lee was saying. It was more incriminatory than he'd feared; apparently the bitch had been eavesdropping, as well as putting two and two together. He ordered Faust to try to interview her so that she could pass a message from him: All would be forgiven if she retracted her statement and then kept her mouth shut. If she didn't, there'd be hell to pay.

However, Connie had refused to be interviewed by the defense attorneys; they couldn't even locate her. So he ordered Bobby Raitz to find her. But as with his attempts to discover where the prosecution had squirreled away Jenna Blair, his man came up empty. Even the senator said that none of the president's moles inside the federal law enforcement agencies had been able to learn the woman's whereabouts.

Fauhomme realized that he was going to need to come up with a plausible story to deal with the evidence arrayed against him. He needed something that would explain it all away by putting the blame on others, as he'd done throughout his career. He'd thought of a plan, but was concerned to note that the administration was making more of an attempt to distance itself from him and Lindsey. He wondered if Faust had reported Lee's betrayal, as well as the other evidence stacking up against him, to the president.

One clear sign came when, a month before the trial, Hilb's statements to the press changed from "the politics of hate" to "letting the justice system we all believe in run its course." In the meantime, the press secretary was issuing "plausible deniability" defenses, such as noting that the president was not involved in the day-to-day running of his campaign, "having left that to his professional campaign manager." Nor could the president, she complained to a still sympathetic late-night television host, be expected to know if his own national security adviser had been "making unilateral plans and decisions without consulting the president."

Although the president continued to "hope for the best" with Fauhomme and Lindsey, Hilb said, he also realized that "in the zeal to do what they believed best in the interests of the American public, mistakes may have been made." However, she was quick to reject suggestions that the president had anything to do with the events in Chechnya, or knew anything about General Allen's concerns, while also denying that he was out of touch with his own team.

"If he has a fault," she said with a tear in her eye, "it's that he tends to view the character of those he trusts in a most favorable light. He's just too doggone loyal for his own good."

One day the senator sent a limousine to bring Fauhomme to a small restaurant at the north end of Manhattan. The place was deserted when he walked in; only the old man was there, sitting in the back while young men in dark suits and aviator sunglasses guarded the doors.

Over steaks and cocktails, the senator said he'd wanted to see Fauhomme "so that I could personally assure you that the . . . um . . . current strain on your relationship with the president is temporary, but necessary. *If* this all blows over, you'll be welcomed back with open arms, but until then the president is, of course, expecting you to keep him out of this as much as possible."

Angry, Fauhomme almost spilled his drink. "If? This sure the hell better blow over," he sputtered. "I think you know that if I go down, everybody's going down."

He'd expected the old man to back off and apologize. But instead the senator's watery eyes suddenly grew cold and hard.

"It's probably not a good idea to threaten the most powerful man in the world," the old man hissed. "Especially for somebody who may be headed to prison, which I'm told can be a very dangerous place."

It took a moment for Fauhomme to recover from the threat. But it was not the time to cower. "Look, you know me, I'm a team player, and if I have to fall on my sword, I'll do it," he said earnestly, but not meaning a word of it. He leaned forward. "I wasn't trying to threaten the president; I'm just talking about the reality if I get convicted. It won't be anything I do, but the shit will come back and hit the White House regardless. If you think nothing's getting done now, just wait to see what happens if the rats on the Hill decide to impeach him. That's what I meant by 'We're all in this together.'" His eyes locked on the old man's. "I can handle some of this, but the most powerful man in the world needs to get involved."

The senator's eyes narrowed. "How do you mean?"

Back at his apartment that night, Fauhomme got drunk, boiled over, and hit the blonde around before passing out. The next morning he woke up to find she was gone, leaving nothing but a note. "You'll be sorry you hit me. I hope they fry you, asshole. BTW, you fat fuck, you're lousy in bed."

Nursing his hangover, Fauhomme was still looking at the note when Faust called with the latest bad news. "Don't worry, we'll fight this . . . and I'm pretty sure we'll win," she assured him.

Fauhomme was not reassured. He was feeling trapped . . . cornered like a fox by hounds . . . only this hunting dog went by the name of Roger "Butch" Karp.

23

"Oyez, oyez, all those having business before Part 38, Supreme Court, New York County, draw near and ye shall be heard. The honorable Supreme Court Justice Charles Hart, Jr., presiding. Your Honor, case on trial is ready to proceed," said Chief Court Clerk Jim Farley.

As Farley called the courtroom to order, the jurist swept in, his black robe billowing behind him as he crossed the distance between the door that led to his robing room and the dais. Glancing at the prosecution and defense tables and then the gallery, he stepped up and took his seat.

Hart was a striking-looking man in his sixties — tall, with tan, chiseled facial features and a full head of wavy blond hair and just enough white at the temples to indicate that he didn't get the color out of a box. Without any preamble or greetings, Hart left everyone standing as he glared at Celeste Faust.

"I asked that the jury not be present for a moment while we have a little discussion, Ms. Faust," Hart said icily. "Did my eyes deceive me or did I read an article in today's *New York Times* in which you were quoted extensively about this case and yesterday's trial events?"

"Well, Your Honor . . ." the attractive young woman with the expensive haircut and tight-fitting designer clothes began to explain.

Hart didn't wait for the rest of her reply. "And have I not issued a gag order prohibiting either party making comments to the press?"

"Yes sir, but —"

"And have I not on several occasions already warned you about violating my order?"

"Your Honor, you have to understand," Faust pleaded, a tight half-smile on her face, her eyes flicking over to the prosecution table where Karp stood patiently. "In a trial of this nature — with its political implications and the DA's overreaching indictment, which was a de facto statement to the press — we are besieged, and I mean *besieged,* with questions from the media that, unanswered, would make it appear that the United States government, and our clients, have something to hide, which they do not. So it may be that in a moment of weakness — and I might add frustrated by the questionable tactics of the district attorney — I said more than I intended when a reporter interrupted my dinner last night in a public restaurant. I do feel that my comments did not reveal any new details and that it would have been rude for me to —"

"Miss Faust, I will not caution you again," Hart interrupted her and continued tersely. "If you persist in this conduct, I will find you in contempt. And if you believe that the district attorney is out of order, then make your objections in court, and I will rule on them. And so far, your batting average isn't very good in that regard. But am I clear about commenting to the press or any other form of media?"

Faust seemed about to reply, but then thought better of it. She ducked her chin and shook her head as if she'd been unfairly singled out but had decided to hold her tongue rather than risk the judge's unjust wrath. "Yes, Your Honor," she said sullenly.

"Good, then let that be the end of it," Hart said. But he wasn't done. He looked out into the gallery, where most of the seats from the second row on back were occupied by the media. "And it has been brought to my attention that some members of the Fourth Estate have been making efforts to contact members of this jury. You know better, and if I find out who among you is attempting to jeopardize this process through such endeavors, I will have that person thrown in the Tombs until the conclusion of this trial. As it is, I am half-inclined to judge you all guilty by association and limit media access to this courtroom to one pool reporter and one television camera. The rest of you would then have to vie with the general public for seats on a first-come, first-serve basis that have up to this point been reserved for credentialed media. So police yourselves or I'll do it for you. Am I understood?"

The media reacted like a classroom full of elementary school students. Some nodded innocently, wide-eyed, as if to imply that the infraction had been committed by someone else, "not me"; others ducked their heads and pretended to be working on notebooks or checking their fingernails for dirt. Nobody wanted to get kicked out of the "Trial of the Millennium" or have to rely on a pool reporter.

"I see we have an understanding," Hart said, then nodded at the court clerk. "If you'll be so kind as to show the jury in, Mr.

Farley, we can get started."

During the judge's scoldings, Karp kept his face expressionless. Inwardly, however, he was smiling. He'd practiced a number of times in front of Hart and considered him one of the best trial judges he'd ever had preside over one of his trials. The judge was Yale undergrad and a Yale Law School graduate. He'd worked in his family's white-shoe Wall Street law firm for a decade before accepting an appointment many years earlier to the bench of the New York State Supreme Court, which was the state's trial court. He was the sort of straightforward, unbiased, no-nonsense judge — a man known for his fairness and calming influence by attorneys on both sides of the aisle — that a trial of this nature desperately needed.

There'd been no surprises in the opening statements three days earlier. Karp had outlined the prosecution's case as minimally and logically as possible: simply put, that Fauhomme and Lindsey had acted in concert with Ray Baum to murder General Sam Allen because he was going to blow the whistle at the congressional hearings on the events in Chechnya. "And when we have finished presenting the evidence — when you have listened to the witnesses, when you have heard and seen all the evidence admitted into this trial — you will be convinced beyond any and all doubt that for the sake of ensuring the president's re-election, and to feed their own addiction to power and to cover up what they'd done, the defendants sitting before you today were willing to sacrifice the truth, our national security, and American lives, including that of General Sam Allen. And what's more, in their conceit, they thought they could get away with it. But ladies and gentlemen of this jury . . . you . . . won't . . . let them."

The defense had countered with an opening statement delivered by Lindsey's attorney, Bill Caulkin, a silver-haired, rheumy-eyed senior partner in a Madison Avenue law firm known for its connections to the current administration in Washington, D.C. He claimed that the prosecution's star witness, Jenna Blair, acting in concert with Connie Rae Lee and Ray Baum, had attempted to blackmail Allen over his sexual affair with Blair. "They threatened to go to his wife and the media, as they had threatened other rich and powerful men with whom Blair slept for money. You'll hear from one of those men, Ariel Shimon, from the witness stand."

However, Caulkin continued, when Allen

balked and threatened to go to the police, the trio decided he needed to die. "And so he was murdered by Baum in the little love nest the general shared frequently with the cold-blooded mistress of this sordid scheme, Jenna Blair, who morbidly watched him die on a webcam and had the nerve to record it all."

Blair, he said, had then conspired with another of the prosecution's witnesses, "a muckraking journalist named Ariadne Stupenagel who saw a big publishing payday," to silence Baum and place the blame on the defendants. "The plan nearly backfired when Baum got the drop on them. And wouldn't you know it, Marlene Ciampi, the wife of the district attorney, showed up in the nick of time to shoot Mr. Baum. . . . How very convenient."

Raising his eyebrows, the old man had started to walk toward the jurors with his hands in his pockets, but stopped and spun slowly to face Karp. "Then, blinded by the 'politics of hate,' the district attorney pulled some questionable maneuvers to entrap my client, Mr. Lindsey, who was attempting to apprehend Ms. Blair, a security risk due to her affair with General Allen and a suspect in his murder. You will hear a number of comments made by Mr. Lindsey at the time, but we ask you to consider whether the DA has chosen to misinterpret those comments, as well as take them out of context."

Caulkin turned his back on Karp and shrugged. "Why? Only Mr. Karp knows for sure. Just as only Mr. Karp knows why he chose to take the word of a prostitute over that of two men who have served their country, and the president, faithfully. I would put to you that the most likely answer is 'politics.' The president of this country, elected by a majority of his fellow citizens in a fair and honest vote, does not belong to the same party as Mr. Karp. Meanwhile, Mr. Fauhomme is the man who put the president in office, and Mr. Lindsey is one of his most trusted advisers. The uncertainty of events in Chechnya — including a routine disagreement on the interpretation of those events among colleagues — became a convenient straw-man motive. But as you will see and hear, it just doesn't make sense. What does make sense is that the murder of General Sam Allen was not some crazy conspiracy straight out of a Hollywood fantasy, but a rather run-of-the-mill blackmail scheme that turned into murder when the victim threatened to go to the police."

Caulkin smiled in a nice grandfatherly way as he walked over to the jury box and leaned on the rail. "My friends, there is an answer as to why the defendants are sitting at that table today, but it's not because they're guilty of murder. And at the conclusion of this trial, we will ask you to tell Mr. Karp that politics has no business in the justice system. General Allen deserves better than that; we all deserve better than that. And you will take a large step toward achieving that by returning a verdict of not guilty."

Karp sat listening impassively to Caulkin's opening statement and personal attack as if the old man was talking about someone other than himself. He knew that as the defense attorney talked, some members of the jury had glanced his way to see if he would react. Would he shake his head? Would he appear angry? Would he chuckle nervously? Instead, he made small notes on a yellow legal pad and waited, expressionless. If the defense wanted to make this about him, he could not have cared less.

In fact, it was already personal to him, even if he didn't let it show on his face. The two men sitting at the defense table weren't just murderers; they hadn't just conspired to kill General Allen, or even the men who died in Chechnya and Dagestan.

They tried to kill my daughter. The thought boiled up in his mind as it had since he heard the entire story of what had happened in Chechnya and Dagestan from his daughter and the man he would soon be calling to the stand. Up to that point he'd been focused on the concept that Allen had been murdered to keep him from testifying to Congress. But he had not discovered the truth about what had actually occurred in Chechnya and the betrayal of the Americans who died, or were taken hostage, there. Not until Lucy told him. Just as he had not realized the personal involvement of the defendants until he learned about "Augie"; up to that point, he thought they'd committed murder to protect the president. He hadn't realized it was also to protect themselves. For a moment he wanted nothing more than to walk over to the defense table and choke the life out of Fauhomme and Lindsey. But, of course, he remained seated, with a look of indifference on his face, as he listened to Caulkin question *his* integrity.

Of the two defense attorneys, he was more impressed with the old man. They'd sparred in the past and Caulkin was usually well-prepared and had one of those deep, resonant voices that played well with juries. He looked like a kindly old grandfather — and used that to good effect to portray himself as the most reasonable person in the courtroom, the jurors' friend, rather than the shrewd defense attorney he was. His opening statement had been well done, considering what he had to work with, and taken lightly it could be dangerous, in that jurors in the modern era were predisposed to think the worst of law enforcement. His assessment of the defense's alternate theory that Allen's murder was to cover up a blackmail ring's activities — in light of some of the evidence that would be presented — was the sort of reasoning that could easily persuade a credulous juror to hold out for a not guilty verdict. All it would take was one, and Caulkin was fishing for that one.

However, Faust had taken the lead in most of the cross-examination of the prosecution witnesses so far, and it was obvious that she considered her colleague to be an inferior litigator. Yet in Karp's experience dealing with former U.S. attorneys, he found that in general they were full of themselves without good cause. They always seemed to come from the big-name law schools where they were invariably tops in their class, but their real-world experience in a courtroom was sadly lacking. Whereas an assistant district attorney in New York County might have a caseload of between thirty-five and fifty cases to be disposed of by way of trial or plea, an assistant U.S. attorney would have one-tenth that number and had the luxury of spending six months chasing semicolons and commas and reading grand jury transcripts before making a command decision.

Celeste Faust fit the mold. As part of his pretrial homework, Karp had read the "scouting report" on her provided by Gilbert Murrow, his chief administrative assistant and a well-trained legal scholar. "Faust graduated magna cum laude from Bryn Mawr College and was law review at Berkeley Law. She went straight into the U.S. Attorney General's Office in Washington, D.C., where she quickly gained a reputation as a willing player in office politics — she's seen as a climber both socially and professionally, as well as openly partisan for the current administration."

In six years at the DOJ, she'd only gone to trial four times as the lead attorney, and a half-dozen times sitting second chair. "She's never lost a case," the report went on, "but my sources at the DOJ say they were all slam dunks, mostly drug and immigration cases. A lot of plea bargaining and dismissals. Although this is unconfirmed, it is also thought among her colleagues that she has written most of the administration's legal responses, including denying press Freedom of Information requests, regarding the events in Chechnya."

Murrow smirked and shook his head when Karp put the report down. "So much for that vaunted 'transparency.' The scuttlebutt is that she was asked by the AG himself to take a leave of absence to represent Fauhomme and that Fauhomme was told in no uncertain terms to can his other attorney and use her if he wanted help from the feds. If it's true, my take is Faust has marching orders to control the fallout on the president. 'Do what you can to get Fauhomme and Lindsey off the hook, but nothing comes back on the Big Man,' " Murrow commented.

After the opening statements, Karp called several technical witnesses, whose purpose was to familiarize the jury with the crime scene and try to take the jury out of the antiseptic courtroom setting and into the real world where Allen's murder and the Loon Lake shootings occurred. Consistent with this process, Karp first called DAO civil engineer Jack Farrell, who had marked in evidence his diagrams of the two major crime scenes. Thereafter, Karp called the NYPD police photographer who photographed those scenes. Then Karp called the first cops to arrive on the scene to further implant the images and accurately corroborate the crime scene photos and diagrams. Some only appeared for a few minutes, such as a representative from a telephone company who brought the documentation to back up his testimony that a call was placed on the night of the murder from the Casablanca Hotel on a cell phone belonging to Ray Baum to a cell phone registered to Rod Fauhomme. "The call lasted approximately three seconds." The initial parade of witnesses was concluded when Karp called the medical examiner to give testimony to the cause and manner of the deceased's death.

Then there were the witnesses who could place Ray Baum, "the man with the tattoo on his forearm," at the Casablanca and in Orvin, including the nosy woman in the hallway and Gertie Malcom, the librarian who, according to Constable Tom Spooner, was a "celebrity" at the Lucky Duck bar and grill. Detective Clay Fulton made a brief appearance to inform the jurors about his investigation, including what he'd been able to find out about Baum's background — the disgraced Marine who, along with his partner, was found with an NSA identification card on his body.

Now it was time to answer the question that, if it wasn't already in the jurors' minds from Caulkin's opening, now would be. And that was what could have possibly been so devastatingly important as to cause the two defendants — powerful, important men in positions of the highest authority — to plan and execute the murder of General Sam Allen.

When the jury had settled into their seats, Judge Hart greeted them and then turned to the prosecution table with a smile as though the morning had begun pleasantly enough. "Mr. Karp, are you ready to present your next witness?"

"Yes, Your Honor," Karp replied, as he turned to the door at the side of the courtroom that led to the witness waiting room and nodded at Detective Clay Fulton, who stood there anticipating his signal to escort the man in.

"The people call David Huff."

24

In spite of another stern look from Judge
Hart, the media in the gallery began buzzing like a faulty transformer when the
former deputy chief of mission for the U.S.
embassy in Grozny entered the courtroom.
They'd known for two weeks that the "surprise witness" was scheduled to testify for
the prosecution, but none of them knew for
sure what he was going to say.

However, Fauhomme, who sat at the
defense table looking only mildly interested
at the man's appearance, knew, because
he'd read Huff's interview with Karp. *Goddamn Lindsey for not pulling the trigger faster
on that drone in Dagestan, and goddamn Ray
Baum for not killing the girl and that bitch
Stupenagel. If it wasn't for them, I wouldn't
be sitting here sweating bullets.*

Fauhomme glanced back at the press in
the gallery with a half-smile on his face that
he thought exuded confidence. *Journalist*

scum. It wasn't so long ago they'd fallen all over themselves to be in his good graces. Laughed at his jokes. Begged to get invited to his parties. They happily ate, drank, and sometimes whored on his tab while fawning over what a great man he was, with such vision for the future of America. And then they wrote what he "suggested" they write.

Now they thought he was done. Washed up like a dead fish on the dirty shores of politics no matter what happened in the trial. The butt of late-night talk show host monologues and Facebook jokes. *They look like a bunch of vultures sitting on a fence waiting for something to die; perched there on the edge of their seats, talking in loud whispers that I can hear . . . laughing at me behind my back,* he thought. He winked at a television reporter who'd spent many a debauched weekend at his beach house; the reporter looked away, embarrassed to have been singled out.

Fauhomme turned back around to watch as Huff walked past him into the well of the courtroom. *Well, fuck them! I'm not going anywhere. Who the hell do they think they're dealing with? I'm the goddamned man of the hour.* He was suddenly so filled with contempt that he could barely conceal the sneer that threatened to take over his face and fought to maintain a look of mild disdain when Huff stopped in front of the witness stand to be sworn in. *I'll show them. I'm going to beat this and then we'll see who doesn't return phone calls. I'm taking names, and I'll be kicking ass again by the midterm election cycle.*

Still, when Huff climbed up on the stand, Fauhomme felt a chill run down his spine. A lot had transpired over the past eight months that had shaken his legendary arrogance.

Two months before the trial, Faust had assured him that it was going to be difficult for Karp to introduce evidence about the events in Chechnya and Dagestan without a witness appearing on the stand. "No testimony about Chechnya, no motive — at least not better than what we're saying really happened."

Then she'd called with the bad news: the man who could provide a motive for murder was going to testify. "Can't we stop him?" Fauhomme had asked as he felt a knot growing in his stomach.

"I think we can and we're going to try — both in front of Judge Hart and at the federal level," Faust said. "But we have to prepare just in case."

Faust had filed a motion at the trial court

level to prevent Huff from testifying on the grounds that his testimony would be solely collateral in nature and not relevant to any of the issues in the case. The U.S. Department of State filed an amicus/interveners motion supporting the defense motion and also asking the court to prohibit the testimony, alleging possible breach of national security.

In support of his opposition, Karp responded, with the jury out of the courtroom, by first arguing that the testimony was relevant since it established the motive for the murder. He further argued with respect to the alleged national security issue that there would not be sources or methods revealed by the testimony, only relevant, documented facts "about the government's and defendants' criminal manipulations and deceit regarding their fellow Americans and the deceased, General Sam Allen." To satisfy the court's inquiry, Karp supplied the court with the transcript of the proposed Huff testimony as an offer of proof.

Karp had, of course, not said anything about Huff to the press. And while the defense attorneys and State Department motions were being fought, the defense kept it quiet, too. But when Judge Hart denied their motions, Faust had "let it slip" to a member of the print media who'd been milling about in the hall outside of the courtroom that Huff was "known to be sympathetic to the opposition party and was angry over being turned down for an ambassador's post after returning from Dagestan."

When Judge Hart cited her for contempt, she complained within earshot of the press that Karp was "running roughshod" over the judiciary. She wondered aloud if her client could get a fair trial "anywhere Roger Karp is the district attorney."

Confronted by the reality of yet another defeat over Huff's testimony, Fauhomme felt panic rise in his throat like bile. He fought it by getting angry. *Fuck these people. And fuck falling on my sword,* he thought. They were supposed to make sure that Huff was stashed away someplace — *like fucking Yemen* — to keep him away from Karp, or give him whatever he wanted.

Faust told Fauhomme that Huff had been promised a good posting, maybe even one of the minor embassies that had already been promised to one of the president's friends, if he decided not to testify. "He knows he's done at State if he testifies for the prosecution," she said.

It didn't work. Not the promises or the threats. "We'll deal with it," Faust assured him again after they lost the motions to suppress his appearance. "There's nothing in his Q&A with Karp that names you or Lindsey." But Fauhomme wasn't convinced.

The morning he learned that Hart had agreed with Karp's motion to allow Huff's testimony, Fauhomme called the senator. "Do something," he'd demanded. But he was told there wasn't much the president could do except more character assassination.

That afternoon, Hilb expressed "the president's disappointment" in the decisions to allow Huff to testify, saying that it set a dangerous precedent. Hilb told press sources off the record that Huff was a disgruntled employee who'd wanted an ambassadorship following the events in Chechnya and Dagestan. "But he was not considered to be ambassador material. That did not sit well with him."

Assistant Secretary of State Helene Vonu again took to the Sunday morning talk shows. She now seemed subdued and defensive, but still she argued that Huff was "not aware of all of the facts" and hinted that he might also be suffering from post-traumatic shock.

Meanwhile, Fauhomme had called what few friends he could still count on in the media, mostly people he had some dirt on, and said he'd appreciate seeing a story about rumors that Huff had been promised an ambassadorship with the next opposition administration. Several "sources close to the State Department," who were in reality Fauhomme, were thus quoted as saying they'd heard Huff boasting at a department dinner welcoming him home that he had friends in high places who'd be taking care of him. "He's rumored to be in line for the post in Berlin, a plum position, if the opposition wins the next election," one newspaper reported.

When he'd done all the manipulating he could, Fauhomme took a deep breath and let it out. *It's going to be okay.* Hadn't he manipulated millions of people to vote for a sitting president with the economy in the toilet and his foreign policy falling apart? He'd certainly be able to manipulate at least one juror into believing he was innocent.

Of course, it had taken a man of his genius to come up with the defense theory that Blair, Lee, and Baum had been operating a blackmail scheme that had turned to murder. And that Stupenagel was an unscrupulous journalist willing to stoop to making up a story about meeting with Allen, and then turning a blind eye, in order to get a book deal.

If the events in Chechnya became a problem, he thought he could sacrifice Lindsey and plead ignorance regarding the activities of the national security adviser. In fact, a lot could be hung on his codefendant; he was the one who had talked to that idiot cop in Orvin, and he was the one recorded at the theater. He'd brought Blair's computer to his condominium, but there was no proof he knew what was on it; just that he'd been told by the NSA to "keep it safe." Lindsey would probably try to cast the blame on him, but who was a jury going to believe was calling the shots, a political operative, a mere campaign manager, or the president's chief security adviser?

Still, Fauhomme had not gotten as far as he had in life by ignoring the details. He would have liked it if Blair and Lee could have been made to "disappear permanently." But Baum had messed that up and his new man, Bobby Raitz, couldn't find them. However, Stupenagel was a "soft target." She hadn't given in to intimidation, but with her expected appearance after Huff and Spooner it was maybe time to eliminate the problem. *I'll have to have a little talk with Raitz.*

However, as Huff sat down in the witness

seat, Fauhomme glanced over at the prosecution table and his heart skipped a beat. Karp was staring at him. *Like he's sizing me up for a fucking coffin.*

The image didn't sit well and Fauhomme's smile faded. He looked down at the legal pad in front of him and picked up a pencil as if he'd suddenly thought of something important to make note of. Sweat beaded up on his fat forehead, his hand trembled, and his stomach knotted. He knew without turning to see that Karp was still watching him. *Get a grip, Rod. He can't touch you. You're the fucking man of the hour, goddammit!*

Having read the transcript of Huff's interview with Karp, his testimony contained no surprises. It was a devastating indictment of the administration's involvement in the Chechen fiasco: from his assertion that the State Department was well aware of an increase in Al Qaeda activity in the area — "It was part of the reason I was there" — to his clandestine efforts to get arms into the hands of Syrian insurgents and Chechen separatists — "The people this administration has been accusing instead of the real terrorists, Al-Sistani and Al Qaeda."

However, Fauhomme did his best to look

as if the testimony was all news to him and as if he was as shocked as everyone else when Huff recounted in vivid detail the battle for the compound. Listening raptly, he shook his head in horror as the diplomat depicted in words and tone what it was like to have brave men dying all around him as his radio operator desperately and futilely called for help. He was conscious that the eyes of the jurors and the spectators in the gallery went from Huff to him and back to Huff as the witness emotionally described the execution of former Navy SEAL Jason Gilbert in the courtyard while a drone buzzed overhead. "And did nothing."

There'd been a brief interlude when the jury was asked to step out of the courtroom while the lawyers argued in front of Judge Hart about Karp's plan to question Huff regarding his ordeal under Al-Sistani and his rescue in Dagestan. Faust had objected and demanded a hearing outside the presence of the jury.

"Your Honor, while we have disagreed with the court's allowing any of the testimony by this witness as irrelevant and inflammatory, the prosecution's theory is that General Allen was killed to prevent him from testifying in front of Congress and to prevent whatever perceived harm that would do to the president's campaign," Faust argued at the bench. "The events in Dagestan occurred well after General Allen's death. The prosecution is once again attempting to appeal to the jury's emotions rather than sticking with the relevant facts."

Judge Hart made a note on a pad he kept on his dais and then looked at Karp. "Mr. Karp?"

"Your Honor, we expect the witness to testify that during the rescue in Dagestan, a Russian double agent named Sergei Nikitin, also known as Bula Umarov, was able to summon an American unmanned aerial vehicle, a drone, to attack the area where the hostages were still in jeopardy. This same agent, Nikitin, was also in the compound pretending to be assisting the American delegation trying to negotiate with Chechen separatist Lom Daudov. The purpose of calling the drone was to kill the witnesses who would expose the White House's and defendants' lies and also protect the defendants from possible disclosure."

Judge Hart thought about it for a minute, but then ruled in favor of Karp. "Please limit yourself, Mr. Karp, to establishing this nexus between what happened regarding the drones and the U.S. government's involvement in these events."

"Yes, Your Honor," Karp had said, and waited for the jury to be recalled before continuing. The prosecutor had quickly led Huff through a series of questions about the rescue in Dagestan and the confrontation between the spy Umarov-Nikitin and some woman named Nadya Malovo. "What, if anything, occurred at that point?"

"Malovo shot Bula Umarov-slash-Nikitin and then told us to run," Huff said.

"Why did she tell you to run?"

"Because the Russian agent Bula Umarov-Nikitin had informed her that a U.S. drone had been contacted and would be attacking the mosque."

"Were you or the other hostage or your rescuers away from the mosque?"

"No. We were all still on the grounds. That's why Malovo said we needed to run. We told the others and got in a truck and had gone maybe a few hundred yards when the missiles struck the mosque."

"And what, if anything, did this indicate to you?"

"That Nadya Malovo was right: a Russian agent was in contact with an American drone operator and whoever the drone operator worked for went forward with the attack knowing that we were not safe."

Pretending to make notes on his legal pad,

Fauhomme kept his face down. Then Karp shifted gears. "Mr. Huff, since your rescue and return to the United States have you had the opportunity to review statements made by the administration regarding the events in Chechnya and Dagestan either to the media or otherwise disseminated?"

"Yes I have."

"Would you say that these reports and statements were accurate?"

"By and large . . . no."

"And would you say that by and large, on many of the major points, they contradict what you've just told the jury?"

"Yes."

"And how would you describe those contradictions?"

Huff shrugged his shoulders and looked over at the defense table. "They lied."

"Please explain."

"I am aware of reports, as well as internal memos within the State Department and with the White House, that have not been shared with the media, the public, or Congress. They're simply fabrications; the memos also indicate that the cover-up was necessary to keep the public misinformed, deluded that Al Qaeda was diminished and on the run."

Karp had walked over until he was standing in front of the defense table looking down on Fauhomme, who made it a point to look up at him as if he wasn't impressed with his opponent. But internally he quailed as the big man's gold-flecked gray eyes locked onto his.

"Mr. Huff, a few minutes ago you said that one of the reasons you were at the compound in Chechnya was an increase in Al Qaeda activity in the area," Karp went on without taking his eyes off Fauhomme.

"Yes."

"However, in the statements to the media, the public, and Congress, would you say that the spokespeople for the president, and the president himself, denied that Al Qaeda was involved in the attack . . . indeed, they denied that Al Qaeda as an effective terrorist organization continues to exist, am I right?"

"Yes."

"Were they being truthful?"

"No. They were not being truthful."

"What in your opinion would prompt them to lie about Al Qaeda being involved?"

This time it was Huff who looked over at Fauhomme and locked eyes. "Because the president had declared that Al Qaeda didn't exist."

"Do you know why that was important?"

"Objection," Faust cried out, rising to her feet. "The very nature of the question calls for the witness to speculate."

Taking his eyes off Fauhomme, Karp turned to the judge. "Quite the contrary, Mr. Huff will give us a firsthand, up-close and personal account of his insider's knowledge regarding these events."

"Objection overruled," Hart said, "you may proceed."

Karp turned back to Huff. "You may answer the question."

"The president was in the middle of an election campaign," Huff said. "Within the State Department it was known that his public ratings in regard to foreign policy were weak; so he declared that due to his leadership Al Qaeda was extinct."

"Was it true?"

"No, it wasn't."

"And in fact, you were at the compound in part because that was not true."

"Yes. Last summer, I was recalled to Washington to be briefed about an apparent increase in Al Qaeda activity in Chechnya and a plan being formulated to deal with it as well as the administration's desire to secretly arm Syrian rebels. The administration was concerned about the former because part of the president's campaign platform was based on having eliminated the threat posed by Al Qaeda. Others had raised the concern that arming Syrian rebels would be putting weapons in the hands of Al Qaeda; we had to find another way without directly involving this administration in an unofficial arms deal. So we worked through classified channels to reach out to Lom Daudov, a Chechen separatist leader of the Free Chechnya movement."

"And you knew that going in."

"Yes."

"And you found that out in a horribly personal way when you learned that the attackers were with Al Qaeda."

Huff had looked down for a moment and then nodded. "Yes, ironic, but yes."

Karp shifted gears again as he strolled over to the jury box and leaned back against the rail. "Mr. Huff, what, if anything, were you told by your superiors, or anyone else, regarding what you should or shouldn't say about your experiences in Chechnya and Dagestan?"

"Assistant Secretary of State Helene Vonu told me that I was not to talk to anyone about this."

"Anyone meaning who?"

"Everybody, but in particular the media, Congress . . . and you."

"And did you remain silent?"

"Until I called your office, yes."

"And what, if anything, has been the result of your coming forward to testify at this trial?"

"I've been placed on administrative leave," Huff replied.

"Mr. Huff, were you derelict in your duty in Chechnya?"

Huff shook his head. "Not as my bosses would have seen it, or as I saw it at the time. It's a messy world and sometimes you get dirty trying to clean it up. But with twenty-twenty hindsight, I wish I had questioned the wisdom of what we were trying to do and maybe stopped it."

"Just a couple more questions, your honor," Karp said, returning to his position at the jury rail. As he did, the disquiet Fauhomme felt deep in his gut made him nauseated. He was afraid, and fear made him hate even more. He wanted Karp dead.

"Mr. Huff," his antagonist asked, walking slowly to the witness stand. "What, if anything, were you offered by my office to testify here today?"

"Nothing. I'm here of my own free will."

"What, if anything, were you offered by anyone else if you declined to testify?"

"After I contacted you and gave a statement, I was called into Vonu's office again. She said that if I refused to testify, the Department of Justice would be able to keep me off the stand, and that if I co-operated with her, I could expect to be appointed as an ambassador in the near future."

"Ambassador," Karp repeated, sounding impressed. "Would that be something you'd want?"

"It's what I've been working toward my entire twenty-three-year career at State."

"And what, if anything, do you expect to happen now that you went ahead and testified?"

"Objection!" Faust argued. "Calls for speculation."

Karp shot back, "Quite astounding that the State Department sought to interfere with this trial. The witness has established predicate and laid a proper foundation with respect to the bribe offered by his bosses that he would have an ambassadorship if he declined to testify. So this is hardly speculative; to the contrary, it's downright direct and painfully pointed."

Judge Hart looked at Faust and said, "You will have the opportunity to deal with this in your case. Objection overruled, please proceed."

"I expect that I am finished at the State Department," Huff said.

Karp looked over at the jurors and kept his eyes on them when he asked, "So why did you agree to testify?"

Huff glanced briefly toward the gallery, and Fauhomme turned to see who he might have been looking at. But he found himself looking at a sea of hostile faces and turned back around.

"My conscience," Huff replied. "Brave men died trying to protect me and then to rescue me. I felt like I owed them more than my silence. And the American people who went to the polls last November believing a lie deserve to know the truth."

The silence that Karp allowed for the response to sink in seemed to last forever for Fauhomme. "Thank you, Mr. Huff. Your Honor, I have no further questions," the prosecutor said at last.

Faust stood up, and Fauhomme's spirits rose. She was the hotshot out of the Justice Department; so far she'd been beaten at every turn by Karp, but she'd assured Fauhomme it was all part of winning the war. She had told him before court that morning that she wasn't going to ask a lot of questions about what happened in Chechnya and Dagestan.

"Our contention in my summation will be that the events may or may not have happened as Huff will describe them, but in any event, they have nothing to do with you and Lindsey," she said. "The more we act like we're trying to make him out to be a liar, the more we look like we're being defensive and have something to hide. Act like you've never heard most of what he says."

Faust at first kept it short and sweet. She asked a few questions as if to understand the events herself, but then she stepped right in it. "Even if we were to accept your account of what occurred in Chechnya and Dagestan as accurate, do you have any evidence, any evidence whatsoever, that Mr. Fauhomme or Mr. Lindsey were responsible for these events?"

"Yes," Huff replied. Faust looked stunned, but before she could speak up the diplomat continued. "We, and by that I mean those of us in the State Department, were well aware that everything was being passed through the NSA and the president's campaign manager. We'd —"

"OBJECTION!" Faust almost screamed, before recovering her wits and addressing the judge in a normal tone. "Your Honor, I ask that the witness's statement be stricken

510

as unresponsive."

"How do you mean?" Hart asked.

"I was asking if he had any real evidence that our clients were linked to the events described by the witness other than that they worked for the administration, like thousands of other people do."

Hart raised an eyebrow and shook his head. "Ms. Faust, you opened the door to this and the witness walked right in. What we in the law profession regard as legally admissible evidence when we prepare our cases and consider what will be, or won't be, admitted according to the rules of evidence is not what a layperson considers 'evidence.' You may not like how he is responding to your question, but he is being directly responsive. You asked the witness if he had *any* evidence to link the defendants to the events he described, and he believes that he does. It will be up to the jury to decide if his testimony is persuasive. Your objection is overruled and the witness may continue with his answer."

Sitting at the defense table, Tucker Lindsey sighed and buried his face in his hands. Fauhomme battled to keep his expression neutral, but he was nearly overwhelmed by the desire to run to the bathroom and throw up.

"Mr. Huff, please continue," Hart said.

Huff nodded. "Before I returned to Chechnya, I was aware that nearly everything was passing through the national security adviser's office, which was to be expected, but also the president's campaign manager, Mr. Fauhomme. Since my return, I have seen memos from Mr. Fauhomme prior to the election directing others in the State Department to insist that Al Qaeda was not responsible for the attack on the compound, or my capture."

Fidgeting in the well of the courtroom while Huff spoke, Faust at first did not seem to realize that he had stopped. When she did, she quickly tried to attack. "Is it true, Mr. Huff, that upon your return you requested an appointment to a post as an ambassador?"

"It's true," Huff replied. "I've made that request several times over the past ten years."

"Is it true that you believed that after everything you went through, you were owed such a posting?"

Huff frowned. "I wouldn't say I was owed," he said. "But I do think I've worked hard to deserve such a post, and done my best and proved my integrity, including during my ordeal in Chechnya and Dagestan, though I was certainly not the only one."

Faust sneered. "Yes, that's right," she said, "there's this unidentified female hostage, this 'Wallflower' whom the district attorney has conjured up several times. Does she even exist?"

Huff looked at the attorney with disdain. "Does she exist? Yes, she exists." Huff paused, trying to keep his emotional grip. "She was a lot braver than I was. In fact," he said, visibly starting to tear up, "she was willing to sacrifice herself for me."

Faust didn't hesitate. "Yes, so we've heard," she said drily, "but not from her. And I don't see her anywhere on the district attorney's witness list. Why not?"

Huff shrugged. "I haven't asked."

"Who is she?"

"Again, all I know is that her first name is Lucy and she was an interpreter for a high-level counterterrorism team that happened to be at the compound when I was there."

"Mr. Karp, can you answer counsel's question as to this woman's existence?" Judge Hart inquired.

Karp stood and nodded reluctantly. "Yes, Your Honor. And I can make her available to the defense to call if they so wish. I did not include her on the witness list for reasons that will be obvious; her name is Lucy Karp and she's my daughter."

25

Sitting at the vanity of her apartment bathroom, Ariadne Stupenagel looked in the mirror and hesitated with her signature red lipstick next to her mouth. She knew how to apply a good foundation to hide the little lines around her eyes and lips; that the proper application of blush covered the tiny veins on her cheeks and nose, and a revolving account at Privé hair salon in the Soho Grand Hotel "kept the gray at bay."

Still, she knew what was beneath the hair color and makeup, just as she knew that under the formfitting blue dress she'd decided on for court, the underwire bra and support girdle belied the fact that gravity and time were taking their inevitable toll. "Ah, Sam, look what the years did to me," she muttered in a low voice.

"What was that, honey?"

Her fiancé, Gilbert Murrow, poked his head out from the walk-in closet, peering at her curiously through his round, John Lennon–style glasses. He was trying to grow a Vandyke, complete with soul patch, to look "more hip," but such transformations were generally beyond him, especially when he was also wearing his standard office attire, which featured a plaid vest, suspenders, and a bow tie.

"Nothing, baby, just talking to myself," she replied with a smile.

Gilbert looked as if he was about to say something, or was trying to think of what he should say under the circumstances, but then gave up and disappeared back into the closet. She bit her lip. Nerd or not, she loved him. Maybe more so because, while he sometimes fretted that his over-the-top girlfriend would wake up and discover he was, in his words, "a boring old pencil pusher in the District Attorney's Office," she'd never met a less pretentious or more intelligent man. She didn't think he was boring at all; he shared her love of early punk rock music, foreign films, seedy jazz clubs, and smoky blues bars. And what he lacked in experience in bed, he more than made up for in enthusiasm. However, she knew he was feeling a little insecure or confused about what he should be doing in regard to her grief over Sam Allen.

After the meeting at the White Horse Tavern, she'd gone home and told Gilbert what Sam had said about Chechnya and the upcoming congressional hearing. She'd left out the part about being former lovers. But whether he caught something in her voice or look, or he was so in tune with her, he guessed there was more than what she'd said. "How did you and Allen meet?" he'd asked quietly. He tried to sound offhand, but she knew he was steeling himself against yet another revelation about some former flame.

Ever since they met, Stupenagel had not tried to hide her hedonistic past from him. It would have been difficult anyway, because a couple of her conquests, including sybaritic assistant district attorney Ray Guma, worked in the DAO. When he'd declared his love for her, Gilbert said that he didn't care about her past; whether this was true or not, she'd still been upfront with him. But for some reason this time, the truth was reluctant to come out. "We were friends a long time ago."

"Friends?"

The question angered her, but she quickly realized that her reaction was probably because she was feeling guilty. She told him the truth. "We were lovers, but like I said it was a long, long time ago. He's been married for more than twenty years, and I haven't heard from him in at least that long. He came to me because I'm a journalist; there was nothing else to it."

Gilbert blinked, but then just nodded. "Okay. Um, it's always good to see an old friend . . . even if it's just business."

As usual, Stupenagel's heart melted whenever her "little man" tried to be brave and hide his jealousies. In fact, his insecurities were sort of a turn-on, which was what she was thinking when she wrapped her arms around him and looked down into his light-blue eyes. "It's just business, Murry Wurry. Sam and I were mostly friends who occasionally romped around in the hay, but you're the only man I want in my bed and in my life. Okay?"

Gilbert had winced. "Okay, but did you have to say 'romped around in the hay'? I've got a bad visual." Then they'd both laughed and gone to bed, where she'd done her best to allay any fears that he was not her one and only.

Well, except that one brief moment in mid-romp when you flashed back to Nairobi and the lean, hard body of Captain Allen, she thought as she faced herself in the mirror.

Three days later, everything changed.

She'd been writing a story about underage sex trafficking–related murders in Manhattan when she got the call from a friend who worked at the Casablanca: Sam Allen was dead. "I overheard the room service manager say it was suicide."

Stunned, she'd thanked her friend and hung up before bursting into tears. But as she regained her composure, Sam Allen's earnest face and voice took over.

"These aren't just any blackmailers. . . . I've been told in no uncertain terms to let it go until after the election. . . . If something were to happen to me, I'd want someone to look in on Jenna. . . . These are pretty nasty people, but they're counting on their scheme to keep me quiet . . . who knows, maybe I'll get run over by a bus on my way to the Capitol."

She scowled. His words weren't those of a man contemplating suicide. He was worried about what his family would be put through if the blackmailers made good on their threats, but mostly he was angry. She knew the man, even after twenty years; he'd been fighting mad, not one who was giving up.

Then her own response had come back at her sounding like prophecy. "I don't like it, Sam, anybody willing to blackmail the acting director of the CIA would probably stoop to just about anything." And so they had; they'd stooped to murder. She'd shoved her sorrow back into her heart and replaced it in her brain with fury and a lust for revenge. They weren't going to get away with it; not on the pages of her newspaper, and not with the justice system. She'd hurried out of the apartment, calling Marlene on the way, and then stormed into Karp's office, only to find that he was already on the trail of the killers.

On the way to Orvin that afternoon, she had not been able to shake the feeling that Sam had known what was coming. That's why he'd made sure to remind her about the cabin on Loon Lake and asked her to look after Jenna Blair. His prescience had saved the life of the woman he loved, though it had cost Stupenagel a bullet in the shoulder that still caused her a lot of pain. Typing with one hand while she healed, she'd transferred her anger into her stories and fought with her emotions to be a journalist, not the friend and ex-lover.

Still, sometimes, in the dark of night, with Gilbert gently snoring next to her, she would get up and wander out onto the apartment balcony to cry. She wept because a great man had been sacrificed for the evil desires of lesser men. She cried for Sam's wife and sons, and for Jenna Blair. Then she sobbed for a young journalist and a brave soldier who'd shared more than a bed . . . and for all the years that had passed since.

For eight months she'd alternated between tears and anger. Just the night before, she'd cried again. Thinking about what she expected to happen in the courtroom that morning, she relived the times she'd spent with Sam, then thought about how he had died and broke down. This time, however, Gilbert awoke and found her on the balcony. She expected him to fumble around in his insecurity for what to say, but he just came up and held her close. Then he took her by the hand and led her back to their bed. "Everything is going to be okay in the end, and if it's not okay . . ." he said as she lay her head on his shoulder and let her tears drip down onto his chest.

". . . it's not the end," she finished. They both loved the Brazilian poet Paulo Coelho and she found that particular line of his comforting as she drifted off to sleep. In the morning she'd awakened thankful for having loved and been loved by such fine men as Sam Allen and Gilbert Murrow.

Looking back at the mirror, Stupenagel scowled at herself. Sam Allen was in the grave, and she was worried about the fine line between just enough foundation and eyeliner, and trying not to look like an aging woman covering up the passage of time. She expertly applied the lipstick and used a tissue to blot the excess. Looking down at the perfect crimson image of her lips on the paper, she sighed, and then neatly folded it and placed it and the lipstick in her purse.

Standing, Stupenagel walked into the living room, where she saw that the morning's *New York Times* was still on the coffee table where she'd left it. Her eyes went to the main headline, FORMER HOSTAGE TELLS JURY WHITE HOUSE LIED ABOUT CHECHNYA, and the subhead below it, *DA admits female hostage his daughter.*

Although not allowed to attend the trial because she was a witness, Stupenagel had heard about the previous day's testimony from Marlene over a glass of wine at the Epistrophy wine bar on Mott Street in SoHo. A big day for the prosecution, and yet she knew that Huff's appearance on the stand almost didn't happen. Butch knew he was going to have difficulty getting the events overseas into evidence if he didn't have a witness to testify to them. He couldn't call Lucy to the stand, and the only person who knew the whole story — even more than Lucy — was David Huff. But he'd been unwilling to talk to Karp, or anybody else outside of his State Department bosses, after returning from Dagestan.

However, Lucy, knowing her father's predicament, asked Jaxon to get her a number for Huff, and she called from the ranch in Taos. "He didn't want to get involved," Marlene told Stupenagel. "But she got pissed and reminded him that people had died protecting him, and that maybe they deserved more than his silence. He thought about it for a day, then called her back and said to give Butch his cell number."

So her husband called the diplomat and asked if he'd agree to be interviewed. "He still wasn't sure," Marlene recalled. "He told Butch that testifying would finish him at the State Department. It's an old boys' club and he told Butch it doesn't matter who's in the White House, you don't throw the boss under the bus. Apparently, the department has a lot of different factions in it and there's an unwritten rule that 'if you don't support my guy when he gets into trouble now, I'm sure as hell not going to support your guy later.' Huff told Butch that if he cooperated he would be breaking that rule and get kicked out of the club."

After court recessed for the day, the media

descended on the beleaguered White House, demanding a response to Huff's allegations. Rosemary Hilb had wearily denied that the president was aware of the events in Chechnya as they transpired, but she conceded that "we may not have been told everything, or been given an accurate account." She said there would be no further word until after the trial. "The president doesn't want to compromise the defendants' rights to a fair trial or the district attorney's duty to seek justice. The president's prayers are with General Allen's family and friends, the jurors, and of course the American people."

So much was made of Huff's testimony in the press, including gloating analyses of what it would mean to the already reeling administration, that the media hardly took notice of the last prosecution witness of the day, Constable Tom Spooner. The *Times* only published a related sidebar story about his testimony on an inside page, but Stupenagel knew that the actual case against Fauhomme and Lindsey relied as much on what he had to say as it did on Huff.

It just wasn't as easy to see what Karp was setting up with Spooner as it was to seize on Huff's dramatic allegations as the story of the day. Unless you were Ariadne Stupenagel and had watched Karp operate in his methodical, precise way dozens of times before.

According to what she gathered from both Marlene and the newspaper account, Spooner had begun his testimony by relating how two women had arrived in the town of Orvin, where he was constable. "They said they were looking for Sam Allen's cabin. My wife recognized one of them, Miss Stupenagel, as a former girlfriend of the general. They seemed nice enough so I pointed them in the right direction."

Marlene said that at that point her husband had turned to face her in the gallery and pointed. "Was the other woman my wife, Marlene Ciampi, who is sitting in the back row to my right? Hold your hand up if you would please, Marlene."

"Butch told me he was going to do that," Marlene said over the second glass of a Hess Select Cabernet Sauvignon. "One way or the other the defense will be making a big deal out of my part in this, so he's beating them to the punch to show he has nothing to hide. So I raised my hand and Tom said, 'Yep, that's Marlene.'"

Spooner went on to talk about the appearance of two men claiming to be federal agents. "One of them bamboozled our town librarian and resident busybody, Gertie

Malcom, into believing they were legit," he testified. "I saw her down at our local watering hole, the Lucky Duck, where she was telling everybody who'd listen about the 'hunk with the Marine Corps tattoo' who'd been flirting with her. I wasn't paying much attention until I heard her say that they'd showed her a photograph of a young woman who she'd seen down at the library earlier that day using the internet. And then she told them the girl might be staying out at Sam Allen's place on Loon Lake."

Marlene shook her head, thinking about what might have happened. "Talk about providence. He said that's when he got a bad feeling and was driving to Loon Lake when he saw me parked on the side of the road. Otherwise, I wouldn't have been back to the cabin in time. My best friend would be dead, and those bastards would have gotten away with killing a lot of good men, Sam Allen included."

As dramatic as the Loon Lake events were, it was Spooner's recorded conversation with Lindsey after the shootings that had been the most damaging. "Just identifying Ray Baum as one of his men was incriminating," Marlene said. "But he also asked about Jenna Blair's computer and told Tom that it contained classified information that no one was to view, which shows that he was aware of what it contained. Butch will have to put it all together for the jury during summations but it was pretty damaging to the defense."

At the end of the evening, the two women had toasted to friendship. "And to love," Stupenagel had added with tears in her eyes. Then she'd gone home and ravaged Gilbert Murrow until he'd sued for mercy and fallen into an exhausted sleep. She was surprised when he recovered enough to come find her crying on the balcony.

She walked over to peer out the apartment window at the sidewalk below. *This trial is far from over, and there are a lot of dots that have to be linked. The defense has its own version of what happened. Bullshit, of course, but in some ways to a gullible juror it could sound plausible.* She mentally shrugged; it was up to Karp to connect the dots; she was just one of many.

"Is he out there?"

For the second time that morning, Gilbert's voice startled her as he walked up and put an arm around her waist. Letting out a deep breath, she leaned against her fiancé. "No, I haven't seen him since the evening before last, when I tried to catch him."

"Him" was a young man, clean-cut and muscular, who had appeared in their Village neighborhood around the time the trial started. They first noticed him loitering across the street, occasionally looking up in what seemed to be solely the direction of the fourth-floor loft of the small walkup they'd moved into a year before. There was nothing extraordinary, or sinister, about the way he looked. He wasn't dressed like a bum or a street drug dealer, nor was he in a suit; just jeans and T-shirt, sometimes a ball-cap. Nothing to draw attention to himself among all the other pedestrians who walked past their building every day and night, except that he was obviously watching and didn't care if they saw him. And that was unnerving.

After writing her stories about the events in Chechnya and Dagestan, Stupenagel received dozens of death threats on her office phone and work email. Some had obviously come from partisan apologists who believed that the president could do no wrong no matter what the evidence said. She figured they were just blowing off steam and their threats were for the most part empty. She and Murrow invested in a state-of-the-art security system, and she carried an electric stun device capable of dropping a bull, much less a man, to the ground like a twitching bag of goo.

But some of the threats had a different tone and feel to them. The callers or writers didn't try to explain why they were angry or felt she needed to be taught the error of her ways with ham-handed intimidation. They were simple warnings: to "keep your mouth shut," "find a reason not to testify . . . leave the country if you want to stay alive," or, "I'm watching you, bitch." Even then she wasn't too worried until she received several similar messages on her private cell phone. She only gave that number to maybe a half-dozen close friends, and they knew not to give it out.

When Gilbert, who could be a bit naïve, wondered aloud how the caller got her number, she'd rolled her eyes. "Who do you think has the power to get into phone records?" she said.

Wide-eyed, he'd nodded. "The government."

Then, right around the time jury selection for the trial began, the young man appeared. She told Marlene about it, who then told Butch, who'd sent Detective Clay Fulton to look into it. The detective thought it was worrisome enough that he suggested posting an officer on the block, but the watcher seemed to know better than to show up. Thinking he might have been scared off, the officer had been withdrawn, only for the stalker to start appearing again. Fulton had actually then tried to catch him, but again he seemed to stay one step ahead.

When no one else but her and Gilbert had seen the young man, Stupenagel started to worry that Fulton and his men thought she was just being paranoid and assigning evil intent to passersby. So she stopped reporting sightings.

Then the evening before last, she went out on the balcony and happened to look down and there he was, standing under a streetlight, staring back up at her. He didn't turn his face as if he'd been caught. Instead, he slowly raised his right hand and made a shooting motion, then turned and walked away.

Enraged to have been threatened in her own neighborhood, Stupenagel had rushed from her apartment, down four flights of stairs, and out onto the street to confront the man with the stun device in her hand. He'd disappeared, so she ran in the direction she last saw him and rounded a corner just in time to see a black sedan pulling away from the curb. "I didn't catch the license number," she later told Gilbert, "but

I'm sure it was a government plate."

"Well, maybe he's given up now that you're going to testify this morning," Gilbert said hopefully.

Stupenagel nodded. "Yeah, you're probably right. But there is one thing from last night . . . it was probably nothing . . ."

"What was nothing?"

"Well, when I was out here . . ."

". . . crying . . ."

"Yes, crying. Or I had stopped and was catching my breath, when I thought I heard some scuffling in the shadows across the street. I was worried that he was back and getting ready to come do something to us. But then the noise stopped as suddenly as it started."

"Did you see anything?"

Stupenagel looked troubled as she thought about it. "Nothing I can be sure of . . . just shadows within shadows. But you know what the funny part is? Seeing that guy had me twisted in knots. But after the noises stopped, the fear was gone. I don't know why, but I'd forgotten about it by the time you got up."

Gilbert turned to kiss her and then pointed out the window. "Looks like our cab is here. Are you ready?"

"Ready as I'll ever be," she said, and then

smiled. "As long as I'm with you, I'm ready for anything."

They had started to walk toward the door when she stopped and began digging in her purse. "I almost forgot," she said. "I made this for you this morning." She handed him the tissue with the bright red imprint of her lips on it.

Gilbert held it carefully, as if examining a delicate piece of art. "You know you've given me about a hundred of these," he said with a chuckle.

Stupenagel laughed but then pouted. "Are you saying you're tired of my little lipstick love messages?"

The little man with the scraggly Vandyke, wearing a nerdish vest and bow tie and peering out of owlish glasses, shook his head. "I have every single one you ever gave me. I keep them safe in a shoebox," he said. "Does that answer your question?"

The tough, brassy journalist reached out to touch his face tenderly. "If I didn't have a date with your boss, I'd drag you back into bed and devour you, Gilbert Murrow!"

Gilbert pushed his glasses up on his nose and grinned. "There's always tonight, my love. There will always be tonight."

26

"So, Miss Stupenagel, did anyone else hear this *alleged* conversation between you and General Allen at the White Horse Tavern?"

Celeste Faust paused in front of the witness stand with her arms crossed as she stared up at the reporter. Trying to recover from her embarrassment of the previous day, she was asking her questions as if she was shooting them at the witness, intending to do harm.

"No. As I told Mr. Karp, we were sitting alone in a booth at the back of the bar; no one else was around us," Stupenagel replied evenly.

"Did anyone see you together?"

Karp's direct examination of the journalist had taken up most of the morning, and Faust had wanted to break for lunch early before beginning her cross-examination. But Judge Hart was always one to keep a trial moving. *"We have an obligation to the jurors to waste as little of their time as possible,"* he said when he called the attorneys to a sidebar at the bench to inform them of his intent to push on and break for lunch at the normal time.

Faust had taken it like she took all other setbacks in the trial, large and small, with a sour look and muttering under her breath. But now, knowing better than to irk Hart, she'd saved her resentment and impatience for Stupenagel.

"I don't know. I'd assume their guy, Ray Baum, did," Stupenagel replied, pointing at the defense table. "Obviously, he was following Sam Allen."

"Or was he one of your fellow conspirators, watching your back while you delivered the blackmail ultimatum to General Allen?" Faust countered with a sneer.

"If you have any proof of that, I hope you're going to be able to show it to the jury," Stupenagel retorted icily. "If not, you're just trying to blow smoke up their —"

"Objection!" Karp interrupted while rising and raising his hand.

Hart raised his eyebrows with an amused look on his face. "To what are you objecting, Mr. Karp, the defense attorney's question or the witness's anticipated . . . um . . .

colorful rejoinder?"

Karp laughed, as did most everyone else in the courtroom, including Stupenagel, Lindsey's lawyer, Bill Caulkin, and the jurors, though not Faust or Fauhomme, whose face had turned crimson when Stupenagel pointed at him. "Both, Your Honor," Karp replied to more laughs.

"Well then, as for Ms. Stupenagel's near-utterance, you objected in the proverbial nick of time, so no harm, no foul, eh? Therefore that objection is denied on the grounds that it is moot," Hart replied. "In regard to your objection to Ms. Faust's question, please proceed."

Stupenagel began that morning when she entered the courtroom wearing a blue dress. The direct examination had followed the script as she struck just the right balance between the former lover who had lost a dear friend and the hard-nosed investigative reporter. Recounting her meeting with Allen in the White Horse Tavern, there were tears when she talked about how they'd met and there were stone-cold responses as she testified about what he'd told her regarding the situation in Chechnya and the blackmail threats to keep him in line.

The same emotional roller-coaster had accompanied her account of the events at

Loon Lake. Anger, fear, and even a little grim satisfaction as Ray Baum and his partner died in a shoot-out on a dark night in upstate New York alternated with the journalist's objective recounting of events.

As she told her part in the story, Karp could tell from looking at the jurors' faces that the narrative was taking shape in their minds. They could see how Gertie Malcom's visit from "the handsome man with the Marine Corps tattoo" fit with the testimony of Huff, Spooner, and Stupenagel. However, the journalist's testimony about her personal involvement in the case was new. Not just for the jurors, some of whom had admitted at jury selection to having read her newspaper accounts, but for the members of the media in the gallery, who listened with their jaws dropping when she talked about hitting Baum with a shovel.

Like an author polishing his manuscript as he went, Karp filled in details around the main story line of his major characters. At one point he'd submitted old photographs Stupenagel gave him of her and Allen together with their arms around each other in Nairobi and Nicaragua. The defense had objected to the photographs as "irrelevant," but he'd insisted that they corroborated her testimony about the nature and length of their relationship, and Hart had agreed to admit them.

Ramping up the drama, and to give the jurors a visual impression they wouldn't soon forget, Karp had asked Stupenagel to step down from the witness stand and walk over to stand in front of the jurors. There he requested that she lower the right strap of her blue dress and show them the pink and puckered scar where Baum's bullet had entered the front of her shoulder three inches from the joint; then he asked her to turn around and show them the crater in her back rib cage where it exited. It made a shooting eight months earlier more real.

After Stupenagel returned to the stand, Karp led her through the remaining Loon Lake events and concluded with questioning her about her newspaper stories. He'd then listened patiently as the defense attorney began her cross-examination.

As with any good novel, in which each chapter might have its own minor complications to be resolved, so did trials, including confrontations between attorneys. Some potential fights he let pass for strategic reasons. However, not all of them.

When he objected to Faust's sneering accusation that Stupenagel was part of the conspiracy to blackmail Allen, he'd decided it was time to step in. Looking back up again at Judge Hart, he was no longer smiling.

"Your Honor," he said, allowing his indignation to seep into his voice, "beginning with the opening statements in this trial, the defense has been making a habit of insinuating . . . no, outright lying . . . to the jury, and the public through their continuing contact with the media in violation of your gag order, that the charges brought against the defendants are political in nature and have no basis in fact. In addition to the many contemptuous and groundless accusations made in regard to my office and me, defense counsel continues to defame. For instance, the defense has just accused the witness of being part of a conspiracy to blackmail the deceased, and by association, the murder of the deceased. But there is not one scintilla of real evidence to support any of these allegations."

Pointing behind him at the defense table while he continued to face Judge Hart, Karp said, "The people's case against the defendants, Rod Fauhomme and Tucker Lindsey, is based solely on the admissible evidentiary facts in accordance with the rules of evidence, not making little speeches and leveling accusations disguised as questions."

Pausing, he then stabbed his finger in the direction of Faust, who had backed away to the other side of the court well. "Defense counsel's use of inflammatory comments during cross-examination is simply an improper effort to influence the jury with speculation, fabrications, and innuendo that the defense presents as though their allegations were already established facts. So I'm asking Your Honor to require an offer of proof from the defense that is factually based and not empty words and conspiracy fantasies. Either they present evidentiary facts — now — or be prohibited from pursuing these lines of inappropriate questioning. Put up or shut up."

Judge Hart barely had enough time to turn toward Faust before she stomped over to stand in front of the judge to reply. "As Mr. Karp is well aware, or should be by this point in his legal career, we are in the stage of the trial when the people are presenting what evidence they have, not the defense. I am rightfully challenging his witnesses' credibility, not presenting our case. If we decide that it's even necessary, we will present our evidence after the people rest."

"Miss Faust, the DA rightfully challenges your accusations. Do you have any factual basis to pursue your alternate theory?"

Judge Hart asked.

Faust just stared in silence.

Judge Hart looked at her balefully. "Well, if you choose not to respond, then I will sustain the objection and caution you yet again that if you persist in the use of that tactic, be prepared to satisfy the offer of proof requirement. Please proceed."

Although his face revealed nothing about what he was thinking, Karp was satisfied that whatever Hart decided, he'd accomplished what he intended. He could not let the defense continue to plant the seed in the jurors' minds during direct examination that the charges were political or that there was a second, more viable theory regarding the murder of Sam Allen without challenging it.

Chagrined, Faust stalked over to the witness stand. "Did anyone else see you and General Allen together?"

"Not to my knowledge."

"So as far as we know, this meeting never happened."

"Is that a question?"

"Let me rephrase," Faust replied. "If no one saw you together, or overheard your conversation, how are we to know that it ever occurred?"

"Just my word, I suppose."

"Ah, right, the word of a *journalist*," Faust snorted. "And we all know we can trust the word of journalists, isn't that right?"

Stupenagel shrugged. "Just like lawyers, some you can; some you can't. I'm telling the truth."

Faust's eyes widened at the retort but then her face hardened and she came back at the witness. "Even if we were to accept your account of this meeting," she said, "did General Allen say who among the, and I quote, 'powers that be' were pressuring him to toe the company line on Chechnya by threatening to reveal his affair with Jenna Blair? Did he give any names?"

"No."

"Can you hazard a guess as to why he wouldn't have told you? I mean, according to your testimony, anyway, he told you all of this classified information about the events in Chechnya, but he didn't name names? Or was it that he didn't really trust one of his little wartime flings?"

"Objection, Your Honor," Karp said, rising partly from his seat. He'd seen Stupenagel tense and wanted to intercept whatever she might say. They'd talked about the probability that the defense would attack her on a personal level and the need for her to keep her cool, but the journalist had a volatile temper and on occasion had a mouth like a longshoreman.

"Sustained," Hart said drily. "Let's keep the superfluous remarks for the newspapers after the trial, Ms. Faust; you asked your question, now let the witness reply." He looked at Stupenagel and nodded. "Your answer, please?"

"I can think of a couple of reasons. He might not have told me because he wasn't ready to go public with it," Stupenagel said. "After all, I'm a journalist and that sort of information would be like having a big piece of chocolate cake in the refrigerator that starts calling to you about midnight. You know there are a lot of reasons you shouldn't eat it, but you'll find the one why you should and the next thing you know, you can't fit into your Victoria's Secret jeans."

The tension in the courtroom passed with a ripple of laughter at Stupenagel's remark. Then with the defense attorney glaring at her, Stupenagel finished her answer. "Or he might not have told me the names in order to protect me. As he said, he wasn't sure how high up this went, other than it was high, and someone willing to threaten a decorated, retired general and acting director of the CIA wouldn't have hesitated to go after a journalist."

"Did anybody try to go after you?" Faust demanded.

Stupenagel hesitated before she replied. "I received several threats over the telephone that were reported to the police."

"Any idea who made these threatening calls?"

"Oh, I have ideas where they originated," Stupenagel replied, "but nothing concrete."

"And yet you're still among us," Faust said. "Apparently these all-powerful people — powerful enough to order drone strikes on the other side of the world — didn't think it was worth the effort to go after a journalist. And if General Allen was so concerned with your safety, why did he tell you anything . . . if he did?"

"Insurance. To make sure the story about what really happened in Chechnya got out if something happened to him," Stupenagel replied. "He knew that I wouldn't be too afraid, or biased, to write the truth. And if something did happen to a friend of mine, he knew I wouldn't rest until I found out who did it." Stupenagel emphasized her point by looking over at the defendants.

Karp turned to follow her gaze with a slight smile. Even if he was the sort of lawyer to coach a witness in courtroom

543

theatrics, and he wasn't, he couldn't have asked for a better performance. Every juror had turned to look at the defendants, too. Lindsey, who thus far had spent most of the trial making notes and passing them to Caulkin, who sat between him and Fauhomme, found a reason to start writing furiously on a legal pad. Meanwhile, his codefendant, Fauhomme, kept his eyes on his attorney.

Faust blinked and cleared her throat. Instead of settling for the answers that mattered to her clients the most — that Allen had not named names and that there were no witnesses to their meeting — she'd asked one too many questions and opened the door to a counterattack from a clever witness.

Trying to regain control of the cross-examination, she pressed quickly on to Stupenagel's efforts to find Blair and the events at Loon Lake. Here she changed her theory of the case slightly. Now the insinuation was that Stupenagel might have been an unwitting participant in the conspiracy between Blair, Connie Rae Lee, and Ray Baum. She asked Stupenagel if it was "possible that Allen was being blackmailed by his girlfriend and her cohorts."

"I suppose it's possible. But he didn't talk

about her like a man who was being black-mailed by the woman he was clearly in love with."

Faust shrugged. "How do you know she didn't make her demands that weekend at the cabin or even his hotel?"

"I've met Miss Blair and heard her talk about Sam . . . General Allen . . . I believe she loved him very much, too."

"Ms. Stupenagel, are you aware that in addition to being a paid escort, Jenna Blair was a professional actress who'd appeared in a number of off-Broadway productions?"

"I'm aware of that."

"Is it possible that she was putting on an act the night you and the district attorney's wife, Marlene Ciampi, found her at the Loon Lake cabin?"

"I don't believe so."

"But it's possible."

"You're not making any sense," Stupenagel said with a scowl. "At the White Horse Tavern he indicated that the threats were coming from someone within the administration who didn't want him to spill the beans on Chechnya. But he did say he wanted to marry Jenna; doesn't sound like a man being blackmailed to me."

"Yes, of course, at this meeting that no one else saw or heard," Faust shot back.

"At least no one who is still alive!"

"That's right," Stupenagel replied. "Because of your clients!"

"Yes, of course, those all-powerful people," Faust scoffed. "And if I'm to understand your testimony, you came up with the idea of looking for Miss Blair at the Loon Lake cabin because you saw a photograph of her and General Allen taken at the lake?"

"That and because Sam asked if I remembered how to get to the cabin."

"Oh, that's right, the oh-so-subtle hint to a woman he once had a fling with."

Stupenagel's eyes flashed but she kept her cool. "That's correct. I think you've got it now."

Faust ignored the retort. "So then you and the district attorney's wife drove to Orvin where you met the local constable, Tom Spooner, and under the false pretext that you were there for nostalgic reasons, you got him to point you in the direction of the cabin?"

"Yes."

"You lied to him about your reason for wanting to go to the cabin."

"Yes. I didn't know if he could be trusted or would help us if he knew why we really wanted to go there."

"You didn't know if you could trust a law

enforcement officer?"

"I didn't know who to trust."

"Other than the wife of the district attorney."

"We're old friends, and Marlene is a private investigator and attorney in New York. She was also one of the best prosecutors in the New York DAO."

"Yes. The DAO her husband runs. Small world, isn't it?"

"It can be."

"Yes, well, let's return to Loon Lake. When you got there your testimony is that Miss Blair had a gun and threatened to shoot you?"

"Yes. She was frightened."

"Afraid of Ray Baum, correct?"

"I don't believe she knew his name. But she was running from a man of his description."

"The man she claimed killed General Allen, correct?"

"Yes."

"Did you ask her if she knew him before Allen was killed?"

"She said she'd never seen him before until the morning after Sam was murdered."

"And that's when she told you the story about having seen this man, Ray Baum, murder the general because it was recorded

547

on her laptop computer?"

"Yes."

"Did you ask her why she recorded the murder of this man she supposedly loved?"

Stupenagel furrowed her brow and hesitated a moment. "It's my understanding that it was an accident. She left the recording app on while she went to take a shower, and that's when the murder occurred."

Faust turned to the jury. "Convenient, wouldn't you say, that she just happened to step out of the room at the time a murder was to occur?"

"Convenient for who? The killer? The men who sent him?" Stupenagel retorted quickly.

Faust spun toward the judge. "Your Honor, I ask that the witness's last comments be stricken from the record as unresponsive and the jury told to disregard them!"

"Miss Faust, you opened that door and the witness has entered the room and shut it," Judge Hart said. "I find the witness's answer responsive to your question; I'll allow it to stand. Please proceed."

White-faced with anger, Faust put her hands on her hips as she faced Stupenagel. "Let me get this straight," she snarled. "Miss Blair is video-camming with Sam Allen, then steps out of the room just in time for the killer to carry out his mission?"

"Yes. That's about it."

"Did you ever think to question her about the timing of these events?"

"No. She explained them. It made sense in light of what Sam told me."

"At this meeting in a bar that no one else saw or heard," Faust repeated, then quickly asked, "Ms. Stupenagel, do you plan to write a book about this?"

"I don't know," she replied. "I may. Writing is how I make my living."

"And wouldn't this be a much bigger book deal if the 'bad guys' are two of the president's closest advisers?"

"I haven't given a deal much thought."

"Well, you'd have to think it would be worth more than your run-of-the-mill true crime."

"I think the murder of a man of Sam Allen's stature is more than run-of-the-mill."

"So you have thought about it?"

"That's not what I said."

"Do you have a book deal?"

"No."

"Have you been approached by one or more publishers to write a book about this case?"

"Yes. That's pretty common in a high-profile case like this."

"And what have you told them?"

"I haven't responded to their inquiries."

"Isn't it true that publishers won't publish a crime book unless there's been a guilty verdict?"

"In general, that's correct," Stupenagel agreed.

"Why?"

"If the defendants are found guilty, they can't sue for libel."

"So you have a financial, and a legal, interest in making sure our clients are convicted?"

"At this time I have neither. But I do have a personal interest in wanting the people who were responsible brought to justice. It doesn't matter to me who or what they are, just so long as they are the ones who did it."

"But it will, won't it?" Faust retorted. "It will matter who pays for this crime. It will matter to your bank account." When Stupenagel didn't answer, she smiled. "No more questions."

Judge Hart looked at the clock on the wall at the back of the courtroom. "We've reached the one o'clock hour, and I think this would be a good time for a break. Be back in one hour and we'll resume at that time. Court is in recess."

Karp hurried outside to grab a hot dog with the works from a street vendor. He intended to go back to his office to eat it, but then looked up the block at the small green newsstand and turned back to the hot dog man. "Make it two."

With hot dogs in hand, Karp walked over to where Dirty Warren Bennett was leaning on the stand looking bored. "Brought you something," he said, handing a hot frank to the surprised man.

Dirty Warren looked as if he might cry as he wiped at his perpetually dripping nose. "Gee, thanks . . . bullshit tits whoop . . . Butch. What's this for?"

"What? Can't a guy buy a friend a hot dog without there being a reason?" Karp said with a wink.

Dirty Warren grinned. "Yeah, you're . . . oh boy oh boy . . . right. I just wasn't . . . goddamn prick . . . expecting it. Thanks again. Hey, by the way, did . . . whoop whoop my ass . . . Stupenagel make it okay to court?"

Karp furrowed his brow. "Yeah. She did. She's on the stand now, though I think we're about to wrap up." He thought about it for a moment. "That's a funny question; why do you ask?"

"Ah, nothing. Just . . . whoop oh boy . . . curious. I'd heard she got some . . . balls . . . threats," the little man replied and quickly changed the subject. "Okay, okay . . . oh boy . . . in the 1957 movie *Gunfight at the O.K. Corral,* Burt Lancaster played . . . itchy scrotum . . . Wyatt Earp but who played Doc Holliday and who . . . whoop whoooop . . . did the director want to play Doc Holliday?"

Karp rolled his eyes. "Funny, I was just thinking about that movie. Sometimes I think you're in the wrong business, you should try fortune-telling. Just don't go into trivia, that question was way too easy. Kirk Douglas played the infamous Doc Holliday."

"Yeah, that was easy . . . I seen that film ten times . . . oh boy dirtbag," Dirty Warren said. "So who was supposed to . . . shit fuck piss . . . play the good doctor?"

Screwing up his face as if stumped, Karp looked up at the sky. He enjoyed letting Warren believe that he'd at long last won a round. But besides being an English teacher, his mother had been a movie buff who loved playing film trivia with her son. "Of all the newsstands, in all the world, I had to come to this one to be asked that question . . ."

"Ah shit . . ." Dirty Warren said, stomping

his foot.

"Why, Humphrey Bogart, of course," Karp said triumphantly. "I suggest you bone up on your movie trivia, your questions are getting easier, not harder."

"Ah crap . . . piss feces damnitall . . . I didn't know I was going to . . . whoop . . . see you," Dirty Warren complained. "I'll get you next time . . . bastard." He leaned close to Karp. "By the way . . . whoop whoop . . . David would like to have a word with you . . . fuck goddammit . . . after the trial. He was none too . . . oh boy oh boy . . . happy about Nadya getting away, but he's relieved Lucy . . . breasts ass piss . . . is okay. So that's a wash. He says . . . whoop . . . he has something to give you."

Wondering what it could be, Karp nodded. "He knows where to find me." Changing the topic of conversation to the Yankees, they finished their hot dogs and then Karp went back inside 100 Centre Street. He located Stupenagel in the witness waiting room. She was sitting on Murrow's lap, crying into his shoulder while he wrapped his arms around her and made small soothing sounds.

"You okay?" Karp asked.

Stupenagel looked at him and sniffed as she nodded, then used a tissue to dab at her nose and eyes. "Jesus, I bet I look like a mess," she said.

"Faust was a little rough on you," Karp noted.

"It wasn't the questions," Stupenagel said. "She's just another lousy lawyer — present company excluded. But saying I was just a fling and that I was trying to make money off of Sam's death . . . that got to me. The bitch better hope she never meets me in a dark alley."

Karp patted her on the shoulder and smiled. "At least make it a dark alley in another city, please," he said. "So you ready to get even?"

Stupenagel smiled. "You bet."

Twenty minutes later, Stupenagel was back on the stand with Karp leaning against the jury box rail. "Miss Stupenagel, so you have a book deal regarding this case?" he asked.

"No."

"Have you asked for a book deal?"

"No."

"Did you file for an indictment against these defendants?"

"Of course not."

"Are you privy to the conversations in my office regarding what charges we do or don't bring against people suspected of crimes?"

"I wish, but no."

"Will it be up to you to reach a verdict on the guilt or innocence of these two men?"

"No. That will be the jury."

"After they've heard *all* of the evidence, correct?"

"That's the way it's done."

Karp came off the rail and turned toward the defense table. "Miss Stupenagel, counsel for the defendant Fauhomme asked you about the recording of General Allen's murder on Miss Blair's laptop."

"Yes."

"And you've had an opportunity to see that recording?"

"I saw it at Loon Lake before Ray Baum and his partner kicked in the door."

"Do you recall if the killer in that recording ever acted as if he knew he was being recorded or watched?"

Stupenagel shook her head. "No. On the contrary, he never looked at the camera or said anything except when he made a telephone call."

Facing the jurors, Karp asked, "I know you've addressed this before but just to be clear, how long have you known, did you know, Sam Allen?"

"More than twenty years."

"When was the first time you saw or spoke

to Ray Baum?"

"At the White Horse Tavern last October. He wasn't there when I walked in, but he was sitting at the bar when I went to pay my tab."

"Did you know him?"

"No, but he started flirting."

"Was there anything about him that stood out from a physical standpoint?"

"Well, he was good-looking, but I guess what I noticed was that he had a Marine Corps tattoo on his right forearm. I even said something about it to him."

"When was the next time you saw or spoke to Ray Baum?"

"About three days later at the cabin on Loon Lake."

"When was the last time you saw Ray Baum?"

"I was standing in the grave he made me and Jenna Blair dig. I hit him with the shovel and then he shot me. I blacked out and fell back into the hole. The next thing I knew, Tom Spooner was looking down at me."

Karp walked over to the prosecution table, where he picked up a plastic bag. "Miss Stupenagel, I am holding People's Exhibit 21. It is a plastic bag containing a DVD recording. Would you look at it, please, and tell the jurors what, if anything, is written on the face of it."

Stupenagel took the bag and glanced at the label before handing it back to Karp. "It says, 'Allen, Congress.' "

Returning the bag to the prosecution table, Karp turned back to the witness stand. "Have you seen that particular DVD before? And if so, where?"

"Yes," Stupenagel said. "It is one of the recordings Sam left in the safe at Loon Lake."

"Do you know what's on the recording?"

"Yes. I watched it with Marlene and Jenna Blair at the cabin."

Karp said, "Could you tell the jurors in general what it contains?"

Stupenagel looked over at the jurors. "It's a video recording Sam . . . General Allen . . . made of the testimony he apparently intended to give before the congressional committee regarding the events in Chechnya."

"Could you tell where the recording was made?"

"Yes. Judging from the background on the recording, it was made in his office at the Loon Lake cabin. You can see the bookcase and some of the wall behind him."

"Does the recording in substance cor-

roborate your testimony today regarding
what he told you at the White Horse Tavern?"

"It's what he told me, but a lot more."

"What do you mean by a lot more?"

"Well, the recording has everything he said
to me," Stupenagel replied. "But he either
didn't tell me everything, or he learned
more between meeting with me and when
he made the recording."

"Do you know when the recording was
made?"

"Yes. It's time and date stamped. It was
made Saturday, the day after we met and
the day before he . . . the day before he was
murdered."

"No further questions, Your Honor."

Judge Hart looked at Faust. "Anything
else?"

The defense attorney rose but stayed
behind her table. "Yes, Your Honor, a few
more questions."

"Then please proceed."

"Miss Stupenagel, have you written and
sold true crime books in the past?"

"Yes."

"And it's quite possible, if not probable,
that you will write a book about this case?"

"It's possible."

"And that could be worth a lot of money?"

"That's possible, too."

Faust walked over to the prosecution table and picked up the DVD of Allen's proposed congressional testimony. She held it up. "Isn't it true that everything you wrote in your stories, and everything you've said here in court — except for the personal stuff, of course — you could have learned by watching this recording?"

"That's true. But why wouldn't I have written more? There's a lot on there that wasn't in my stories."

Faust shrugged. "I don't know. You tell me. Maybe you were only told some of what the recording said."

"By whom?"

Smiling, Faust tossed the bag back down on the prosecution table. "I'd say someone who had a copy of the recording. Wouldn't that make sense?"

"Not at all," Stupenagel said, shaking her head in disbelief.

"Mr. Karp, any further questions?" Judge Hart asked.

"Just one question, Your Honor. Miss Stupenagel, do you recall what General Allen was wearing that day at the White Horse Tavern?"

Stupenagel smiled at the memory. "Yes. He was 'in disguise' and wearing an old sweatshirt, jeans, cheap sunglasses, and a Yankee ballcap that had seen better days."

Karp nodded, then turned to Judge Hart. "Your Honor, may this witness be dismissed? She wants to sit in the gallery and watch the rest of the proceedings."

The judge looked over at Faust. "Any objections?"

Busy making notes, the defense attorney didn't bother to look up. "No," she said. "I'm sure she wants to take notes for her book."

After that the reporter was allowed to step from the stand. Without looking to either side, she walked past the defense and prosecution tables, down the aisle of the gallery section, and took a seat in the back next to Marlene as Karp announced, "The people call Tabor Cowden."

A young, well-built man with sandy hair and a nervous smile entered the courtroom from the side door leading across a narrow hallway to the witness room and took the stand. "Mr. Cowden, would you please tell the jury what you do for a living?"

"Uh, yeah, I tend bar at the White Horse Tavern on Hudson Street."

27

Karp knew that the dramatic narrative of the case against the two defendants was swiftly moving toward the final chapters. Unlike a book, he couldn't jump ahead to read what the defense intended to say or do when they presented their case. But just as some novels foreshadowed what was to come, he believed he had a pretty good idea of their strategy based on their public pretrial statements, their jury selection questions during voir dire, their questioning of the people's witnesses, and their own witness list.

So he was prepared for all eventualities and ready to counter Faust's intimation during her cross-examination of Stupenagel that she was either making up her meeting with Allen or in collusion with Ray Baum by calling White Horse Tavern bartender Tabor Cowden to the stand. "Mr. Cowden, last November you were interviewed by a

Detective Clay Fulton, do you recall that?"

"Yeah, the big black guy. He was one tough-looking dude; I could use a guy like that as a bouncer on Saturday nights."

Karp smiled. "I'll let Detective Fulton know in case he wants to moonlight. But in the meantime, do you remember him asking you if you recalled seeing Ariadne Stupenagel in the bar a couple of weeks earlier?"

"Yeah."

"Do you recall your answer?"

"I told him that I seen her. She's pretty hard to miss," Cowden replied to chuckles in the gallery. Stupenagel had never been a wallflower in dress or attitude among her colleagues, or anyone else, for that matter. "She used to come in a lot more, but I hadn't seen her in a while, so I noticed."

"Do you remember whether Detective Fulton asked if she was sitting with anyone?"

Cowden nodded. "Yeah, I told him that I didn't know. I was behind the bar; she got a beer and went and sat down in the back. I can't see back there."

"Do you remember Detective Fulton asking you if there were other people in the bar?"

"You mean about the guy sitting at the bar?"

"He's one, and I'll get to him in a minute; however, do you remember describing anyone else?"

Cowden furrowed his brow and then brightened. "Oh, yeah. Another guy came in after Ariadne. I'd say he was middle-aged, not real big but still one of those guys who carries himself like you don't want to mess with him. I remember he was wearing sunglasses — the cheap kind you buy off a vendor on Sixth Avenue — but not much about his clothes. He was definitely wearing an old, beat-up Yankee ballcap; I remember that because I'm a fan. Don't come wearing a Red Sox hat into my bar, or I'll eighty-six your ass double-quick."

"As it should be." Karp laughed. "Do you remember where the man in the Yankee ballcap sat?"

Shaking his head, Cowden said, "Nah, he didn't sit at the bar. But I don't remember seeing him again. I got busy not long after that so he might have slipped out the back."

Karp walked over to the prosecution table and picked up a photograph and returned to the witness stand. "You mentioned another man, a younger guy, who did sit at the bar. Was he sitting there when Ariadne

Stupenagel came in?"

"No."

"How about when the man in the ballcap arrived?"

"The young guy came in after the guy in the ballcap. He walked toward the back at first but then he returned and sat down at the bar."

"Do you remember describing him for Detective Fulton?"

"Yeah. He was young, maybe thirty or so. Clean-cut, not particularly friendly. He had a tattoo on his forearm."

"You know what sort of tattoo?"

"Yeah, the Marine eagle, globe, and anchors. My dad was a Marine."

"You talk to him?"

"A little. Like I said, he wasn't real friendly. Mostly just, 'Hey, how ya doin'?' That sort of stuff. But he got all chatty when Ariadne came up to pay her bill."

"Chatty how?"

"For starters he was hittin' on her like he hadn't seen a woman in a year," Cowden said. "I mean laying it on thick."

"How did Miss Stupenagel react?"

Cowden glanced back at where Stupenagel was sitting in the rear of the courtroom with Marlene. "Well, the guy was a stud so I figure she was liking the attention. But in the end she shut him down. She said she had a boyfriend to go home to; and good for her, the guy was a creep."

"How do you mean?"

"Well, after she left he asked if I knew who she was."

"Did you tell him?"

"Uh, yeah, I mean everybody knows who Ariadne Stupenagel is," Cowden said, "at least in this town. So I figured it wouldn't hurt to tell him her name and that she was a famous newspaper writer. But he kept asking all these other questions like where she lived, who she worked for . . . that sort of thing. Only now he was getting under my skin so I told him I didn't give out that sort of personal information."

Karp held up the photograph with its back to the witness. "Do you remember being shown a photo lineup by Detective Fulton the day he talked to you?"

"Yeah, the detective showed me like five or six photographs of different guys."

"And were you able to identify the young man with the Marine tattoo sitting at the bar?"

"Yeah, right away."

Karp turned the photograph around and handed it up to Cowden. "Is this the man you identified?"

Cowden was already nodding before Karp finished his question. "Yeah, that's the guy."

"Mr. Cowden, would you turn the photograph over and tell me what, if anything, is written on the back?"

Doing as he was told, Cowden looked back up. "Yeah, there's a date and my initials. Detective Fulton had me write that there after I identified the guy."

Taking the photograph back, Karp looked at the court stenographer. "Let the record reflect that the witness identified People's Exhibit 25 which has been previously identified by Tom Spooner and Ariadne Stupenagel as Ray Baum."

Bill Caulkin quickly muttered, "No objections."

"Mr. Cowden, were you shown a second set of photographs that day?" Karp asked.

"Yeah."

"And were you able to identify any of those as the man in the ballcap?"

"Nope."

"Thank you, Mr. Cowden. No further questions."

As Karp sat down, Caulkin rose to handle the cross-examination. He moved out from around the defense table as if arthritis was killing him, though Karp knew for a fact that the sixty-six-year-old played racquetball several times a week at the West River Health & Racquet Club on the Upper West Side. "Mr. Cowden, were you told that among the photographs you couldn't identify was one of General Sam Allen?"

"Oh, I recognized him because he'd been all over the news," Cowden answered. "But I couldn't say if he was the guy in the baseball cap."

"So you don't know if General Allen was in the bar that day, or any day?"

"No, I honestly can't say."

"And you can't say if Miss Stupenagel met with anyone besides chatting to the young man sitting at the bar?"

"That's right."

Caulkin walked slowly in front of the jury with one hand on the rail. "Mr. Cowden, I believe your testimony is that Miss Stupenagel has been a regular at the White Horse Tavern?"

"Well, she used to be," Cowden replied. "I hadn't seen her for quite a while before this."

"But it wouldn't have been unusual for her to walk into the bar and have a beer on any given day?"

Cowden shrugged. "Not particularly."

"Were you standing right there when Miss Stupenagel and Mr. Baum were having their conversation?"

"Not right in front of them," Cowden said, "I was washing glasses down at the sink."

"So you weren't really focused on what they were doing and saying?"

"Oh, I could hear them pretty good. I was checking out the dude's pickup lines."

"Were you in a position to see if they passed any notes, or maybe said something under their breath?"

"What? You mean secretly?"

"Yes, maybe talking out loud for your consumption, but otherwise communicating secretly."

Cowden looked as if he thought the defense attorney was crazy and shook his head. "Yeah, I guess. But that sounds pretty ridiculous."

Karp tried not to smile at the response. *It does sound ridiculous. Couldn't have said it better myself, and the jury will pick up on that,* he thought.

Realizing the same thing, Caulkin blinked a couple of times at the answer, then simply turned to the judge and said, "No further questions."

Hart looked back at Karp. "Mr. Karp?"

Standing, Karp remained behind the table. "Mr. Cowden, how long have you known Miss Stupenagel?"

"Oh, man . . . let's see, I started working there eight years ago and she was a regular back then."

"So, eight years. Have you ever seen her with Ray Baum before that day?"

"Never. I've never seen him before at all."

"Did Miss Stupenagel act in any way as though she knew Mr. Baum when she came to pay her tab?"

"No. I'd say the opposite. She didn't say anything to him until he started to hit on her."

"And again her reaction was?"

"She mostly laughed. She said she was old enough to be his older sister or something like that . . . typical funny Ariadne. Then she said she had a boyfriend and was going home."

"And your testimony was that after she left he began asking personal questions about her?"

"Yes."

"He wanted to know her name?"

"Yep."

"Where she lived?"

"That's right. But I didn't tell him . . . actually I don't know."

"And what she did for a living?"

"Yes."

"And when you told him she was a journalist, what was his reaction?"

Cowden thought about it for a moment. "He got kind of a funny look on his face. He wasn't smiling anymore and left right after that."

After Cowden stepped down, Karp nodded to the court clerk, Jim Farley, who rolled a television out in front of the jury box. He'd waited until this moment to show the jury the recording Allen made of the testimony he'd planned giving to the congressional committee on Chechnya so that they'd understand how it fit into the case he was making against the defendants. Karp painstakingly set the scene, and included small, but important, details such as the police photographer who identified photographs he'd taken at the Loon Lake cabin study from the same angle Allen's camera had been so that the jurors could see where the tape was made, and thus corroborate, Stupenagel's testimony.

The defense had, of course, protested allowing the tape to be shown to the jury, arguing that it was addressing collateral issues and was not proof that what Allen intended to testify to "was in any way subject to the administration censure."

Karp responded, "Your Honor, it goes to

the heart of establishing motive for the defendants' murder of General Allen."

Hart then ruled. "I find that the probative value of motive outweighs any collateral effect. It will be up to the jury to determine its factual persuasiveness, if any."

The lights in the courtroom went dark as General Sam Allen's handsome, tan face appeared on the television screen. "My name is Samuel H. Allen, lieutenant general U.S. Army retired. What follows is a recording of the testimony I intend to swear to under oath in front of the congressional committee hearing on what occurred at the U.S. compound outside of Zandaq, Chechnya. If you are viewing this recording instead of having watched my testimony before the congressional committee on Chechnya then I have been prevented from appearing in person.

"What I'm about to say is not easy. I've spent my entire adult life in the service of this country's military and civilian leaders, especially my commander-in-chief, the president of the United States. I may not have always agreed with a president's decision or policy, but I have always carried out my orders to the best of my ability and honored the office of the president, if not the man. So it is with great difficulty and soul-searching that I have reached this decision to break from that tradition. However, the demands of my conscience, prodded by the needless deaths of Americans, and the debasement of this country's security, leave me no choice."

General Allen paused and looked for a long moment into the camera before continuing. "It is my opinion that the American public has been lied to regarding the events in Chechnya, including this administration's role in what happened, as well as the attempt to cover up a needless tragedy.

"I will leave it to those responsible to reveal their reasons for their actions. My purpose here is to recount the facts as I know them and, where applicable, point out where these facts differ from what Congress, and the American people, have been told. . . ."

As Allen laid out his evidence, Karp positioned himself so that he could study the faces of the jurors. He could see in their eyes and expressions that the general's revelations from beyond the grave fit into the testimonial evidence they'd already heard from the other witnesses. With each point made by the general, their brows furrowed and they began stealing looks at the defendants. Meanwhile, Fauhomme and

Lindsey, as well as their attorneys, pretended in the half-light to be engrossed in what Allen had to say, as though they'd never seen the recording before. Of course they had, during the discovery process and then again during the pretrial hearings.

Allen's statement took nearly an hour of crisp, detailed, unemotional exposition. Then, looking up from his notes, the general at last let anger show on his face, as if he could no longer control it. "Four days ago, I was called to a meeting with the president's national security adviser, Tucker Lindsey, and the president's national campaign manager, Rod Fauhomme. At that time I informed them of my concerns regarding the 'official' version of the events in Chechnya. I was then told in no uncertain terms that I was not to deviate from the administration's talking points at the hearing before the congressional committee. If I did, I was told that certain private matters would be surreptitiously revealed to the public that would harm my family, my position as the acting director of the CIA, and my reputation."

Sighing, Allen put aside his notes. "As for my reputation, to quote Shakespeare's Othello, '. . . he that filches from me my good name robs me of that which not enriches him and makes me poor indeed.' But in the end, I'm the one who put himself into this position so that innocent others could be injured by my actions. However, as a result of both the methods used to try to ensure my silence, as well as my own actions, I feel I have no choice but to step down from my position as acting director of the CIA and withdraw my name from further consideration. Thank you and God bless America."

28

Facing the rear of the courtroom, Fauhomme glared for a moment at Ariadne Stupenagel and Karp's wife. He wanted to fix their faces in his mind; after all, he hadn't gotten to where he was in life by forgetting or forgiving people who crossed him.

Where you are in life? Are you crazy? You're sitting in a courtroom with a murder case hanging over your head. Can't you feel the noose tightening?

Fauhomme reached up and loosened his tie as he fought the feeling of panic and an uncomfortable tightness in his chest brought on by the voice in his head. It was the same voice he used to use to deride and debase others, but now like a junkyard dog it had turned on him.

The two women in the back of the courtroom met his gaze with hard looks of their own. He averted his eyes to the rest of the gallery, but there wasn't a friendly face in the crowd. With a shudder he turned back around.

The attorneys were all up at the judge's dais arguing, and he couldn't remember why. The trial was just grinding on and every day seemed to bring a new defeat. He looked over at Tucker Lindsey, who sat staring at the table in front of him with his red-rimmed eyes. More to have someone to talk to than because he empathized with Lindsey, he said, "Don't worry. It will get better when we present our case."

Lindsey's pale face flushed as he raised his head slowly and then turned to Fauhomme. "We're fucked," he whispered. "And it's your fault." Then his expression went blank again and he resumed staring at the table.

The venom in his codefendant's voice rattled Fauhomme, who was still trying to decide how he would retort when the lawyers finished their business. Faust and Caulkin returned to their seats, having obviously lost whatever argument they were trying to make. They looked almost as defeated as Lindsey when Karp announced, "The people call Connie Rae Lee."

Mustering a smile, Fauhomme turned to look as the tall brunette entered the courtroom. He'd fantasized that she would appear in court and then refuse to testify against him. After all, they'd shared some good times. He'd taken her places and introduced her to people she would never have met if it wasn't for him. She'd told him more than once he was a great lover and . . . their eyes met and he realized that his fantasy was not about to become reality.

When she edged into the room she looked frightened, but when she saw him her face hardened and her jaw set. Her eyes flashed in anger, wiping the smile from his face. He felt her pass behind him, and his skin crawled as if he expected her to plunge a knife into his back. Instead, she opened the gate between the gallery and the well of the court and walked purposefully up to the court clerk to be sworn in. Climbing up on the witness stand, she looked at him again with contempt.

A mixture of fear and rage coursed through his body. *Here's another one to put on the enemies list,* he thought. The voice started laughing so hard that he hardly heard the first introductory questions and answers, and he had to concentrate to hear the next question.

"Miss Lee, would you please tell the jury what your relationship to the defendant,

Rod Fauhomme, was in October of last year."

"He was my boyfriend."

"At that time how long had he been your boyfriend?"

"A little more than three years."

"And did you know the other defendant, Tucker Lindsey, as well at that time?"

"Not well," Lee replied. "I saw him at some parties and political functions. I knew he was the president's national security adviser and that he and Rod talked a lot. But that was it. I never sat down and had a cup of coffee with him or anything like that."

"You said the defendant, Fauhomme, was your boyfriend. Would you describe the nature of that relationship?"

Lee shrugged her shoulders. "He lives . . . lived . . . in Washington, D.C., and I'm here in New York, so I saw him whenever he came to town, and sometimes I would go down there. He paid for my condominium on the Upper West Side and gave me an allowance so I wouldn't have to work."

"What did the defendant do for a living?"

"He runs political campaigns, including the president's. I think he gets paid for television talk shows and the consulting he does, too, but he didn't tell me much about where his money all came from. I just know that he had a lot of it."

"During last year's presidential campaign, how would you describe your boyfriend's involvement in the day-to-day process?"

"He's a control freak," Lee said. "He also thinks he's the smartest guy in every room he walks into. Everything passed through him. I once watched him scream at some volunteer college students at a rally for not approving their signs with him first. Anything, or anybody, that was going to be on television or in the newspapers had to be run by him. He used to brag to me that even the generals at the Pentagon had to brief him about what was going on. He had the media so scared that they'd call him and read him their stories, and he'd tell them how to write their quotes."

"Did he at any time ask you to assist him with his job?"

"Yes. He expected me to be the hostess for parties he threw here in New York."

"And what were your duties at these parties?"

"Oh, the usual stuff like arranging for the caterer, passing the invitation list through him, getting in touch with people, and making sure there was plenty of alcohol. Lots and lots of alcohol."

"Anything else? Maybe not quite so

'usual'?"

Lee flushed slightly. "Well, a lot of these parties were for wealthy people that he was hitting up for campaign donations or political support. Anyway, they were mostly men, so I was supposed to make sure there were a lot of pretty women there, too."

"Who were these women?"

"Some were friends or girls I met at my yoga studio — I'm an instructor — or at the theater where I sometimes acted. Others were just girls I'd meet and if I thought they were a good fit, I'd get their names and phone numbers and invite them to the parties."

"Besides attending these parties, did you ever ask any of these other young women if they would be willing to do more than just show up?"

Lee bit her lip and nodded.

Karp moved in front of the witness stand. "I'm afraid you'll have to speak up so that the stenographer can record your answer."

"Yes," Lee said quietly. "Sometimes the men at the parties would be single, or away from home, and they'd express an interest in female companionship."

"Did this companionship include sex?"

Again Lee nodded, but added, "If the men wanted that, then yes."

"Were the women paid to have sex with these men?"

"Yes."

"Did the men pay the women for sex?"

This time Lee shook her head. "No. At least not directly, though they were contributing large amounts of money to these funds Rod controlled."

"How were the women paid?"

"Rod would give me the money, and I would put it into an account, and then transfer the money from there into their accounts."

Karp strolled over until he was a few feet from the defense table and looking at Fauhomme. "This man, the defendant Rod Fauhomme, would give you money to pay young women to have sex with the men invited to these parties?"

"Yes."

Hearing a small commotion behind him, Fauhomme turned in time to see several members of the media get up and leave the courtroom. He knew why. Testimony that the president's campaign manager had paid young women to have sex with important men was about to hit the morning news cycle. He shook his head and turned back around.

In the meantime, Karp kept pressing.

"Was the purpose of this just to keep these wealthy men happy?"

"Only partly," Lee replied. "But Rod also expected the girls to report to me about things they might learn from the men that would interest him."

"What sort of things?"

"Just about anything. If they were considering supporting another candidate. Or who they were doing business with. How much money they were thinking about donating. A lot of them were associated with big corporations or were from other countries, and he'd want to know their secrets. Like I said, he's a control freak, and the more he knows, the more he can control."

"How much would these women be paid?"

"It depended," Lee answered. "A thousand per date, maybe five thousand for a week."

"Depended on what?"

"If it was just going back to the guy's hotel it might be a thousand," Lee responded. "But if they called me with something Rod particularly liked, he might tell me to 'give them a bonus.' Certain guys were simply worth more than others — more money to donate, or more secrets."

"How would these women get this information?"

"Whatever came up in conversations, pillow talk," Lee replied.

"What, if anything, would Fauhomme do with this information?"

"I don't know," Lee said. "I'd sometimes overhear him talking to someone on the phone about expecting a big donation or that something he'd heard from me needed to be discussed. But if I asked him what he wanted with the information, he'd tell me to mind my own business."

"Do you know a young woman named Jenna Blair?"

"Yes. I've known Jenna for several years. We've been in some off-Broadway theater productions together; we both came to New York to be actresses and became friends."

"Did you at some point ask Jenna to attend one of these parties?"

"Yes," Lee said. "Rod had seen her a couple of times at my apartment, and he asked me to invite her."

"Any particular reason?"

"Well, Jenna's pretty and has that sort of sporty, athletic look that some men like. Most of the other girls were your typical model or actress types. But not every guy is attracted to that and Rod thought she would be a good fit."

"And did she attend one of these parties?"

"Yes. I told her she might meet some important people with connections. I didn't tell her about getting paid for sex."

"And did one of the men at this party ask to date her?"

"Yes. An Israeli businessman named Ariel Shimon was real interested in her. He asked me to ask her if he could take her out."

"Was he expected to pay for her sexual favors?"

"No. It was just sort of understood that the girls at Rod's parties were available for that if the men wanted."

"Did you tell Miss Blair about Mr. Shimon's interest?"

"Yes."

"Did she agree to go out with him?"

"Not at first, especially when I told her that she'd be paid if she also had sex with him and reported anything he said."

"How'd she react to that?"

"I don't think she believed me at first," Lee said. "It wasn't like she was a call girl who knew the score. So my offer came out of the blue. But I knew she was hurting for money and also wanted to go to law school someday. I thought there was a chance she'd go for it. Ariel's a good-looking guy for his age, and rich. But she just laughed it off and went home."

"Did she eventually agree to go out with Mr. Shimon?"

"Yes. He wooed her and she went out with him."

"Did they eventually become lovers?"

"Yes, after several dates."

"And was she paid?"

"I think it surprised her, but yes, I told her that the money had been deposited in her account."

"Why do you think it surprised her? Wasn't that what she'd been told?"

"Well, yes, but I think she genuinely liked Ariel and went out with him for the fun of it."

"And did she eventually report any of this 'pillow talk' that the defendant, Rod Fauhomme, was interested in?"

"Yes. She wasn't comfortable doing that, but I convinced her it was harmless, like getting a tip for the stock market before everyone else."

"And what would you do with that information?"

"I would tell Rod," Lee replied. "He said that as soon as I heard from her — or any of the other girls, for that matter — I was supposed to tell him. He'd get angry if I forgot or put it off."

"Why was Fauhomme interested in what

Mr. Shimon had to say?"

Lee shrugged. "He didn't tell me specifically. But he had a couple of drinks once when we were alone and he said that Ariel was a big-shot Israeli defense contractor and trying to get into politics. He said that Israelis have a big influence on Jewish voters in this country and it was important to keep him happy."

"You said that Jenna Blair seemed shocked, or surprised, when you told her money was in her account. Did she give the money back?"

"No. She kept it. She told me later that she knew he was married and going back to Israel so she was just a fling for him and she got some money for law school and a good time out of it. It was a win-win for both sides."

"And did Mr. Shimon eventually return to Israel?"

"Yes. I believe he was here for a few weeks, maybe a month."

"And what was Miss Blair's reaction to his leaving?"

"I think she was hurt," Lee said. "Especially the way he did it. He gave her an expensive bracelet and basically said, 'Thanks for the good times, don't contact me, good-bye.' And that was it."

"Did Miss Blair attend any more parties and agree to go out with any other men?"

"Not at first," Lee said. "But eventually I talked her into it. She was sort of picky about the men she'd see; if she didn't like them or wasn't attracted, she wouldn't go out with them. I don't think she was ever really comfortable with it, but she wanted to go to law school and didn't see another way."

Fauhomme was relieved when Karp walked away from the defense table to stand at the jury rail. "Did you know General Sam Allen?"

Lee nodded. "I knew who he was from television, and then I met him over the Fourth of July weekend at Rod's beach house on Long Island. Rod had a big party and Sam was one of the guests."

"Was Jenna Blair also present at this party?"

"Yes."

"Do you know how she came to be there?"

"I don't know the specifics, but a little while before the party — maybe a week — Rod asked me to have her stop by my apartment so that he could talk to her in private. He even made me leave. All I know for sure is that she was at the party and I didn't invite her."

"Was she there to meet General Allen?"

"Yes. Rod did tell me to make sure they were introduced and seated next to each other at the dinner table. He also told me to let her know that Allen was going for a run on the beach in the morning and that she should use that opportunity to spend more time with him."

"So you understood that this was a setup for Miss Blair to meet General Allen?"

"Yes. I knew what was happening."

"And was this setup successful?"

Lee nodded again. "Yes, but in ways I don't think even Rod thought it would be. It was clear from the beginning that they liked each other. Sam was in great shape and Jenna runs and surfs and climbs mountains . . . just his kind of girl. And he was handsome, charming, smart, and, I think, lonely. If it wasn't love at first sight, it was close."

"Did Jenna Blair and Sam Allen establish a relationship?"

"Yes. They began seeing each other . . . dating."

"And was Jenna Blair paid for this as well?"

Lee shook her head. "No. She told Rod she didn't want the money and that she was done."

"How do you know?"

"Sam and Jenna spent the second night together that weekend at Rod's beach house. After Sam left in the morning, Rod went to talk to Jenna to see how it went. When he came back to the main house, he was pissed off and swearing up a storm. He said, 'That little whore has decided to develop a conscience at the wrong time. Talk some sense into her.'"

"Those were his words? 'That little whore has decided to develop a conscience at the wrong time'?"

"Yes. His exact words."

"And he told you to talk some sense into her?"

Lee nodded. "Yes. So I met her for lunch. She said that after the night at the beach house she didn't expect to hear from Sam. She thought he wouldn't want to have anything to do with her now that they'd . . . now that they'd slept together. But he'd called a couple of days later, and they'd been seeing each other ever since. She was obviously head-over-heels. So I went back and told Rod that she wasn't going to spy for him and didn't want his money."

"How did Rod — the defendant, Fauhomme — take the news?"

"He'd been drinking and got angry. He

said it was my fault."

As Karp continued questioning Lee, Fauhomme noted how the prosecutor had to tiptoe around one subject. He'd been charged with domestic violence for hitting Lee the night of the election. The District of Columbia prosecutor had put off going to trial until the New York case was over, but in one of the few "victories" won by his lawyers, Karp wasn't allowed to mention the assault charge.

"What, if anything, did the defendant, Fauhomme, do after that in regard to Ms. Blair's refusal to participate further in his scheme?" Karp asked.

"He thought about it for a little while. Then he said he had a Plan B."

"Do you know what Plan B entailed?"

"Not exactly, except I know it involved Ray Baum."

Karp walked over to the prosecution table and picked up a photograph. "Can you identify the man in this photograph, People's Exhibit 25?" he asked, holding it up so that she could see it.

"That's Baum."

"What was Mr. Baum's relationship with the defendant, Fauhomme?"

"Basically, his right-hand man," Lee answered. "He traveled with him. He'd stay in a hotel near my place whenever Rod was with me. He was sort of a bodyguard, but he did a lot of stuff. Anything Rod needed done, Baum did it."

"You said you know that the defendant's Plan B involved Mr. Baum. How do you know that?"

"Because after he got done . . ." At a look from Karp, Lee changed what she was going to say to, "After he got mad at me, he called Baum and told him to come over. When Baum got to my place, they went back into the office. They didn't close the door all the way and I heard Rod tell Baum to get photographs of Sam and Jenna together."

"Is that all?"

"That's all I heard. One of them closed the door the rest of the way."

"When was this?" Karp asked.

Lee thought about it for a moment then replied, "Well, sometime after the Fourth of July party. I remember it took a little time before I could get together with Jenna, and by that time she'd been going out with Sam for . . . I don't know, a few weeks. So late July? Early August?"

Karp nodded. "Let me skip ahead a little bit to October," he said. "Was there an occasion when you walked in on a conversation the defendant, Fauhomme, was having in the office of his home in Washington, D.C., with the defendant, Lindsey?"

Lee looked over at the defense table and frowned. "Yes. I knew he was talking to Lindsey and Ray Baum. They'd both come over about noon."

"Was anyone else present?"

"Well, not in his office. But two of Lindsey's men were parked outside and one of them came to the door once."

"Okay, so explain to the jury why you entered the room."

"Well, I was walking past the office when I heard Rod yelling."

"What, if anything, was he saying?"

"I heard him yell, 'Wrong! They're not fucking Al Qaeda!' It got a little muffled but then I heard a loud bang, so I decided to poke my head in and see what was going on."

"What, if anything, did you see?"

"I saw Rod, Tucker Lindsey, and Ray Baum watching the television."

"Could you tell what they were watching?"

"Not exactly. It was black and white, maybe some green. I could see little white images of what looked like tiny people running around on it. I didn't get much of a chance to see it."

"Why not?"

"Rod screamed at me to get out. He could be a real bastard sometimes and treated me like crap," she said.

Fauhomme felt his face flushing and swallowed hard when his former girlfriend, the one he'd imagined crawling back to him, shot him a hate-filled look. "He thinks I'm stupid, but I'm not. I listened and I saw a lot of what was going on around me."

"Did you leave the room?"

"After he screamed at me, yes, of course."

"Was this about the time one of the men who'd been waiting outside came to the door?"

"Yes, it was right after that. He knocked on the door and said he needed to speak to Tucker Lindsey right away. I showed him to the office. He knocked on the door and Rod shouted, 'Now what?' He probably thought it was me. But the guy opened the door."

"Did you hear anything about what he had to say?"

"I was standing a little behind him where Rod couldn't see me," Lee said. "I heard him say that he had a message or something about Chechnya, but then he went in and shut the door behind him."

"Did he stay long?"

"No, just a couple of minutes. He left without saying anything, but he gave me kind of a funny look on the way out."

Standing against the rail in front of the jurors, Karp looked over as Fauhomme shifted uncomfortably in his seat. "You said this man mentioned something about Chechnya," the prosecutor said. "Was there something about Chechnya that you later associated with what you saw on the television?"

Lee nodded. "Yeah, that was the day that attack happened over there . . . the one where some Americans got killed and some others got taken."

"By 'over there,' do you mean in Chechnya?"

"Yes, Chechnya."

"What was the defendant Fauhomme's reaction to the events in Chechnya?"

Fauhomme winced every time Karp described him as "the defendant," which was just about any chance he got. It wasn't just a description, it was an accusation the tall man hurled at him.

"Oh, he was pissed off," Lee said. "It was only a little before the presidential elections and I'd hear him muttering to himself about how all the 'idiots were going to fuck it all up.' I was around a lot then — he liked to take me to all the dinner parties and events to show me off — and he was always having these little conversations, and I'd overhear things. Like about Chechnya. And Al Qaeda. He was real uptight if somebody brought up Al Qaeda. I remember we were having a small reception at my place and this tough-guy actor made a joke about the ghost of Al Qaeda attacking us in Chechnya, and Rod went through the roof. He told the guy to follow him out to the balcony, then closed the door; but me and all the other guests could see that he was yelling at the poor guy."

Karp walked over to stand in front of Lee. "Did Sam Allen ever come up in the conversations about Chechnya?"

"Yes, Rod was mad because Allen was causing problems . . . that's what he said, 'That fucker's causing problems.' "

"What, if anything, did the defendant, Fauhomme, ask you to do in regard to General Allen?"

"He told me to call Jenna and find out what Allen was saying about Chechnya and who he was talking to."

"And did you?"

"I called her and asked in a sort of round-about way if Sam ever said much of anything about Chechnya. But she wouldn't say and

595

told me that if I wanted to stay friends, I'd quit trying to get her to spy on him."

"Was there some other mention of Sam Allen in regard to Chechnya between the two defendants, Mr. Fauhomme and Mr. Lindsey?"

As he spoke, Karp walked back toward the defense table. Fauhomme watched him come over and tried to look defiant as his enemy approached. *Don't let them see you're afraid,* he thought. *But you are afraid,* the voice in his head replied. *You are very afraid.*

"Yeah, there was some meeting he went to . . . I think at Lindsey's office. I could tell he was worried when he came back from that meeting."

"How could you tell?"

"Well, for one thing he called Ray Baum to come over. I could tell Rod was sort of scared or nervous so I was paying attention. I listened at his office door when he told Ray to follow Allen. He said, 'If he drinks a cup of coffee, I want to know about it, and who he's drinking it with.' "

"How did you learn that Sam Allen had died?" Karp asked, looking from Fauhomme to Lindsey and then back at the witness stand.

"It was a few days later, after the weekend, a Monday, I think. I was back in New York.

Rod was there, too. I'd just come back from yoga class and when I came in, Rod was sitting in his favorite chair smoking one of his smelly cigars and watching the television."

"Was he doing anything in particular?"

Lee pursed her lips and shook her head. "Not really. Just sitting there watching. It took me a second to realize that the news was about Sam Allen. He'd been found dead in a hotel. I couldn't believe it."

"Did the defendant, Fauhomme, say anything at all?"

"I gasped and he just pointed at the television with his cigar and said, 'Sam Allen's dead . . . that's too bad.' "

"And what, if anything, did you think about his reaction?"

"I thought it was weird. I started to cry and he just looked at me like I was crazy and told me to knock it off or go to my room. I even asked him, 'Why are you acting like this? Sam's dead!' And he just kind of shrugged and said, 'People die all the time.' I was stunned. He just seemed so cold."

"What happened next?"

"I thought about Jenna and that she must be heartbroken. I tried to call her but didn't get an answer. I got scared, like maybe something happened to her, too. Then she called me. She was hysterical. She screamed that Sam had been murdered. I was like, 'What? What?' The television didn't say anything about murder."

"Where was the defendant, Fauhomme, during this phone call?"

"He was sitting in his chair but got up quick when I asked her why she thought it was murder. He put his head next to mine so he could hear what she was saying. She started talking about how she'd left her webcam on and recorded the murder. Rod turned sort of white and started writing me these notes. He said he was sending someone over to help her, and that if Sam was murdered, it might have something to do with the Chechnya stuff. He sent Ray Baum."

"How do you know that?"

"I was standing there when he called him. Then he went into his office. I heard him tell Baum that he was an idiot. A little while later, maybe an hour, he got another call — I think from Baum because he called him an idiot again. He was in his office but he was practically screaming when he said, 'Find her, goddammit, and get that fucking computer. You hear me, or you're fucking finished.'"

Lee hesitated. "Uh, sorry about the language, but that's what he said."

"That's okay," Karp said. "The jurors understand that you're just trying to be accurate. What, if anything, did Fauhomme say to you after that?"

"He came out of his office and saw me standing there," Lee said. "His face was purple, he'd been yelling so loud. But he kind of pulled himself together and was actually nice. He said that Jenna was missing and that he was worried about her safety. He said that if I heard from her I was to tell him right away. He said it was a matter of life and death."

"What was he like over the next twenty-four hours or so?"

"He was a wreck. Tucker Lindsey flew in from D.C. and stayed at a hotel near my place; they holed up a lot in Rod's office. Then Jenna called."

"What, if anything, did you do then?"

"I walked into Rod's office and pointed at my phone so that he would know it was her."

"Why did you do that?"

"I thought Jenna was in danger."

"But why not tell her you were talking to Rod?"

"He told me not to; he said he was worried that whoever killed Allen was trying to use Jenna to smear the president. And he said they might be able to hear my phone calls and he didn't want them to know that he was after them. I still . . . I still believed in the president and that Rod, whatever he was as a boyfriend, which wasn't much, he cared about this country. Anyway, in those days I did pretty much whatever I was told."

"So go on, please, tell the jury what you said to Jenna and then what happened next."

As Lee began to recall Blair's telephone call that set up the meeting at the theater, Lindsey slumped in his seat. "I hate you," he whispered to his codefendant.

"The feeling's mutual, you faggot," Fauhomme whispered back. "You queers just don't have what it takes."

"I hope that keeps you warm in prison," Lindsey shot back. "I think you're going to meet a lot of queers who will give you more than you can handle."

For once in his life, Fauhomme was speechless.

29

The first question Karp needed to settle when Lee appeared in his office the day after the election was whether she was Fauhomme's accomplice and therefore should be charged with the crime or was an unwitting pawn in his game. Hard questioning had convinced him that it was the latter, but that didn't ensure that she was going to hold up in court.

In fact, when Lee finished her account and he told her she was going to have to testify against her former boyfriend, she'd quailed in fear. "You don't know what you're up against," she'd cried. "He's friends with the president and is capable of anything, anything. And Lindsey, he comes off as this mild-mannered gay guy, but he's cold as a fish and he'd step on his mother's throat if it accomplished what he wants."

"Not to worry," Karp said. "You let me deal with those characters. All you have to do is tell the whole truth. You understand?" She'd just nodded, looking into Karp's eyes.

Now, eight months later, Karp ended his direct examination of Lee by playing the recording of the telephone call Blair had placed to her at his request following the events at Loon Lake. Another chapter was about to be closed, and then there would be just one more, but he didn't want to look too far ahead.

As the trial had proceeded, he realized that he could lead Faust into mistakes like a chess grandmaster trapping an overeager neophyte. The strategy behind the way he moved his "pieces" of evidence wasn't always evident in the moment, but was part of a gambit leading to eventual checkmate. He sensed that Faust would trap herself if he continued to present what she would see as openings in his case.

"Jenna! We've been so worried! Where have you been? Rod sent one of his security guys to your apartment last week, and you were gone. It looked like somebody had torn the place apart!"

"A man . . . the man I told you about who killed Sam . . . he showed up first. He must have been listening to my telephone calls. I recognized his tattoo on the security camera, but I went down the fire escape and got away. I was so scared; I didn't know who to turn to . . ."

"Oh, honey, you should have called me again. Rod . . . and the president's national security adviser, Tucker Lindsey, I overheard them talking. They didn't want to worry me, but they think that man works for the terrorists!"

Karp had stopped the recording at that point to ask, "Was the man with the tattoo Ray Baum?"

"Yes."

"And did you actually hear the defendants say that they believed Baum worked for terrorists?"

"Yes. They said it right in front of me. I think now that they wanted me to hear that so I would tell Jenna."

"So to be clear, they knew that she was talking about Ray Baum, a man who worked for your boyfriend at the time, Rod Fauhomme, and had NSA identification cards issued to him by Tucker Lindsey?"

"Yes."

"And that it was not some unknown 'terrorist' who was after her and her computer?"

"That's correct."

Karp started the recording again and watched the jury as Blair breathlessly described how the man with the tattoo found her at the cabin on Loon Lake and how she then lost him after a car chase. "Jenna, listen to me. Do you still have your computer? Rod thinks that's what they're after!"

Again Karp stopped the recording. "Why did you say that?"

"Rod was right there, and he wrote a note telling me what to say. And then he told me to tell her that Tucker Lindsey would meet her and make sure she was safe."

"And that's when you set up the meeting at the theater on 13th Street?"

"Yes."

Karp wrapped up the direct examination of Lee and turned her over to Faust for cross-examination. As he returned to his seat, he looked back at where Stupenagel and Marlene were sitting, but his eyes locked on a young man two rows behind them on the other side of the aisle. He was obviously staring at Stupenagel; then he turned his head and met Karp's eyes before looking quickly away. Conscious of the reports of a young man stalking the reporter outside her apartment, Karp made a mental note to ask Fulton to check on the guy. But for now he needed to focus on Faust as she cross-examined Lee.

As anticipated, the defense attorney's

main thrust was to paint Lee as part of a prostitution blackmail ring. "I believe your testimony was that my client, Mr. Fauhomme, gave you the money that you then deposited in your account?" Faust asked at one point.

"That's correct."

"And that you then paid these women who worked for you."

"They didn't work for me —"

"No? You arranged for them to appear at parties and sleep with wealthy men and then gave them money for it. In fact, that's pretty much the job description of a madam, wouldn't you say?"

"I was doing what Rod asked and he gave me the money to pay them."

"You were a pimp, right?"

"I guess that's one term for it."

"And these girls — your friends and acquaintances — they fit the description of prostitutes, or call girls if you will, right?"

Lee had hung her head. "Yes, that's correct."

Faust had sneered as she stalked up to the witness stand and stared up at Lee. "Do you have any proof that Mr. Fauhomme gave you the money you used to pay these women? Any receipts? Any canceled checks?"

"No. He always gave me cash."

"Are there any records to indicate that he transferred money from his account to you?"

"Like I said, he gave me cash."

"But there's no proof of it," Faust said, and raised a sheaf of papers she'd been carrying. "But right here are documents, Defense Exhibit M, that show that you deposited large amounts of cash over several years." She handed the papers to Lee. "Would you tell the jury please whose signature is on these copies of the deposit slips."

Lee hardly looked at the papers. Karp had told her this would happen and had shown her the documents before the trial. "Just tell the truth, and keep your answers short," he'd cautioned her. "It may get tough; it may be embarrassing; you might get angry or want to explain. But that will just play into the hands of the defense attorney. Stick with the simple truth, and you'll be okay."

"They're my signatures."

"And who was the only person with access to that account?"

"Me."

"Is Mr. Fauhomme a signatory on that account?"

"No. He told me to set it up and —"

"We've heard your explanation, Miss Lee."

Lee frowned and replied angrily, "Where else would I get that kind of money?"

Karp's face remained impassive, but inside he cringed. Sometimes a witness's natural reactions couldn't be helped, but Lee had walked right into Faust's line of fire.

The defense attorney smiled sardonically. "Where? Didn't you just say you were a pimp and that these women were essentially prostitutes? Don't men pay for prostitutes?"

"That's not true," Lee insisted. "Rod gave me the money and told me how much to pay the girls."

"But there is no proof of that. However, there is proof that you put cash in your account and you paid the prostitutes, isn't that right?"

Lee glared at Faust. "Yes."

Faust turned to walk toward the jury with her back to Lee. "And I can think of one more source for that cash. What about blackmail, Miss Lee, were these men blackmailed?"

"No!" Lee exclaimed.

"Did you threaten to expose their sordid little affairs?"

"You're making that up!" Lee yelled.

"Am I?" Faust shot back, raising her voice

and pointing her finger at Lee. "What would you say if Ariel Shimon, the man you said was the first of Jenna Blair's conquests, gave us a statement — and in fact will soon be on that stand to testify — that you black-mailed him for large sums of money?"

"He's lying!"

Faust moved on. "Tell the jury about your relationship with Ray Baum."

Lee frowned. "How do you mean?"

"What I mean," Faust said with a smirk, "is was it romantic? Sexual?"

"What? No! He worked for Rod. I only saw him when Rod was around. I didn't like him."

"But according to your testimony, you said you knew that Rod was going to send him over to Jenna Blair's apartment after she called you about Allen's death?"

"Yes, because Rod told me to say that he was sending someone. I was in shock and didn't think that it might be Ray Baum."

"Your friend's supposedly in a panic about having witnessed the murder of her lover, and you're just passing on notes from my client?"

"Yes."

"Miss Lee, did this conversation happen at all?" Faust said. "Or at least in the way you described it? Or was Miss Blair checking in now that the deed was done?"

"Objection, Your Honor, in form and substance," Karp said. "First, these are multiple questions, she can only answer one at a time. But more important, there's that same suggestion of some sort of misconduct."

"Objection sustained," Judge Hart said. "Please rephrase your questions and refrain from making unfounded allegations."

"Very well, let's move on," Faust said with a knowing smile. "Did you know about Sam Allen's cabin in Orvin?"

"I think I may have heard Jenna mention it before."

"Did Ray Baum know about it?"

"Apparently. He went there."

"How did he know how to find it, if you didn't tell him?"

"I don't know. Rod didn't say anything to me about what was going on."

"Or did you all know about the cabin because Jenna told you that's where she would go sometimes with General Allen?"

"I knew that. But I don't know where Baum got the information. I never told him or talked to him or Rod about it. To be honest, I didn't remember it at the time."

"That's your story and you're sticking with it?" Faust said.

"Miss Faust," Judge Hart said, "is that a question or a comment? Because if it's the latter, please refrain."

"Yes, Judge," Faust said. "Miss Lee, was Ray Baum part of your blackmail ring? Your muscle?"

"There was no blackmail ring. Baum was Rod's man. I had as little to do with him as possible."

"And Ray Baum isn't here to tell us anything different, is he?"

"I guess not."

"You guess not? He was shot and killed after allegedly trying to force Jenna Blair and Ariadne Stupenagel into digging their own grave, apparently intending to murder them. At least that's what the jury was told by Miss Stupenagel."

"That's what I've heard."

"From the district attorney. Did he feed you this story?" Faust said angrily.

"OBJECTION!" Karp said as he jumped to his feet.

"There you go again, Miss Faust. How many times do I have to warn you about making allegations without a legitimate offer of proof? Sustained," the judge said, shaking his head.

"Miss Lee, is it possible that this was a

falling-out among your little blackmail ring?"

"There was no blackmail ring."

"Maybe Ray Baum knew where to find Miss Blair because you sent him to kill her, is that right, Miss Lee?" Faust said, her voice rising to almost a shout.

Lee looked as if she was about to shout back, but then she glanced at Karp, who gave her a small nod. She visibly relaxed. "There was no blackmail scheme. I hardly knew Ray Baum. And you're making all of this up."

The witness's regaining control seemed to take the wind out of Faust, who, given the court's admonitions, gave up after a few more questions. Then Karp rose for redirect, keeping it short and simple.

"Miss Lee, who sent Tucker Lindsey to meet Jenna Blair at the theater on 13th Street?"

"Rod told me to tell her that Lindsey would meet her at the theater."

"Were you ever in a position to direct the president's national security adviser or the defendant Fauhomme to engage in any such schemes involving murder or blackmail?"

The question seemed to melt Lee's resolve to be strong. She sobbed. "No. I'm just a yoga instructor and a lousy actress."

Karp walked up to the witness stand and grabbed a box of tissues, which he offered to Lee. "It's okay," he said gently, "take a moment."

The young woman blew her nose and dabbed at the tears. At last she nodded. "Thank you."

"You're welcome," Karp replied. "Are you ready to go on?"

When the young woman nodded, Karp turned to Judge Hart and said, "Your Honor, at this time it seems abundantly appropriate for the people to play for the jury People's Exhibit 32, a recording of a conversation between the witness and Jenna Blair on the morning following Sam Allen's murder."

Faust's eyes grew large and Caulkin turned red as she jumped to her feet. "Objection, Your Honor, we have no record of this on the evidence list given to us by the district attorney."

"Your Honor, please accept this as a matter of legitimate rebuttal concerning, particularly, counsel's attempted impeachment of the witness. Once again counsel has delved into the realm of fantasy in which she continues to assert without any evidence that the witness and others were involved in a conspiracy to murder General Allen,"

Karp said patiently, as if schooling a young law student. "She just attacked the witness's account of this conversation and intimated again that whatever was said was somehow self-incriminatory. This recording should clear that up."

"Miss Faust, I will not repeat any more admonitions. You opened the door. I'll allow it," Judge Hart said tiredly.

Karp walked over to the prosecution table, where he pressed a button that would play the recording for those in the courtroom to hear. His computer tech, the same one who'd been insulted by the FBI agents at the murder scene, had discovered an app on Lee's telephone that recorded all of her conversations and stored them in a database.

As Jenna Blair's desperate voice rang out in the otherwise silent courtroom, Karp smiled to himself. He'd taken another piece from his opponent's board, and the black king was in sight, sitting at the defense table with his head in his hands. And there were more traps to come.

"Connie, oh, my God, Connie . . . he was murdered!"

30

The young woman sat in the witness chair with her head bowed and tears streaming down her face and dripping onto the stand in front of her. It was a little after noon and Jenna Blair had been on the stand for nearly four hours while Karp questioned her. She was exhausted, and her grief was palpable in the silent courtroom.

When he met with her that morning before the trial resumed, she looked as if she'd been crying and hadn't slept since arriving in New York from New Mexico, which she admitted was true. "I was okay in Taos," she said. "Maybe it was being around Lucy and Ned, and living in such beautiful natural surroundings, but I slept, for the most part. When I cried, they seemed to be cleansing tears and I would be at peace, for the moment anyway. But since I've been back in New York, I've only dozed, and my tears feel hot and bitter."

Karp told her that it was okay to be afraid and nervous about her testimony. "I won't sugarcoat it, the defense is going to come after you with everything they got," he said. "They're going to call you names and accuse you of everything from prostitution to murder. I'll be able to head some of it off at the pass, but not all; it will get rough."

However, instead of worrying her, his warnings seemed to give her more resolve. "I don't care what they call me — some of it is even true — or what they accuse me of doing. I know the truth and they can't take that away," she said. "I'm sad and anxious, but I'm not afraid. In fact, mostly what I am is angry. Those men took something precious from me that I will never be able to replace, and it's not just Sam, though my heart is broken and right now it doesn't feel like I'll ever be whole again. But they also robbed me of my trust. I was pretty apolitical before this; I suppose that because I'm young I leaned more to being a liberal. But in the end, I figured that in spite of all the things that get said, the people in power all have the country's best interests at heart, and just disagree on how to accomplish that. But it's not true. They only care about their own interests, and some of them are even willing to kill a man like Sam Allen to protect those."

Although new tears had sprung to her eyes as she spoke, she'd looked at him and smiled. "I'll be okay out there today, Mr. Karp. I won't let you, or Sam, down."

Blair was true to her word. With Karp feeding her questions, she had calmly described how a small-town girl from Colorado who came to New York City to be an actress had instead become "essentially a call girl," beginning with the Israeli businessman Ariel Shimon. "I accepted money for dating wealthy, and sometimes powerful, men, which usually led to sex," she said. "I began to see it all as just a business deal."

When asked where the money came from, without hesitation Blair said she knew that Fauhomme supplied it. "Connie told me," she said. "And she'd also tell me sometimes how pleased he was with the reports I gave her, or because one of the guys had told him that he was happy with me."

Everything changed when she was introduced to Sam Allen. She told the jury about the meeting with Fauhomme when he said the president wanted to know if the general could be counted on to be a team player. So she'd agreed to meet Allen and "see where it led, as I had done with the other men I'd dated for Fauhomme." For the first time in her testimony, Blair had faltered and choked up. "But Sam was like no other man I've ever met. He had the spirit and love of life of a young man, but the depth and soul that I've never found in guys my age."

Blair said she fell in love quickly. "And it was the best day of my life when he told me that he loved me, too."

At that point in her testimony, Karp had altered the course of the questioning just slightly when he asked, "What, if anything, did he say to you about the events in Chechnya?"

Describing how they'd been at the bed and breakfast in Virginia when he heard the news, she said, "He was angry that it took several hours for Lindsey to tell him about the attack. He was in charge of the CIA but it was like they were trying to keep a lid on it." But he was soon consumed with getting to the bottom of what occurred, which affected the amount of time they could spend together.

"I was okay with it," she said. "I understood that if there was anything he loved more than his family, or me, it was our country. He didn't tell me much, but I knew he felt that he and the American people weren't being told the truth, and he was going to dig until he found out what it was. I didn't realize how deeply he felt about it until I saw that tape he made at the cabin after he . . . after he died. Only then did I realize what he was dealing with, and why they killed him."

Returning to his original line of questioning, Karp asked, "Did there come a time when you realized that something about your relationship with General Allen needed to change?"

"Yes," she replied. "I'd been thinking about it for some time, but it came to a head that last weekend at the cabin on Loon Lake. We were both pretty preoccupied. He had the congressional hearing coming up, and, though I didn't realize it at the time, he was being blackmailed by Fauhomme and Lindsey. . . .

"Anyway, he had his confirmation hearings coming up after the election and the last thing he needed was a scandal," Blair said. "And to be honest, I couldn't live with it anymore. Maybe it sounds funny coming from a . . ." She sighed before going on. ". . . coming from someone who'd worked as a call girl, but I was having a hard time dealing with the fact that he was married, and I know he was having a hard time with it, too. Having an affair was not a natural state for Sam Allen to be in. So I told him

618

that I thought it was best that we take a break until after the hearings . . . and that if he wanted to continue to see me, he needed to do the right thing and divorce his wife. I wasn't going to be the 'other woman' anymore."

"Was that an ultimatum, 'Divorce your wife or I'm gone'?" Karp asked.

Blair shook her head. "It wasn't like that," she said. "I loved him very much. It was more like giving him an out if he wanted it. And I think we both needed to step back for our sanity and clear up these things in our lives. I'd also made up my mind to tell him about what I had been doing for Rod Fauhomme. He deserved to know, so I told him there was something important I needed to discuss with him — something that might change the way he looked at me — but I didn't want to do it until after the congressional hearing."

During the trip home from the cabin, they'd both been lost in thought. He'd dropped her off and then gone to the Casablanca "to work on his presentation," but had contacted her via webcam that evening, wanting to talk. "I remember he was getting sleepy, which was unusual for Sam; he was usually the Energizer Bunny. But he said he'd been drinking scotch, and I knew he'd been dealing with a lot of stress. I told him that I was just getting in the shower and would call him in twenty or thirty minutes when I got out."

Blair's voice grew husky as she struggled to finish. "That was the last thing we ever said to each other." It was too much, and she buried her head in her hands and wept.

Karp waited for a minute so that she could gather herself before gently moving her on. "What did you do after your shower?"

Lifting her head from her hands, Blair wiped her nose with a tissue. "I came back to my computer; my screen had gone dark, but I noticed that it was still recording his room. I thought he might still be on but all I could see were shadows. I thought he'd gone to bed."

"How did you learn that Sam Allen was dead?"

Blair took several deep breaths. "I was in a coffee shop," she said. "He hadn't texted me . . . he always sent me a text every morning . . . so I thought he'd left early to go see his friend at West Point and just forgot. I was going to give him a hard time about it." She stopped and smiled at the memory. "But then I saw the news . . . Sam was dead. Somebody, I don't remember if it was the news or someone standing around me, said it was suicide, but I didn't believe it. Sam Allen was not the sort of man to quit or give up on anything. So I looked at the recording on my computer to see if there was some clue that he was suicidal, but what I saw . . ."

Again the young woman stopped. She tried to speak, but her voice came out first as a sort of thin keening. Karp walked up to the stand and poured her a glass of water, which she accepted gratefully.

"You were saying that you saw . . ." Karp encouraged her.

Blair nodded sadly. "I saw a man . . . the man with the tattoo on his arm . . . murder Sam," she said, her voice now a monotone.

"This man?" Karp asked, holding up the photograph of Ray Baum already entered into evidence.

"Yes, that's him," she answered.

After seeing the murder on her laptop, Blair explained, she'd called Connie Rae Lee. "I didn't know who else to turn to," she said. "I was scared and thought that maybe Rod Fauhomme would be able to help because he was the president's friend. Connie said Rod was sending a security man over; I was looking at the camera feed from the outside of my apartment building when I saw these two guys pull up in a dark car. But one of them was the man with the tattoo. I knew I'd been betrayed, so I ran for it."

Karp led her through the events in Orvin. "I was scared to death," Blair testified. "I didn't know where to go. But then for some reason an email Sam sent me while I was in the shower popped into my head. It was a line from *The Last of the Mohicans:* 'No matter how long it takes, no matter how far, I will find you.' And the numbers, 121078, which is my birthday. That's when I knew he sent it for a reason, and I had to get to the Loon Lake cabin." As the jury sat in rapt attention, Blair explained how Allen's safe was hidden behind a false front in the bookcase, and then what she'd found in the safe.

Once again Karp got the sense of leading the jury through the pages of a detective novel in which the things they'd all read earlier were now fitting together, filling out and completing the story. The arrival of Stupenagel and Marlene. The doors being kicked in by Baum and his partner. Digging her own grave and the shoot-out.

"After the events that night at Loon Lake, did you and I talk at some length?" Karp asked.

"Yes, for several hours, and I told you

everything I just said," Blair replied.

"And did I ask you to place a call to Connie Rae Lee and say that you wanted to give someone in authority your laptop so that you would be safe?"

"Yes. She told me I would be met by Lindsey and that he would take care of me."

Karp walked over to the defense table and pointed. "You're talking about the defendant, Tucker Lindsey, the man sitting here? Had you ever met him before?"

"Yes, that's him. And yes, I met him at the same dinner party where I was introduced to Sam at Fauhomme's house on Long Island."

When Karp pointed at Lindsey, the defendant had not raised his head but continued writing on a legal pad as if he was not even in the same room. Shaking his head, Karp turned back to the witness stand, where he continued questioning Blair about the events at the theater until at last he reached the point where he intended to play the recording: the recording of Sam Allen's murder.

Throughout it all, Blair had held up amazingly well. But now she sat with her head down, exhausted and on the edge of more tears. However, she wasn't the only woman in the courtroom who dreaded this moment. Turning toward the gallery, Karp nodded at a gray-haired woman dressed in a dark dress who sat stoically between two grim-faced young men.

He'd talked to Sam Allen's wife, Martha Allen, in his office before the trial and told her some of what he expected would come out during the testimony. "I want you to know so that you're prepared if you are going to attend," he'd said.

She'd listened to his explanation with grace and dignity before speaking. "When all of this started to come out, I won't say that it didn't hurt," she told him. "Of course I was aware that Sam and I had grown apart. But it was one of those things where it was just easier to ignore than do anything about it. I loved him very much, and I know that in his way he loved me, too. We had a good life and raised two fine boys to be exceptional young men."

She was silent for a moment before adding, "You know, I don't blame that young woman or even my husband, though I wish he'd said something sooner. I know Sam, and living a lie had to eat at him, even if he was just waiting for our youngest to get out of high school before he asked for a divorce. He was quite a catch, and she must have been something herself to keep up with him.

But she couldn't have seduced him if he wasn't ready to be seduced, so I hope they both found some happiness before . . ."

At that point, she had bowed her head and started to cry quietly. Karp handed her a tissue. "Can I get you something?" he asked.

"No, no, thank you," she'd replied as she pulled herself together. "It's okay. I'm okay. I really am. I'm a little tired of having the media camped out on my front lawn and reading about how I let myself go and the tabloid headlines about Sam and the girl . . . Jenna. So the tears come and go, but I have some fine memories and my sons to sustain me."

"Will you be attending the trial?"

Allen had picked up her head. The tears disappeared and her eyes narrowed into angry slits. "Of course, I'll be there, Mr. Karp," she said tightly. "I'll be there for Sam and for our sons. I want to hear for myself if those two sons of bitches had anything to do with his death, and if they did, I hope you fry them."

Martha Allen hadn't missed a day, sitting in the seats reserved for her and her sons in the first row behind the prosecution table. When Jenna Blair was called to the stand, she'd listened intently but without any apparent emotion while ignoring the stares

625

and whispers from the media and spectators in the gallery. There was only one part
of the trial that she didn't want to see or
hear — the recording from Blair's computer
of her husband's murder. So at a signal
from Karp, she got up and walked out of
the courtroom.

Karp watched her leave and then addressed Judge Hart. "If it please the court, I
now intend to play a recording from the
witness's laptop computer, People's Exhibit
29," he said.

Faust jumped to her feet. "I object," she
exclaimed. "This recording is not on the
people's evidence list, and we were not
given a copy, in violation of the rules of
evidence."

"Mr. Karp, how do you respond?" Hart
asked.

Karp sternly replied, "Your Honor, the
defense was not given a copy of the recording because they already are in possession
of the original." He turned just in time to
watch four sets of jaws at the defense table
drop simultaneously.

The judge looked bemused. "Care to explain?"

"Sure, Your Honor," Karp replied. "Miss
Blair's computer was loaded by a computer
technician from my office with a GPS track-

ing device in its software. The device was activated when the laptop was opened at the apartment of Connie Rae Lee approximately one hour after the defendant Lindsey seized it. The computer remained there for several days and was then transported to Arlington, Virginia, where it was placed in a safe-deposit box registered to the defendant Rod Fauhomme at a branch of the Bank of Virginia. Several months ago, the computer was again moved and currently resides at the law offices of Caulkin, Burrows, and McInish on Fifth Avenue. I believe that the defense has had plenty of time to view what's on the recording."

"Counsel?" Hart asked, looking over at the defense table.

Faust and Caulkin put their heads together and whispered fervently. "I'll withdraw my objection," Faust said with a smile. "We were planning on putting the computer and the recording into evidence when we presented our case anyway."

Although Faust thought she was being cagey, Karp knew what she was up to and why the change of heart. Taken out of context, the webcam conversation between Allen and Blair could be interpreted as Blair having said something at Loon Lake that he wanted to discuss. Such as a blackmail threat. And that she'd known the murder was being recorded and had watched out of some sick desire.

In fact, he'd anticipated this reaction from the defense and was prepared to put it all into context. But more than just the dry facts went into building a case. Jurors in part judge the validity of testimony based on their assessment of a witness's demeanor. It was why Huff's testimony was so powerful — not just his recounting of the events, but his tearful, moving acknowledgment that the men who died trying to save him "deserved better than my silence." And that was why Karp told Blair that instead of playing the recording of Allen's death before or after she was on the stand, he would play it during, so that the jury could *see* the truth about her relationship with Sam Allen.

Although he knew it had to be tearing her heart out, Blair did her best to watch the recording. She bit her lip when Baum entered the room and patted her unconscious lover's cheek and said, "Sleepy, old man?" And covered her mouth, but not her eyes, when he took a syringe from a small case he carried in his jacket pocket and then tilted the general's head back and forced his jaws open. A small cry escaped her lips, echoed by others from members of the jury and those in the gallery, as the killer injected the poison. But still she watched as the man she loved was dragged from his chair and disappeared from the camera's view.

Baum moved back into the camera's view and sat down at the computer and typed, and Blair's hand dropped from her mouth. Then, when the killer smiled, not realizing he'd been recorded, and took out his cell phone, punched in a number, and said, "It's done," her eyes hardened and she stared with hatred at the two defendants, who studiously kept their eyes on the television screen.

When it was over, Karp asked her a few questions before turning her over to the defense. Faust rose, and as he'd predicted, she spent two hours attacking Blair's character and trying to paint a demeaning image of her. She was a whore. A blackmailer. A murderess. She'd concocted her story to fit what the district attorney wanted to hear to escape punishment by pointing at "two innocent men" as the killers.

Karp had intervened with objections when necessary, buying Blair small moments of reprieve from the relentless and remorseless assault. But for the most part he let Faust wear herself out like a boxer who spends too much of his energy in the earlier rounds only to have nothing left at the final bell. And when Faust with a sneer finally was done, there was not a sympathetic face among the jurors for her clients. Only contempt.

Still, Karp left nothing to chance and moved in for the coup de grâce during redirect. But first he nodded to Fulton, who was standing in the back of the courtroom. The big detective stepped out and then returned, escorting Martha Allen, who'd said she wanted to be present during this time.

When she was settled in her seat, Karp turned back to the witness. "Miss Blair, I note you are wearing a diamond ring on your left hand; is that an engagement ring?"

Blair looked down at her hand and nodded. "It was supposed to be."

"Who bought the ring for you?"

"Sam."

"Did he give it to you personally?"

The young woman shook her head and wiped at her eyes. "No, he never got the chance."

Karp left the next question hanging and walked over to the prosecution table, where he picked up a DVD. "Your Honor, this is a second recording made by General Sam Allen at the cabin on Loon Lake, made shortly after the recording already submitted into evidence as People's Exhibit 29."

"Objection, Your Honor," Faust said.

"Yes, Miss Faust?"

"Just a moment, Your Honor," Faust said. There was a flurry at the defense table as the two attorneys hurriedly pored over their paperwork and conferred. Then Faust spoke up. "Your Honor, we object to this as improper redirect, and we have no record of a second recording."

"Mr. Karp?" Hart asked.

"Your Honor, as I said, this recording was made by the deceased as a personal message to Miss Blair, made on the morning of the day he was murdered, while he was still at the cabin," Karp said. "Beginning with their opening statements, as well as the cross-examination of Miss Stupenagel, Miss Lee, and now Miss Blair, the defense has continually intimated without one scintilla of evidence that Miss Lee, Miss Blair, and Ray Baum were in league to blackmail Sam Allen and then, when that did not work, to murder him. I had not planned on offering this recording except now to correct this false narrative insinuation. Miss Faust has again implied that the conversation between Allen and Miss Blair that was recorded on her laptop is in reference to a blackmail attempt. I would ask that the jury be allowed to view this message from the general to Miss Blair so that the jurors can make up their own minds as to the state of the relationship between the deceased and this witness."

Judge Hart shook his head. "Miss Faust, this may be an additional consequence of your inability to adhere to my admonitions and to satisfy the fundamentals of a legal offer of proof required, given the thrust of your defense. I'll allow it; please proceed."

The recording began with Sam Allen sitting in a chair on the front porch of the Loon Lake cabin. He was dressed in an old army sweatshirt and a beat-up Yankee ballcap. He smiled.

"Hello, my love," he said. "It's Sunday morning here at Loon Lake. You're still asleep and I wanted to say these things before you wake."

The general's smile faded and he looked troubled. "If you're watching this, then something has happened to me. Something drastic, because nothing short of that could keep me from you so that I could say these things when we get together after the hearings."

Allen looked out over the lake and the call of a loon could be heard in the background.

He sighed. "It has been my hope that we would have a long and loving life together. That you would get your law degree and hang that shingle in downtown Orvin and leave it to me to watch our children. I have hoped that you would never have to watch this recording, but if it has come to that, then I have some things that need to be said."

He turned back to the camera, his eyes wet with tears. "First, I'm sorry. I believe in my heart that we were meant to meet, fall in love, and make a life together. However, I went about this the wrong way, and in doing so have disrespected my wife and you. I should have asked for a divorce before I began with you; Martha is a good woman, a fine friend, a great mother, and she deserved better from me. I can only hope that someday she will forgive me. At the same time, I need to apologize to you. I kept asking you to wait for the 'right time,' after my son got out of high school, then after the congressional hearings, then after my confirmation hearings."

Allen stopped talking for a moment as he stared steadily at the camera. "But in love, as with many things in life, there is no right time, there is only now. Not only should I have done right by Martha, but I should have asked you to be my wife regardless of these other issues."

Holding up a small jewelry box, Allen said, "You will find this in the safe. I intended it to accompany my proposal, but if I can't be with you, I want you to have it as a small token of the enormous . . . and undying . . . love and respect I have for you."

The loon cried out again and Allen turned toward it. "I have arranged so that my wife and sons will never want for anything, but I am hoping that Martha will understand when my will is read and she learns that I've left this cabin to you. I hope that someday you will come here with someone who loves you as much as I do, and that your children and grandchildren will play on this porch where once I held you in the moonlight. And sometimes when the loon calls, you will feel me near, because no matter how long it takes, no matter how far, I will find you."

Allen paused and took a deep breath before smiling. "Just like in the movies."

31

A lot of wet eyes watched Jenna Blair leave
the witness stand and walk with her head
up out of the hushed courtroom. When she
was gone Karp turned to Judge Hart and
said, "Your Honor, that concludes the
people's case."

The judge immediately sent the jury home
and then listened as Faust made the per-
functory motion to have the case dismissed,
saying that the prosecution had not proved
the defendants' guilt beyond a reasonable
doubt. Hart had snorted. "I realize that it's
sort of a tradition to make such a motion,
Miss Faust, but I'd say you have your work
cut out for you. Motion denied. I'll see
everybody here and ready to go at nine in
the morning sharp."

Karp rushed from the courtroom to the
witness waiting room to speak to Blair
before she left. But when he knocked and
entered, he was surprised to see Martha

Allen standing with her arms around the sobbing younger woman. "It's okay, dear, we all loved him," Mrs. Allen said as she gave him a nod, and he quietly backed out of the room.

"We can catch up tomorrow," he said as the door clicked behind him.

In the morning, he found Jenna Blair waiting for him outside his office door. She was leaving for New Mexico at noon. "Lucy and Ned have offered to let me hang around a little longer until the press moves on to their next scandal," she said before wistfully adding, "I'd like to go to the cabin on Loon Lake — I hope I can live there someday — but for now there wouldn't be a moment's peace, and to be honest, I'd be a little afraid. Mr. Fulton told me there's been some death threats. I guess some people don't want to hear the truth." She held out her hand. "So this is good-bye for now, Mr. Karp, and I wanted to thank you."

Karp took her hand and shook it warmly. "You're welcome, though I'm the one who should be thanking you," he said. "Without you I don't know that we would have ever been able to get to the bottom of this. You've been very brave." He hesitated, looking for the right words to say. "I'm so sorry for your loss, but I hope you'll take Sam's words to heart and find someone to love you."

Tears brimmed in Blair's eyes, but she nodded. "It seems impossible now, but maybe someday," she said.

"Sure you don't want to stick around and see justice done?" Karp said, already knowing what her answer would be.

"No," she replied. "I've said what I needed to say. I got a good start on grieving when I was in New Mexico, but the trial was always hanging over my head. Now, I'm looking forward to spending a lot of time remembering what it was like to be loved by such a good man. I'm sure you'll handle the bad guys just fine on your own."

An hour later, Karp was sitting at the prosecution table watching as Faust opened the defense case by calling Ariel Shimon to the witness stand. He entered the courtroom wearing what appeared to be a fifteen-hundred-dollar Armani suit and equally expensive shoes. He flashed a bright smile, but he couldn't hide a bad case of nerves when he took his seat and tried to pour himself a glass of water but knocked it over.

Also dressed more as she would be going to a dinner party in Washington, D.C., than a New York courtroom, Faust smiled. "That's okay, Mr. Shimon, we realize this is an uncomfortable situation for you. But could you begin by telling the jurors a little bit about yourself?"

Shimon tried to smile back but was not very convincing. "Yes, I am an Israeli. A former colonel in the Israeli army and am currently a businessman specializing in defense contracts."

"Are you married? Do you have a family back in Israel?"

Shifting uncomfortably and licking his lips nervously, Shimon nodded. "Yes, I have been married for twenty-two years and have two children in Tel Aviv."

"Are you in politics? Or have you ever had political aspirations?"

Again, Shimon nodded. "I did . . . until this."

Faust turned toward the defense table. "Mr. Shimon, do you know our clients, Rod Fauhomme and Tucker Lindsey?"

"I've met Mr. Lindsey once at a White House dinner," Shimon said. "And I've known Mr. Fauhomme for six or seven years."

"Would you say you were on friendly terms with Mr. Fauhomme?"

Shimon shrugged slightly. "Friendly enough. During some of that time I was unofficially representing some people in Israel who were interested in American politics, so naturally I became acquainted with the president's campaign manager."

"Did you ever attend parties hosted by Mr. Fauhomme or his girlfriend at the time, Connie Rae Lee?"

"I did."

"And did you at one of these parties meet a young woman named Jenna Blair?"

Shimon blushed. "Yes, Miss Blair was introduced to me by Miss Lee."

"Would you say you initiated the contact with Miss Blair or was it the other way around?"

"Oh, it was definitely the other way around," Shimon said. "Miss Lee asked me how long I was going to be in town and if I needed female companionship. I said no. But a little later at the party, she brought Miss Blair over and then left her there with me."

"And how would you have described Miss Blair's reaction to you?"

"Aggressive," Shimon said. "We're not used to such aggressive women in Israel, so I thought it was just the American way."

"Was she sexually aggressive?"

Shimon licked his lips again and nodded. "Very. A lot of innuendo and flirting."

"And how did you respond?"

"Well, I . . . I . . . oh, this is embarrassing," the Israeli said, acting the part. "But I'd had a few drinks and was a long way from home. The attention of a pretty young woman was very flattering."

"How did the evening end?"

Shimon heaved a sigh. "She asked if I would give her a ride home. I had a car with a driver and thought, 'Why not?' I had a lot to drink by that time and was feeling no pain."

"And?"

"And while we were driving to her apartment, she began kissing me and touching me . . . you know, in a suggestive way. When we reached her apartment, she asked if I wanted to come up for a nightcap." He sighed again. "I am ashamed to say, we ended up in bed."

Faust nodded. "So you had sex. Did you ever see Miss Blair again?"

Shimon's face grew hard. "Just once. She called the next day — how she got my number I didn't know — and said that we had to meet. I told her that the night before had been a mistake. My wife and I had been having difficulties, but I loved her and felt great shame. But she insisted. She said it was important to my future. So we met at a coffee shop."

"Was there anyone there but you and Miss Blair?"

"Yes, Miss Lee and a man she introduced as Ray, just Ray."

"What was the purpose of this meeting?"

Shimon passed a hand across his tan face. "I was shown a computer," he said. "There was a video on the computer of myself and Miss Blair having sex. I said, 'What is this?' And Miss Lee said, 'This is what will destroy you if you do not do what we say.' "

"And what was it that they said you had to do?"

"I had to pay them five thousand dollars in cash every week or they would send the video to an Israeli television station and to my wife."

"You were blackmailed?"

"Yes. I made a mistake — once — but I felt I had to pay for my family's sake. So I paid."

"How long did this go on for?"

Shimon shrugged. "About three weeks."

"So you paid roughly fifteen thousand dollars for a one-night stand?"

Hanging his head, Shimon nodded. "Yes."

"You said you paid the extortion money for three weeks. What happened after that?"

"I said, 'No more. I will not pay one cent more. And if you don't stop, I will go to the police!' "

"Were you bluffing?"

"Yes. I would have continued to pay. I did not want to hurt my wife."

"What did Miss Lee, Miss Blair, and this man named Ray do?"

"Nothing. They just went away and nothing happened. I felt like such a fool."

"You mentioned that you had political aspirations until this. Did something happen to those aspirations?"

Shimon nodded sadly. "Yes. I decided I would not run for office. I would have this blackmail hanging over my head forever and I did not want to become a target again."

After a few more questions, Faust turned the witness over to Karp, who rose and walked over to the jury rail, which he leaned against. "Mr. Shimon, do you have any records of these payments you made?" he asked, knowing he was echoing Faust's questions to Lee.

"No. Everything was in cash."

"So there are no records of you withdrawing five thousand dollars in cash from your bank, or cashing a check for five thousand dollars?" Karp asked.

"I wrote checks on my account in Israel and cashed them here," Shimon said.

"At which bank?"

Shimon acted as if he was trying to remember. "Different banks. I don't remember which ones; it's been a long time, several years."

"Did you bring those canceled checks with you?" Karp asked.

"Uh, no, I wasn't asked to bring them."

Karp looked surprised. "You mean to tell me that defense counsel didn't ask you to bring the proof that you withdrew fifteen thousand dollars over the course of three weeks to pay for this one-night stand?"

"I probably wouldn't still have them anyway," Shimon replied, his eyes darting over to the defense table.

"No, but wouldn't your bank have statements going back that far?"

"Possibly, I don't know . . . I . . ."

"But you weren't asked to bring those?"

"No."

"So in other words, you have no documentation to back up what you just told the jury?"

"They have my word. I am telling the truth," Shimon said, trying to sound offended.

"And did you tell your wife the truth when you went home?"

"What?"

"Did you tell your wife that you'd had sex

with another woman and then paid her and her friends fifteen thousand dollars to keep it a secret?"

"Um, no."

"So you tell the truth when it's convenient to you, is that right?" Karp asked.

"I am telling the truth now."

"Yes, when it's convenient to you. And what if I was to tell you that a waiter at Asiate and the doorman at the Plaza remember you and Miss Blair together?"

This time it was Karp who was bluffing. None of the waiters currently at Asiate had been there three years earlier, and none of the doormen at the Plaza had been able to identify a photograph of Blair shown to them by Fulton. The detective had also had no luck finding Blair's roommate from that time.

Shimon's eyes widened and he looked over at Faust, whose face had grown tight. She didn't know Karp was bluffing either. "They would be mistaken. Or maybe they saw me with someone else."

"More women that you didn't tell your wife about?" Karp said.

"No. I . . . uh . . . I only saw one, Jenna. Just once."

Karp walked over to the prosecution table, where he picked up a plastic bag containing a diamond tennis bracelet. "Mr. Shimon, Jenna Blair testified that you gave her this tennis bracelet on the night you dumped her, is that true?"

Shimon shook his head. "No. I never bought such a thing."

"No? You didn't purchase this at Macy's and give it to your mistress, Jenna Blair?"

Looking at the jurors, Shimon tried another smile. "No, why would I buy a diamond bracelet for someone I hardly knew who was trying to blackmail me?"

Karp raised an eyebrow and smiled. "Exactly, Mr. Shimon, why would you?"

Strolling over to stand in front of the witness, Karp looked puzzled. "A couple of things are troubling me about your testifying here today, Mr. Shimon?"

Shimon flashed the nervous smile again. "And what would that be?"

"Well, for one thing, how did the defense know that this had happened to you? Did you tell the defendants three years ago?"

"No. I read about the trouble Mr. Fauhomme was in and then I thought that maybe it was related to what happened to me. So I called."

"Did you go to the police all those years ago?"

"No; like I said, I didn't want anyone to know."

"But it's okay now," Karp interjected. "And you know, that's another thing that's been bothering me since I realized you were on the defense witness list."

"Why is that?"

"It's just that I've been trying to figure out what they have on an Israeli business-man to make him come all the way back to the United States and testify at a murder trial about a one-night stand."

"I don't understand."

"That's the point, neither do I. Isn't your wife going to find out? Your kids? If you had any political aspirations, I'd imagine this about does them in, wouldn't you agree?"

"I imagine."

"Then I can only surmise that it must be something big, something worse than a quick fling in New York City three years ago. What is it, Mr. Shimon? What do they have?"

"Objection, Your Honor," Faust said.

"I'll withdraw the question," Karp said. "I don't think I'm going to get an honest answer anyway."

32

Tucker Lindsey's hand shook as he poured himself a glass of water on the witness stand, spilling a little as he brought it to his lips. As his attorney, Bill Caulkin, took a break in the questioning to look over his notes, he hazarded a glance over at Karp, but quickly looked away as if he was a schoolboy who'd been caught doing something naughty. The cool reserve he'd always presented to the American public as the president's national security adviser was a thing of the past, and Karp took note of it.

As trials went on, Karp studied how a defendant's demeanor changed. It varied, of course, but generally, the weight of the evidence, particularly the defendant's "inner secrets" — that evidence that the defendant believed would never be revealed — had the most profound effect on his mood. Without appearing to pay much attention, he watched how defendants interacted with their attorneys and sometimes, in a case such as this one, with their codefendants. He studied their body language, listened to their voices, and gauged their faces to see how they were sleeping or to search for the telltale signs of their being medicated.

Of the two defendants in this trial, Rod Fauhomme had exhibited the widest variety of behavioral changes. In the beginning, he manifested confidence and contempt for the charges brought against him and for Karp himself. He was constantly writing notes, many of which he'd pass to his attorney, as if directing his defense. His interaction with Lindsey was minimal but always with a macho, take-charge flair. But as the prosecution's case had gone forward and the evidence against him — carefully laid out by Karp — mounted, and his attorney's attempts at countering the prosecution were thrown back in her face, cracks appeared in his deportment, like the fissures in a dam about to give way. With each witness and every motion denied, anger, worry, and even fear would play across his face before he had a chance to control them.

By the time Karp rested the people's case, Fauhomme's florid countenance often had the look of a hunted animal. His eyes darted around and his smile looked more like a grimace. He frequently turned during breaks to glance back at the gallery, not as if he was searching for friendly faces but more like a deer looking for danger. He hardly spoke to his attorney, though he glared at her often, and he and his codefendant might as well have been sitting in different rooms for all the interaction they had.

Tucker Lindsey had also changed, but in a different way. He'd begun the trial as one might expect a national security adviser used to dealing with high stakes. He was cool and collected to the point where it often appeared that he was listening to an interesting discussion that hardly involved him. His body language indicated that he didn't care at all for Fauhomme or have much faith in Faust, but more as if they were two people who didn't matter to him than with any real acrimony. He'd occasionally leaned his head over to listen to Caulkin, but otherwise was basically as he was in life, haughtily self-assured.

However, as with Fauhomme, as the trial went on and the case against them piled up, the arrogant veneer gave way to fearful concern. Soon after Huff's testimony he would sit through the entire proceedings with his head down and his hands on his lap or on the table in front of him, hardly moving except to pour a glass of water. The neatly coiffed hair and designer clothes gave way to a rumpled look, and sometimes he appeared to not have shaved. He'd grown noticeably thinner, with the hollows of his cheeks becoming more pronounced.

Karp noticed when he walked over to the defense table that if Lindsey looked up, it was with red-rimmed eyes, beneath which dark circles appeared as if painted on. His body language portrayed a man who heard the bell tolling his doom and had given up, or whose conscience was robbing him of sleep.

In the past, Karp had often seen defendants flag and take on the look of beaten men during the people's case; after all, that's when the deck would appear stacked against them. But then they would perk up when their attorneys began to present their case and at least appear to level the playing field. However, for Lindsey, the appearance of Ariel Shimon, who was followed by two more men who claimed they'd been blackmailed by Blair, Lee, and Baum — and had been as easily dispatched during cross-examination — had done little to change his deportment or appearance.

Karp had wondered if the defendants would take the stand and expose themselves to cross-examination. With all the trump cards in his advocacy arsenal, combined with his aggressive competitiveness, he hoped that one or both would try to challenge him.

After their last witness appeared the previous afternoon, the defense attorneys had put their heads together and then told Judge Hart that they'd like some time to confer with their clients over whether they'd appear on the stand. Hart had given them until the morning.

When court reconvened, Hart asked if they'd reached a decision, at which point Caulkin said he would be calling Lindsey but that Fauhomme had not yet decided. A few minutes later, with the jury seated, Lindsey stood, buttoned his suit coat, and then, like a man summoned to his execution who just wanted to get it over with, took a seat on the witness stand.

During the direct examination, Lindsey had toed the company line by testifying that much of the testimony from prosecution witnesses had been misinterpreted or taken out of context. "For instance, the event described by Miss Lee in which she walked in on a meeting among myself, Mr. Fauhomme, and Mr. Baum did happen," he testified. "However, her chronology was inaccurate. We were actually discussing the president's performance during the debate on foreign policy the previous week when one of my men interrupted us with a report he'd just received on the events that had been transpiring in Chechnya. We were watching a taped version of the aerial reconnaissance vehicle's view of the events — not a real-time transmission. Miss Lee walked in on us *after* the recording was delivered and *that's* what she saw."

"What about her claim that she overheard Mr. Fauhomme exclaim something in regard to Al Qaeda?" Caulkin asked.

"To be honest," Lindsey said, "I don't remember him saying that in particular. However, my focus was on what was going on in Chechnya, and the safety of Americans, not who was responsible at that particular moment."

"Can you explain why you were looking at a recording from the drone several hours after the attack as opposed to in real time?" Caulkin asked.

Lindsey shook his head slightly. "I'm afraid the man who can answer that is dead. The recording was delivered to us by General Allen's agency."

"Was it common for Mr. Fauhomme to be present during what had to be a top priority event for you?"

"Like I said, we were there discussing foreign policy as it applied to the campaign," Lindsey said, looking over at his codefendant without much expression. "I needed to see what was going on and I was at Mr. Fauhomme's office. However, it was not uncommon for him to sit in on foreign policy discussions. It was a busy time for the president leading up to the election, and he relied on a lot of his closest advisers to keep him abreast of what was going on. Mr. Fauhomme obviously had a role in helping the president address some of these matters — both domestic and foreign policy — as they came up. I saw nothing unusual or untoward in that."

"And what about Mr. Baum?" Caulkin asked. "Much has been made about his questionable background and why he possessed NSA identification cards if he was working for Mr. Fauhomme."

Lindsey bit his lip. "Unfortunately, we did not do a good job of vetting Mr. Baum," he said. "He came recommended to us — I believe by some of his former officers in the Marine Corps, who led us to believe that the charges against him in Afghanistan, which by the way were dismissed, had been overblown. Mr. Fauhomme indicated that he needed someone who could be trusted with sensitive matters, as well as someone who could work as his personal security. Mr. Baum volunteered. He never really worked for the NSA, but it allowed Mr. Fauhomme to have a liaison who had the necessary low-level security clearance he needed. Unfortunately, it appears that Mr. Baum, in concert with Miss Blair and Miss Lee, decided to work his own game."

Caulkin brought up Stupenagel's testimony regarding a source named "Augie" who had told her that orders had come from "you and Mr. Fauhomme" to attack the trucks bearing the American hostages at the Zandaq compound and then again the mosque in Dagestan before it could be ascertained that the hostages were safe.

"That's nonsense," Lindsey said with a scowl. "As I pointed out, we were not watching the attack on the compound in Zandaq in real time. It was too late to do anything regarding those events by the time we viewed the recording, much less attack our own people. As for Dagestan, well, I think the proof of the pudding is that Deputy Chief of Mission David Huff and the hostage we've now been told is the district attorney's daughter are both alive and well. Believe me, if someone had wanted them to die during that attack, they would not be alive today. The president's decision to order the attack came after the hostages were free and clear."

"Why then would someone make that assertion — if they did — to Miss Stupenagel?" Caulkin asked.

Lindsey shrugged. "You'd have to ask this 'Augie,' but it sounds to me like someone covering his butt at the CIA."

Lindsey conceded that many of the original talking points regarding the attack on the Zandaq compound were "inaccurate." But he blamed that on the administration's well-worn rhetoric about "the fog of war" and "a fluid situation" compounded by the difficulty of not having enough "human intelligence gathering on the ground." Part of his implication was that the CIA was at fault, and by association, the leadership of General Sam Allen.

"I don't want to disparage General Allen," Lindsey said. "He is a true American hero. However, he was new to the job and the agency was — how shall I put this — in turmoil due to the complete inadequacy of his predecessor, as well as the deterioration of the agency during previous administrations."

Lindsey confirmed that he and Fauhomme

had met with Allen at the latter's request to discuss concerns regarding the events in Chechnya. "In my mind, it was nothing more than a quite normal disagreement between colleagues, which happens all the time with intelligence agencies based on who has what information," he said. "I'm not saying that General Allen was completely wrong, but I did feel he was making assumptions based on disjointed, incomplete, and sometimes refutable facts."

"I'm taking it that this was a pretty heated discussion?"

"Yes, it was," Lindsey conceded. "General Allen came from a background where his opinions and decisions were rarely, if ever, challenged. He was a man of action; *act now and ask questions later.* For better or worse, that's not how we operate in the intelligence-gathering world. We prefer to wait for all of the facts before making decisions, or even discussing the events; however, the media was all over this one, and the decision was made to try to give the American public our best assessment. In that situation, it is no surprise that we erred on some of the facts. However, at the time, General Allen got his back up, and to be honest, left in a huff. It was the last time I ever spoke to him."

"Was General Allen at any time threatened with blackmail by you and Mr. Fauhomme regarding his relationship with Miss Blair?" Caulkin asked.

Lindsey looked as if he'd been asked an incredibly stupid question. "Absolutely not," he said dismissively. "I was aware of the affair and concerned. As one of the president's closest advisers I was worried about the possible repercussions on the president if the press found out. In fact, I was in New York when the general died, talking to Mr. Fauhomme about how to approach the subject with General Allen, as well as trying to find a common ground regarding Chechnya, when Sam Allen was killed."

"I understand that you've met Miss Blair," Caulkin said. "Could you tell us your impressions of her?"

Lindsey twisted his lips. "She and Miss Lee were both what we in politics call 'power groupies,' " he said. "They're like rock-and-roll band groupies but they gravitate to people with political power; money is important, too, but it's almost secondary. We see them a lot in political circles. Some of them are fairly harmless, such as the obsessed housewife who volunteers for everything and is gaga for the candidate.

Some just want to be where the action is, or they're collecting notches on their bedpost like a baseball fan collects player cards. But others have more sinister motives . . . powerful men are susceptible to blackmail if they give in to temptation."

Looking over at Fauhomme, Lindsey said, "I never told Rod this, I figured it was his business and I know he truly cared for her, but I always felt that Lee was one of these political groupies and that she was taking him for a ride. He was spending a lot of money on her — shopping trips and vacations — but it was never enough. And he once told me that she was putting a lot of pressure on him to take her to White House functions and introduce her to important people, which was entirely inappropriate."

"And what about Miss Blair?"

"Like she said, I met her at Mr. Fauhomme's party on Long Island," Lindsey replied. "But I could tell right away that she was sizing up some of the men who were there. She zeroed in on the general pretty quick and then stuck to him like white on rice. It was pretty shameless the way she threw herself at him, whether he was exercising or reading a book in a hammock; she made sure she sat next to him at the dinners and followed him around like a . . .

well, I think everybody knows what I mean. You heard how she dragged him off into the dunes after knowing him for, what? Twenty-four hours? And knowing he was a married man? She wasn't exactly a paragon of virtue."

"But what about her tearful testimony and all that talk about true love?"

Lindsey rolled his eyes. "Yeah, well, she said she came to New York to be an actress, and I guess she landed a starring role. I have to say, she pulled the wool over a lot of people's eyes. I know Rod liked her — that's why she was at the party — and the general was certainly taken by her."

Caulkin walked over to the defense table to look at his notes, then turned back to the witness stand. "Would there have been any reason for General Allen to believe that his stance on the events in Chechnya would pose a threat to him?"

Lindsey looked thoughtful for a moment and then shrugged again. "General Allen was the acting director of the CIA and faced confirmation hearings. He made it quite clear in many circles that he expected to get the job. He might have seen this difference of opinions as posing an obstacle to his goals."

"Was he expected to stick to the party line

at the congressional committee hearings?" Caulkin asked.

Lindsey spread his hands as if the answer wasn't as clear-cut as all that. "Well, in any administration, a certain amount of common concurrence is expected. We all can disagree and voice those disagreements, but in the end, the president is the boss," he said. "As in any company, disagreements are generally kept in-house, but a united front is presented to the rest of the world. That's called loyalty. But if General Allen felt compelled to give his opinion to the committee, no one would have stopped him."

Quiet for a moment as though to consider his next statement carefully, Lindsey then went on. "I have wondered since his death if he felt that Mr. Fauhomme and I would sabotage his chances for confirmation because of this disagreement. After all, he knew that we have the president's trust and confidence. I think he made his tape so that if the president changed his mind regarding his appointment, it could be 'leaked' to the press as if he'd been prevented from giving his opinion."

"Is there anything else?"

"Well, if he was being blackmailed by these women and Mr. Baum, then that might have had him rattled as well. He knew that Baum worked for Mr. Fauhomme, and that Lee was Rod's girlfriend. Sam Allen was under a lot of pressure, even more than I knew, and a guilty mind jumps to a lot of paranoid conclusions."

Caulkin strolled over to stand in front of the witness with his arms crossed loosely. "Mr. Lindsey, the district attorney has made a great deal about some of your actions following the death of General Allen. One was your conversation with Constable Spooner after you learned from the FBI that Ray Baum had died in a car accident. Would you care to explain that?"

"Certainly," Lindsey said, "though it's a long story. Anyway, following the discussion with General Allen regarding his proposed testimony to Congress, Mr. Fauhomme and I concurred that the general was exhibiting some rather unusual behavior. Then the morning of Allen's murder, I received a call from Mr. Fauhomme indicating that he'd overheard a telephone conversation between Miss Lee and Miss Blair in which they seemed to be discussing a video recording about General Allen. He didn't put two and two together until he turned on the television and saw the news about the general's death. He called me in something of a panic

— I was in New York and staying at a nearby hotel — and that's when I said he needed to send Ray Baum to Miss Blair's apartment to talk to her about this."

"Mr. Baum? Why not the police?" Caulkin asked as if surprised.

"At that point the best information we had was that this was a suicide," Lindsey replied. "I have to say that some alarm bells were going off in my head — I haven't been in the intelligence game all this time for nothing — and I wondered if this video had anything to do with the general taking his life. We didn't know anything about Mr. Baum's role as the killer, and he was the person we could get to her the fastest. Rod told me that in hindsight he wondered why Baum seemed so eager to go to Miss Blair's apartment."

"So what does this have to do with your conversation with Constable Spooner?" Caulkin asked.

Lindsey nodded. "We were starting to put two and two together as far as Miss Blair and Mr. Baum having some connection, possibly with Miss Lee, though to be honest, Rod didn't want to believe that. I mean, Miss Blair just happens to be able to outwit and outrun someone she supposedly had no reason to suspect, except for a tattoo she saw on a grainy security camera? Mr. Baum had disappeared and we couldn't contact him. The next thing we know, I got a call from the FBI saying he'd died in a car crash and that I needed to contact Constable Spooner. Call it my spy paranoia, or a hunch, but Baum showing up in Orvin? Why was he in Orvin, except that he knew he could find Miss Blair there? Suddenly it was clear to me that he'd arranged to meet her there."

"But what about the shootings?"

Lindsey shrugged. "Wouldn't be the first time there was a falling-out among killers."

"And Miss Stupenagel and Mrs. Ciampi?"

"I have no idea, really," Lindsey said. "Miss Stupenagel could be telling the truth — she was looking for Miss Blair, too, and figured out where she was hiding. Or . . . well, I'll leave it to others to speculate."

"What about the things you said to Constable Spooner?"

"Again, I tend to think in worst-case scenarios," Lindsey said. "The whole situation was murky. I've got a dead general who was the acting director of America's biggest spy agency; I have a woman on the run who supposedly has some sort of recording involving the general, and I have no idea if it includes sensitive classified material; and

I have a rogue NSA agent involved in a car crash. I didn't know who to trust or what information I could share with a small-town law officer."

Caulkin walked over to the defense table and checked several items on a legal pad. Up on the stand, Lindsey attempted to pour himself a glass of water, but his hand trembled so much that he just put it back down. His attorney then closed his notepad like a professor finishing his lecture for the day. "Mr. Lindsey, you're a very well educated man. A Rhodes scholar. A Ph.D. in International Studies. Could you have made more money in the private sector?"

Lindsey smiled slightly. "That's not hard compared to a government salary."

"So then I have to ask you, why did you decide to dedicate your life to public service?" Caulkin asked.

Lindsey blinked back what appeared to be genuine tears. "I wanted to serve my country," he said, his voice husky with emotion, "and the American people."

"Thank you, Mr. Lindsey," Caulkin said, sounding a little choked up himself. "I have no further questions."

Judge Hart nodded and looked at his watch. "I have a few administrative details I need to deal with, so let's take a thirty-minute break. Court is in recess."

As everyone stood while the judge departed, Karp looked behind to his wife and Stupenagel and was at first alarmed, and then puzzled, when he saw the young man who'd been watching the women walk quickly up to the reporter. He handed her something and then turned and left. Stupenagel looked at whatever was in her hand and then up at Karp before turning and running after the man.

Something in her expression said to Karp that he was expected to follow her. Still, it took him a little bit to work his way through the crowd and out into the hallway. At first he didn't see anything but then he spotted his wife down the hall, waving. He hurried to her, but she went around a corner ahead of him.

Striding as fast as his long legs and a bum knee could move, he rounded the corner and saw his wife, Stupenagel, and the young man in a heated conversation at the end of a hall next to a window. The young man was startled when he saw Karp and began to turn away, but Stupenagel grabbed him by the arm. "You owe it to him," she insisted.

"I gave you the tapes," he said, looking at Karp.

"It's not enough, damn it," the reporter shot back.

"What's going on here?" Karp demanded.

Stupenagel looked at the young man. He stared at her for a moment but then nodded. She turned to Karp. "Butch, I want you to meet Augie . . . *the* Augie . . . he just gave me these two recordings," she said, holding up a pair of DVDs. "He says they depict a drone's-eye view of the terrorist attack in Zandaq and the drone strike in Dagestan."

"Is that true?" Karp asked.

The young man hesitated and then nodded. "Yeah," he said, and then held out his hand. "Augie Nieto. I think you might want to hear what I have to say."

After a brief chat with Nieto, Karp informed Jim Farley, the court clerk, that an emergency required his attention and that he'd be in his office during the break. He asked Farley to inform Judge Hart that he might need an extra half hour to handle the matter, which, of course, he would put on the record when court reconvened.

An hour later, Karp returned to court. Judge Hart gave him a funny look. "Everything okay?"

Karp smiled. "Yes, Your Honor, thank you for your consideration and during the course of this afternoon's proceedings it will become clear why I requested the extra time. Your Honor, with the court's permission, I am now prepared to cross-examine this witness."

The judge's eyes narrowed for a moment, but then he said, "Okay, please proceed."

Karp took up his favorite position standing beside the jury and placed his notes on the ledge. "Mr. Lindsey, as the president's national security adviser, how is it that you did such a poor job of vetting Ray Baum?"

Lindsey frowned. "As I noted, I believe that he came with a recommendation from his former Marine Corps officers."

Holding up his yellow legal pad and a pencil, Karp asked, "Can you provide the names of these officers, or where they might be stationed?"

"Not at the moment," Lindsey said. "I might be able to dig them up later."

"Later?" Karp asked. "You mean after this trial is over. How about this evening, Mr. Lindsey; perhaps you could find them this evening and get back to me so that we can contact them."

"I suppose I could try," Lindsey said.

"Thank you, I'd appreciate that," Karp said. "But again, as the president's spymaster, how is it that you were aware that the president's married appointee to head the nation's top spy agency was having an affair with someone you've labeled a 'power groupie' and yet had not said or done anything about it?"

"I was . . . uh . . . in New York to talk to Mr. Fauhomme."

"The president's campaign manager. So this was more of a campaign concern as opposed to a national security issue?"

"Well, both, in a way."

"Both? So then you were talking to Mr. Fauhomme about the possible ramifications for the campaign, but who did you discuss this with from a national security standpoint?"

Lindsey furrowed his brow. "What do you mean?"

"Well, did you contact your counterpart in the FBI? And if so, could you provide me with that name?" Karp said, again raising his yellow pad and pencil as though to write.

"No, I hadn't gotten that far," Lindsey said.

"So the campaign was a greater priority than national security?"

"I wouldn't say that."

"I think you just did. But let's move on," Karp retorted. "So if I understood your testimony, the defendant Rod Fauhomme overheard Miss Lee talking to Miss Blair about some video of General Allen and then when he realized that Allen was dead in a New York hotel — apparently from suicide — the alarms went off and you told your codefendant to send Mr. Baum, a man you admittedly did a poor job of vetting, to what? Apprehend her? He's not a police officer. Or just to get that recording?"

"I guess just to ascertain what the conversation about a video recording of the general might be," Lindsey said.

Karp looked puzzled. "What made you think it was something other than what a girlfriend might have of her boyfriend?"

"Oh," Lindsey said. "I guess there was some indication that the recording depicted the general's murder."

Karp's eyebrows shot up. "So now there's an indication that this recording could be evidence in a murder investigation, but instead of sending the police, or, say, the FBI, you told Fauhomme to send his man Ray Baum."

"Or maybe Rod said he was sending Ray," Lindsey stumbled. "I don't remember the sequence."

"It's hard to remember a lie, isn't it, Mr. Lindsey? Or as a master spy, do you register the difference?" Karp said.

"To be sure, I do," Lindsey shot back before Caulkin could object.

"Would it surprise you to know that my office did not determine, or say, that this was a murder investigation until the day after General Allen's body was found?"

"Like I said, I believe Miss Blair said something to Miss Lee about it."

"Indeed, we know from their testimony that Miss Blair had seen the murder on her laptop and called Miss Lee. But you said that Fauhomme only told you that he overheard a conversation about there being a recording."

"There might have been more to it than that . . . yes, I think there was something about a murder," Lindsey said. He was starting to lose the shell of confidence he'd displayed when first called to the stand and was taking on the look of a cornered animal.

"But you didn't call the police or tell Mr. Fauhomme to call the police?"

"I was concerned there might be a security issue."

"Why? What led you to think that?"

"The general was the acting director of the CIA and this woman had a video of him. And now he was dead."

"Okay. So Ray Baum trots on over to Miss Blair's apartment but she escapes — or, as you suggested, he let her escape," Karp said.

"Perhaps."

"Yes, perhaps. She goes missing and then so does Ray Baum?"

"That's right."

"Did you have reason to believe that she was involved in the death of Sam Allen?"

"Well, she disappeared right after."

"What made you jump to the conclusion that she was a fugitive from justice as opposed to maybe a witness or just a frightened young woman whose lover had been murdered?"

"Well, I didn't know, but we certainly wanted to question her."

"But that's not what you told Constable Tom Spooner," Karp said. He walked over to the prosecution table and picked up a sheaf of papers. "I'm holding a copy of People's Exhibit 18, the transcript of your conversation with Constable Spooner the day after Ray Baum was killed while trying to murder Miss Blair." He walked back to the witness stand and handed it to Lindsey.

"Would you turn to page six, please," Karp said. "Are you there?"

"Yes."

"Could you read what I have highlighted, starting with line ten," Karp said.

" 'Do me a favor and secure the area

around the cabin — no one in or out,' "
Lindsey read. " 'We'll have another team up
there as soon as possible. We are also looking for a fugitive. White female, blond, hazel
eyes, about thirty years of age. Her name is
Jenna Blair but she may be using an alias.' "

"Thank you," Karp said. "So you described her as a fugitive. Fugitive from
what? A hunch that she was involved in a
murder that you didn't even know was a
murder yet?"

Lindsey shrugged. "I was using the term
fugitive loosely. I just meant she was wanted
for questioning."

"Okay, turn to page three and read lines
four through seven," Karp said.

" 'Can you tell me if there was a laptop
computer located in the car?' " Lindsey began.

"Let me stop you there," Karp interjected.
"You're the one asking the question, correct?"

"Yes."

"Okay, now you want to explain why you
wanted her laptop?"

"Because of the recording on it."

Karp looked taken aback. "But wait a
minute, you didn't say anything about
knowing this recording was on her laptop."

"It might have come up. Like I said, I was

focused on finding the girl and learning what I could as fast as possible."

"Turn to page nine, please, and read lines one through three," Karp said.

" 'This is a national security case and we don't want it compromised,' " Lindsey read. " 'Same thing with that computer; if it's located, no one is to touch it; it contains highly classified material.' "

"So did you just have a hunch that there was highly classified material on that computer," Karp asked, "or were you worried that it had evidence of a murder that you were involved in?"

"Like I said, General Allen was acting director of the CIA and I had to see what was recorded," Lindsey responded, sticking to the script.

Karp walked back to the prosecution table and picked up another sheaf of papers. He held them up. "This is People's Exhibit 19," he said. "It's the transcript of a recording made of you and your team outside the 13th Street Repertory Theater."

He handed the transcript to Lindsey. "Would you remind the jury what you were doing there?"

"We were there to apprehend Miss Blair and recover her computer," Lindsey replied sullenly as he looked at the pages.

"Turn to page three, please, and read only the line highlighted in yellow. This is you speaking."

" 'If she runs, take her down,' " Lindsey read.

"And what did you mean, 'Take her down'?"

"I meant capture her."

"Really? Read the next line only please."

" 'And try not to hit any civilians.' "

"If you were only trying to capture her, why were you concerned about civilians?"

"I had no idea if she was armed," Lindsey said.

"Okay, turn to page ten, and begin reading until I tell you to stop," Karp said.

" 'You need to come with me, Jenna, I can protect you. . . . How? Sam was a general and he ran the CIA and they still killed him. How are you going to protect me? . . . We'll put you in the witness protection program. You can't keep running.' "

"Okay, stop," Karp said. "So now she's a witness, not a security threat or a killer?"

"I didn't know," Lindsey replied. "I was trying to get her to give up."

"Continue reading, please," Karp said.

" 'Witness protection? Witness against who? That guy? You know and I know he wasn't acting on his own. Sam told me that people were upset with him because he wasn't going to go along with the "official" story on Chechnya. . . . What people? . . . He didn't say. I think he was trying to protect me. But he said he was being blackmailed because of his relationship with me.' "

"Okay, stop," Karp interrupted.

"She's a good actress," Lindsey said, but his head hung.

"Yeah, I'd say she deserves a Tony," Karp replied sarcastically. "Please turn to page thirteen, and read starting with line five."

" 'I wouldn't know about that. What I do know is that you're playing a very dangerous game, and if you don't come with me now, I can't be responsible for what happens to you. . . . What's going to happen to me? . . . Nothing if you come with me. . . . What are you going to do with that recording? . . . We'll find this man . . . and if others are involved, we'll go after them too. The FBI will. . . . Is that who you're going to give the recording to? The FBI? . . . Yes. It's a bureau investigation now.' "

"Stop," Karp demanded. "Mr. Lindsey, you said you were after the laptop computer, right?"

"Yes."

"What did you do with it?"

Lindsey stared at him and shook his head. "You know what I did. You had a GPS tracker. I took it to Rod's apartment. It's in my lawyer's office."

"So you never turned it over to the FBI?"

"No."

"Why not?"

Again Lindsey just stared at him. He shook his head again, then glared at Fauhomme. "We were concerned that if we brought another agency in, there might be a leak, and we weren't sure who was involved."

"Read the last line of the last sentence on that page," Karp said tersely.

Lindsey looked down and started to speak but then had to stop and cleared his throat. " 'Seal the doors. And get in here. I want that bitch now!' "

Karp walked up to the witness stand and held out his hand for the transcripts. Lindsey handed them over without raising his head.

Nor did he look up when Karp asked his next question. "This was all about protecting the president's re-election bid, wasn't it?"

Lindsey let out a large sigh but didn't answer.

"It all started with a lie about what happened in Chechnya, didn't it?" Karp persisted.

"That's not true," Lindsey said quietly.

"It's not?" Karp said. "Mr. Lindsey, let me ask you this. You've testified that you only saw the attack on the Zandaq compound after the fact, is that true?"

"Yes."

"And that you had no knowledge of a call from someone named Wallflower, who has been identified as Lucy Karp, until after the fact, is that true?"

"Yes."

"And that there were no orders given to fire upon trucks bearing the hostages in Chechnya, or on the mosque in Dagestan until it was clear that the hostages were safe, is that true?"

"Yes."

Karp walked up to the witness stand until he was only a few feet from the visibly trembling and red-faced national security adviser. "What if I was to tell you that I am going to call a witness in rebuttal who can prove that you are a liar?"

"Who?" Lindsey gasped.

Karp whirled to look at the gallery. "Augie Nieto, would you please stand up!"

As the gallery murmured, the young man stood up. Karp turned back to Lindsey.

"I'm sure you recognize Augie Nieto. What do you say, Mr. Lindsey?"

Lindsey stared for a long time at the young man. Tears appeared in his eyes and he struggled to speak, then he hung his head.

"Mr. Lindsey," Karp said calmly. "Your attorney asked why you got involved in public service. I ask you now to recall your answer and then tell the jurors the truth."

Slowly Lindsey began to nod his head and then lifted his chin until he was looking Karp in the eyes. He blinked several times, then passed a hand across his face as if wiping sleep from his eyes. "Most of what I said before was a lie . . ."

As the courtroom erupted, with reporters running for the hall to make their calls and the defense attorneys screaming objections, Karp smiled with grim satisfaction. "Then, Mr. Lindsey, I believe it is time for you to start telling the truth."

EPILOGUE

Karp finished his brisk early morning walk and punched in the security code to open the street-level door leading into the building that housed the loft. He was about to walk in when he was stopped by a shout.

"Hey, Butch! Hold on . . . whoop whoop . . . I brought you the *Sunday Times* . . . piss balls . . . special delivery," Dirty Warren shouted as he came around the corner from Grand Street. "Thought you might . . . crap oh boy . . . want to get an early start on this one! Wow . . . oh boy whoop . . . read all about it!"

"Thanks, Warren, you didn't have to do that," Karp said with a smile. He nodded at the foyer. "Want to come up for a cup of joe?"

Dirty Warren's pale blue eyes lit up like diamonds behind the thick lenses of his glasses. "Really? A cup of coffee . . . bastard whoop whoop . . . in your place? Gee, thanks, Butch, that . . . scratch my balls . . . means a lot." He looked at his watch and his face fell. "But I got to take a . . . whoop whoop . . . rain check. I have an appointment with our friend, David Grale, he wants to know how . . . holy crap fuckers . . . your new prisoner is doing."

Karp nodded. Several nights ago, someone had pressed the front door buzzer, but there was no one in the security camera. A few minutes later, the buzzer went off again, but there was still no one in the camera's view. Thinking it might be some neighborhood kids who could use a good scare, he went down with Marlene's gigantic Presa Canario dog, Gilgamesh, to check it out and give them something to think about.

However, when he reached the sidewalk, there was no one in sight. He was about to turn around and go back into the building when Gilgamesh suddenly whined and began pulling him down the block. Reaching the alley, the dog sat and stared into the dark with his nub of a tail twitching back and forth.

"Hello, is there anybody there?" Karp asked.

A shadow separated itself from the others and walked toward him. "Hello, Butch," Grale said, his pale, skeletal face suddenly illuminated by the streetlight.

"Good evening, David," Karp had replied, wondering what had occasioned this visit from the King of the Mole People.

Grale soon answered. "Am I to understand that Nadya Malovo escaped?"

Karp nodded. "Yes, but because of her, Lucy survived and Al-Sistani is dead."

Nodding solemnly, Grale said, "Somewhere there is a spark of decency in her, though the evil that surrounds it is usually stronger. But none of us are done with her, not yet. I can feel it to the depths of my soul. But whether it will be for good or ill, only God knows."

"I'm afraid you're right," Karp replied. "But I guess we'll deal with that when it happens."

"Indeed," Grale said. "But I didn't come here tonight solely for that reason. I brought you a present." With that he yanked on a long chain that Karp had not noticed, the end of which disappeared into the gloom of the alley. "Heel, dog!" he commanded.

A combination whimper snarl emerged from the shadows, followed by the appearance of a man crawling on his hands and knees. A collar was around his neck, attached to the chain Grale now handed to Karp. "He's yours to do with as you please," the mad monk said. "I have a new dog now. I found him wandering the streets outside of Ariadne Stupenagel's apartment back during your recent trial. I believe he'll do for now."

With that Grale had stepped back into the shadows just as an unmarked police car driven by Officer J. P. Murphy pulled up. "Sorry, sir, I didn't know you were coming out to walk the dog," Murphy said, getting out of the car. "I thought I saw something odd down the street so I drove around the block. And . . . oh, my God . . . what the hell is that?" The officer pointed at Andrew Kane, who crouched in the alley entrance.

"A lost soul," Karp said. "If you'd be so kind as to call for emergency backup and have this individual transported to the psychiatric ward at Bellevue Hospital and notify Dr. Morris — he's in charge — I'd appreciate it."

Karp patted Dirty Warren on the shoulder. "Tell him the prisoner is still at Bellevue undergoing evaluation. And give him my thanks, he did the right thing."

"Sure thing . . . whoop . . . Butch," Dirty Warren said with a grin. "And don't forget . . . oh boy ass . . . that rain check."

"I won't," Karp said, and held up the

newspaper. "Thanks again."

Riding the elevator up to the fourth-floor loft, Karp thought about Lucy's spiritually motivated understanding that her family was designated a team to confront, combat, and defeat evil. He was still thinking about it when he opened the door to see that Marlene and the twins had been joined around the kitchen table by Ariadne Stupenagel and Gilbert Murrow.

"Look what the cat drug in," Stupenagel said.

"Hi, honey," Marlene called out. "I was just reading Ariadne's story about the trial to the boys."

"Oh, boy, did she at least spell my name right this time?"

"She did more than that," Marlene said. "She made you out to be some sort of superhero."

"Great, just what I need," Karp said, rolling his eyes.

"Yeah, listen to this," Marlene said, and then in her best stage voice read, " 'The dramatic collapse of National Security Adviser Tucker Lindsey on the stand culminated in his confession to his and Fauhomme's roles in the cover-up of the events in Chechnya and Dagestan, as well as in the murder of General Sam Allen.

" 'With the jury excused from the room, Judge Hart questioned Lindsey to determine if he was mentally competent. "Your Honor, I understand the nature of the charges against me. Yes, I am quite capable of assisting my lawyer in my own defense, and I take full responsibility for the consequences of what I intend to say," Lindsey said. Thereafter the judge called the jury back and allowed Karp to proceed with his questioning.

" 'When Karp asked Lindsey about the motivation for the murder, Lindsey replied, "It was feared that if the truth came out, the president would lose the election." Lindsey denied knowing beforehand that Fauhomme had directed Ray Baum to murder the general; however, he admitted to assisting in covering up the crime and trying to pin the blame on others. "I was knee deep in it," Lindsey testified, "and saw no other way out."

" 'Following the cross-examination of Lindsey and attempts by both defense attorneys to literally redirect him, Hart again sent the jury from the courtroom. He then asked if in light of his confession on the stand, Lindsey wanted to change his plea. In one of the most dramatic courtroom scenes this reporter has ever witnessed, the national security adviser, once one of the most powerful men in this country, tearfully pleaded guilty to the crime of murder, at which point his codefendant, Rod Fauhomme, stood up and began screaming at Karp. "Who are you to judge me? I'm the fucking man of the hour. I know what's best for this country. What does it matter if one man dies if progress is made?" The former campaign manager was then subdued by court security personnel.

" 'Karp went on to explain to the court the reason for his earlier request for a delay. In essence, he informed the court that he had a new witness — a witness who turned out to be the equivalent of drawing an inside straight flush in a high-stakes poker game. He then called Augie Nieto, a high-level administrator with a private company contracted by the NSA to run their drone program. Nieto testified that Lindsey and Fauhomme watched the attack in real time and ignored calls for help. The drone overhead was armed, contradicting the administration's earlier claims that it wasn't, and it was online and able to respond. However, drone operators were told to stand down. Only later were they ordered by Fauhomme and Lindsey to fire on the hostages. He said that he passed the information about the attack on the compound in Chechnya to General Allen late Friday night, two days before he was murdered. The attack on the mosque in Dagestan, according to Nieto, was also intended to annihilate all terrorists, hostages, and witnesses.

" 'Asked after the trial why he waited to come forward until the eleventh hour, Nieto said that he was originally led to believe that telling the truth would have dire national security implications for the United States. "However, I could not sit there and listen to Lindsey lie, knowing that Fauhomme would do the same. Sam Allen was a better man than either of those two could ever be, and I felt like I had his blood and those of the other brave men who died in Chechnya and Dagestan on my hands."

" 'Reached for comment following Nieto's appearance, White House press secretary Rosemary Hilb stuck to the script and denied his allegations. "Aware that the justice process is still continuing and there could be appeals if there is a conviction," she said, "the president will withhold further comment at this time." ' "

Marlene snorted derisively, then continued to read. " 'The trial concluded with the attorneys giving their summations. The defense, represented by former Assistant Attorney General Celeste Faust, stuck to the original story line that Allen was murdered by a conspiracy composed of his girlfriend, Jenna Blair, Fauhomme's girlfriend, Connie Rae Lee, and disgraced Marine Ray Baum. She fought the small details, such as claiming that there was no proof that Fauhomme was the person who answered the call Baum placed from Allen's room. "It was all part of the setup to make him take the fall." She insisted that Lindsey's confession was motivated by a desire to "save himself, and in all likelihood he was the puppeteer behind the other co-conspirators. Ask yourselves, who had the power to pull this off, the president's national security adviser, or a politico, a lowly campaign manager?"

" 'However, in his summation, Karp described Fauhomme as "a kingmaker who thought of himself as the real power behind the throne." In what has become a classic theme for the district attorney, Karp told the jurors that they could determine the truth "not from what I say, or what any individual witness says, but how each witness, each document or recording accepted into evidence, every technical or scientific piece of evidence, corroborates the rest. That's how you'll know the truth." After several hours, broken only by short intermissions, Karp at last came to his grand finale.' "

Karp sighed. "Oh, boy, haven't you read enough?"

"No," Marlene said. "I think the boys should hear this. Oooh, this is good . . . 'Standing in front of the jurors like Moses delivering the Ten Commandments to the wandering tribes of Israel . . .' "

"I think I'd better leave now," Karp said.

"Stick around," Stupenagel said, "it gets better."

"As I was saying . . . 'wandering tribes of Israel, Karp delivered a sermon worthy of a Sunday Baptist revival. "This case is extremely significant not only for you as jurors, but also for the people, our fellow citizens. We have learned from the evidence in this case, beyond any and all doubt, the true nature of the character of these defendants." ' "

" 'Slowly walking along the jury rail, looking each juror in the eyes, he asked, "So who are they?" He whirled and pointed at the defendants. "We know from the evidence that they lie, they hide the truth; that they mislead the public and accuse anyone who dares challenge them of being politically motivated or guilty of the crimes that they themselves committed." Then he turned back to the jury. "Here in this court we witnessed in grave detail the defense accusing Jenna Blair and Connie Rae Lee of murder, and myself and my office of manipulating the process and unfairly charging them with a heinous crime. The defendants, and those they work for, do these things because they are guilty of extreme arrogance, believing — or having convinced themselves — that they know what's right for all of us. Sometimes they'll do it for money; sometimes they'll do it to enhance their resumes; but always, it's about the power. We know what they are; they are evil. So isn't it fitting that we confront them in this courtroom? Why?" Karp allowed his question to sink in before his answer. "Because a trial is a solemn and sacred search for the truth under the rules of evidence.

" ' "So who are we? The best way, it seems to me, to describe who we are is to understand where we came from." A few decibels at a time, Karp allowed his voice to rise. "We are the product of American exceptionalism. That is not some arrogant or superior concept. Not at all. It came to America with the Puritans, who saw themselves like the Children of Israel from the Old Testament. They fled oppression in

Europe, engaged in a perilous journey across the vast ocean, and came to what they regarded as the Promised Land. One of their leaders, John Winthrop, who founded the Massachusetts Bay Colony, said in 1630, in substance, *We are the city on the hill and we will be judged by the Almighty with respect to how we live our lives.* So this concept of American exceptionalism is a moral and spiritual belief system. We are a moral people. We try to institutionalize virtue and recognize that evil exists and it must be confronted and defeated. That's who we are. That's where we came from. It's in our spiritual DNA.

" ' "What does that mean?" Karp asked the rapt jurors and the gallery. "It means we don't leave our brothers and sisters on the battlefield to be mutilated and slaughtered. We rescue them when they are in peril. We don't lie to cover up our mistakes. We admit them and try to rectify them and only then do we move on. That's who we are as a people. We must continue to be a moral and spiritual force for good."

" 'Karp walked into the well of the courtroom and held his hands out to his sides as if to encompass not just the physical surroundings but the people in attendance. "In this courtroom that means you have the opportunity to strip these defendants of their deceit, their manipulations, their lies, and their fatal conceit. We can all agree that good conscience demands, common sense requires, and justice cries out that the defendant Fauhomme, like his codefendant Lindsey who admitted as much on the stand, is guilty of murder." He then returned to his seat as silence enveloped the courtroom.' "

Marlene looked up from the paper, her eyes wet with pride. "Wow, honey, that was really good."

"That was cool, Dad," the twins chimed in.

"There's more," Stupenagel said. "Go on."

Marlene dutifully began to read again. " 'Sent to deliberate, the jury took less than three hours to reach their verdict: guilty as charged. Pale and shaking, Fauhomme collapsed into his chair. The convicted man then half-walked and was half-carried by the team of court officers from the courtroom. His last words before he disappeared from sight: "I'm a dead man. They'll never let me live." And then he was gone.

" 'Meanwhile, in the two weeks since the trial, Karp is still pursuing bigger quarry. Although he won't comment on the workings of the grand jury, a source close to the

DAO . . .' "

"Gilbert!" Karp said with a scowl.

Murrow's eyes got big. "It wasn't me, I swear," he cried out.

"Forget it, Karp, I'd never expose the love of my life like that," Stupenagel said. "I have spies everywhere. Read on, Marlene."

" '. . . a source close to the DAO says that Tucker Lindsey has been revealing details about others involved in the cover-up and the administration's deceit while misleading the American public regarding the terror attack in Zandaq and the events in Dagestan. More indictments are sure to follow. In fact, two days ago, Israeli businessman Ariel Shimon was indicted by the attorney general of Israel for illegal arms sales to Iran. Lindsey testified at the trial that the administration had used knowledge of the sales to coerce Shimon into lying for the defense. As for Rod Fauhomme, he remains in administrative segregation in the Tombs awaiting final sentencing before Judge Charles Hart, Jr.' "

Marlene closed the newspaper and patted her friend Stupenagel's hand. "You done good, girl," she said. "That was a great story. So, how's the book going?"

"Signed on the dotted line last night," Stupenagel said. "It's going to be nice to be able to put it all together, along with a lot of detail I didn't know or couldn't fit."

"I hope we'll get a signed copy," Marlene said. She looked up at her husband. "What do you think, honey?"

Karp tossed the *Sunday Times* that Dirty Warren had given him on the table. A large bold headline blared from the top of the page: IMPEACHMENT HEARINGS BEGIN.

"Sic semper tyrannis," he said. "And so it begins again."

ABOUT THE AUTHOR

Robert K. Tanenbaum is one of the country's most respected and successful trial lawyers and has never lost a felony case. He has held such prestigious positions as bureau chief of the criminal courts and homicide bureau in the New York District Attorney's Office. He was also deputy chief counsel to the congressional committee investigations into the assassinations of President John F. Kennedy and Reverend Martin Luther King. He taught for several years advanced criminal procedure at his alma mater, the University of California at Berkeley, Boalt Hall School of Law. His previous works include the novels *Tragic*, *Bad Faith*, *Outrage*, *Betrayed*, and the true crime book *Echoes of My Soul*.

The employees of Thorndike Press hope you have enjoyed this Large Print book. All our Thorndike, Wheeler, and Kennebec Large Print titles are designed for easy reading, and all our books are made to last. Other Thorndike Press Large Print books are available at your library, through selected bookstores, or directly from us.

For information about titles, please call:
(800) 223-1244

or visit our Web site at:
http://gale.cengage.com/thorndike

To share your comments, please write:
Publisher
Thorndike Press
10 Water St., Suite 310
Waterville, ME 04901